Shadow of Treachery

by

Gray Laidlaw

Order this book online at www.trafford.com
or email orders@trafford.com

Most Trafford titles are also available at major online book retailers.

Note for Librarians: A cataloguing record for this book is available from Library
and Archives Canada at www.collectionscanada.ca/amicus/index-e.html

Printed in Victoria, BC, Canada.

ISBN: 978-1-4269-0000-6 (sc)

*Our mission is to efficiently provide the world's finest, most comprehensive book publishing
service, enabling every author to experience success. To find out how to publish your
book, your way, and have it available worldwide, visit us online at www.trafford.com*

Trafford rev. 10/20/2009

www.trafford.com

North America & international
toll-free: 1 888 232 4444 (USA & Canada)
phone: 250 383 6864 ♦ fax: 812 355 4082

For Margaret, my dear wife

Prologue

It was an errant ray of sunshine which wakened me on that surprising morning in late March at the start of my Easter holidays from university. I was in my grandparents' house which was the only home I had ever known as both my parents had died in an accident when I was only six months old. I love my grandparents and consider myself lucky to have been brought up by them. This may seem to be ungenerous to my parents, but I never knew them and I suppose that I was then so young it must have been easy for me to form new bonds.

I glanced at my watch and realised that I had better hurry down to breakfast. I had been to a party the previous evening and I had slept rather late. When I got down I found it rather strange to see Grannie and Granddad looking intently at the *Daily Telegraph*, and giving me only a quick nod of greeting. Usually in the morning my grandmother showed her upbringing by making the pre-breakfast meeting a somewhat formal affair, and her invariable routine was, "Good morning my dear, I hope you slept well." And this was followed by the ritual of a kiss on both cheeks, plus one in the middle for luck. But this morning was different, just a muttered, "Good morning Yvette", hardly raising her eyes from the paper before returning to scanning it with Granddad.

So I was rather puzzled as I ate breakfast, and I heard snatches of whispered remarks from Grannie in her soft French accent, "Are you sure, Andrew...? Are you quite sure?

I may say I think you are right, but it is so long ago…"

Granddad's reply, in his clipped British military voice was easier to overhear, "It seems incredible…I know you and I only saw him once, but it must be him, just look at the cleft chin, the pale eyes and the cap of black hair. Also notice that the place and the dates fit. Hélène, my dear, even at this late stage of our lives, I fear that we must finally act."

"To think that if we are right he's got away with it for all these long years…Oh, Andrew, what should we do?"

At last she turned to me, "Yvette, I'm sorry that we have been very rude this morning, but there is an item in the paper which has brought back a lot of most unpleasant memories. Please bear with us dear, but we are not yet ready to talk to you about it. We may have to speak to some other people first, but I promise that we'll explain things soon."

And with that I had to be satisfied, but I saw that Granddad took the paper with him when he retired to his study after the meal. I know that curiosity killed the cat, but I couldn't resist taking a walk into the village and buying another copy of the paper and reading it while I had a cup of coffee in a café. I scanned it carefully but could not see any item which could possibly fit in with their obvious distress. One possibility was something in the obituaries, but these involved an elderly actor, an even more elderly author, and a jazz musician who had died of AIDS at an early age – not a very hopeful lot. The news section was no better, as the editorial dealt mainly with a cabinet reshuffle necessitated by the sudden death of the Secretary of State for Defence and his replacement by Michael Marshall, a rising star in politics, and the son of Lord Hempson who was fast becoming the Grand Old Man of the party. Only on the sports page did I find something of interest, in the shape of an article about the US Masters which was due to be played at Augusta in the following week.

So it was with my curiosity still unsatisfied that, after a country walk, I made my way home for lunch. When I got there I could see that they had come to some conclusion. Typical of Granddad, any serious matter had to be dealt with correctly – one of his endearing characteristics – and I smiled to myself as he said, "Yvette, come and sit down and have a glass of sherry. Hélène and I have some things to tell you."

He bustled over to the sideboard and poured out the drinks, *La Ina* for me and for himself, but *Dubonnet* for Grannie who would never allow anything as vulgar as a drink from Spain to sully her lips. It was she who spoke first as she gazed at me over her half moon pince-nez, her only concession to old age, "Yvette, my dear, as you probably realised this morning Andrew and I have had a most unpleasant shock. Something from long ago which we thought was dead and buried has suddenly come alive, very much alive. It is a long tale. A few years ago when you began to be curious about the adventures which your grandfather and I had in France in 1944, we wrote our wartime experiences down for you. That seems appropriate at the time, but I'm afraid they weren't the full stories. We left out a lot of unpleasant bits. We thought then they should really only concern the two of us, but unfortunately that is no longer true, and so, as we are no longer young and fit, we hope to persuade you to take our place in doing what must now be done!"

That was the last thing I expected to hear, and I was just about to break in when Grannie silenced me with a gesture, "Just hear me out, child, we're not quite ready to explain things to you, so please don't be impatient. But I must warn you that you are going to have to be like the young Alice in Alice and Wonderland who was told that she would have to believe a lot of impossible things before breakfast, but in your case it will be after dinner. You see there are some people we would like to talk with, and unfortunately the most important one is in America so it will be a day or two till we can get hold of him. But although we cannot complete all our plans till then, Andrew and I feel that we should start now and tell you the background to the affair, why it is so important, and why we both hope that you will agree to be involved. But before I begin the tale – and Andrew too will tell you of his part in it – we want to have a quiet talk together, and we also have these other calls to make. So please be patient, dear, and we'll talk after dinner. I wonder if you will use this afternoon to read over again what we have already given you, and this evening we'll make a new start and include all the unpleasant bits!"

And that was that, so I had to nurse my unsatisfied curiosity all afternoon and, to pass the time, I took myself up to my bedroom then tried – and failed – to work out scenarios which could explain things. I could reread, of course, about their adventures in France, back in 1944, when they met and managed to flee together, first to Spain and then to Portugal, before flying back to England. Grannie had been involved in the French resistance movement helping allied airmen. I had also known that, ever since I was a little girl, Granddad had been some kind of hero since he had been awarded the DSO. However, I knew none of the details as both were reluctant to talk at any length about their experiences, and after a while I had just given up asking. In any case young people are really not interested in what, to them, is ancient history. What I did appreciate was that my grandfather had known how lucky he was to meet Grannie in these dangerous war-time days, which was shown by the fact that he had persuaded her to marry him while they were still in Portugal during their escape.

After the war, Granddad stayed on in the army. My father, John Dallachy, was an only child. There had been problems when he was born, and after that there could be no more children. Following Granddad's footsteps, my father became a regular army officer, also in the Argylls. Shortly after I was born, Granddad took retirement from some kind of staff work as a Brigadier at the Defence Ministry and settled in Henley-in-Arden in a charming little house. This gave my father and his young bride the opportunity to enjoy a short holiday and to leave me in the care of his parents who were eager to fuss over their infant granddaughter. Tragically, their return flight crashed and both my parents were killed, and what was to have been a temporary arrangement for my grandparents, suddenly turned to a permanent commitment. At that time my grandparents were in their late fifties, but they must have been still young in heart. I suppose that in some way I helped them overcome their grief at the loss of their son and I became the daughter they never had.

One wonderful thing they did for me was to ensure that I grew up bi-lingual, as when I was young Grannie never spoke to me other than in her native French and Granddad used English despite the fact that he was trilingual, having been brought up in Alsace in the 1920's and '30's. At that time more German than French was spoken there, so he had to use German at school, and then English and French at home with his Scottish father and his French mother.

Although Grannie was the major influence in my life, Granddad did one good thing by infecting me with his own passion for golf, and then ensuring that I played it well. This, certainly, was the reason that I chose to follow him by going to St Andrews University when I was eighteen to take an Arts degree.

Anyway, I spent that afternoon thinking over what I knew of my grandparents and reached the conclusion that, apart from creating the loving environment in which they had raised me, I really knew very little. Certainly, their consternation this morning was a complete mystery and Grannie's indication that I would be asked to help them in some way had me totally baffled. I confess that I was also bit excited by the unexpected turn of events and it was in this mood of eager anticipation that I went down to dinner.

That spring evening was one of those bonus ones stolen from high summer, and I could see that three chairs and a table had been arranged on the terrace outside, overlooking the garden. It was there, when the meal was over, that we sat down with a pot of coffee and glasses of *Grande Champagne Cognac* – Grannie had never lost her belief in the merits of a digestif after the evening meal. Granddad was sitting close beside her, as so often he was, and it touched me to see how strong the bond between them was.

It was to him that she spoke first, "Well, Andrew, this is a surprise, isn't it. Imagine finding ourselves after so many years about to tell our story to Yvette. It is some forty-seven years now since that meeting at Mélitour, back in 1956, when we all decided that the mystery – whatever it was – should die with us…but now? Who knows?"

I felt that this was the first of these impossible things I had to believe, as their adventure had been in 1944, and now she was talking about 1956, but I had more sense than to interrupt her, and she turned to me with a smile, and began almost hesitantly, "My dear child, you are so very young, and it is difficult for you to imagine that we were once young too, but I was almost the same age – twenty-one, going on twenty-two – as you now are, when the great adventure of my life began.

"Until now Andrew and I have only given you a brief out-
line of the happier parts of that adventure, of how in the
spring of 1944 – when he was an army major – he was passed
down an escape line to the Chateau de Mélitour where, as you
know, I was working as a nursemaid. We have glossed over
much of what happened and we have done this because there
is a dark side to the story which we, and the others concerned,
decided to keep to ourselves. But now something has come
up, something so surprising that we must tell you everything,
even though some parts of it are still painful to me today although nearly sixty years have passed. I must also tell you that,
sadly, some of the suffering still goes on. If I am going to explain it all to you, I must start when I was even younger that
you now are, when I was almost sixteen, and going to be interviewed for a job at the Chateau."

"But Grannie," I broke in, "I hope you are going to tell
me why you never once took me to your part of France. You
and Granddad always had some excuse not to go there, despite the fact that we took most of our holidays in France. I'm
sure that you will remember that at last I stopped asking…as I
could see that it was forbidden ground."

She turned and looked at Granddad for a moment, and
then back to me, "Yes, Yvette, we saw how puzzled you were,
and often wondered if we should tell you everything. Maybe
we should have done that but, as I've told you, we and the
others involved decided, back in 1956, that no good would
come of our bringing the affair out into the open. Maybe we
were right, maybe not, however as from today things have
changed and our secret must now be yours as well. Let me
start from the beginning…"

Before I continue, let me explain that the wartime experiences which follow, as told to me my grandmother and grand-

father that evening and on subsequent occasions, provide the background to my own adventure. That adventure would change my life and so it has been personally important that I should have accurately reported here the words which first Grannie and then Granddad used. I am confident that I have been true to myself, but if I have gone wrong anywhere, I'm sure that I haven't lost the sense of what was said.

Anyway, let me get on with Grannie's story…

Chapter One

She paused, as if reluctant to begin, but then shrugged her shoulders and turned to Granddad, "Isn't it absurd, Andrew, I find myself almost frightened to begin, so give me a top-up of Cognac. I need, not Dutch courage, but some good French stuff!"

So it was with a refilled glass in her hand that at last she began. "You already know a lot of my story. What I have decided to do is to go over it all, but only go into detail about the difficult bits which are new to you and some of these are in fact the very best!" She paused again before going on, "Back to the beginning. I was born in the little town of Chaource – in fact hardly a town, just a big village – set in the Department of Yonne bang in the middle of France. The Department begins south of Troyes, and extends for about 60 kilometres. It was then, and still is, almost entirely agricultural land or forests with a smattering of small villages. The only towns of any size are Tonnere, with about 6,000 people and Auxerre, much larger at about six times the size. The important thing to remember is the sparse population, and about sixty years ago, within a radius of 20 kilometres from Chaource, there can't have been more than just a few hundred people. This remoteness, I can tell you, was to be very useful to us during the war.

"In Chaource my father had a cabinet-making business. My good fortune was that the old Comte de Mélitour had discovered his skill a long time ago, and it was because of this contact that I was invited to go and see the young Comtesse in connection with the post of nursemaid to her baby son Albert. My story begins on a day in April in 1938, when I was sixteen and got on my bike to ride the ten kilometres from my home for the interview at the Chateau de Mélitour. It was a bright summer day, and when I rode through the great entrance gates of the Chateau grounds it was like entering a Garden of Eden – it was so perfect. The grounds were in fact small compared to some of the great houses, extending as they did to only some ten hectares, but they were big to me, and with six gardeners there wasn't a weed to be seen, and the extensive lawns were like bowling greens. You will remember from what you have read that the family, apart from their great estate, also own La Maison d'Argent, one of the major department stores in Paris. I have told you of the happy pre-war years with Albert my young charge and my growing friendship with Marie-Claire, the young Comtesse de Mélitour. But all that was to end when her husband the Comte was killed in May 1940 while serving with the French army.

"Gone now was the happy young Comtesse, and although she still arranged the affairs of the Chateau as expertly as before, she did it like an automaton. It was when the first Germans came to see her that I realised what was now her driving force – hatred of the Germans who had despoiled her beloved France and killed her dear husband. That first visit might not have gone off too badly if it had been made only by the very polite middle aged Colonel, who explained that he had simply come to assure her that she would not be inconvenienced. Unfortunately, however, he was accompanied by a Lieutenant Hermann Kretzer, an almost impossibly smart and arrogant young man who looked every inch a Nazi."

She paused for a moment and said, "These ranks of course

are wrong, I should call them Oberst, and Oberleutnant, but I'll just Anglicise them to Colonel and Lieutenant. The Colonel was then on crutches waiting, he told us, to get an artificial foot, and then went on to say that he had been crippled when his unit was shot up by a British fighter plane. As the Colonel said this I noticed a grimace of hatred pass over the young Lieutenant's face, and I realised that whatever his feelings were for the French, it was for the British that he reserved his real hatred.

"It was after they drove off that the barrier of employer to servant suddenly broke down. Having been icily polite till they drove off, she suddenly burst into floods of tears and I found myself with my arms around her, mingling my tears with hers , and we formed an alliance that afternoon – one oddly enough that we never felt the need to put into words – that we would do everything possible to hurt the bastards. But what could we do? We lived in a remote Chateau, surrounded by miles and miles of fields, mostly wheat and other cereal crops, and in between the fields some woodland areas. There were no vineyards as the areas of Chablis and Burgundy were further to the south. Life had to go on, but it was a kind of suspended animation, with our only source of joy coming from the development of young Albert.

"It was, in fact, nearly two years later, after the nights of the 30th and 31st of May 1942 that, in a way, Marie-Claire came alive again. These were the nights on which the RAF struck Cologne and Essen, massing over a thousand bombers in each raid. We listened to the news from the BBC on an illegal radio she had in her bedroom, and when she excitedly threw her arms round me, saying, 'Isn't it wonderful, Hélène, now at last the British are giving these damn Germans some of their own medicine. Let's have a drink to celebrate.'

"As I remember it that one drink became two – or maybe more – as we shared our hopes that these great bombing raids would change the direction of the war. Abruptly she stopped talking and then, with a little shout of triumph, exclaimed, 'Hélène, suddenly I know what we can do to help!' And she then went on to explain what, in retrospect, seemed so obvious, 'Undoubtedly, these raids will be very hazardous. Formations of bombers make an easy target for German defences and I fear that many of these aircraft will be shot down. The outcome for the bomber crews will most likely be a horrible death, but surely there will be some who manage to parachute to safety, and also try – somehow – to escape capture and return home. Their aid will be my cause and, my dear Hélène, I wish that it to be yours too.'

"And that," said Grannie, "was the beginning. Surprisingly, the intention was easily put into practice because Marie-Claire was well respected within the region. Soon both of us became involved with an escape route for Allied airmen, who were trying to get down to Spain. Once confidence in Marie-Claire was established, and her abilities recognised, she was appointed to be the leader of our local group, but this was not without problems because she had be absolutely certain about the loyalty of the Chateau staff. You should realise that, in those dreadful days, it was sadly true that many in France thought that the war was over, and they might as well become as friendly as they could with the Germans, and do nothing to annoy them. Fortunately there were no problems with the inside staff as since the war had started two men had retired, and two of the women had married, leaving just two young women that Marie-Claire had known since childhood. There was Alicia who taken over as cook, and Michelle who did the other housework. But Marie-Claire still worried about the gardeners, and although two had left, there remained two younger lads about whom she was doubtful and two middle-aged brothers, both of whom were army veterans of the 1914-1918 war, on whom she felt she could rely.

"In fact it didn't take her long to solve the problem as the Chateau owned several farms, so she spoke to the young men, saying that she had arranged work for them on one of the farms, explaining that food production was now all-important. When this was arranged she took the older men aside and explained what she proposed to do as regards the escape line. As she expected they were enthusiastic and were keen to help in any way they could. I was at this meeting, and I had better mention their names – George and Pierre Martins – as one day they were to save my life and that of my dear Andrew, your grandfather."

I couldn't help breaking in, "Tell me more, Grannie!" But she shook her head, saying, "Just be patient, my dear, we'll come to that event in good time, but not for quite a while yet, so let's get on with that meeting with the two of them. Georges told us one thing which was to become very important later. He and his brother had both brought back a souvenir from the 1914-18 war, a revolver each. He explained that they were clumsy great things, Webley 45s, which they had picked up from dead British officers, complete with bullets. The Comtesse laughed and thanked them for their offer, but reminded them that if we were to get involved in a shooting war, all would then be lost. Our only hope, she emphasised, was to work underground, and to do nothing which might arouse German suspicion."

She stopped again and said, "You have already read about the setting up of our escape group, about how we were responsible to a British officer who we only knew as M. Ombre

— the shadow. The whole organisation was set up on a 'need to know' basis, so if any of us were picked up by the Germans there was little we could tell them — just the names of the few people here — so the rest of the line would be safe. Marie-Claire told us that M. Ombre carried a suicide pill just in case he was picked up. I think that I can skip the next two years, as you have already read about them and our many successes, but I would just remind you of one occasion when Marie-Claire invited the old German Colonel and Lt. Kretzer to dinner. It was important to her to appear friendly towards them. Kretzer tried to get fresh with me and I slapped his face, and that didn't at all get me into his good books. Then on another evening she and I were asked to have dinner with them in their headquarters near Tonnere."

She paused there, and suddenly a thought was triggered in my mind, and I said, "Look, Grannie, you've now covered the four years — 1938 to 1942 — and you are now going on from there. It all began when you were just sixteen but you haven't mentioned any of your friends, and not a single boyfriend. Your story is fascinating, and I hope that I can write it down sometime, but you really must paint in some of the background, particularly about what you did in your spare time. Whatever you were, you would never have been a wallflower!"

"I would remind you," Grannie smiled, "that you have never been very forthcoming yourself when it came to talking about your boyfriends. When we do manage to drag anything about them from you, it is as if you are talking about cardboard characters!"

"Touché, Grannie," I said, "but I'm getting to be a big girl now, not as shy as I used to be, so I'll trade. Right now I'm twenty-one, almost the age you were when your big adventure took place, and although — as you know — I've had several boy-friends, none have been really serious, so maybe I did see them as cardboard characters."

I paused there, but suddenly felt that a confidence of mine might get something in return, so I went on, "Incidentally, it may surprise you to know that I must be an old-fashioned girl as I am still a virgin!" Granddad laughed, "Well, Hélène, you've no excuses now, you must tell all, including all that X Certificate stuff you've never told me about, but not right now as I think it is time we went in as it is getting cold,"

That was a very good suggestion so in we went and settled ourselves around the living-room fire after which I said, "Yes, do go on, Grannie!" She looked at us severely, but there was a twinkle in her eyes, "I'm, afraid, Yvette, that you are going to be sadly disappointed as there is only one X in my young love-life, and that is Andrew! Anyway, as he well knows, I too was a virgin when I first came to him! What a night this is for con-fessions! Before we go to bed I'll tell you a sad little story. Back in the winter of 1941-42 both my parents – your great grandparents-died, my father first and then my mother just a week later. It was as if she didn't want to live on alone. They had been incomers to Chaource, so that left me with no rela-tives in the town and in fact only one other anywhere, my much elder brother who was married and lived in Reims. You may remember me telling you that he too died some 25 years ago, before you were born. Anyway, after my parent's death my only ostensible reason for visiting Chaource was to shop. But there was also a private reason – to meet a young man, Joseph Blum. None of what I am going to tell you is news to my dear Andrew, as he knew it all even before we were mar-ried. The Blums were our next door neighbours in Chaource, a delightful Jewish family, and his parents and mine were close friends. Generations of Blums had lived in the town and I suppose that, in a sense, they were bad Jews, as none of them were – at least overtly – religious, and over the years many of them had married Gentiles. Joseph and I had been friends since early childhood but, as I have said, we were an innocent young couple and, although we came to love each other we never got much further than kissing and petting – as you call it these days. Things might well have been different, and indeed we might have got married, but Joseph was adamant that so long as the Germans were in control it was impossible, saying that any formal link with a Jew was perilous, and marriage would have been the worst of all as it would place me in the same category as himself.

"He was a gentle boy and by 1942 he was in his third year at the University of Reims studying to be a vet, but not for pampered cats and dogs, because his interests lay in the field of horses and farm animals. The demands of his studies meant that I only saw him during the university holidays. When we met at the start of his summer vacation for that year I could see that he had become seriously worried, not so much for himself, but for his parents. He told me that if the worst came to the worst, he could run, but they couldn't. There was good reason for his worries as our newspapers were already beginning to parrot those horrible anti-Semitic German lies. He returned to the university deeply fearful for the safety of his family. Things got much worse after November 1942. Maybe, Yvette, you'll have read that the Allies invaded North Africa then, and in response the Germans occupied the whole of France, taking control over the area to the south which had previously had a semblance of autonomy under the puppet French government in Vichy. At the same time the German grip on the country became much tighter.

"I had been looking forward to seeing Joseph during the

Christmas holidays, but it was not to be. When he came home it was to find that his parents and some other relatives had, just the previous day, been arrested and taken away. But when they came for him, he was ready. He knew where his father had hidden a gun, brought back from the 1914-18 war, just like our old gardeners had done, and he shot two German soldiers and their Sergeant before turning the gun on himself."

Grannie stopped there, and shook her head sadly, "...and that Yvette is the story of my first love, a gentle young man who died in a blaze of glory. He has never been forgotten in Chaource, and fresh flowers are still placed on his grave. But, if I did not find luck in my first love, how very lucky I have been with my second." I saw her look over at Granddad, and he reached over and held her hand for a moment, and they both smiled at each other before she turned back to me. "...and that's enough for tonight!"

Chapter Two

Next morning the weather had reverted to winter, so I had no excuse but to get down to my books and do some much-needed revision, after all it was now less than three months until my final exams in June. But after lunch when I was looking forward – with no great pleasure – to doing some more work, I was surprised by Grannie saying, "Yvette, while your grandfather goes off for his usual post-prandial snooze it will give me a chance to go on with some of the bad bits in my story, and I warn you they will be difficult for me to tell – and for you to hear. The account will take me up to the time when I first met Andrew. If I do it without him beside me I won't embarrass him, as I have to say some nice things about him." Granddad looked over at me as he got up to go, saying, "I can guess some of the things she'll talk about, as she always works on the principle that flattery will get you anywhere – and that's how she got me!"

But, trust Grannie, she got in the last word. "Just push off Andrew, and leave us alone!"

So it was just the two of us, sitting beside each other on a couch near the fireplace, as she went on. "I suppose that we were remarkably lucky, as right through 1943 and into 1944 we continued with our work, and although I never counted them we must have received and passed on some two hundred or so airmen. The flow gradually increased especially after the United States joined the war and we began to receive Americans as well. It gave us enormous satisfaction to hear of the increasing number of air raids, the destruction of so many German cities and of the death of so many Germans, so we were proud to help our clients who had done all this for us."

She stopped there and leaned over to take my hand. "I hope Yvette that you aren't too shocked by these bloodthirsty feelings we had then, but just try to imagine what had happened to France, and to our loved ones. How could we fail to hate the Germans, and believe in the saying of the time, 'The only good German is a dead German.' But I'm afraid that we were getting overconfident, after all we had got on for some two years without disaster, but sadly it couldn't last, and it started with an accident to young Albert.

"The Comtesse and I still used our bicycles as did other members in our group, and to make things look normal she sometimes took Albert, a tough 7-year-old, with us. What could be more innocent than a mother and child out with the nursemaid?

"It was early in April when he had his accident on one of these outings, and it was such a silly one. We had been visiting a farm which occasionally we used to hide some of our clients and, as we were leaving, a hen ran across the road in front of him. He swerved to avoid it, but it was a dirt road and his front wheel skidded, causing him to fall heavily, and break his leg. It turned out to be an awkward break, and the poor little chap had to be plastered from hip to ankle.

Just a day or two after that a message came to the Comtesse in the late afternoon. She called me into her office, and told me that she had to meet our British controller, M. Ombre the following day. This was odd, as although he kept a watching brief over all the parts of the escape chain for which he was responsible, he seldom met people, unless to deal with a special operation. However the heads of all the groups in his area were to meet in a woodman's hut in the forest between Chaource and Bar-sur-Sein, and she had to be there by eleven o'clock, so would need to leave immediately after breakfast.

"When she came back there was a sparkle in her eyes, and I knew that the news must be good. In fact it really wasn't all that good, just that we were going to be busier than ever. We had heard on the radio about heavy Allied air attacks, particularly in the Pas de Calais area, and the warning was that because it was well defended, many planes were likely to get shot down. None of us knew of course, that three quite separate air attack operations were being carried out. First there were general and wide-spread attacks on the French railway system and on road bridges so as to hamper German troop movements, then there were the attacks in the Pas de Calais as part of the deception plan to persuade the Germans that the invasion would come by that, the shortest route, and the third were concentrated attacks on the launch sites for the V1 flying bombs, although of course we didn't even know then that they existed. All three operations were very successful, and when the flying bomb attacks began in June, our fighters were better prepared than they might have been."

She paused then, and looked over at me. "And I can also tell you, Yvette, that the RAF shot down far more of these flying bombs than they might have done, thanks to the bravery of my Andrew!" She was about to go on, but I broke in, "Is that why he was awarded his DSO? Will you tell me about that? Is it a part of your story?" However again she just shook her head, saying, "All these explanations will come when it is appropriate for them to do so. After all we have to ensure that you hear the whole story. We feel that it is only if you do so that we will be able to persuade you to act on our behalf."

Here again was this suggestion that I was to get involved, and all I could do was to mutter a reluctant, "OK, Grannie," and to sit back and listen some more.

"Now let me return to my story and continue from where I was so rudely interrupted," she went on with a smile to me, "the agent, M. Ombre, told the Comtesse that the British were now going to adopt a more hands-on approach, as a rehearsal of what would happen when the Allies were in France. He was in fact being moved to a base near the coast, and his place in our area was being taken by a young British officer who was also present at the meeting. The Comtesse didn't say so in as many words, but I could see that she preferred M. Ombre. The new man – a British army officer just like M. Ombre – spoke perfect colloquial French, and his nom de guerre was to be M. Brume (the Mist). She spoke some more about him, and she confessed to being worried as he seemed so young for the job, but she then laughed and wondered if the new agent had his own worries about how young she was. He was apparently quite handsome, tall with black hair, and a rather deeply cleft chin.

"But on to more important things because here is what the Comtesse then went on to say to me, 'Hélène, you must often have thought about how I hold your life in my hands, and also all the lives of the other members of our group. We've all heard stories about German interrogation methods and how they treat their prisoners. I always felt that we might be lucky in this area as the Colonel was an officer from the old school, but the news is that he has been sent away, and we are in the hands of Major Kretzer. That's right – Major – with the departure of the Colonel he has been promoted to major. I shudder to think what that bastard would do to us if he were to find that we had been smuggling aircrews right past his nose. We have discussed this before; the real hazard to the group is if I were to be picked up, as I know the names and addresses of all our members. Anyway, I took the opportunity today to ask our new controller, M. Brume, if he could get me one of the suicide pills. At first he was doubtful, but then said that he understood my concern, and gave one to me.'"

Grannie stopped and glanced at me, "I can remember sitting there feeling absolutely horrified, but Marie-Claire then went on and said with a smile, 'Don't look so sad, Hélène, it is a load off my mind, and probably nothing will ever happen, but death is infinitely preferable to captivity – and what would then be in store for me. I can also tell you that I am now going to make arrangements with my lawyer in Tonnere about Albert, just in case the worst does happen. His grandmother, my mother-in-law, is still in Cannes, and she is the obvious person to act as his guardian, helped by you, Hélène, if that is possible.' It was a bad time, dear Yvette, and I can remember that day as if it were yesterday. I sat there, almost overcome with horror at hearing my dear mistress and friend talking of the possibility of her early death in such a matter-of-fact manner, but she brushed aside my halting words of comfort, just saying, 'I told you a few moments ago, Hélène, not to look so sad. Remember that we all have our parts to play, and none of the others need know about this. So cheer up and be your normal bright self at dinner time.'"

Grannie paused again, and I could see a faraway look in her eyes as if she were reliving those dreadful times, and she now spoke very quietly. "Looking back at the far-off spring of 1944, everything seemed to happen at once. Albert's accident was early in April, and Marie-Claire's meeting with the new British agent was on the 13th of April. Then two days later she went off again to have a meeting with her opposite number in

Troyes. When she came back I could see that she was the bearer of bad tidings. He had told her that the group to our north, based on Calons-sur-Marne, was in trouble, with several of its members having been arrested, so the word was to keep our heads down and be careful.

"We were by then living very much as a family, and it was three days later, on the 18th, just as we were finishing dinner, when she chose to tell the three of us – Michelle, Alicia, and me – some dreadful news. But, typical of her, she chose to sweeten the pill, quite literally! We were about to start the sweet course – delicious plates of strawberries from the glass house – when she pulled the cork of a wine bottle on which I could read the label, Château d'Yquem 1927, one of the greatest Sauternes in the world, pure golden magic.

"As she poured it out she said, 'I hope that this lovely wine will do something to compensate for the dreadful news I have to tell you. There has been a disaster in the area to the south of ours, between Auxerre and Bourges. The controller there was a very old friend of the Mélitour family, and I know him well. He was a general in the First Army in 1940, and my dear Jean-Pierre was under his command. He was so devastated then by the catastrophe of 1940 that he retired immediately after the Armistice, coming to live in Sancerre. Until yesterday all had gone well, but there must have been some breach of security as, very early in the morning, German soldiers came to his house to arrest him. Fortunately for us, and for the rest of his group, he had a gun and managed to kill one of them, before turning the gun on himself. Certainly his heroism would seem to have saved us as there have been no moves in our direction, so we can only hope that we remain safe.'

"That wasn't all the bad news, as she went on, 'Until recently I had been getting more and more optimistic that our network would survive undiscovered until the Allies opened the Second Front and cleansed France once more. However, last month I made a deal with a senior British agent who came to visit us, and I told him that in exchange for my continued cooperation I wanted false papers for Albert and myself, and also for the three of you. It was my hope that, if the worst came to the worst, they would give all of us a chance of escape, if we were lucky enough to get any warning of trouble. I have been so confident, perhaps foolishly so, that I decided not to tell you anything about it. But this new event is certainly a clear warning that there may be trouble ahead. So far as I am concerned, of course, this avenue of escape is not at present open to me, not while Albert still has his leg in plaster, so for now let's concentrate on the three of you.'

"I can remember that it was quite a while before she went on, 'I have here papers for each of you, and you will see that you are described as shop girls, and that you work in La Maison d'Argent, our family shop in Paris. The manager, M. Duchene, knows of this, and he has a key to a small apartment in which you can live. So please study these papers carefully. You must each learn your new identities as well as those of the other two, just in case you are questioned separately. I have agonised whether or not I should ask you to go now, but I think that we owe it to the others in the group not to do anything immediately, in case it is a false alarm and that the Germans are not on to us. But as soon as there is a whiff of danger − be off! I wouldn't expect the Germans to come in by other than the front door, so get everything prepared now so that you can run at the drop of a hat. For a start I suggest that you park your bicycles in the stable in the back courtyard with just the bare minimum of things already packed in the pannier bags. Keep these papers with you at all times so that you can make for your bikes and be off through the woods at the back. With the maze of little roads around here I think you have a very good chance of getting away. So remember, don't wait for permission – just GO!'

"She then went to her desk and produced three envelopes, one for each of us. 'Here are your papers, and you will see that I have also enclosed some francs as you'll need money on your journey to Paris…any questions?' Any questions? Of course we had questions, but the main one we were too ashamed to put into words. Why was she favouring us with special concern and neglecting the other members of our group?

"As if reading our minds, she said, 'The others should be alright. Just remember that I was careful to pick girls who were not from this immediate district, and although you may have met some of them, they do not know your names, just as you don't know theirs, so there shouldn't be anything to give them away. The only two here who are in the know are our gardeners, Georges and Pierre who would certainly come under suspicion were I to be arrested. But I have warned them what they must do. They are both very good at pretending to be dim-witted sons of the soil, so I'm sure that they will be convincing if they ever have to plead ignorance of the whole affair.'

"She paused there and told us to get busy and read up about our new identities, and about half an hour later she said, 'That's enough for now, I suggest you go up now and sort out what you want in your pannier bags, and then get them packed. From now on you must be ready to go instantly.' It was a beautiful spring evening and out in the courtyard, where we when to pack our bags, there wasn't a breath of wind or any sounds. It was all so peaceful that it seemed a sacrilege to be making these preparations. Ironically, just as we were finishing a nightingale chose to start its song, so maybe it wasn't surprising that the poignancy of the contrast between this lovely song, the talk about betrayal and death, and the shadow of the evil Major Kretzer hanging over us, left us all with tears on our cheeks.

"The next morning was an anti-climax. Nothing happened, but we were an anxious and unhappy household. Then early in the afternoon something did come to break the calm of the day. The phone rang, and Marie-Claire answered it. It was just a brief call, but I saw a shadow come over her face, followed by a look of despair. She said very little, just, 'I am so very sorry but yes, tell Paul I'll meet him there as soon as possible...bon chance...'"

I could see that the events of that day were still very clear to Grannie, and she went on to tell me that the Comtesse had slowly put the phone down then turned to Grannie and quietly said that she must immediately find Michelle and Alicia and tell them to come at once for the news was very bad.

Grannie continued with her account of the drama, "When the three of us had hurriedly assembled before the Comtesse she told us that the call had been from the secretary of the controller of our neighbouring group, based in Troyes. Half an hour ago the Germans had moved in and arrested his two deputies. By good fortune she and the controller had been visiting a friend just across the road, and had seen what was happening. Also his car had been in a nearby garage, so he was going to try to escape and make for Etourvy. Marie-Claire then explained to us about a secret house there which was stocked with dried food and water in which he could hide for a long time.

"The Comtesse then went on to say, 'There was more to that telephone call. It was explained that he has something very important to tell me. The unexpected German action against those unfortunate groups in our region over the last few days has caused me to suspect that there is a traitor in our midst. Of course it is impossible to talk openly over the telephone but I was lead to understand that my suspicions had been correct and that the controller in Troyes must have found out who it is. Anyway, his secretary tells me that he feels that he must immediately speak to me. So, I am now going to cycle over to the safe house in Etourvy to learn at first hand was he has discovered. Now, girls, just in case I need your help, will the three of you please risk staying here till I get back? But you must remember – go at once if anything suspicious happens!'

"When she rode off I did some sums, and reckoned that if all went well with the Troyes controller's car trip, he would probably arrive in Etourvy before she got there and that she would get back not later that about five o'clock. I wasn't far wrong as not long after five I saw her racing up the drive, then flinging her bicycle down at the front steps and running into the house calling, 'Come at once, girls!'

"I shall never forget her look of anguish. Obviously she had cycled as fast as she could, so she was breathless, and her words tumbled out in fits and starts, 'we meet in ten minutes...I must wash...then there is something I must do...'

When we assembled again, she seemed to be more composed. 'It's awful, when I got to Etourvy I met the man from Troyes and he was able to confirm that there is indeed a traitor in the organisation and, as a consequence, the whole chain is being torn apart. That is the bad news, but there is good news. He also gave me a package containing his notes which explain who the traitor is together with a vital bit of evidence to prove it. Because of the present situation I felt that I daren't keep the package with me, as it is far too precious – and dangerous. So on my way back here I hid it where it is most unlikely to be discovered, but where it will be easy for you three to find, if you have the necessary instructions. For now it looks very much as though our time here is over, and I have decided to tell you nothing more, not even the name of the traitor. In fact I dare not do so as the less you know the safer you will be. If the Germans were ever to hear of it they would I am sure, just deal with things in one way – a quick death for anybody who might be privy to the information. However as things are coming to an end here, this information is now only of value for one thing – REVENGE. Even though I cannot tell you now, I would not like the information to die with me, so I have written a short letter addressed to the three of you, telling you where to find the package with the proof of the traitor's identity. I then tore the letter into three pieces, and put one piece into each of these three envelopes.'

"She stood up and gave each of us one of the envelopes, saying, 'The solemn commitment, girls, to which I hope you will agree, is a very simple one, and is the same for each of you.

(1) That you will not open your envelopes until both the following conditions are met:

    (a) that I am dead, and

    (b) that the war is over.

(2) That if and when both items of (1) are satisfied, the three of you will then try to meet and piece together the three pieces of the note. This will tell you where to find the package.

(3) I cannot know what the circumstances will then be, so I leave it to you whether or not you destroy the evidence, or whether you pass it on to whatever authority is then the appropriate one in a post-war France.'

"She actually counted these points off on her fingers as she made them and, despite her exhaustion and emotional turmoil, she smiled while she spoke as if she found her precision somehow amusing. 'Of course, I fervently wish to live thought the war and deal with the matter myself. In that case I shall try to get in touch with you. Hopefully, I will be able to tell you that he too has survived so that you will witness my exposure of the bastard. I only wish that I could kill him myself!'"

Grannie stopped there, and I could see that she was back again in that awful afternoon, and thinking about how they had all hated the Germans, and also this unknown traitor. "You know," she went on, "war is an awful thing. All three of us, and Marie-Claire too, would happily have killed the traitor with our bare hands, whoever he was." She then opened her handbag, which was always beside her, and produced a plain white envelope, at which she looked thoughtfully. "So here is my envelope, still sealed as it has been since 1944, and until yesterday, Yvette, I thought that this matter was dead and buried, but now things have changed. I should go to Paris to talk things over with the other two, Alicia and Michelle, who also are concerned, but unfortunately neither Andrew nor I feel up to the journey. What I hope is that I can persuade you to take on the obligation which Marie-Claire put on my shoulders all those years ago. It may surprise you to know that she is still alive!"

"But Grannie," I said, "the war has now been over for nearly sixty years, and if as you tell me, the Comtesse is still alive and has done nothing all this time, why should you bother now? After all, her instructions to you only come into effect after she has died – and you've just said that she hasn't! Also to suggest that I should be involved is surely absurd? I'm sure you know I would do anything for you or for Granddad, but why? Why all this? It is ancient history now, and who will be interested?"

She reached over and took my hand, "Not quite so, dear, although I could wish that it were. Will you be patient and hear the rest of it? There is still more to tell you about that afternoon, as first Alicia and Michelle had to get their bikes and ride off to the shelter of the woods. It was an emotional parting and I wished I could have gone with them. But I couldn't as I had one more job to do, and I hoped to join them in the evening in a safe house we had in a neighbouring village.

"You see the Comtesse had taken me aside and said, 'Unfortunately for you, Hélène, there is one more thing which I would like you to do. When I was in Etourvy a message was passed to me that a British soldier – a Major – who must have been involved in some under-cover operation, had got to Troyes this afternoon. Despite all their problems they managed an arrangement to send him here, to Chaource. He is being brought down by a truck bringing a load of wine as, very conveniently, it is market day tomorrow. It will come at about 7 o'clock tonight, and unload behind the market building. We now, of course, have a problem as we cannot pass him south through Auxerre, and the best option I can think of is for you to meet and take him to the safe house in Etourvy, and he can wait there till the heat is off. I confess I don't like the plan and the delay in getting him away, but I can't think of anything better. So will you please take on this last task? Pick up one of the spare bicycles in Chaource, meet him, and ride with him to Etourvy?'

"I can tell you my nod of acceptance was a reluctant one, but nod I did, and she hurried on, 'Good, I was sure I could rely on you, so here is a little map of Etourvy to show you where the house is, just up on the left from that little square in the middle of the village.' As you will realise, Yvette, it was an emotional time for us. We three girls had a chance, a very good chance, of escape, but Marie-Claire could not consider leaving her dear son, and we could only hope that she did not need to use her suicide pill. My distress must have shown as she put her arms round me, and comforted me like a mother with her child, but soon she gently pushed me away, saying, 'We have no time for the luxury of tears, we must be brave, and it is time now that you left for Chaource. But before you do, let's stop in the garden as I must tell Georges and Pierre how things are, and it would be nice if you would say au revoir to them.'"

Grannie looked up at me before going on, "I haven't said much about these two, but as I have told you they were loyal servants of the old school, and when she told them her news it was like the end of the world to them. She explained that if anything happened to her, the Dowager Comtesse would come back to care for Albert, and look after the estate till he grew to manhood. As always, it was Georges who was the spokesman, and Pierre always did what his elder brother told him to do.

"'Madame la Comtesse, it has been a privilege for Pierre and me to have served you and your family since we were young lads. I was employed by your husband's father back in 1908, and Pierre followed two years later, but in all these years this is the saddest time. Just to think that we beat the Bosch back in 1918, and were foolish enough then to let them get off their knees. Pray God we won't be so foolish this time.' Suddenly his voice broke, choked with emotion, and having been so formal he suddenly stepped forward and put his hand on

her shoulder, saying 'Madame, as I told you when all this began two years ago, Pierre and I have guns. Old they may be
but they can still kill, and if we can help at any time you have
only to ask or give us a sign.'

"Marie-Claire took his hand, and stretched out her other
hand to Pierre, 'My dear old friends, I am deeply touched, and
I greatly appreciate your loyalty, but I am afraid that two guns,
even in such capable hands as yours, will not be enough,
but...' She stopped there, then looked thoughtfully at Georges, and went on to say, 'But now there IS something which
you can do.' She went on to explain about my going off to
meet a British soldier in Chaource with instructions to take
him to Etourvy, and the ever-present possibility of my meeting up with a German motorbike and sidecar patrol. I can't
remember her exact words, but in modern parlance, she asked
them to ride shotgun to me and the soldier.

"I could see that it was like a fix to a drug addict as their
eyes brightened at the chance to DO something, and immediately Georges changed from being a gardener to being the efficient Corporal which he had been almost thirty years before.
He straightened his shoulders, and said to me, 'Mlle. Hélène, it
will be a privilege to help you. Go now and meet your soldier
in Chaource at 7 o'clock as arranged, and you won't see a sight
nor a sound of us. I'll ride ahead to scout for any trouble, and
Pierre will be at a safe distance behind, ready to come up and
help if required. We mustn't ride as a tight group. This, I can
tell you, has given us back our pride, especially as we may get a
chance to shoot one of the bastards.'

"It was just the tonic that I needed, and I laughed as I said
to Georges, 'Maybe you would like to come across some
Germans, but I'm looking forward to a nice quiet trip to
Etourvy where I can drop off the soldier, and then make for

my rendezvous with Michelle and Alicia.' George asked where they would be waiting and I replied, 'Up in one of our estate cottages, near Germigny'. That seemed to satisfy him, 'Right, we'll escort you to Etourvy, and then take you to meet your friends.' Marie-Claire managed a smile at us before saying, 'That's enough talk, you really must all get off now, all three of you, or you'll be late.'

"After all that had gone before, my leave taking from Marie-Claire was oddly formal. She just placed a kiss on each of my cheeks. 'I won't say adieu, my dear, it must only be au revoir. Keep safe, dear Hélène, now off you go.'"

Grannie paused again for a moment, and I broke in, "Before you go on, one thing puzzles me. You have talked about the Comtesse and your friends, but you have hardly even mentioned your charge, young Albert. By this time he must have been about seven, so what about him, what about farewells to him?"

Grannie was still for a moment, as if lost for words, and before she could speak Granddad came into the room, and having heard my question he smiled at her and said, "Hélène, I told you that now you shouldn't try to hide anything. Anyway, if there was fault that day just remember a large part of it was mine. After all, you wanted to stay but I was the one who dragged you away from him!"

It was as if with my question, I'd turned over a stone and found something nasty underneath, "Look I've no business and no wish to pry. Don't worry if there are some things you wish to keep to yourselves. We all have some areas which we want to keep personal and private."

But, as I was talking I could see that she had come to a conclusion, as she sat up straight and gave a nod to Granddad, as if to thank him for what he had said. "Yvette, in answer to

your question, the reason why I have not mentioned Albert is
that I am ashamed. I try to blot the whole thing out of my
mind, and I've been trying to do so now for nearly sixty years.
I'm sure Freud would love to have studied me. The fact is that
he was a wonderful little boy, he depended on me and to him
I must have been like a second mother. I was proud that he
loved me, but yet I ran away when he most needed me, and
when his safe childhood world was falling apart. Maybe if I
had stayed, the disaster might not have been so overwhelming.
I don't know, but that thought remains with me like a shadow
to this very day. I haven't in fact seen Albert since 1956 when
he was nineteen. He certainly had not forgiven me then, but I
live in hope that the years will have taken away some of the
pain. Indeed, our intention is to ask you to visit him and,
when you do, I pray that you will find him more forgiving."

Things seemed to be moving to the point of absurdity. We
had been talking about 1944, and here was 1956 cropping up
again. "Grannie," I said, "why on earth should I want to talk
to Albert? Your story has been set in 1944 when he was seven,
so now he must be in his sixties. What possible interest can he
have in meeting me?"

"Yvette, I will tell you everything, but for now let's leave it
till this evening – we've talked enough this afternoon." As I
had been speaking I'd seen Granddad coming over to sit beside her and they gave each other a little nod as if to agree
something and it was she who spoke. "Just be patient till this
evening, as a lot more will be explained then." I still had reservations. "Your story, Grannie, is fascinating, and I'll wait till
tonight to hear the rest, but one other thing puzzles me. When
speaking about the Comtesse you sometimes use her title, but
often you change to call her Marie-Claire…why not always the
same?"

"But that, Yvette, is easy to answer. You see I was proud to call her my friend, but also she was my boss, both when I was her servant and when she was, in a way, my commanding officer, and so even now there is this duality when I think of her." And with that I had to be satisfied. But I was looking forward to the evening.

Chapter Three

When we sat down that evening I saw that again they were sitting together on the couch, as if to support each other, and she shook her head sadly, saying, "I'm afraid that there is still much to tell you, which I must relate in some detail, as otherwise you may end up thinking, as I suspect you now do, that the whole thing is a bee in an old lady's bonnet…but it ain't! Now, where was I? Ah yes, I had just got to the point when I was about to go off to Chaource on my bike to meet the British soldier, and I didn't then know that I was going to run away and desert young Albert, just when he most needed me.

"To begin with all went well. I got into the town in plenty of time and decided to go into a little *épicerie* to do some shopping. It had occurred to me that Michelle and Alicia had dashed off without taking any food with them, so I bought enough so that we could have some kind of a meal when I joined them and even threw in a bottle of wine so that we could toast our escape.

"After that I only had to collect the spare bicycle and make my way to the little street behind the market. Then, exactly on time, I saw an ancient Citroen truck come chugging up the street towards me, and stop at the market entrance. The load, I could see, consisted of barrels of wine and a stack of bottled wine in cases. I had seen the driver on other occasions, and he muttered to me, 'This is your man, but lest anyone is looking he'd better help me with this lot.'

"They made light of the job, and I could see that the soldier seemed to be a strong young chap, tall and well built, with a shock of red hair, dressed in rather smart, but casual clothes, and that, Yvette, was the first time I saw my dear Andrew."

She paused there, and took a sip from her glass, "When they finished I heard him give a quick word of thanks to the driver before coming to me, and I was relieved when he addressed me in perfect French."

She turned to Granddad, "What was it you said to me, dear?"

"I can't remember, but I certainly know what I wanted to say."

"Oh," said Grannie, "and what might that have been?"

Granddad twinkled, "Just how brave you were in risking your life to help me, and, incidentally, that you were the most beautiful girl in the whole world!"

Grannie smiled, and then leaned over and kissed his cheek, "You're an old charmer, and as I've often said, you must have kissed the Blarney stone. But, as for me, I certainly thought that you were a very handsome young man.

"But we had no time for talk, as Georges and Pierre came up the street, pedalling like mad, and stopped beside us. 'Mlle. Hélène,' Georges gasped, 'it is terrible. Soon after you left, that damn Major Kretzer and his new Aide, a lieutenant, came to the Chateau in a car, along with four soldiers in a truck with a canvas roof. We thought we'd better wait to see what was going to happen, but they were in the house for just a few minutes before going off with the Comtesse, and taking young Albert with them. It was just as she had feared, but why? Why did they take the boy as well?'

"I can tell you Yvette that the news horrified me, but I had the sense to realise that I could do nothing to help, and all I could do was to get on with my job. I explained very briefly to the soldier – I'll pay him the compliment of calling him Andrew after this – what the situation was, and what was planned for him. I then went on to tell Georges and Pierre to go straight to their house as it was essential that they behaved normally in case any suspicion fell on them. They would have none of it. 'Mlle. Hélène, and you Sir, it is our privilege to help you. I'll go off now to scout ahead of you, and Pierre will follow behind. Let's be off, the sooner we get away from here the better.'

"So off we went, and as we rode I told Andrew in more detail about the arrangements, and I could see that he was far from pleased at the suggestion that he should hide in Etourvy along with the controller from Troyes. Andrew, it's your turn now, and you'd better tell Yvette what you said."

"To begin with, I was very disappointed that I was only going to have such a short time with this very attractive girl, but I also didn't at all relish the idea of going to ground and hiding, because there was a certain amount of urgency about my journey. I explained that I had good papers showing me as a student at Reims, so it was quite reasonable for me to be taking a cycling holiday during the Easter holidays. I also felt that my host in Etourvy would be glad to be rid of me, and so I suggested that if I could just keep the bike I would stay there for just one night and be off on my way to Spain in the morning."

Then Grannie continued her story. "It took us only about three quarters of an hour to get very nearly to the outskirts of Etourvy, by which time the sun had set, but there was a little light from an almost full moon. I was just congratulating myself that my job was nearly done when I was surprised to see

Georges tearing back to stop us.

"'Don't go any further,' he panted, 'I'd just got to the square in the middle of the village when the same lot who came to the Chateau drove down from that row of houses you were making for, and then headed off on the road to Tonnere. I could see that there was a man with them in civilian clothes who must have been your contact, but I was too far away to help or use my gun!'

"I couldn't think what to do for the best, but I saw Andrew look at Georges with interest, 'You've got a gun, what kind?'

"'It's an old one,' Georges said proudly, and he showed it to Andrew, 'but it is in good order, and Pierre has one the same – and we have bullets as well.'

"'They are beautiful,' Andrew said, 'and where do you think they will have taken the Comtesse and this other man?'

"That was something I could answer, 'It will almost certainly be to a big house which they use as their headquarters, and also as their mess. It is just on this side of Tonnere, about fifteen kilometres from here. You see, for security reasons, the Comtesse pretended to be on good terms with the Germans, so I know the house, as she and I dined there on one occasion.'

"Andrew looked pleased, 'Did you now? Tell me about the house.'

"I told him that it was a solid modern one, but not very big. 'It is set back from the road and they have surrounded the grounds with a high tough wire-mesh fence. The only entrance to the grounds is guarded by an armed sentry.'

"'Any idea how many soldiers there will be there?'

"'Well, unless there has been a change, there won't be more than six or seven, including the sentry, plus of course

Major Kretzer and his new side-kick. But why are you interested in all this, surely we can't do anything to help?'

'"That's as maybe!' said Andrew, 'Tell me, Georges and Pierre, how would you like to start a little war? I haven't got a gun – yet – but I have a very lethal knife, and with a little luck I can kill that sentry and get his gun. Then with three guns plus surprise we should be able to have quite a lot of fun. Are you two game?'

"You can guess, Yvette, what their reply was, and the three of them held a council of war, making their plans and totally excluding me from any part in the enterprise. It was, I can tell you, the first evidence I had of what a male chauvinistic pig your grandfather was, and I'm afraid that he isn't much better now! I couldn't stand it, of course, so I broke into their cosy confab. 'Just a minute, British soldier – what's your name, oh yes, Andrew – kindly remember that I've risked my neck in getting you this far, so if you imagine that you are going to abandon me while the three of you go off to start your little war you've got another think coming!'

"I can tell you, Yvette," she went on, "that your Grandfather had the grace to look a little embarrassed. 'I'm sorry, Hélène,' he said, 'just tell me where you want us to take you, and after that you'll be free of us, and whatever mischief we try to get up to.'

'"You've got it wrong, Andrew. I'm coming with you. Just remember that I've had four years now to learn to hate the Germans. And don't give me that disapproving look; having me in your party gives it a certain respectability, and also a somewhat un-warlike appearance.'

"As I spoke I began to get the germ of an idea. 'I also think that you can use me to advantage. Surely we can come up with some way for me to distract the sentry's attention sufficiently long enough for you to creep up on him and cut his throat with that knife of yours? We daren't use the guns – that would be like poking a stick into a hornet's nest.'

"'Bully for you,' he said, 'we'll talk some more while we are cycling.'

"But I could see that both Georges and Pierre were un-happy. 'Mlle. Hélène,' Georges said, 'this is no work for a woman. We are off now to kill young men – Germans they may be but still they are men – and I would hate to see you involved.'

"I saw Pierre give an emphatic nod of agreement, but I went over to them, and put an arm around each of their shoulders. 'Surely you have heard what the Germans do to girls like me when they catch us helping British or American men to escape? No? Well, if they are lucky they get killed, but if they are unfortunate enough to be at all pretty, then they are sent to field brothels for the pleasure of the German troops. So don't worry about any qualms I might have – and certainly I don't have – about killing the bastards!'"

"I can tell you," Andrew broke in, "that it was only then that I realised what a firebrand this pretty and so innocent-looking girl was, and she certainly silenced Georges. In short measure we were cycling along a dark and deserted road. Bad new spreads fast and obviously all the locals were sensibly staying home and keeping out of trouble." I looked at my dear sweet grandmother and my staid and very respectable grandfa-ther, and it seemed incredible to hear what they had been ca-pable of doing, these quite different youngsters, and I under-stood the awfulness of war and what it does to people.

But Grannie was going on with her story, "We didn't see a vehicle, or a person, even as we cycled along through the vil-lage of Mélisey. The trouble started when we were within five kilometres of the Germans' house and I heard a sound which terrified me. As I may have told you, the Germans often used motor-cycle and sidecar combinations in which two soldiers patrolled the countryside, and the sound of their engines was quite distinctive. This is what I'd heard. By ill luck we had just passed a large clump of trees and were on a long stretch of road with wheat fields on either side, and the crops were far too small to give any change of concealment. Andrew saw my look of alarm and, as we looked back, we could see the glimmer of war-time driving lights. He reached over, grabbing my arm, almost tumbling me off my bike, and said, 'Off your bike, Hélène, best thing we can do is to pretend to be a courting couple.'

"And before I really knew what was happening we were standing at the edge of the road, and his arms were around me. Looking down the road I saw that Pierre seemed to have disappeared, no doubt ducking into that clump of trees we had passed, and the machine rushing up the road towards us. 'Look happy!' Andrew whispered, and suddenly my lips were crushed by the most passionate kiss of my young life, and even in that moment of terror I rather liked it! As the machine stopped beside us, Andrew drew back, and we both stood blinking in the light of a big torch held by the soldier in the side car. He jumped out, still keeping the beam on us and said to the driver – in German of course – as he too got off, 'Hans, I think that we could have some fun with this bitch , her boy friend would seem to have warmed her up nicely.'"

"Did you understand him? Did he really say that?" I broke in, "I've never heard you speaking German."

"Oh, I understood all right. Living with the Germans for all those years it had been easy to pick up enough to get by, but he could have spoken any language and his meaning would have been quite clear. But then Andrew surprised me by speaking to the soldier in fluent German, and he spoke so humbly, 'Look, Sir, I am a student in Reims and this lady is my fiancée, please be generous and let us go.'

"As he spoke I looked at the driver, and saw the two stripes of a corporal on his sleeve. He ignored Andrew, and looked suspiciously at me before turning and speaking to his mate, 'Gerhard, just remember that there are three girls missing from Château Mélitour. Could this be one of them? Your papers please!'

"He made to walk over to me, but then jumped back as his mate said, 'Wait a minute Hans, the reason the Major wants us to pick up these girls is because he suspects that they may be helping this escaping British spy there is so much fuss about. Maybe he is this bloke?' From being casual they were suddenly very much on the alert, and I saw two guns appear, and point towards us. Then I heard an urgent whisper from Andrew, 'Hélène – FAINT!'

"Well, I'm not much good at amateur theatricals, and although I didn't know what was happening I reckon that my faint was quite convincing. It was then natural that Andrew would bend down to me and, as he did so, I heard two tremendous explosions and something whine over my head, and a wet spray splash onto my face.

"What I hadn't seen, but Andrew had, was that Georges and Pierre had crept towards us from opposite directions, through the field on the other side of the road, and Andrew had realised that they couldn't fire while we were on our feet, as the bullets from these great revolvers would go straight through a man. The corporal was obviously dead, but the soldier was writhing on the ground and screaming with pain. Pierre blew the back of his head off.

"In those first moments all I could feel was overwhelming relief, and I ran over to Georges and Pierre and gave them smacking kisses on their lips, saying, 'How can I ever thank you — we were both dead or worse if you hadn't appeared.' Then Andrew put his hand on my shoulder, 'Hey! What about me?' But as I turned to kiss him, he drew back and laughed, 'Mlle. Hélène, much though I want to kiss you, I do think that first I should wipe your face!' He produced a hankie and tenderly wiped my face, saying, 'That's better, I wouldn't have liked the taste of all that German blood and guts!'

"I looked at the mess on his hankie and realised with a shudder of horror just what that wet spray on my face had been, and I shut my eyes for a moment, as if to hide myself from everything. I felt his arms go round me, but I had to tear myself away to be sick, not the kind of sickness that I had known before, this time it was as if all my insides were coming up. When I was more or less recovered he gently helped me to my feet again and for a moment he held me close.

"'Death is awful, isn't it, but it was their lives or ours. Now you see why Georges and Pierre and I all wanted to take you to meet your friends, and I'm sure that you agree that now we should do so. Our enterprise will certainly involve more killing, maybe them, maybe us, and it is no work for a young girl, even for one as brave as you. So tell us where to go, and we'll see that you get there safely.'

"For a moment I was tempted, all this seemed like a nightmare, but as I looked down at the bodies of the two young soldiers I didn't see them, instead, in my mind's eye, I saw the body of Joseph my first love, and also the bodies of the countless millions who had died under the German jackboot."

"But Grannie," I broke in, "surely you can't blame all the

Germans? I've read that it was only the fanatical Nazis who were responsible for horrors like the death camps."

"My dear Yvette," she said, "you can say that – even believe it – looking back as you do from the safe platform of the twenty-first century, but even though that is becoming a fashionable belief today, it is wrong, just as you are wrong. No, the truth is that almost to a man and a woman the Germans lined up behind Hitler when the band began to play. So, put yourself in my place as I stood on that dark and deserted road with two old soldiers and a young man whom I'd known for only two hours. I can tell you that if you'd lived under the Germans as I'd done, I reckon that you would have acted as I did."

She smiled at me before going on, "'It's an attractive offer,' I said to Andrew, 'but no thanks! Suddenly I've got some steel in my backbone. When boys are taken on a hunt for the first time they are blooded. Well, tonight I have been, and you need have no fears that I'll be squeamish.' Then Andrew – bless him! – gave me a warm smile, before saying, 'Atta girl, now how about that kiss?'

"And, damn it, I found myself liking that kiss far more than I felt I should, as then I hardly knew him!" She stopped there, and gave an almost girlish giggle, saying, "Little did I then know how very well I was soon to get to know him."

"However," she went on seriously, "although he could now accept me on the team, Georges and Pierre were still unhappy, as to them war was still an exclusively male privilege. But I was also touched to see that they really cared for my wellbeing. However at last they did agree for me to come with them, and they may have been influenced by the fact that I could probably help them with the sentry.

"The scheme was, of course, a very obvious one. When we got near the German HQ, Andrew would make his way through the fields to the other side of the sentry post and, on cue, I would come up pushing my bike with a flat tyre. The sentry couldn't fail to come out from his hut to have a look, and this would give Andrew the chance to creep up and use that knife of his to cut his throat. All this, of course, could be done in silence so as not to raise any alarm."

Grannie had said all this in such a matter-of-fact way that I found it hard to believe what she was saying. There they were, she a sweet old lady, the archetype of the perfect grand-mother, and he an old-fashioned gentleman, and the only fa-ther figure I had ever known. It was impossible to picture her, covered with German blood and guts, calmly discussing with Granddad how he could best cut a young man's throat, and I think that she could read my thoughts, as she leaned over and took my hand, "See, my hands are quite clean now…it was all a very long time ago."

She paused for a moment, then went on with a laugh, "Now, Yvette, as you well know, good news isn't worth re-porting, so I won't say much about what happened then, just that at first everything went without a hitch. We had hidden the bodies of the two soldiers, and their machine, in a copse of trees, and then reached the German HQ without any trou-ble. Once we got there the sentry was no problem at all, thanks to my dear Andrew and his very sharp knife! Fortu-nately the sentry was a tall young man, so this enabled Andrew to dress in his trousers and tunic and become a very convinc-ing German soldier. We had also become a very well-armed band, Georges and Pierre had reloaded their guns, and An-drew and I each had a Mauser hand-gun taken from the sol-diers. Then, in addition, Andrew now had a Schmeisser sub-machine gun from the sentry.

"They of course knew about guns, but I'd never pulled a

trigger in my life. Andrew's lesson, however, was brief and to the point, 'Any fool can use a hand-gun, just think of it as an extension of your fingers. All you have to do is point, and fire.'

"It all sounded so very simple, but I fervently hoped that I'd never need to put his advice to the test. Anyway, as I stood there, watching the men dragging away the body of the sentry, and hiding it under a bush, I had the queerest feeling that I was a raw young actress about to go on the stage for the first time. From the entrance gate I could see the curve of the drive leading to a wide area of gravel outside the house. It wasn't a traditional French chateau, far from it, as it was quite modern with a plethora of bathrooms and a most efficient central heating system, which no doubt, was why the Germans had requisitioned it. The windows to the front were closely curtained, and at first it was impossible to tell whether or not they were lighted. But as I watched, I saw a curtain move slightly in one of a line of windows and for a moment there was a flicker of light.

"'Do you know what room that is?' Andrew whispered. 'Yes, there is a large drawing room cum reception room on two levels. The upper half opens off the entrance hall, and from it a short flight of stairs leads to the larger lower bit. On the night when we had dinner there they used the upper part as a dining room, and the lower part was used both for pre-dinner drinks and for coffee and drinks after dinner.'

"'Well,' said Andrew, 'something is certainly happening there…we'll see.' I could also tell them that the soldiers' quarters were to the rear, so we took a wide sweep over the grass, avoiding the gravel of the drive, where I could see an army truck parked near the front door, then round the house to the back door, where I hid behind a buttress. I had no part to play in the first phase.

"There was a small outside light, and I saw Andrew, looking every inch the figure of a smart young German soldier, go and knock at the door while Georges and Pierre flattened themselves against the wall on either side of it, each with a gun in his hand. The door opened, and I saw a rather puzzled expression on the face of the soldier, and he made some kind of enquiry. Now, as I've told you, Yvette, Andrew's German was then colloquially perfect, and he said in a very curt tone, 'Good evening, I have an urgent dispatch for Major Kretzer.'

"Whatever the soldier's reply was it was cut off with a gasp of astonishment when he found himself confronted by two elderly men armed with large guns, and he had the sense to stay quiet. They had equipped themselves with a length of cloth and some rope which they'd found in the sidecar, and soon the soldier was securely bound and gagged.

"Now it was my turn. I ran over to join them, and we tiptoed along a passage from where we could hear voices, and also the sound of a military band, probably a radio set tuned to one of the German propaganda programmes for the troops. The door to the room – the kitchen as it turned out – was ajar. My three men burst through it and I saw what had been a peaceful scene, three young soldiers sitting round a large table with steins of beer in their hands. I couldn't blame them for looking both astonished and frightened as they were faced with two men with enormous revolvers and another with a Schmeisser, despite the fact that he was in German uniform. Andrew's speech in German was short, and very much to the point, 'One cheep from any of you, and he is dead!'

"I knew what part I had to play, so I looked around and found some dish towels for improvised gags and some strong cord to tie them up securely to their chairs, always of course being careful to stay behind them so as not to interrupt the field of fire. The soldier who had answered the door was led in and bound like the other three.

"'Good,' Andrew whispered, 'Now Georges and Pierre, just to begin with, you two stay here and look after this lot, while Hélène and I do some reconnoitring. We'll be very quiet so don't follow us unless there are sounds of trouble. We can gamble, I think, that Kretzer and his new man will now be interrogating the Comtesse and the chap who was in Etourvy , and doing so on their own. Bastards like that don't want any observers to their villainy.'

"Another door from the kitchen opened on to a passage with store rooms on either side, and at the end a very solid door, obviously one meant to keep the servants in their place. Andrew eased it open, and I saw that we were in the front hall of the house and on the right was the door into the two-level reception room. Suddenly, and horribly, the silence was broken by an agonised scream, and we heard Kretzer shout, 'Numero deux!'

"I was about to dash over to the door, but Andrew held me back. 'Quietly, we must take them unawares.' We tip-toed over to the door and eased it open. At once we could hear other sounds, the pitiful sobbing of Marie-Claire and, almost worse, the frightened wailing of young Albert. Fortunately for us the upper room was unlit, and Andrew signalled me to lie prone, and we slithered across the parquet and peered through an ornamental railing and over the edge."

Grannie paused for a moment, and then went on, "I shall never forget what I saw; it was like a scene from *Grand Guignol*. There were three of them, Kretzer, his new Lieutenant whose name I didn't know, and a young civilian. I can still remember that, even in that awful moment, I noticed he was quite handsome, with a deeply cleft chin and a cap of black hair, and was very correctly dressed in a lounge suit.

"They were all looking at Marie-Claire, secured to a wooden chair, her legs tied to the chair legs, and her arms to its arms. She was sobbing pitifully and horribly, and I saw the reason. Her right hand was dripping with blood, and Kretzer was holding a pair of pliers with one of her nails in its jaws. As we looked he shouted at her, 'You've got eight more to go, why don't you tell me now where the British soldier is? Your misfortune is that this old fool here died before he could tell us.'

"I then noticed another figure – obviously dead – who had been tied hand and foot to a chair like Marie-Claire. He was, or rather had been, an elderly man, presumably the controller from Troyes. Sadly, there was also little Albert, lying on a chaise-longue with his poor leg stretched out, encased in its plaster cast.

"I saw Andrew sight his gun on Kretzer, but he whispered, 'I daren't fire yet as your Comtesse is behind him, but when I fire go for the young officer.' Almost as he said that, Kretzer seemed to lose his temper. 'You silly bitch, I'm in a hurry and I must catch this man. Now you've got no escape, that precious pill of yours wasn't much good, was it, I changed it to a harmless one! But if you don't mind your own pain, what about your son's?' He pulled a gun from a holster on his belt, reversed it, and using it like a hammer smashed Albert's plaster cast. His scream of pain went through us like a knife and Marie-Claire made a super-human effort to free herself. That of course was impossible, but the violent jerk she gave upset her chair and she fell, unable to help herself. There was a ghastly crunch as her head hit the stone fireplace and, for a moment, there was a stunned silence broken immediately by the tearing rattle of Andrew's gun, and Kretzer was almost cut in half by the hail of bullets.

"The sound of the two shots from my gun seemed almost insignificant by comparison, but the soldier clutched his shoulder and then collapsed in a heap, hitting his head on a very solid table as he fell. That just left the civilian who was standing behind a table, near one of the windows. I sighted my gun and my finger was tightening on the trigger just as Andrew also turned. But the man's reflexes were quick, and he ducked behind the table and then crashed, feet first, through a window. Just for a moment one of his shoulders came into view and we both fired, but couldn't see the result, and Andrew fired another long burst before dashing down the stairs to follow him. It was all so ghastly that I froze, unable to move. I saw Andrew peer through the broken window, and shout up to me, 'He's got away, but there is some blood here so he won't get far. At least one of our shots must have got him and also he was cut as he went through the window. But come down now, and see if you can help.'

"As he spoke Georges and Pierre rushed in, and I saw them look with approval at the remains of Kretzer and the body of my victim, lying so still in death, but then with concern at the others. I went down the stairs into the charnel house. I had never even seen a dead body before tonight, and here were three of them, and although I had a moment of revulsion at the sight of the man I had killed, any feelings of regret were washed away by the sight of Marie-Claire and Albert. I saw Andrew have a quick word with Georges and Pierre as, with their help, he gently freed her from the broken chair and carried her over to a couch, but she seemed deeply unconscious.

"I went over and knelt down beside poor little Albert, but

he was hysterical and beyond all comforting. Andrew looked as us, saying, 'This is a fine pickle, isn't it? Our only hope is to get these two to a hospital which will treat them, and not give them back to the Germans, any ideas, Hélène?' As he'd been talking I had been racking my brains, and I remembered that the family physician lived in Tonnere, and was the head of a clinic, really a small hospital, and I even remembered his phone number. I explained to Andrew what I had in mind, and as I went over to the phone I heard him giving some instructions to Georges and Pierre, and then something about the German truck. As I picked up the phone, despite the horrors around me, an absurd idea came into my head, and Andrew saw me smile. 'What the hell are you laughing at?' It must have been hysteria on my part, but despite all the need for haste, I said, 'I was just wondering if I should leave the Germans any money for this call!'

At that point, Granddad broke in, "I can tell you that I began to wonder if this gorgeous girl was a complete idiot. Here we were, with three dead, and two people in urgent need of hospital treatment, and she was concerning herself with how to pay for the call. He then turned to Grannie, "I hope, dear, that I wasn't too rude to you!"

"Rude!" she said, "You were insufferable...but maybe I did deserve it. Anyway the bit of lost time didn't seem to matter as our good luck was that the doctor himself answered, and I said, 'Dr. Jeanfils, it's Hélène...it is terribly urgent, don't interrupt...just listen!' When I finished, he was equally brief, 'That's awful, but do you have any transport?' And just as he said that I heard the engine of the German truck being started, and I realised that either Georges or Pierre must be outside and busy so I said, 'Yes we have.' At the other end, he replied, 'Good, bring them to the clinic as soon as you can, I'll be there to meet you.'

"Suddenly everything went into top gear, for there was the sound of four shots and with a feeling of disgust I realised that the bound and gagged soldiers in the kitchen had been shot. I turned angrily to Andrew, 'Surely it wasn't necessary to kill them; they were helpless!' But he just shook his head, rather sadly, pointed out that the soldiers had all seen Georges and Pierre, and to leave them alive would have been to sign their own death warrants.

"It made a dreadful kind of good sense," she said, "but that is another thing which I have tried to forget, but never can. I still wonder about the four young wives, and maybe families too, which they probably had then, back in Germany.

"But, I'm getting distracted…let me go on. We went out to the German truck, but then I realised that I had put my gun down when I picked up Albert, so I ran back into the house to get it. But, just as I picked it up I couldn't help looking at the young soldier I'd killed, and was aghast to see that his eyes were open, and that he was looking at me. So now it was my turn to be an executioner, just as Georges and Pierre had been, and I forced myself to raise my gun. But, just as I was about to pull the trigger, I saw him make an effort to speak, 'Mlle.,' he whispered in quite good French, 'I know why you killed the others. I don't mourn Major Kretzer, he was an animal, and what he did to your Comtesse and her child was dreadful. I am ashamed of my country, but your hands too are not clean. Just remember that the four in the kitchen were not like him, they were just simple young lads, and were no danger to you and your friends. Now, if you want to pull that trigger then do so at once, but if you spare me, I promise not to raise the alarm, and to say nothing which could help the authorities to trace you and your friends. My story will be that I was shot at the very beginning and never saw any of you. So can you find it in your heart to trust me?'

Grannie paused, and I wondered what she was going to say, "I'm afraid, Yvette, that I then showed what a poor soldier I was, as I knelt beside him and said, 'Are you badly hurt?'

"'No, Mlle., I don't think you have fired a gun before but, despite that, both your shots got me in the shoulder. It is painful, but not serious, and my good fortune was that when I fell I hit my head on the table. I have a nice big lump on my head to prove it, so I can plead being unconscious all the time while you were here.'

"For a moment I felt an odd sense of rapport with the young officer, and I wished that we had time to talk, but there were others waiting for me, 'Let's shake hands,' I said, 'there has been enough killing. You've made a promise, and God damn you to hell if you break it!'

"We solemnly shook hands, and he smiled at me, 'I wish things could have been different, I would have been honoured to be your friend, but go now, your colleagues are waiting, bon chance!' And then, Yvette, like a complete idiot, I left him, and went out to the truck."

But I then broke in by saying, "Don't say that, Grannie, I think you were jolly brave, and quite right to save him." She smiled at me, "Oh, not shooting him was right, but what I didn't think of was that he must have known the identity of the traitor, and it was a racing certainty that he was the civilian who had dived through the window and made his escape. It just didn't occur to me then to ask him about the man, and if it had only done so, then a lot of things would have been quite different.

"We had a quick council of war before leaving. Our bicycles were hidden at the bottom of the drive, Andrew's and mine we could pick up in our German truck, and the canvas roof made it like a small van. As for Georges and Pierre we persuaded them that their work was done, and done superbly , and that they should make their way towards home, but only to go there if it seemed safe, and otherwise to lie up somewhere for the night. In any case they had to get to Mélitour at their usual time in the morning just as if nothing had happened. Their story had to be that they knew nothing of the Comtesse being taken away.

"All now was haste. Andrew went over and lifted Marie-Claire while I picked up Albert. I tried to be careful but I couldn't help moving his leg, and he gave a scream of pain, which must have triggered a reflex in Marie-Claire, even deeply unconscious as she was. I saw her eyes open and she first looked up in horror at the German soldier holding her in his arms, then at the three of us, Georges and Pierre, and me with Albert screaming in pain. But in just a moment her head dropped and she was unconscious again. Sadly there was nothing we could do for either of them, but just try to get them to the hospital as quickly as possible. After a quick but emotional parting from Georges and Pierre we watched the old stalwarts ride off. I began to tremble, and Andrew saw my distress. He put an arm round my shoulders and I felt his breath warm on my wet cheek, 'You've been wonderful, Hélène; just bear up for a little longer. We'll get these two to the hospital, and then the Dallachy Continental Tours Service will get you to Spain in double quick time – just you wait and see!'

"And that, Yvette, was the first time that I knew what my married name was going to be!"

Grannie paused again, and said, "I've told you that entire bit in some detail because it is the core of our stories, Andrew's and mine, but I'll try and be as brief as I can for what is still to come. To begin with we had to drive that German truck the eight kilometres into Tonnere, and for little Albert, every bump was a new agony. All I could do was to hold him tightly in my arms, and tell him that we were going to see nice Dr. Jeanfils who would put leg right again. Poor little chap, his safe childhood had been shattered, he had seen his mother being arrested by a German, who then tortured an elderly man to death, and then tortured his mother, before smashing his leg. After that had come the horror of the gun shots and the bloody death of Kretzer beside him. It also occurred to me that he must be confused by the fact that Andrew was in German uniform, so how could he be safe when he was being driven by a German? I did my best to reassure him, but I could see that my presence was his only comfort, I was a rock of safety in a nightmare world, and he clung on to me tightly.

"Andrew drove quietly, sitting up smart and straight in the driving seat – every inch a proud German soldier. The clinic was set back from the road with a private driveway and, as we drove up, I saw Dr. Jeanfils on the steps to meet us but he stepped back in alarm at the sight of a German truck and driver. However I leaned out of the window and explained things and then eased myself out with Albert. He came over to me, and whispered, 'You've been wonderful, Hélène, I'll do all I can for them.'

"It didn't take him long to say to me, 'I don't like the look of the Comtesse, her hand will heal, but she has a depressed skull fracture, and God only know what damage has been done. I can't risk operating myself – it isn't my field – but one of the best brain surgeons in France works in Auxerre. Fortunately he is a patriot, and I'm sure I can get him to do what is necessary, and to be discreet.'

"He then came over and looked at Albert, still held in my

arms, no longer hysterical, but sobbing quietly and sunk into misery. He then eased him from my arms on to the bed and examined his leg. He looked sadly at me, after examining his leg, 'What monster would do this to a little boy?' Then to him, 'You've had a bad time, Albert, they were nasty men, but Hélène and her friends have killed them so you've nothing to be frightened about now. I am going to fix your leg up again, it will be sore for a while, but it will get better…I promise…I am going to give you a prick with this needle, and it will take the pain away.'

"I saw Albert get the injection, and smoothed his hair, saying, 'You'll be all right now my pet, you'll go to sleep now and Dr. Jeanfils will make your leg better soon.' The injection then began to take effect, but suddenly he fought it, 'You'll stay with me, Hélène, won't you?' I could only shake my head sadly, 'I wish I could, but the Germans are hunting me, and I must go…' He gazed at me in horror, 'But, Hélène, you MUST STAY…Must Stay…must stay…must…' and then he was asleep.

"I turned to Andrew, as I knew then what I had to do, 'Look, I really have to stay here to look after him. I've cared for him since he was just a little boy, I can't leave him now when he needs me so much.' But Dr. Jeanfils looked at me with alarm, 'Hélène that is impossible. It will be hard enough to hide these two without you as a further complication, as they must be looking for you…no, you certainly cannot stay!'

"Andrew then solved everything by gripping my arm so tightly that I gave an exclamation of pain, 'Dr Jeanfils,' he said, 'don't worry, we're off now, and I hope that all goes well with your patients…and remember – you've never seen us!' And he then ran back to the truck, almost dragging me behind him."

She stopped suddenly, and said to me, "Could I have

stopped him? I think, maybe, I might have been able to. But I didn't. All I know is that Albert was then to think that I had deserted him, and probably still does, although, with the benefit of hindsight, I don't really think I had any alternative. But despite that, it has worried me through all these long years.

"Anyway, and I confess without too much of a struggle from me, we got back to the truck, and Andrew almost threw me into the cab, saying, 'I'll need you eventually to tell me where to go, but for now get down and stay out of sight as long as we are in the town.' I can tell you, Yvette, that suddenly I was too tired to fight, and I cowered down as we drove through, and then out of Tonnere."

She suddenly stopped. "Well I reckon that is a very good place on which to stop things tonight. Let's settle down with nice big cups of tea!"

But I had a better idea, and said, "You aren't the only one, Grannie, who needs to get her strength back – I've been riveted by your story tonight – and I hadn't before realised how bad thing were for the two of you. But, as for your suggestion of tea, I think we deserve something stronger than that…agreed?"

"Do you know," Granddad said, "there are just a few occasions when Yvette says something really quite sensible!"

"That's as maybe," Grannie smiled, "but remember, dear, that tomorrow you have to get your monthly check-up, so don't drink too much."

This was news to me, so she had to explain – somewhat to Granddad's displeasure – that he had had a minor heart attack in January, soon after I'd gone off for the Easter term, and that he was still to some extent under the doctor's orders. As for him he assured me that the attack had been very minor, and that there was nothing at all to worry about.

Chapter Four

With Granddad having his medical in the afternoon, it was next evening before we could sit down together again, and Grannie surprised me by saying, "Yvette, we are now going to be even more indebted to you!" And she went on to tell me that Granddad's tests had shown that he needed to take things very easy for some months, and that this had led to a change in their plans.

I was alarmed by the news of Granddad's health but I knew that he would shy away from any discussion. But I was also getting a bit annoyed at these references to 'plans' without being told what they entailed, so I demanded point blank, "Now tell me just what plans are you talking about?"

It was Granddad's turn to avoid the issue, "Look, Yvette, I'm not dead yet, so will you please just give us today , and maybe a little bit of tomorrow, to finish our sagas, and then decide what – if anything – you'll agree to do for us , OK?"

And with that I had to be satisfied, and Grannie went on with her story. "So there we were, driving in that truck out of Tonnere, and Andrew said to me 'You can come up now, and let's look at the bright side. As I see it, until the alarm is raised we should be quite safe in this truck, what with me in this uniform – also we are very well armed.'

"And indeed we were as we both had a Mauser and he had the Schmeisser beside him. 'You see,' he went on, 'despite all that has happened it can't be more than three quarters of an hour since I shot Kretzer and you shot his lieutenant, and although that civilian escaped it will be some time before he can alert the Germans, so I think that gives us quite a while yet. Let's make the most of it and get as far south as we can, but avoiding towns.'

"As he said that I could have wished that I were still down under the dashboard, because I was just too scared to tell him that I had left a fully conscious German officer at the house, and that I hadn't even thought to tear out the telephone. Then Andrew made it worse when he said, 'You know, I did make one mistake, I should have cut the telephone line, just in case any other Germans came to the house, but that's unlikely so I don't think we should worry about it.'

"I couldn't bear to think of my foolishness, and to change the subject I said, 'But it is so very far to Spain, at least seven hundred kilometres. How can we possibly get that far?'

"'First things first!' he said cheerfully, 'We can use this truck for quite a while yet as it has plenty of petrol, and it being dark is a help. In fact if necessary we could even drive without lights as there is a nice full moon. But when we do stop we must hide the truck and lie up somewhere for the night, and get on our bikes in the morning for the long ride to Spain. I could wish that we had a road map, but we don't. For now all we can do is to head south-west, and Spain is a nice big country! There will be signposts to help us. These papers of ours, you a shop girl from Paris, and me a student from Reims, would look odd if we were to try to buy rail tickets to anywhere near the border, so we'd better stick to our bikes. If we push ourselves, we can cycle maybe as much as a hundred kilometres a day, so we can do the journey in a week, if you can put up with my company for as long as that!'

"Even that little joke didn't raise my spirits, and I sat in quiet misery. We drove on through the night with Andrew pushing the truck as fast as he could while I tried to keep us headed South but off the main roads. Eventually Andrew said that we couldn't risk using the truck anymore because the alarm had almost certainly been raised. We slowed down a bit to look for a suitable place to get rid of the truck but almost immediate the search became urgent as we saw bright car lights in the distance, coming towards us. 'Damn,' he said, 'with lights like that it must be a German vehicle.' But the fates were with us as he saw a little track leading off into the forest, so he stamped on the brakes, swerved into it, and a little way up he was able to turn left behind a screen of trees and out of sight of the road. He turned off our lights and the engine, and whispered to me, 'Cross your fingers, let's hope that they didn't see us.' I heard the noise of the vehicle coming towards us, nearer and nearer, but then it passed our little escape road and went on its way. 'Phew!' said Andrew, 'that was a close call, but this is a super place.' And so it was; the strip of trees was only some twenty meters wide, but it was impenetrably dense. Between us and the next bit of forest was a small lake, with a dam of some kind as I could see a sluice and some control gear, and also a small hut backing on to the forest, no doubt used by the water engineers. I saw Andrew go over and peer into the water, and he was smiling as he came back. 'This is perfect, the water is quite deep and there is a place where we can easily get the truck over the edge and into the water. That's one of our problems solved, so let's get busy.'

"I was glad to have something to do, if only to take my mind off things – the horror of Marie-Claire and Albert, and the nagging worry about the soldier whose life I had spared. Had he broken his promise of silence? We got our bikes out of the truck, and the thought came to me that we were certainly travelling light. I had just a few clothes and toilet things in the pannier bag of my bike which I had packed for my escape to Paris. As for Andrew, he had just a small pack with him. And that was all, except for the parcel of food I'd bought in Chaource, and as I saw it I felt my tummy have a little rumble to itself.

"As I was doing this I saw Andrew go over to the little hut and put his shoulder to the door which opened with a protesting noise of splintering wood. 'We're in luck,' he called, 'it is clean and there is even a small couch to sleep on. If only they had left us some food for dinner it would be perfect.' I looked happily at my bag of food, and wine too I remembered, and laughed as I said, 'The age of miracles is not past as I've got a meal here, but I refuse to eat it with a German. So for God's sake get out of these German clothes – here is your bag – and don't come back till you are properly dressed. You see, when I was waiting for you in Chaource I bought this food to eat with my girl friends this evening after I got rid of you, and I still haven't managed to do so!'

'You're a great partner Hélène, so please stick around. It all sounds wonderful, but first let's get this damn truck out of sight.' It wasn't in fact too difficult as all we had to do was to drive it to the edge, then Andrew opened the hand throttle and jammed it into gear and it jumped forward and teetered for an agonising moment on the edge before toppling into the water with a tremendous splash. I can tell you that Andrew then stood back with the superior smile that all men in the world assume when they manage to DO something, and he turned to me and said, 'That's a good job done, and if you'll get the dinner ready, I'm going for a swim, this uniform smells and I feel dirty.'

"That was me put very firmly in my place, and I saw him

go off, very modestly, into the trees and, as I unpacked, I saw a white figure in the distance, and heard the splash as he dived in. Suddenly I too felt dirty , and no wonder as I hadn't even washed my face since it had been splashed with German blood and guts, so right where I was I stripped off my clothes and dived in. But...ouch! I'd gone in just at the place where we'd pushed the truck into the water, and I could smell a dis-gusting mixture of petrol and oil. So I hastily swam away, and I still wonder if it was conscious or unconscious thought which led me to swim towards Andrew."

She couldn't then go on, as Granddad was laughing at her, and he then turned to me, 'I can tell you, Yvette, that the first thing I knew was when this beautiful naked woodland dryad – or nymph or whatever – suddenly appeared in the water be-side me and what could I do but put my arms round her..." "And," said Grannie, "we both sank because he was too stu-pid to realise what would happen when he embraced me."

"But," said Granddad, "don't get the impression that she was cross with me as we were both laughing when we sur-faced, and she said to me, 'I don't mind you embracing me, but please don't drown me!'...that's right, isn't it?"

They turned and smiled at each other, and I could see that this was to them a treasured memory, and it was with a smile on her face that Grannie went on, "As I'm sure you will real-ise, Yvette, it was, to say the least, an unusual situation, and suddenly I was madly embarrassed, so I turned and swam back at my fastest crawl, got to the side, and got myself dressed in clean clothes. But before doing so I had, with great difficulty, to dry myself as all I had was a very small towel. But it gave me time to think, and I just couldn't believe what I'd done. I'd had a very strict upbringing, and yet I had almost flaunted my nakedness to a man I'd only just met, and I wondered what on earth he would think of me! It was all very confusing.

"I gave myself a shake, and told myself to forget it, and to get on with the food, such as it was. Preparing the so-called dinner wasn't too difficult, as I happened to have an old knife in my pannier bag, but as for food all I had was bread, butter, charcuterie, a few lettuce leaves, and some tomatoes and cheese, but at least I did have a bottle of wine, although it was only an undistinguished vin du pays. Then I remembered that we had no glasses and, worse still, no corkscrew. Just as I had come to this unfortunate conclusion, Andrew appeared looking very much the student on holiday, in flannel trousers and an open-necked shirt. However he looked happily at my meagre collection of food.

"'You are a magician; I'm ravenous and you've saved my life!' 'Maybe,' I laughed, 'and I've also got a bottle of wine, but no corkscrew, and even if we were to get it open we've nothing to drink out of!' 'No problem, Hélène, you see I am a good boy scout.' And he produced one of those knives full of gadgets, such as one to get stones out of horses' hooves, and it also had a corkscrew. 'As for drinking,' he went on, 'I don't at all mind sharing it with you straight from the bottle – if of course you don't object.'

"I was oddly shy, after my display of nakedness, as we sat side by side on the old couch in the hut, but as we laughed and choked as we tried to pour the wine down our throats, I found that I was relaxing, and all the horrors of the day seemed to slip far behind me. Then, after we had finished the meal and the wine it seemed the most natural thing in the world to find Andrew's arm round me, and he whispered, 'I enjoyed that first kiss, so how about another one now?'

"Time seemed to stand still as we kissed, I felt his mouth open slightly and his tongue tease my lips, and then I found my tongue eagerly joining his. It was sheer bliss, but then he suddenly pulled away. 'Hélène, this is not fair to you, I am taking advantage of all that has happened today, and we must stop while I still can.'"

She paused and looked at me with a rueful smile before she went on, "I can tell you, Yvette, that I was disappointed. I was overcome by urges which I'd never felt before, and I said, 'I don't understand, Andrew, what you mean by not taking advantage of me, damn it I want this as much as you do!'

"But he looked at me, and shook his head. 'Hélène, don't you realise why Spanish gentlemen are so keen to take their ladies to bull fights?'

"It was so absurd that I couldn't help laughing. 'Andrew, you've lost me. What the hell do bullfights matter to us, and what on earth is the point you are trying – and failing – to make?'

"'It is very relevant to us,' he said very seriously, 'you see, old Mother Nature has planted in all of us a strange duality between death and sex. It is just as if the old girl wanted to ensure that death is always followed by new life, and just remember all that killing in the bullring, and what we've seen today.'

"'Andrew my dear,' I said with complete conviction, 'you may well be right, and if you are then who are we to go against our natures? I have only known you for a few short hours, but to me it is like a lifetime, and everything I know about you is good. I can tell you know that I am a virgin, but I shall regret it so long as I live if we do not lie together tonight and make love.'

"He kissed me gently. 'Hélène, my very own lovely Hélène, these Spanish gentlemen must be right, that death is the ultimate aphrodisiac, as I feel just as you do. But I can tell you that I didn't need any aphrodisiac to make me want to make love with you. You are the girl of my dreams, the one I felt I'd never be lucky enough to meet, and I can only hope that we'll be spared to spend the rest of our lives together.'

"I can tell you Yvette," she went on, "that there was just one thing which stopped me being the happiest girl in the world."

"What was that, Grannie?"

"Just a simple thing. I wondered innocent as I was, whether it was possible for two people to lie together on such a very narrow couch, and I asked Andrew what he thought."

"That was very sweet Grannie," I broke in, "how lucky you were, and how romantic, just like a scene in a film of a love story."

"Romantic my foot, so do you know what this so-and-so, your grandfather, said? Well, I'll tell you. Certainly he did kiss me, but it was a bit perfunctory and, having just given the couch a casual look said, 'I'm sure we'll manage, but now I must go for a pee, and I suggest that you do the same.'

"But when we came back to the hut again it was, at first, just like an X Certificate romantic film as he took me in his arms and began to unbutton my blouse, but now it was my turn to upset the idyll. You see, I felt that I could never be really close to him if I didn't tell him about the German officer I'd left still alive back at the house. I was so afraid that he would be angry, but it was just the opposite. He took my face in his hands, and gently smoothed my hair back, saying, 'Hélène, my dear, if you had shot that young man I would have to have told you that you were right to do so, but it would have been like a shadow between us. There must be some charity, even in war, and I am very glad that you showed it. I can tell you that I hated it when Georges and Pierre shot these four soldiers, bound and gagged as they were, but they, after all, were going to live on in the district, and they couldn't risk being identified. Your soldier was different – and it looks as though he has kept his word because we've got away – and I'm very glad that you were brave enough not to shoot.'"

She stopped there, and I wondered what intimate details I was now going to hear, but she was suddenly my very respectable grandmother again as she said, "As this, most certainly, is not an extract from an X Certificate film, I'm saying nothing more about that night, except to say that we really did manage very well on that narrow couch. Maybe it was uncomfortable, but I can't remember that. All I know is that it was the most wonderful night of my life, and it is my dream that your dear father was conceived then on that narrow couch in that little hut – certainly we gave him several chances.

"Of course in all the best films we should have wakened each other next morning with tender kisses, and the promise of more loving to come, but we were not so lucky, as what wakened us was the sound of an engine and the crunch of tyres on the grass. In a moment we had both jumped up and peered out of the tiny window. We saw that the vehicle was a truck with a large load, all covered by a tarpaulin, and the driver was getting out of his cab. The reason for his being off the road was soon obvious as he went over to a small tree to urinate, but that wasn't enough as he then pulled down his trousers and pants, and squatted down. Andrew turned to me with a smile, and whispered, 'I wish that he would hurry up, as I think we both could be doing with following his example!'

"I stayed where I was, but Andrew picked up his clothes and began to pull them on quickly. He was back beside me, with a gun in his hand, just as the man finished, and we saw him pick up a tussock of grass to clean himself with before pulling up his trousers again. 'Good,' said Andrew, 'Now he'll be off.' But he wasn't, as he walked over to the water's edge and lit a cigarette. But then, to our dismay, he seemed to see something of interest on the grass, and walked over to the water's edge and knelt down as he peered into the water. I wondered if the water was clear enough for him to see the truck, and was surprised to see him stand up and look towards our hut, before raising both his arms above his head, and calling out, 'Good morning, the two of you in the hut, and please believe me that I am your friend!'

"Andrew hesitated for only a moment before he eased the broken door open and walked out, almost theatrically laying down his gun on a rock outside the door. As I watched I saw him walk over to the stranger and in a moment heard the almost inaudible sound of their voices. I was of course eager to hear what they were talking about, but I also realised that first things came first. It was one thing to be naked in front of my lover, but quite different to be in that situation with a stranger, so I modestly eased the door shut and looked around frantically to find where my clothes were, as they had been scattered all around the hut in the urgency of Andrew undressing me.

"At last I managed to get myself decent and went outside, to find them sitting side by side on the grass, in what looked like perfect amity, and I was introduced to a M. Maurice Bernard, and he smiled at me, before saying, 'It is a great pleasure for me to meet you Mademoiselle, and I must explain why I happened to come here. You see, I had a call of nature...' He paused there, and laughed, 'But, of course, you must have seen that! However perhaps I should also explain how I came to be on this minor road.'

"We soon learned that he wasn't just a truck driver, but in fact that he owned a small haulage company in Dijon, and the previous afternoon he had loaded a large consignment of wines in Beaune. He had then driven to Avallon to spend the night with his parents who lived there. He went on to tell us that his father was the head of the Gendarmerie in the town, and that a most urgent message had been received in the evening to say that a young man, believed to be a British spy, with the help of a local girl, had murdered a German officer and six German soldiers in cold blood, and then wounded a second officer. They had also stolen a German truck. Because of the seriousness of the affair, a reward of fifty thousand francs was offered for information leading to their arrest.

"'It was pure chance,' he went on, 'that I took this road, and was heading for the main road at Clamercy when I just had to stop. You see, my mother had got hold of some real coffee, and I drank too many bowls of it at breakfast. Anyway, it was a nice morning and, when I had finished my business, I looked around, and what did I see but some tyre tracks leading to the water's edge, and a German truck showing up as clear as a bell in the pure waters of the dam.' He suddenly went all formal, 'Monsieur, may I shake your hand, as I would like to congratulate you on killing seven of the bastards.' Then to me, 'Mademoiselle, may I also have the privilege of giving you my salutations?'

"Andrew broke in before he could say more, 'You'd better congratulate her as well, as she shot one of them!'

"'In that case, it is even more of a privilege.' And he politely kissed me on both cheeks.

"It was such an extraordinary morning that I surprised myself by saying, 'That was nice, but how about the one in the middle!' That gave him a good excuse to put his arms around me, and to give me a smacking kiss, and he smiled at me before saying, 'Well, certainly this has been my lucky morning, but I am afraid I have some very bad news for you. You see, the roads are now impossible for you on those bicycles which I can see over there, as the Germans have patrols everywhere. I was stopped in Vézelay, but fortunately one of my father's men was there, and could vouch for me. He also told the German officer that I was going on a long journey, and got the officer to give me a note to the effect that my vehicle had been stopped and searched, and was in the clear. He very kindly gave me this just to save me time, in case I was stopped again.'

"'I wonder,' he went on thoughtfully, 'if this gives me a chance to help you. I may say that I play no heroic part in the Resistance, but I sometimes help by moving equipment, and sometimes people. So, tell me, where are you making for?'

"'Why do you ask,' Andrew laughed, 'to Spain, of course, from where we hope to get to Portugal.'

"It was M. Bernard's turn to laugh, 'Well, I did wonder, but certainly the Gods are smiling on you today. Can you guess where I am going with this load of wine? I can tell you that all of it is of the very best quality, some even from the finest vineyard in the world, the *Domaine de la Romanée-Conti*...no? Why, to Lisbon of course! You see, half of the old crowned heads of Europe have found a good life there in Estoril, just along the coast, and that good life includes the finest of wines.'"

Grannie stopped there and stretched herself, "And that is all I'm now going to tell you in detail about our journey, we have to save some time, all you need know is that he agreed to take us to Madrid, where we would be safe. As you well know, we did escape, but we were faced with two extremely uncomfortable days, hidden in the back of the truck in among all the cases of wine. But it gave us a unique chance to get to know about each other. It really was too ridiculous, here I was in love with Andrew, and having made love with him, and yet I knew nothing at all about him. Of course he was in the same situation about me. While we talked on the long journey I told him the story of my young life, and he told me of his early days in Alsace with his Scottish father and German-French mother. Then how they were killed in a car crash in 1933 when he was just fifteen and was taken to live with his Scottish grandparents in Gairloch in the Scottish highlands where they had a croft. Then came St. Andrews university and in 1939 he joined the army, where he was soon found to be fluent in three languages. Then, to my surprise, he stopped his personal history, saying, 'A lot of what I then did I cannot tell you, and certainly nothing about what I was doing before we met. So long as there is even a possibility that we'll be captured, it is safer if you do not know.'

"And with that I had to be satisfied. But also, of course, we talked about our adventure together, and in particular we wondered about the identity of the young man who had crashed out of the window and whom we had certainly managed to wound. It seemed to us rather odd that he, as a civilian, had been there. Why would Kretzer have allowed anybody but German soldiers to be present when prisoners were being tortured?" Grannie stopped there, then went on very seriously, "It was then that I remembered the description which Marie-Claire had given us of the new British agent, M. Brume, as being tall with black hair and a cleft chin, and although I mentioned it we didn't think it could possibly be him.

"Anyway we crossed into Spain on the evening of the second day, and Maurice dropped us on the outskirts of Madrid at about four in the morning, giving us a handful of pesetas so that we could get a bus into the city, and the refuge of the

British embassy. It was an emotional time when we parted. How do you thank someone who has done so much and risked his life to save yours? I don't remember what was said, but whatever it was it came straight from the heart.

"But back to us. There was no red carpet treatment when we got to the British embassy, and who could blame the young officer at the entrance, as there we were dirty, smelly and dishevelled, still in the same clothes we'd worn on the journey. Then, as for papers, they showed me as a Parisian shop girl and Andrew as a student from Reims. Until then I had only heard Andrew speak in French, apart from a few words in German, but now he spoke English. Certainly I could speak it after a fashion as Marie-Claire had spent a lot of time teaching me so that I could talk to the escapees, but the English which he then spoke was new to me. Now of course I know that it is a gift which the British have, to assume a tone and a choice of words which demand instant obedience. This, I believe, is the reason why they were able to build such a huge empire, and why the French and the Germans never managed to do so. I can't remember what exactly he said, and I'm sure after all this time that he doesn't either, but it was something like, "Please don't waste my time. I am Major Andrew Dallachy. Go and get the Military Attaché, wake him if necessary, and tell him that Waverley is here.'

"It seemed to galvanise the Duty Officer into action and in just a few minutes he was back with an elderly man, still in pyjamas and a dressing gown, who showed all the signs of nursing a hangover and of failing to do it much good.

"He looked doubtfully at Andrew, and dismissively at me, and said, 'I understand that you claim to be Major Andrew Dallachy, code name Waverley.' He stopped for a moment and fished a piece of paper out of his rather shabby dressing gown pocket. 'Tell me the code number.'

"'One seven zero eight.'

"This obviously was correct, and he held out his hand to Andrew, 'Major Dallachy, I congratulate you on managing to get here, and so quickly. It is a privilege to meet you. I am Colonel McPherson, and I know what you require us to do, as we received confidential instructions from London in the hope that you...'

"But Andrew interrupted him, 'Look, Colonel, could we continue this conversation when we are comfortably seated? We've had a hell of a journey, and for me a large whisky would be just right, and I think a cognac for Hélène here would be equally welcome.'

"'Of course, of course!' And he led us into the building, and into some kind of sitting room, and gave instructions about our drinks to the Duty Officer. But I did notice that he looked rather doubtfully at me.

"And that, Yvette," Grannie said, "was the end of all the pleasantries!"

"But why, Grannie," I broke in, "surely all your troubles would then be over?"

"But no, not at all! The Colonel then said, 'Major Dallachy, I would love to hear details of your escape from France and no doubt you will be giving a full report about it in due course, but for now we have no time to waste. I'll get reservations for us on the Lisbon train this morning, and I'll arrange a passport for you to cover the journey and for your entry into Portugal. I'll come with you, of course, just to ensure that there are no problems. I'll also contact Lisbon at once and they, I am sure, will arrange a plane to take you to England tonight.'

"'Now' he went on, 'this young lady is French is she

not…? Good…I'll have time before we leave this morning to arrange things for her, probably with the Free French Legation here. I'm sure they will look after her.'

"He stopped there and turned to me, 'It is obvious, Mademoiselle, that you have helped the Major in his escape from France, and that we owe you a considerable debt of gratitude. I can tell you that your actions will not go unreported.' I was bitterly disappointed, I had just assumed that I would go on with Andrew, but now I could see that the chains of bureaucracy were being tied round me. How on earth could I get to Britain before the war was over – whenever the heck that would be – and what would I do in the mean time in this strange Spanish city of Madrid?

"But Andrew, bless him, would have none of it. 'I suggest, Colonel, that some of that gratitude is called for now. I would never have got here if Hélène had not risked her life on my behalf, and I can tell you that we are going to be married.'

"That wasn't entirely news to me, as we had whispered statements and commitments of love during our short time together. He smiled at me as he said, 'You really are going to marry me, aren't you Hélène?'

"I was suddenly so filled with joy that I was tongue-tied. I couldn't even remember how to say 'yes' in English…and all I could do was to burst into tears and say 'Oui, certainement oui!' as I nodded my head.

"Now, as I have told you before, Andrew has an unfortunate habit of changing far too quickly from romance to practicality. He gave me just a quick nod and said to the Colonel, 'Good, that's settled, so there will be three of us on the train this morning, and you'd better also warn Lisbon that there will be two on the plane to England tonight.'

"But the Colonel was horror-struck, 'Major, that is quite

impossible. She is French, and these papers she has are no damn good. Also there is the problem that she must be very much wanted by the Germans, and because of that I think it would be unwise of her to make her number with the French embassy here, where I'm sorry to say there are many who are overtly pro-German. So that leaves the Free French, but, knowing them, I'm afraid it will be weeks before they get round to doing anything by way of getting her a passport.'

"'However,' and he turned to me, 'please don't worry, you are our responsibility and I'll see that you get comfortable quarters, and also provide funds.'

"I felt Andrew tighten his grip on my hand, as if to reassure me, and he said, 'Colonel, I'm afraid that I meant what I said about Hélène coming with me to Lisbon. If she doesn't go, then I don't go, which will be very unfortunate, and very unpopular back in London.'

"I almost felt sorry for the Colonel. 'Major Dallachy, I can sympathise with you at having to leave your charming fiancée behind, but you will have to do so. I don't need to tell you that there is a war on, and it is absolutely impossible to get her a French passport for the journey in the time that we have. It is now getting on for seven o'clock, neither the French embassy nor consulate will be open before nine, and our train leaves at ten. With some countries it might be possible but the French – particularly with the problem of the Free French – are so careful, that they would never step out of line and issue a passport immediately.'

"'Well, Colonel,' said Andrew, 'I can appreciate your problem, but I have a very simple solution. Just issue her with a British passport in the name of Mrs. Andrew Dallachy, and then arrange with Lisbon to have a tame padre to meet us in the embassy – and marry us – when we get there late this afternoon. Certainly the passport will initially be false, but it will be genuine before the day is out.'

"The Colonel suddenly became human. 'You are a hard man, Major, but looking at Hélène I can well see why you don't want to leave her behind. I'll have a word with the Ambassador, and I'm inclined to think that he'll agree to your suggestion.' He stopped and beamed at me, and so it was arranged.

"When we've got more time I'll tell you all the details, but just one thing may amuse you. It was after we got ourselves off to wash and change that morning before breakfast that I came back into the room where Andrew was talking to the Colonel, who suddenly said, 'Are you joking Major? Surely there must be more in your message to London in our most secure cipher than "Four hundred along and shoe size three thousand"? What the hell does it mean?' I heard Andrew give a brief confirmation, but no explanation, and then the conversation had to end as they saw me, and I had more sense than to make any enquiries. All continued to go well, we got to Lisbon by train, then we got married, before being flown to England that evening – very uncomfortably – in a rather battered old Bristol Blenheim which I was told had once been a bomber.

"Anyway, there we were, landing in England on a beautiful sunny morning, and I imagined myself the happiest girl in the world. Andrew must have noticed my rapt expression as he gave me a loving squeeze and kissed my cheek. 'You're really safe now, welcome to Britain my lovely wife!'

"You know," Grannie said, "he really can be quite nice sometimes. But, again my euphoria didn't last long. We were met by three people, a quite elderly civilian and two RAF officers – a Group Captain and a Wing Commander I later learned – and they took us to a room in a building nearby where they began to talk very urgently to Andrew. It wasn't that they completely ignored me, they were too polite for that, but it was obvious that I came very low in their priorities. After just a few moments, I heard the Group Captain say, 'Major Dallachy, we won't waste any time talking here. After breakfast you are going straight to Farnborough where a team is waiting to analyse your report.'

"He then looked rather doubtfully at me, 'Mademoiselle, I understand that you were able to help Major Dallachy in his escape, and we are most grateful. I'll arrange for another car to take you to London so that you can make your number with the Free French, and we'll give you a float of money as there must be lot of things you need to buy.'

"I saw the civilian whisper something to him and he nodded saying, 'I've just been reminded that you'll need Clothing Coupons. Maybe you don't know that clothes are rationed at present. I'll also arrange for these and for Major Dallachy to be advised where you will be staying in London as, no doubt, he will want to see you again. However this will not be soon, as he has a lot to do at present.'

"What a let-down, just like, or maybe worse, than the Madrid bit. However, as before, my dear Andrew sorted it out. 'Group Captain Jenkins, I am afraid that you have not been fully briefed. Hélène and I were married yesterday in the British embassy in Lisbon, and we have all the papers here. She is British, and more to the point she is my wife. After all we have been through there is no way that we are going to be parted now – war or no war! So she too comes to Farnborough and we can stay at a hotel nearby. Certainly I'll spend my days with your RAF team, but I'm going to spend the nights with her!'

"There was a moment of surprised silence, and I was mortified to find myself blushing, but Andrew laughed, saying 'Don't look so embarrassed darling, we are married now so it is quite legal. Anyway, gentlemen, why don't the three of you do your duty and kiss the bride!' It was the elderly civilian who made the most of the invitation, and having done so he took my arm, saying, 'Before we leave, let me take you over to the mess where I know they have arranged a good old fashioned English breakfast to welcome you!'

"And that was my introduction to the ghastly meal which the British call breakfast. However Yvette, I think we should stop there as I feel that is quite enough for tonight. You'll be glad to know that we are nearly at the end now of what you have to know about our joint adventures, and the rest you can read about…OK?"

And that was it, with no more explanations.

Chapter Five

Next day the weather was so miserable that after lunch Grannie said, "We haven't long now before the end of our stories, so I can now tell you my last bit, and after dinner tonight Andrew can tell you the really important things. So now I'll go back to April 1944 when we were in Farnborough.

"For the rest of the week he did whatever he had to do, and I was content, very content, to be by myself and just walk around the town and spend some of the money and to use up some of the big bundle of Clothing Coupons I'd been given. Sometimes I walked out into the country, and it was magic to do so without the fear of a German hand on my shoulder. That was during the day, and the nights were wonderful. However there was a tiny shadow between us, as Andrew would still tell me nothing about what he had been doing in France and what he was doing here. He did tell me, though, that he hoped to get leave soon, and that we would go up and stay with his Scottish grandparents. We had spoken to them on the phone, and they were overjoyed to hear that he was home and safe. Apparently he had not been reported as missing, but they had been concerned about him. They were very sweet to me – speaking slowly and clearly for my benefit – although I could hear that they were surprised by his sudden marriage.

"But one thing which his grandfather said rather puzzled me. 'You can understand Hélène that we have been very wor-

ried about him as he had just come on leave about ten days
ago, when he was suddenly dragged away. His departure was
so sudden and dramatic that we knew what he was involved in
must be very urgent and important.'

"But when I taxed Andrew with it, he just smiled and said,
'Hélène, I'll do a deal with you. When we are on leave I'll take
you to a lonely moor where nobody is near us, and then I'll tell
you everything. What I have discovered is such a deadly secret,
and so much depends on it, that I daren't burden you with it.
The very outcome of the war might depend on the Germans
not finding out what I discovered.'

"It was on the Friday night that he came back to the hotel
in the late afternoon, very smartly dressed in his army uniform, and I was in the bedroom when he arrived. Throwing
his cap on a chair he said, 'Hélène, I've finished here, I've now
got fourteen days leave, and the people here have managed
somehow to book sleepers for us on the night train to Inverness. I'll phone Granddad now, and I'm sure that he will drive
over there to meet us at the station. It is a beautiful drive from
Gairloch, and I'm sure they will want to see you as soon as
they can.'

"He stopped there and explained to me about petrol ra-
tioning in Britain, but said that he had been given a lot of
coupons so petrol wasn't a problem. 'You see,' he went on,
'we're being well looked after, as RAE are taking us to London and the railway station by car. That means we'll have an
early dinner here, and there is enough of time before that, if
we hurry, for us to make love.' Those early days of our marriage were wonderful."

She stopped for a moment, and I could see that her mind
was back sixty odd years ago. "Nowadays you young people
think nothing of catching a train and of getting a seat or a

sleeping berth, but the war-time trains were slow, and almost unbelievably overcrowded. To get a seat then was a miracle, and even to sit on your suitcase in the corridor was almost a luxury. But Andrew must then have been moving in exalted circles, as for our journey to Inverness we had the ultimate luxury of two adjoining first class sleepers. Certainly they were separate, but there was a communicating door, so that was all right. We arrived in Inverness early the following afternoon after a fifteen hour journey, and lucky to be there so quickly. I didn't know it then, but the whole of the train services in the country were under severe strain due to the preparations for the Second Front and the invasion of France, which was then just six weeks away. Andrew's grandparents, John and Mary Dallachy, were on the platform to meet us – they looked much younger than I had expected – and such was the warmth of their reception that I found myself with tears on my cheeks. Mary had seen this and she put her arm round me, then kissed my cheek saying, 'My dear, see, I have kissed the tears away, and let's have no more of them. You are very welcome, Hélène, and I hope that you will come to love us as much as we shall love you. Andrew has been all that we have in this world, and we are very pleased that he has now found such a lovely wife.'

Grannie stopped again, and fished a hankie out of her pocket, saying, "Darn it, here I am crying again, just remembering their welcome all these years ago. There I was, a strange foreign girl whom their beloved Andrew had only just met, and whom he had married in quite indecent haste, but they were so generous, and so comforting to me. That little speech of Mary's set the scene for our visit, and for all that followed. I am so sorry, Yvette, that they were dead before you arrived, as they were wonderful people.

"I had imagined that they would live in some very humble dwelling on a bleak Scottish hillside, and certainly I saw many such hillsides as we drove from Inverness. But there were compensations, beautiful lakes – which I was told I must now call lochs – and there was a grandeur in the scenery quite unlike anything that I had seen before. It was all new and wonderful to me. Finally we drove along the ten-mile stretch of Loch Maree, and on to the sea at Gairloch, a little Highland town and a refuge for holidaymakers. You'll remember, Yvette, that we have taken you there, and showed you their house, and very handsome it was, set back from the road in its own grounds. That was a surprise for me, and Andrew seeing this turned to his grandfather, saying, 'I'm afraid, Granddad, that I have misled Hélène, as I told her that you lived in a croft , and not a house like this.'

"I was soon to learn that there had been a croft at one time, but old John had been very successful, and they had been able to extend it into this lovely home. They had also retained the land on which they kept small herd of dairy cows, the milk from which they turned into creamy butter and delectable cheese. I only wish I could get some of it now. Our holiday was uneventful until one beautiful day when Andrew and I went off for a walk with a picnic lunch. It was after we had eaten it, and found a sheltered spot in the heather where we could lie down, that Andrew at last told me what he had been up to.

"However, in the best tradition of soap operas I think I'll stop there. From now on it will be Andrew's story and not mine, and tonight he can tell you how he came to be involved."

So it was that I had once more to wait in suspension until after dinner for the story to continue. It was a cold and wet evening so we settled down for coffee in front of the fire. I had expected that Grannie would at least start the business off but it was Granddad who spoke, saying, "I've got some good news for you, as you will be able to read quite a bit of my story, which will be better than listening to me droning on. I'll first need to set the scene, and then give you some papers to read. I'm pretty sure, Yvette, that you must hope that I'll keep this short, but first I'm afraid I'll have to start with my early army days.

"The war broke out on 3rd, September 1939 and within a few days a flood of students went up to St. Andrews to go to the University Recruiting Board, and to offer their services. They took me on at once as a potential army officer, but it wasn't until November that I was commissioned as a Second Lieutenant. Then came initial training, and I didn't get to my regiment in France till the end of April 1940 , just in time to join the great retreat to Dunkirk, and I was one of the lucky quarter million as I got home without a scratch.

"It was a time then when the Free French forces were being organised and somebody must have noticed languages in my army records, and that having been raised in Alsace, French was my first language, English my second and German my third. The result was that I was detached as a liaison officer, and sent to the Free French HQ in St. Stephen's House in London.

"It should have been both a rewarding and an interesting time, helping these brave exiles but I'm afraid that it wasn't. Quite naturally they were humiliated by the way that their armies had been over-run by the Germans, and tried their best to shift the blame to the British. In fact I soon found that I was being looked upon more as a spy than a colleague, and soon I was so fed up that I asked a chap I knew at the War

Office if there was anywhere else where my languages could be used. It was my good luck that I asked the question at just the right time.

"It was then, when things were desperate, that Churchill made one of his inspired decisions and the Special Operations Executive was formed with the objective – in his own words – to set Europe alight. So all sorts of ideas were being considered about how to bring the war to the Germans, and I got involved in one of them. It started with a call for an interview in an office in Baker Street. There were three on the panel and the whole interview was conducted in French. You may find it interesting, Yvette, to learn the names of the three people who interviewed me. The first, a Mr. Thomas Cadet, will mean nothing to you, but he was the BBC correspondent in Paris before the war. You may possibly have heard of the second, Mr. Maurice Buckmaster who later became the head SOE with the rank of colonel. The last panel member, who subsequently became notorious, was Mr. Kim Philby of the Foreign Office. I sometimes wonder if my name ever got back to Russia in his reports to his Soviet masters.

"Anyway, I must have been approved as I was posted immediately to the SOE and to a Survival Course where I learned how to kill people in all sorts of ways, and also how to live off the land. That was in the late autumn of 1940, and I had quite an interesting time after that. In 1941 I went to France, first setting up a maquis group near Reims, and then becoming involved in various operations both in that area and in Alsace – where I still knew people – until in April 1944 when I was withdrawn from France by Lysander and went up to Gairloch to spend a two-week leave with my grandparents. All was going well until the morning of 15th April 1944 – just think of that date in connection with Grannie's story – when I got up early and took myself off with the fishing rod before anyone was awake. I learned afterwards that it must have been only a few minutes after I left that my grandfather picked up the phone to find the Duty Officer of my unit demanding to speak to me, and he was far from pleased to find that I was away and worse, that I hadn't left a message to say where I was going.

"That was when the affair moved into high gear. Grandfather was ordered to enlist the help of the local policeman to try to trace me and also to go to the Gairloch golf course where a helicopter would land in about an hour's time. If I had not been traced by that time then either he or the policeman had to fly with the machine and indicate the possible areas where I might be found. I can tell you, Yvette, that it was quite extraordinary in 1944, when helicopters were still somewhat experimental and extremely rare. However a long search wasn't necessary as the bobby knew me, and guessed correctly where I would be – fishing quite illegally of course – so I was returned home on a very much less hi-tec machine, on the back step of his old bicycle. I was then allowed just a few minutes to get into uniform, pack my bag, and then be chased off to the golf course, just in time to meet the helicopter, after which I was wafted over the hills to the airfield of RAF Lossiemouth. I still knew nothing about why there was all this fuss, but I was rushed to a waiting Mosquito – that beautiful twin-engine fighter-bomber which was so successful towards the end of the war. This one, though, was rather a special one, being the photographic reconnaissance variant stripped of all armaments, in smooth blue camouflage, and also stripped of everything else they could think of, in a quest for speed and yet more speed.

"I can still remember that flight, it sounds like nothing

now, but less than an hour and a half after taking off we were landing at RAF Farnborough. On the way down I had quizzed the pilot, but he knew nothing. However he did say, 'It must be a bloody important meeting you're going to, as my navigator and I were all ready for take-off this morning to get some new pictures of the Tirpitz in her Norwegian fjord, when our mission was aborted. Instead I was told that I had to take a VIP down to Farnborough, and you, Major, would seem to be that VIP – congratulations!'

Granddad stopped there and looked at me with a broad smile. "You'll be glad, Yvette, to hear that I'm going to stop there as I know that you've had quite enough of hearing Grannie and me rambling on about our adventures. But that doesn't matter because the good news is that I wrote down the rest of my story about a year ago. Probably you won't have heard of an organisation called the *Second World War Experience Centre* which was set up in Leeds by a Dr. Peter Liddle, which has been very successful in getting old fogies like me to tell our stories before we died. So here is a copy of the paper which I did for them. Once you have read it you'll be finished except for just a little more about 1944. Tomorrow, maybe in the afternoon, I can tell you that part and also what happened in 1956."

He stopped again and smiled at me, "I bet you're still wondering how the hell that far-off year should concern you, but I'll just leave it there for now." As Granddad had said, I was tired so I took the clip of papers to bed with me, intending to put them aside till morning.

I have placed a copy of Granddad's letter in Appendix One. When I glanced at the first page it was all so extraordinary that I just couldn't put it down and I read it to the end, and then did so again. But even then I was still puzzled. Certainly I now knew about his bravery and why he had received the DSO, but I was no clearer as to the help which he and Grannie seemed to want from me. Also, why had he stopped his letter at the time when he met Grannie, surely the adventure they had lived through in getting to Portugal was worth reporting?

Anyway my last thoughts, before getting to sleep, were that they must now really tell me about the ancient wrong which they wanted to put right.

Chapter Six

When I got down to breakfast it was with my curiosity buds sharpened, and after the morning salutations Granddad said, as indeed I had expected he would, "No questions now, we'll talk after breakfast."

So it was with the three of us round the sitting room fire that I started things by saying, "Granddad, what a wonderful story. I had never realised before what a hero you were. Why haven't you and Grannie told me before about your adventures? And why did you stop your letter to Dr. Liddle at the time when the two of you met without telling him the rest of your amazing experiences?"

He shook his head rather sadly, "Can't you guess dear? Remember that they took place nearly sixty years ago, and people now are very different to what we then were. As you know, within a few hours of our meeting we contrived to kill seven Germans, four of whom were tied up and helpless. That wouldn't go down too well would it? No I think that some stories – or at least a part of them – should be dead and buried, but you are an exception, as there is now a good reason why you have to know it all. Be patient, we are nearly finished."

I was suddenly embarrassed as I realised what my own thoughts had been. He leaned over and took my hand, "Don't say anything, my dear, war is an awful business, so just thank God that you have not been faced with decisions like that. But anyway, cheer up, as the war bit is almost over!"

He stopped there for a moment before saying to Grannie, "So, it's back to us again my dear, on that first leave up in Gairloch after we got back from France, and what could have been better for you than to stay up there with my grandparents?"

"And there I did stay," Grannie broke in, "and your father was born early in February 1945. So, if you do your sums, you will realise that it is quite possible that he was conceived on that very first night of high drama...disgraceful, wasn't it!" They both laughed, and I could see that the memory of the joys of that night of nearly sixty years ago still gave them pleasure, and I found myself wondering whether the night when I lost my virginity would be equally memorable.

Little did I then know that it would run pretty close!

But, as my mind wandered, I realised Granddad was going on, "My war effort after April 1944 was most uninteresting as I was appointed to a staff job at the War Office, but in October I was back in Gairloch again on leave and we decided to try to find out how things were in France. Now phoning to and from there was almost impossible as all the lines were still under military control. First we tried to contact her two friends – Michelle and Alicia – but they seemed to have disappeared in Paris. We knew that the Mélitour area had been freed by the Allies towards the end of August, so Hélène tried writing to Marie-Claire in the hope that she had recovered. In early November she received a reply." He stopped there, and gave me a letter, brittle and yellow with age. A transcript of the letter follows, translated into English:

```
                        Chateau de Mélitour
                        Department of Yonne,
                                      France
                        25th October 1944
```

Dear Madame Dallachy,
    The Dowager Comtesse de Mélitour has instructed me
to write in reply to your letter to the Comtesse
dated 14th October and to congratulate you on your
marriage.
    She has been living in the Chateau for some time
now, with Albert her grandson. His leg is now healed,
but he will probably walk with a slight limp for the
rest of his life.
    The news of the Comtesse is not good, as she is
still far from well and often has to go into hospital
in Auxerre where she is undergoing treatment.
    Because of the circumstances of your departure,
and of the consequences for the Comtesse and for
Albert, I am instructed to tell you that you are no
longer welcome here, and that no further
correspondence will be entertained.
Yours faithfully,
M. Francois Norman
(Secretarie)

"That's an awful letter, Grannie," I said, "Do you know
why she wrote in these dreadful terms?"

"No Yvette, we had no idea at all, and that is why I then
got the idea of asking Andrew to go there, and find out what
had gone wrong."

Granddad laughed, "I can tell you Yvette, that if you
played your cards right at the War Office you could, given
time, do almost anything. But it took me until late January of
1945 to find an American unit near Chaource, and to invent a
reason for a liaison visit. After a couple of days of wasting

their time I knew that they would be glad to be rid of me. So when I made an excuse of meeting old friends, they happily lent me a jeep stocked up with several jerrycans of petrol, and driving to Chaource was no problem.

"I got there on a bright Sunday afternoon and could even feel a touch of spring in the air. Hélène had given me the address of the two old gardeners with the suggestion that I should first make my number with them, and try to find out what was wrong, and how right she turned out to be. I stopped near the village market and I could see some curious looks at the Jeep with its large American stars, and there I was in British uniform. For a while I just sat there, remembering that evening only some nine months previously when we had met, and all that had happened since then. But I told myself to snap out of it, and drove to the address I'd been given, then jumped out and rang the bell.

"It was Georges who opened the door, and I saw him give a quick puzzled look, but then there was a great beam of welcome, and an excited shout, 'Pierre, come and see who's here!' They both greeted me as a comrade returning from the wars, but like the old soldiers they were – at least to begin with – respectful of my rank. Hélène had told me that there was a small hotel in the village, but they would have none of that.

"'Nonsense, Major,' Georges said, 'we shall be honoured if you stay with us. I may say that we have heard of your marriage to Mlle. Hélène, and she would never forgive us if we allowed her husband to lodge in the village.' I remember then that Georges paused before going on, 'I presume, Major, that you are here to find out how things are at the Chateau...Yes?...Well, we have a lot to tell you. But first let's sit down and have a drink together.'

"They took me through the house and into a little garden,

very much a gardener's garden, nary a weed to be seen, and already showing a carpet of crocuses and early daffodils. 'Let's sit out in the sun,' Georges said, 'it is warm enough, and, I have some Chablis from the Mélitour vineyards.'

"As you have heard, Georges always liked to arrange things, and he insisted that I told them my story before they told me theirs. So I did, right from the time when we parted outside the German·HQ, and I went into some detail about our escape through France, and our arrival in Madrid. But then I just said that we then got a train to Lisbon, and managed to get a flight to England. But Georges then said, 'And when did you marry Mlle. Hélène?'

"So I had to explain that we had fallen in love during our journey, and that we had got married in Lisbon, not very long after we had met. Suddenly Georges became the down-to-earth poilu of thirty years before. He dug Pierre in his ribs and said with a laugh, 'You are a lucky man, Major, Mlle. Hélène was a ripe peach, ready for plucking!' But then he stopped abruptly, 'My apologies, Major, that was rude of me. All I wanted to say was that she was a lovely girl.'

"But I could laugh with him 'Don't apologise, Georges, you are quite right in what you first said, and I certainly know how lucky I was then, and how lucky I am now. Perhaps you would like to do some simple arithmetic when I tell you that our first child is expected in just two weeks from now.' I saw them do a quick count, and we all laughed, even Pierre being motivated to make a remark, 'That was quick work Major!'"

But Granddad couldn't go on, as Grannie broke in, peering at me as she did so over her pince-nez, "This is quite an education for you, Yvette, and maybe you don't already know how vulgar men are on their own, when they begin to talk about women. 'A ripe peach ready for plucking', indeed!"

Then she stopped and blew a kiss to Granddad, "But I am glad that you agreed with him, my dear!"

There was a pause, and Granddad winked at me before he went on, "That ,Yvette, was a pleasant interlude, but there wasn't much else to laugh about. Georges and Pierre were able to tell me their story, one which began very well as they had no immediate problems after our adventure together, but later there was a tremendous fuss about all the German deaths and our escape. However they also told me that Marie-Claire and Albert had been successfully hidden away till the Allies came in August, when the Germans just faded away. It was then that the Dowager Comtesse managed to come up from Cannes, and two days after that an ambulance arrived at the Chateau bringing the Comtesse and Albert. Dr. Jeanfils had done a wonderful job. Apparently he had managed to treat her in his clinic, and he had also arranged for Albert to be hidden in a farm near Tanlay, so by then the boy was well on the way to recovery. But, as for the Comtesse, it was very sad, as they told me that she was now like a three-year-old child, thankfully a happy one, but no longer the wonderful woman she once was.

"They then went on to tell me that only a few days after Marie-Claire and Albert came back they were told that the Dowager Comtesse wanted to see them. Albert was beside her. However when they went towards him, just to say how good it was to see him again, they were astonished when he cowered back and went to hide behind his grandmother, screaming a torrent of words and something about them being with the Germans, and how they and Hélène had deserted him. It had gone on until a maid was summoned to lead him away.

"The old Comtesse had then gone on to say 'You two can

see what you have done, your stupid actions have left my grandson with a leg which will never be quite right, and his mother with awful injuries from which she will probably never recover. I know, of course, that you have been servants of the estate for many years, but now I cannot bear the sight of you. Put down your tools now, and GO! I want you off the estate this morning.'

"Georges then went on to tell me that none of their arguments helped in any way, as she just wouldn't listen to them, and said, 'I can only hope, Major that you have more luck, but I doubt it. Pierre and I know her of old, and once she makes up her mind she never changes it. So there we were after thirty-six years of service, sacked for no good reason. It was fortunate for us however that our abilities are well known in the district and, on the very next day, we were offered jobs at the Château de la Cordelière, just a few miles up the road to Bar sur Seine. We are better paid there, so we haven't done too badly after all. But we still miss Mélitour, although it is a sad house now.'

"By common consent we then talked of other things, nothing more about our adventures, and although there was a shadow hanging over us I very much enjoyed my time with them that evening. It was pleasant to hear how grateful they were that Britain held out against the Germans back in 1940. At that time this was by no means the opinion of most of the French to whom I had spoken. The popular view then seemed to be that things would have been fine if we had just made peace in 1940 as they had, because the Germans would then have struck their tents and gone off, leaving France as it had been before the war.

"Anyway, next morning it was again bright and sunny, and I cheered up as I made my way along the road from Chaource to the Chateau which Hélène knew so well. When I went through the entrance gates I could see that the Dowager Comtesse had things well in hand. The gravel on the long driveway was raked smooth, with neatly clipped edges, and on the side a group of young gardeners were engaged on topiary work which no doubt had been neglected during the last five years. It was a sight which showed me that, although for Britain the war had still to be fought and won, here in France, now cleared of Germans, it had already been forgotten.

"On the previous day I had driven down in my battledress, but I had packed my best uniform and made sure that my buttons were bright and shining. A good impression I had felt, was important. But I am afraid things started very badly. I stopped the Jeep with its American stars at the entrance and went up and rang the bell. I was greeted by a manservant, and had just announced myself, 'Major Andrew Dallachy to see the Dowager Comtesse.'

"But young Albert, curious like all children, rushed past me to see the Jeep. Then he turned and looked at me, first with a doubtful expression, but then doubt changed to certainty, and then to terror. He rushed back into the house, and I heard him calling, 'Gr..mere…Gr..mere…it's a German!'

"Eventually I was taken through to see her, but I got no smile of welcome. 'Major Dallachy, you are no doubt aware that I wrote to your wife some months ago. I told her that she is no longer welcome here. Surely you realise that this also applies to you? You have already seen the unfortunate effect your presence here has had on my grandson, so please say what you have to say, and make it as short as possible.'

"I can't remember my exact words, but I tried to persuade her that everything Hélène and I had done had been for the best in an appalling situation. In particular I emphasised that the two of us, with the old gardeners, had set out to free her daughter and young Albert. I told her that we had already killed three German soldiers even before we got inside the German HQ. I then explained how, with me then dressed in German uniform, we dealt with the guards and crept into the torture chamber just a few moments too late to avert the tragedy.

"'It was just as we got there,' I said, 'that we heard Marie-Claire scream as Kretzer tore the second of her nails off, after which he seemed to lose his temper and smashed the plaster cast on Albert's leg. I can tell you, Madame, that at first I couldn't fire as Marie-Claire was behind him, but she made a super-human effort to free herself, which caused her chair to overturn, and she hit her head on the fireplace as she fell. The resulting confusion enabled me to shoot Kretzer, and for Hélène to shoot the other German officer. There was another man there, presumably the traitor who betrayed the escape organisation. He managed to escape, but not before we had shot and wounded him.'

"I emphasised to the Comtesse the awful injury to Marie-Claire took place before any action of ours. I told her that before we got her to that friendly doctor in Tonnere who looked after her and Albert so well, we had to shoot four more German soldiers. I also told her that Hélène, my dear wife, was very conscious of the fact that Albert wanted her to stay with him, but what could she do? The doctor had enough problems in trying to hide the Comtesse and Albert, without having a young woman on his hands – much wanted by the Germans – as well.

"For what it is worth I said, 'Just maybe she would have stayed, but I made up her mind for her, and dragged her away. It was the right decision – the only possible one – and I do not apologise for it. You will see, Madame, why Albert is so frightened by seeing me. It is because he has only previously seen me disguised in German uniform, so it is hardly surprising that he is confused.'

"It was a while before she looked up. 'Major, I have not heard your story before. I can see that I should have asked the gardeners, and it is I who should apologise to you and also to Hélène. I have been so distressed by this tragedy which has turned my dear daughter-in-law from a vibrant young woman into a pitiful idiot that I'm afraid I haven't been thinking straight. You mentioned how confused young Albert is, and who, at his age, could understand all the whys and wherefores of what happened that night? So it isn't surprising that he is terrified when he sees you. To him you must just be one element in a nightmare which will always be with him, and in which there are no good people. And one can also understand why he is bitter about Hélène who, as he sees it, abandoned him to strangers.

"'Oh, it is a damnable business, Major, and now having heard your story I am completely satisfied that what you and Hélène did was for the best, and that I and my family owe you both a debt of gratitude. But, despite that, I am sorry to say that I think it best – at least for the present – if neither of you comes here. You have seen poor little Albert, and although Marie-Claire is usually peaceful in her dream world, she too is hysterical if she gets any reminder of that awful night. The first time I saw this was when I asked Georges and Pierre to come to see me, shortly after she was brought back here, and just the sight of them caused an appalling and most distressing reaction.

"I know that you have seen them, and they may wonder why I treated them like I did. I just could not risk them staying on the estate. What I did, though, was to arrange jobs for them with friends of mine at nearby Château de la Cordelière, and although they were going to be well paid, I add 50% to their wages without them knowing it. They deserve the best, these two, and I am only sorry that I had to do what I did.'

"She stopped then and excused herself, saying that she wanted to get something, and when she returned it was with a slim jewel case, saying, 'I'd like Hélène to have this. I know that she was a dear friend of Marie-Claire, and it is wonderful to know now that she did not betray that friendship.' She then opened the case, and I saw the necklace which became Hélène's favourite, the same one she is wearing now."

He stopped there, and Grannie gave a quick nod before unclasping the necklace, and giving it to me, a choker with two strands of pearls and a middle strand of black pearls, with an elaborate clasp studded with diamonds and pearls. "Put it on, Yvette," she said, "and when you go to Mélitour, as I hope you will some day, I am sure that there will be people who still remember that Marie-Claire often wore it, and it may give you a certain cachet if you now do so. I have worn it for nearly sixty years and it is time for a change. It is yours now, dear, and I am very happy to give it to you."

I just didn't know what to say. How could I let her give me her favourite adornment, so I stammered out, 'Grannie, it is very sweet of you, but I can't possibly accept it; how could I recognise you without it. And as for wearing it if I go to Mélitour – why should I go there? Although I have been fascinated to hear, at last, about your adventures, I really don't see any reason why I should go to France, especially now when I have only ten days left of my Easter holidays, and so much work still to do."

To my surprise my remark didn't seem to bother her, and

she made no effort to argue with me. "I know, my dear, we have both seen your reservations, but just hear the story to the end. You see, for better or for worse, we decided to tell you everything in chronological order, and so far we are only up to 1945, so there are still nearly sixty years to cover!"

She laughed then and patted my hand, "But don't worry, there isn't in fact a lot more to tell, although the most important bit of all comes at the very end. Andrew is finishing 1945, and this afternoon we'll tell you the rest, about an episode in 1956, and then what has come up only in the last few days. Andrew, carry on now, and as for you Yvette, please put on your necklace without any more argument!"

"Well," Granddad continued, "just a week after that trip to Mélitour I was called in by my CO at the War Office to be told Hélène was seriously ill, and that I had been granted immediate compassionate leave. She was then in the last weeks of her pregnancy and had somehow missed her footing on a stair, and had fallen heavily. This brought about a very messy delivery of your father, and some damage was done which meant there could be no more children. When I got to Gairloch some two days later I found that my baby son was in good shape but that Hélène had got septicaemia, and for a while it was touch and go whether or not she would live. But, thank God, she made it, and a few days later she was well enough to hear the details of my visit to Mélitour. I was worried lest my mixture of news would upset her but it was a time when – like me – she knew what things were really important. We had a healthy son, we were alive and in love, and to Hell with everything else!

"Anyway, when she was well enough, she wrote to the old Comtesse to thank her for the gift, and said that if ever things changed she and I would be glad to come to see her. She also wrote to the Mélitour store in Paris, La Maison d'Argent, and was able to get from them the addresses of her two friends, Michelle and Alicia. Like her they hadn't wasted their time; both had both married, and lived near each other in St. Germain.

"There was an exchange of letters, and the three of them decided that although Marie-Claire was very ill she was still alive, so they should respect her wishes and do nothing about the three parts of the letter. To join them together again they felt, would be a betrayal of trust and anyway, after VE Day on the 8th of May, all we wanted to do was to forget the war."

He stopped there, and smiled at me, "So, Yvette, that is my bit of the story finished, and as you know, I then took a permanent commission and for the next eleven years I spent quite a lot of time in Germany, where Hélène could follow me, and then during the time that I was in Korea she came back and lived in Gairloch. By 1956 I was back in London, and it was then that she received a letter from the old Comtesse. But that is her story, and you'll hear it this afternoon. Right now I think it is time for a drink."

Chapter Seven

It was after lunch when we sat down again for Grannie to finish her story and to bring it up to the present. But, sadly, although I couldn't know it then, the present was not to be the end of it. She started on a bright note, "Cheer up, Yvette, you have been very patient, and there isn't a lot more to come. I can tell you that the years 1945 to 1956 were important for us. Those early years of marriage, and being young and in love, were wonderful, and when you are that age you think that they will go on forever. By 1956 Andrew was 37, by which time he was a full Colonel. John, your father, was eleven and was entered for Wellington College when he got to twelve. He had, of course, been raised in army surroundings and he idolised your Grandfather. He was a fine boy, and it is tragic that you never knew him.

"Andrew had arranged leave in August of that year, and we spent it in what for all three of us was our favourite place – where else but in Gairloch – with John and Mary his grandparents. It had been nearly five years since we had last been there for a long holiday and I was amused to see that old John made it his business to repair a gap, a serious one to him, in his great-grandson's education by teaching him to fish, and to do it skilfully. I may say that he had previously done his best with Andrew, but he was not too happy with his prowess.

"'Damn it,' he said one day, 'he was nearly fifteen before I started to teach him, far too old, and it is essential to start early. Even young John is too old, but at least he is four years younger than his father was, so there is hope for him!'

"Well, he succeeded, and on most days very old John and very young John went off to unknown and probably illegal locations, and seldom came back without at least one to show for it," and she pointed across the room to a glass case on the living room wall with a stuffed salmon still gleaming as if just out of the water, and I well knew the inscription on the brass plate:

A salmon of weight 21lb. 14oz. Caught by John Andrew Dallachy, aged eleven, on the 7th day of August 1956 in a river near Gairloch

It was a matter of family legend that the exact location could not be stated, as they shouldn't have been on that river.

"We are an unfortunate family, aren't we?" she went on, "We don't have many relations. I never knew my grandparents and my parents both died when I was only nineteen. Andrew's died when he was even younger, and it was his grandparents who were the only relatives for us and for your father. Then, as if that wasn't bad enough, it was your misfortune to be even more deprived, as you never even recall seeing your father and mother."

I gave her hand a squeeze, and said, "Do you know, Grannie, I have never wept over the loss of my parents, why should I have done so – I never knew them – and you and Granddad have always been so wonderful to me. But hearing this family history has brought things home to me. I'm sad today, but I shall always be grateful to both of you for all you have done over the years, and now for telling me your stories. But I'm fine now, so let's get on with 1956."

"OK!" she smiled, "Let's do just that. It was when we

were still up at Gairloch when I was surprised to get a letter
from the old Comtesse. Here it is, read it." I unfolded the
thick creamy paper, and this is what I read (translated from
French):

Chateau de Mélitour
Department of Yonne,
France
7th August 1956

My Dear Hélène,

    I hope that both you and your husband will now
have forgiven me for my attitude back in 1944 and
1945. It was however a very difficult time both for
me and for my family.

    Since then I am sorry to say that my major problem
remains unresolved as my dear Marie-Claire still
lives in a dream world of her own. My consolation is
the continuing joy I find in Albert, my beloved
grandson, who you last saw as a frightened little boy
of seven. Now he is a handsome young man of nineteen
with only the trace of a limp to remind him of those
awful days of 1944.

    Hélène, I write to you now to ask a favour of you
and your husband. We have recently consulted a young
doctor who has gained a reputation as a world-class
expert on brain injuries, and he feels that there is
a chance of improving Marie-Claire's condition. The
new treatments which he intends trying involve
shocks, both electrical and otherwise, and he has
asked if you and your husband could possibly come to
Mélitour. What he wants is for Marie-Claire to see
you dressed as near as is possible to what you were
wearing on that awful night. The two old gardeners
would also be there, as would your husband.

    I realise of course that you will not now have
these old clothes, but if you could have something
made up I would of course reimburse you for all the

expenses which you and your husband incur, and for
all your travel costs. As for what your husband
should wear, the doctor feels that a German uniform
would be too much, and would like him to be in
British army dress.

I also realise that your husband is a serving
officer, so his time is not his own, but I do hope
that you will be able to come with him, and we can
fit in with any time convenient to you.

Do please come if you possibly can, Hélène, I
seize every chance to help poor Marie-Claire.

There followed some notes about travel arrangements, and
a suggestion that if we came by train, they would send a car to
Troyes to meet us.

Once I had finished, Grannie continued, "It was a plea
which we could not refuse, and I phoned the old Comtesse
that same night to make arrangements. Fortunately Andrew
had some leave still to come, so things moved quickly and it
took just two days for me – with the help of a lady friend in
Gairloch – to run up a dress which was very similar to the one
which I had worn back in 1944."

"Very similar!" Granddad broke in, "It was exactly as I
remembered, and I can tell you, Yvette, that I had tears in my
eyes. She was again the lovely brave girl I fell in love with, indecently quickly, twelve years before."

They smiled at each other, and I wondered if I would ever
be so lucky as to marry, and look back some forty or fifty
years with the pleasure that these two still found. But I
couldn't pursue the thought, as Grannie was going on with the
story.

"I think it was only some four or five days after we got the
letter that Andrew and I set off, leaving young John with his
great-grandparents. It was a long journey in those days, first to

Inverness by car and an early morning flight to London, then
train and boat to Paris where we stopped for the night. In the
morning we took the train to Troyes, where we were met by a
chauffeur driving a magnificent limousine which I recalled
from pre-war days. I even remembered the young Comte,
Marie-Claire's husband, driving it back from the Paris Motor
Show of 1938. It was a legendary make, a Hispano-Suiza, and
certainly for Andrew a ride in that magnificent car made him
forget the hardships of the journey.

"I confess, though, that I was sad and disappointed that
Albert had not come to meet us as it could only mean that he
had still not forgiven me. When we got to the Chateau it was
as if it had remained in a time warp since the days before the
war. The driveway and the gardens were as immaculate as on
that far-off day in 1938 when I cycled up to be interviewed for
a job.

"And there was a very haughty major-domo — unlike the
old one — who showed us into the same salon where I first
met Marie-Claire. Our greeting from the old Comtesse could
not have been warmer, and she still seemed very much the
charming if somewhat grand lady whom I had known before
the war on her visits to the Chateau. Albert was also there,
now a handsome young man, but although he was polite, it
was the politeness of a stranger, and this distressed me. Surely,
I felt, although he must know the truth, he nevertheless must
still feel that I deserted him when he most needed me.

"We stayed at the Chateau for two days before we saw
Marie-Claire. The doctor arrived that afternoon and he ex-
plained to us what we had to do. We waited till the evening
when he set up a tableau vivant of Andrew and me, along with
Georges and Pierre who had been brought over from
Chaource. The four of us stood in embarrassed silence, with

Albert in the background, until at last we heard footsteps and the old Comtesse came in with Marie-Claire, leading her by the hand as if she were a small child. It was an awful shock for me, remembering her vibrant personality, but now although her appearance was little changed; it was as though she was a wax-work dummy. Her eyes were still as large and blue as ever, but there was nothing behind them. She looked slowly round at me, at Andrew, then at Georges and Pierre, and I thought I could see a slight narrowing of her eyes as if she were puzzled.

"Then as instructed by the doctor, I stepped forward in my new-old dress, saying, 'Marie-Claire, do you remember me? I'm Hélène.'

"For a moment she froze, but then I saw horror in her eyes as she gazed wildly at me, then at the others. It was dreadfully like the way she had looked as we left that German HQ when she was briefly roused by Albert's screams, and she gave a pitiful moan , 'Non…non…non…' before slipping to the ground in a dead faint. It was a very sad moment, bad enough for us, but how much worse for Albert and the old Comtesse. I could imagine what a continuing nightmare life must be for them, and for the first time I could feel some sympathy with Albert's reserve towards us. He must know that the disaster was not our fault, but I could understand the feeling that somehow we should have managed to do something. None of us could find much to say after Marie-Claire was taken away, but later in the evening the doctor did try again by taking me up on my own to her room. But when she saw me she cowered away in terror. So that, very sadly, was that.

"Soon afterwards the doctor went to bed, and Andrew and I decided to tell Albert and the Comtesse about the torn-up letter, the three pieces of which had been given to me and to Michelle and Alicia. I finished by asking them if they would like us to get together with them so that we could read the letter and see whether it led us to the bastard who had betrayed us and caused all this misery. I had expected, and so did Andrew, that they would be enthusiastic in finding who was responsible, but they were not. At the time I could see that Albert would have gone on with it, but the old Comtesse asked if we would wait till the morning before hearing her decision. So we all went off to bed wondering what the outcome would be.

"In the morning after breakfast Albert said that his Grandmother would speak for both of them. She made quite a long speech. She talked about what a sad life they had, and ended by saying, 'My dear Albert lives as normal a life as he can, and I am content to live here and let the world go by. Now if we were to dig back to those awful days of 1944, and we did find evidence of treachery and who was responsible for it, we would be besieged by journalists and reporters, probably British and American as well as French, AND I WILL NOT HAVE IT. We've suffered enough, and exposing some unfortunate Frenchman now, twelve years after the event, isn't going to cure Marie-Claire, and nothing else would make the exercise worthwhile. So please destroy your part of the letter, and it would be a great service both to Albert and to me if you could find time to travel back through Paris, and see your two old friends and persuade them to do the same. Neither Albert nor I want anything to arise which would remind us of those awful days.'

"So that was that, on all counts our visit had been a failure, and we said our farewells, warm and gracious from the old Comtesse, cool and formal from Albert. I am sure we all knew that we would never meet again.

"We got to Paris that afternoon and were able to meet Michelle and Alicia for dinner, with their husbands. I may say that I was glad to find that they seemed as pleased with their men as I was with mine! I had briefed Andrew, so as arranged he took the other two men aside after dinner so that we three girls could talk together about old times.

"We spent a long time reminiscing and catching up on our respective lives. When we came to the matter of Marie-Claire's letter, I explained the request from the old Comtesse and Albert that we should each destroy our pieces. I think that Michelle and I would have agreed to do so, but Alicia would have none of it. 'This is the wrong time to make such a decision,' she said, 'The old Comtesse and Marie-Claire aren't going to live forever, and after they are dead maybe Albert will change his mind. So let's wait.'

"And that's just what we did. We each have kept our portion of that letter for over forty years – and now thank God for that! Just before getting to the end, I should tell you that we have had no contact in all these years with Mélitour, but I have received news from time to time from Michelle and Alicia who still have friends in Chaource. And as for Mélitour, shortly before she died the old Comtesse saw Albert marry, in 1970, when he was 34. He has two children, a girl, Maria, born in 1974 and a boy, Jean-Pierre, named after his grandfather, born in 1978. The position now is that Albert's wife is dead, and the girl is now married and lives in Paris. Albert lives alone with his son, Jean-Pierre, who runs the estate and the farms; he has a degree in agriculture from Reims University. It would seem that Albert has done well in business as the store in Paris, La Maison d'Argent, continues to prosper, and now there are branches in Reims, Lille and Lyon. He has been in

New York recently in connection with the possible opening of a store there.

"But as for poor Marie-Claire there is no good news, she is just the same and is tended by living-in nurses. She is like a child while everyone around her gets old."

Grannie then said, "Now Yvette. You must pay attention, as I am about to tell you the reason why Andrew and I have told you all this ancient history. Until last week we both felt that it was dead and buried, and should stay that way. But you must remember that day when we saw something in the *Daily Telegraph*? It was an article about the appointment of a new Secretary of State for Defence, see, here it is!"

I couldn't help laughing, "Grannie, you told me that I was going to be like the young Alice who had believed impossible things. Well I have tried, but I'm afraid that I have to quit here! How on earth can he come into any story of yours? I did in fact read the article on that day, the only criticism of him was that since he is in only in his early forties he may be too young for the job. Anyway I'm baffled, how can he possibly have any link with what happened during the war?"

But Grannie just smiled at me, and then said, "Just read through the article again dear and see if anything strikes you now."

I skimmed through it, how young Michael Marshall had first become an MP when he was only twenty-five, and subsequently how he had progressed smoothly up the ladder of power, now being appointed to the same job which his father, Lord Hempson, had held, back in the 1960's. There was also some speculation that he might well become Prime Minister sometime, a position which his father had narrowly failed to win. None of this seemed of interest, but then, towards the end of the article, a paragraph leapt out of the page:

"Some critics of the appointment are saying that Michael Marshall has insufficient experience in defence matters, but he must have soaked up a lot of useful knowledge from his father. The advice that Lord Hempson could have give him goes a long way back as he had an army background with a distinguished career in the Second World War. He joined the army in 1940 and, after home service as a Lieutenant, joined the Special Operations Executive in 1944. In the spring of that year he was engaged in hazardous operations in France, working with French Resistance groups in connection with escape lines for Allied aircrew. In April 1944 his operation was raided by German troops. During the attack, despite receiving a serious wound in the shoulder, he managed to hold onto his position for enough time to allow his French friends who were with him the opportunity to flee. Unfortunately he was captured and spent the rest of the war in a POW camp reserved for prisoners who might try to escape."

At the head of the article were three photographs, one of the new young Minister, another showing the head of the distinguished elderly Lord Hempson, and a third of a young Lieutenant Henry Marshall, dated 1943, showing a rather handsome man immaculately dressed in army uniform. He was wearing a forage cap and around it I could see his thick dark hair. My mind went back to a conversation I had heard about a deeply cleft chin, and there it was in the photograph.

"Grannie, you surely don't think that Lord Hempson was your traitor?"

She nodded her head, "Yes, Yvette, that is just what we do think. I know, of course that Andrew and I are relying on a brief sighting in that awful room before he crashed out of the window and both of us caught him with shots. But if he is not the man, then it is someone exactly like him, and these looks are rare. Then there is also that description which Marie-Claire gave me, back in 1944, of the new British officer – tall with black hair and a deeply cleft chin – so we both have come to the conclusion that in all probability a young Lord Hempson was in fact M. Brume, the new British officer in our area, and also that he was the traitor who betrayed our escape line."

"It is," she went on, "a great pity that neither of us has seen a photograph of him as a young man before, remember that we were abroad for much of the time, but it does mention a shoulder wound and Andrew and I certainly caused at least one! The clincher is that he was in France at just the right time. I may say that I have managed to get from the *Daily Telegraph* a copy of that picture. Here it is, and I can tell you that we are sure that he is the man."

I looked at the photograph, and it was certainly a very clear one. Granddad then smiled at me and said, "I can see, Yvette, that you aren't yet convinced, and I agree that we need some real hard evidence. This is where you come in. Just to begin with I hope to persuade you to go to London tomorrow. I wish that I could go but I am under doctor's orders, but I have used my old rank to pull some strings in the Ministry of Defence. They will turn up some of their old records for you. I haven't gone into any details and of course I didn't mention anything about our suspicions. I said only that you are interested in seeing the records of the escape line that Hélène, your grandmother, was involved in.

"I would hope that the records will show details of Marshall's work in the escape lines, and that he too worked in the right area. We are probably right about this, as the *Daily Telegraph* presumably got their story from the MOD. He must have been able to concoct some kind of fairy story and get it accepted as history. I think we must accept that he was a

POW, but it is possible that after the Germans turned him they gave him a plausible cover story so that he would appear whiter than white after the war. Anyway, if there was a cover-up then maybe you'll discover some inconsistencies in the records, and who better than a highly intelligent young girl like you to spot them."

But I stopped him there, as despite my previous reservations, I was suddenly convinced that there might well be something in their suspicions. "Grannie and Granddad, flattery will get you anywhere, but in this case it isn't necessary. You are a clever old pair of schemers, and you must have known that by telling me your stories in such detail you would arouse my interest. Just let me say that I have taken your bait hook line and sinker! So, in answer to your question, yes of course, I'll go to London tomorrow. Fancy a traitor, who was our Defence Minister, now having a son in the same position, it's disgusting. It will be fascinating if I do find some of the evidence you are looking for, and certainly I'll also go to France to see your friends if we find real grounds for your suspicions. I'm right am I not – that is your plan for me, isn't it?"

They both beamed at me, and he said, "I don't normally approve of drinking champagne as an aperitif, but this is special, and I may say that I put a bottle in the fridge this morning just in case you agreed to help. Anyway now that we have managed to interest you in our quest, I think we should drink a toast to your success."

"Granddad," I said, "you're wrong, I'm not just interested, I am fascinated, and I can also tell you that I'm looking forward enormously to some detective work. But now, tell me, I know that you've both been busy this week – I couldn't help overhearing some long telephone conversations, some of which I think were in French – so what have you been up to?"

"He didn't answer immediately as he went off to get the bottle and then fiddled with the cork which came out with a satisfactory pop. He poured out the drinks, and as he passed round the glasses, said, "Let's sit round the fire and then drink my toast, a very simple one," he raised his glass, "TO THE TRUTH!"

As we clinked glasses I could hardly believe that here I was, a very down-to-earth girl with little interest in history, and even less in the war of two generations ago, looking forward to researching the activities of a few people deep in France nearly sixty years back, involving incidents that were not worth even a footnote in the history books. Then it occurred to me that if I were successful the story of a traitor becoming the British Defence Minister, and fathering a son for the same job, would certainly be more than just a footnote. Also Granddad had hit the nail on the head when he said that the fascination was in looking for that most elusive thing – truth – and I was determined to find it.

He settled back comfortably in his chair, and I waited eagerly for what he had to tell me. "I can tell you, Yvette, that Hélène and I have gambled on you being sufficiently interested to take up the trail on our behalf, so we have made several preliminary arrangements. Hélène has spoken to Michelle and Alicia, and unless your visit tomorrow to the MOD shows that our suspicions are unjustified, they will be happy to see you and to open their letters with hers.

"We were also able this morning to speak with Albert, or to give him his correct title Comte de Mélitour, and as I told you he is just back from a trip to America. I explained our conviction that Lord Hempson was the villain, back in 1944, and that we were trying to persuade you to act on our behalf.

He agreed that if you do see Hélène's old friends, you can
bring the old letter for him to see, and said that you would be
most welcome to stay at the Chateau. Perhaps I should have
mentioned earlier that both Michelle and Alicia are more or
less housebound, so it all depends on you and whatever assistance you receive at Mélitour."

He stopped there, then leaned over and took my hand, "I
know, of course, that you have only just a week left of your
holiday, and we are both very grateful that you are willing to
give us some of your time. Now this is Sunday, and if I phone
the MOD in the morning, they will be ready for you when you
go down. Then on Tuesday we can discuss what you have
found, if anything, and on Wednesday you can fly to Paris if
things look hopeful. Finally on Thursday you can go to Mélitour if the letter has any information which is still useful after
all these long years. You needn't spend much time there as
either the package will have survived or be lost forever. I expect that you should get back by Saturday, or Sunday at the
latest."

It all sounded so very easy, and how could I know that this
simple timetable would go so very wrong.

Chapter Eight

So, after all this clever story-telling by Grannie and Grand-dad, I was off to London on the train next morning full of hope and excitement. My introduction at the MOD was to a Mr. James Butler and, after various security checks, I was taken along miles of corridors to his office. I had rather expected that he would be a rather junior civil servant – why should somebody senior be involved in such a routine request – so I was surprised to see that the office was large and quite luxuriously furnished, with easy chairs and a coffee table next to the large fireplace, in addition to a more business-like area with a large desk and visitors' chairs.

It certainly occurred to me that Granddad must still have some clout at the Ministry for such an important man to take the time to see me. Important he might be, but he soon made sure that I was at my ease. Coffee and biscuits arrived like magic, and over the small talk I could relax and have a good look at my host. He looked to be in his late fifties, very much a civil servant mandarin – certainly dressed like one – but his manner was pleasantly informal. It was when we had finished our coffee and moved away from the easy chairs that he steepled his fingers and looked across the desk at me. "Now, Yvette, I understand that your grandfather has asked us to look out what records we have about the French escape line that your grandmother was involved in. May I ask you why he wants to do this? He has, after all, waited nearly sixty years to do so, and I wonder why he wants us to look for information now?"

I don't know why – after all it was a quite reasonable question – but a little warning bell rang in my mind. Was it the rather intent look in his eyes? I didn't know, and I rather surprised myself in my reply. "I'm sorry, Mr. Butler, if we are being a nuisance, but it is all my fault! You see, Grannie has often spoken about her adventures, and I thought it would be interesting to see what records there are – if any – about the organisation run by the Comtesse de Mélitour, which, after all, did enable my grandfather to escape to Spain with the V1 secrets – and to marry my grandmother for good measure!"

He laughed, "Yes it was a romantic story, wasn't it, and they were damn lucky to get away. But for now I'll get my archivists to buckle down to work and we should have something to show you early this afternoon. But please do not expect very much detail as you will appreciate that few records were made in France, and such records as we have were patched together after the war. So, why don't you go off now and do some shopping, and I would be delighted if you would meet me for lunch, shall we say Simpson's in the Strand at half past twelve? We'll get back here soon after two, by which time there should be something for you to look at."

I was astonished by the invitation and demurred as best I could, but he would have none of it. "Do please come, it would be such a pleasant change from eating with my colleagues here. It isn't often that I get the chance to entertain such a lovely young girl and I can tell you that my stock will rise enormously!"

Well, I didn't go shopping. It was a nice morning, so I walked down to the Embankment and found a seat where I could watch the boats on the river, and just think. My reception from Mr. Butler was so much out of line with what I had expected that it worried me, and it would seem that he must already have looked up some records himself. How else could he make the remark about it being a romantic story? But nothing I could come up with made sense, and it was with a very large bump of curiosity that I went to meet him for lunch.

He was every inch a gracious host, arranging a very nice lunch, and I found myself relaxing especially as we soon found a common interest in golf. Then, when he found that I was at St. Andrews and played for the ladies' team he smiled and said, "Do you know, I could wish that I were maybe thirty-seven years younger – or that you were the same number of years older – you see, I too was a student there, and graduated in 1966, and I was a member of the university team, just as you are now."

So we really had a lot to talk about, I thoroughly enjoyed the meal, except for one thing which jarred. He kept pressing drinks on me, and I had difficulty sticking to just one glass of sherry and two of wine – and no post-prandial cognac. I smiled to myself as it seemed to me that he was like a young man trying to soften up his girl friend, but then a nastier thought came unbidden. Could he be trying to cloud my mind before I saw the papers? I told myself not to be so silly, but the niggle of doubt remained.

We got back to the Ministry soon after two o'clock, and he said to his secretary, "Ask Mr. Roberts to bring me the documents which he has found." In a few minutes there was a knock at the door and a young man came in with a thin sheaf of papers in plastic enclosure , and I saw Mr. Butler look at him with obvious displeasure, "Why are you here, where is Roberts?"

The young man explained that his colleague had been

called away urgently as his wife had gone into premature labour, and that she had been rushed to hospital. I could see
that my host was not at all concerned about his assistant's
domestic problem, but seemed instead to have one of his own,
as he said, "But these are the original documents, I asked
Roberts to get me photocopies."

I heard the young man saying that he had not been advised of this, and I was puzzled about the exchange. Why
shouldn't I see the originals? So I said, "Mr. Butler I've been
enough of a nuisance already. All I want is a quick glance
through them, and I can do this in your office in just a few
minutes. You have already told me that only a few records are
available, so it shouldn't take long." I held out my hand for the
papers, and for a moment he hesitated, but then he realised
that he really had no option and handed them to me with a
curt, "Do please be very careful!"

I took the thin plastic folder, which obviously contained
only a very few sheets of paper, then went over and sat in one
of the armchairs at the fireplace. I was just about to slip the
sheets out of the folder when I saw a small neat label stuck on
the outside.

France 1944

ESCAPE LINES: Troyes - Tonnere - Auxerre

Original papers reported missing, presumably destroyed in error. Replacements
prepared in 1968 by Mr. James Butler.

As I looked at this in surprise I suddenly realised why he
had wanted photocopies, as these would have come without
this revealing plastic folder. As I pondered I heard the young
man being dismissed and Mr. Butler came over and sat in a
chair beside me.

"I did warn you that you would not find much information. However, when I see the folder I remember the loss of this particular file some thirty-five years ago, and one of my early jobs here was to do the best I could, by way of rewriting the papers. Fortunately I had read the originals, and could remember everything that was of any importance."

He sounded sincere, but I was convinced that he was lying. He must have remembered all about it, to have given the instruction about photocopies, and I also realised that someone – or something – had alerted him when Granddad had made his enquiries. But I just smiled, and thanked him for the information, and slipped the sheets out of the folder. There were only two of them, with large typescript and wide margins. The language was flowery, using several words where one would have sufficed, and the result was that it could all have been written on just one sheet – maybe less.

It gave the names of the various Controllers, including the Comtesse de Mélitour, and mentioned that two British officers had sometimes been involved, and gave their code names as Ombre and Brume, but their real names were not given. It also paid tribute to the two years that the line had operated and to the number of aircrew who were helped on their way to freedom, and ended by saying that security had always been lax, and that the Germans had moved in during April 1944, and that under the command of a Major Kretzer they had arrested and shot most of the senior people. It ended on a bright note by saying that a British SOE officer, Major Dallachy, who had himself been escaping down the line, managed to collect a group of Frenchmen, and then to steal some German arms, before shooting Major Kretzer and killing several of his troops.

As I finished I laid down the papers on a small table beside me, and Mr. Butler said, "Not very much, is there? But you will see that it does pay tribute to what your grandfather did by wiping out a nest of Germans – quite a remarkable feat."

I was very angry, but I tried to conceal it when I said, "Certainly he did well, but why doesn't it say anything about my grandmother, without whom he would never have managed to get away? Incidentally, why didn't you speak to my grandfather before writing this very incomplete report – after all he was still in the army at the time – and he could have filled in many details."

I could see that Mr. Butler was embarrassed, but he was still suave and pleasant to me, "Obviously we should have done, but I was then a very junior junior, and I had clear instructions just to write down what I could. You must remember, Yvette, that the war had been over for more than twenty years and there were few people here by then who were interested in crossing all the 't's and dotting all the 'i's, in what was becoming ancient history. At that time they had more pressing problems with the French, what with old de Gaulle who was then trying to keep us out of the EEC."

I couldn't quite think what to say then, certainly I didn't believe him, but I couldn't say it. However I had one important question for him. "You mentioned in this paper you wrote about the two British officers, and their code names – Ombre and Brume – do you happen to know, and if not can you find out, what their names were? It would be very interesting for my grandparents to know this."

He frowned, I saw his eyes flicker for a moment, and the thought came to me that he wouldn't have made a good poker player. But he composed himself, and his reply was almost believable, "No certainly not, you see the war of resistance in France was a very dirty one, and the identities of all these SOE officers is still highly classified information, even after all these years. This has been done to protect all these brave soldiers from the nit-picking criticisms of young pinkoes and lefties who have never done anything more dangerous than crossing a road. I may say that there is another reason which would infuriate the followers of Germaine Greer, which arises because they were in France for several years with all these attractive French girls, and there had to be some consequences. So, part of the secrecy is to protect them from paternity claims."

He stopped there before smiling at me and going on, "War is a dirty business, isn't it Yvette? But these papers do at least recognise your grandfather's heroism."

Suddenly I really got cross. It was obvious that some kind of cover-up had been arranged in 1968. Could it have been to hide young Lord Hempson's involvement in the affair? It also occurred to me that Granddad's approach to the Ministry must have caused some alarm bells to ring, and it was due to this – and not because of any influence he still had here – that I had been dealt with by such a senior official. After all, Hempson's son was now the Minister. All this went through my head in just a microsecond, and I couldn't resist taking that self-satisfied look off his face, so I said, "As you've pointed out, there certainly isn't much information here, which is disappointing as there is nothing about how the Germans penetrated the security of the escape line, and so caused many deaths. I may say that the question of who betrayed the line to the Germans is of great interest to my grandparents, and I am sure you will be glad to hear that I hope very soon to fill in these gaps. If I can get the truth of the matter it would be an interesting fragment of war history, so maybe you would like me to come back to see you again if I am successful?"

Again his lack of a poker face betrayed him, and I could see how unwelcome my news was, "What on earth do you mean, Yvette. How are you possibly going to find secrets of nearly sixty years ago?"

"Quite easily. You see, on the very day when the line was betrayed the Comtesse de Mélitour called my Grandmother in, along two others of her organisation, and told them that she had buried a package which would identify the traitor. I can also tell you that later in the day my grandfather shot Major Kretzer when he was torturing the Comtesse, and my grandmother shot and wounded another of them. And that wasn't all. With the help of the two gardeners from the chateau they contrived to kill another six Germans and also to wound the man whom they believe had betrayed the escape line. It is a wonderful story and well worth telling even now. What is also very important is that something has now come up, and we believe that – even after all these years – we can find instructions as to where this package is, so I am off to France on Wednesday. I may say that I am first going to Paris to see two of Grannie's old friends, and after that to stay at the Chateau de Mélitour for a few days. Incidentally, did you know that the real heroine of the affair, Marie-Claire Comtesse de Mélitour, is still alive?"

"Still alive?" he stuttered, "I thought she would have been dead a long time ago, but anyway, she's mad, isn't she?"

So much, I thought for his not knowing much about things, and I decided that I would turn the screw a little further, and that a little untruth would be in order. "Well I haven't yet met her, but my grandmother knew her, and I believe that she has some lucid moments, and so she may be able to help us."

After that I won't say that he was rude to me, but certainly

Gray Laidlaw   127

I was helped on my way pretty smartly. I got the odd impression that he didn't quite know how to treat me, and that he wanted further instruction, but from whom?

Back home that night the three of us tried to make sense of my day. As for my being seen by Mr. Butler, Granddad said that it certainly was not his doing. All he had done was speak to the French section of the War Historical Department for the Defence Ministry, and he had expected that it would be dealt with as a matter of routine, nothing at all like being attended to by a high level executive who would give me lunch at Simpson's.

"All these idiots have done," he said, "is to make us surer than ever that Lord Hempson, a pillar of the establishment, must have something to hide, and for my bet he is the bastard who betrayed the line. I reckon that the Germans must have got hold of him, and got him to work for them in return for saving his own skin. Then as a kind of quid pro quo they must have taken him in as a POW, after we had shot him in the shoulder, with a story of being captured during a fracas with Partisans. When he was released after the war who would even think of investigating the story? So, my girl, you go off on Wednesday and prove it!"

With our suspicions newly confirmed, that evening Hélène phoned Alicia (now a widow), and arranged that I would stay in Paris with her on Wednesday night, and she insisted that her grandson would meet me at the airport. She was the generation who still thought that young ladies had to be escorted, so later I phoned to confirm my flight number, and my arrival time. She seemed to be very excited at the prospect of piecing the bits of the letter together, and told me that Michelle would join us for dinner so that we could have a kind of grand opening of the envelopes.

When the call ended I looked over at Grannie. "It seems such a pity that you can't be in Paris on Wednesday, it will be fascinating to see what we find, and I shall feel almost an interloper when I open your envelope."

"Don't worry about that," she smiled, "the only thing now which is important both to Andrew and to me is that at last we are going to DO something. It has been a great mistake to leave it so long, but back in 1956 the old Dowager Comtesse was anxious that we should leave well alone. Then, as the years went by, the whole affair began to seem less important, and it was only that old photograph in the paper the other day which has stirred us up again. So, as Andrew said – go to it!"

By common agreement we said nothing about the affair on Tuesday the next day, and I was able to get down to some much-needed work. My degree examinations were now only some ten weeks away, and I was determined not to disgrace myself. With that in mind I almost doubled the weight of my packing by taking a few text books so that I could read them in any spare time I could find while I was in France.

Chapter Nine

Then, on Wednesday I was off to Paris. It was a pleasant spring afternoon when I landed at Charles de Gaulle airport. It occurred to me that I was going to have to forget my English for the next few days, and thought how lucky I was that Grannie had brought me up to be bilingual.

Philippe Dupont, Alicia's grandson, met me. He turned out to be a cheerful young man in his early twenties, and he seemed as excited as I was regarding my quest, especially when I told him of my odd reception at the MOD. "You know, Yvette, it is like an adventure story in a book, maybe I'll write it sometime!"

"Are you an author, Philippe?"

"Well, I am and I am not! Fact is that I have written two books, but no publisher is interested...as yet. So far my writing is just a hobby, as I am training to be a lawyer, and I can only write in my spare time. But I have managed to get a few pieces accepted in newspapers, but unfortunately the money I've earned is only peanuts. However, just in the last few days, the *Paris Post* has arranged to give me a small retainer, and I've hopes that I'll have some successes with them."

I always love visiting Paris, and as we talked I was able to admire the beautiful avenues and buildings which make the city such a joy. Then, having told me about himself, he enquired about me, and when I mentioned St. Andrews University I found that he had been there while on a holiday in Scotland. "Just to see the town," he smiled, "not to play golf. I can tell you that one of the few English sayings which I can remember is that a round of golf is a pleasant walk spoiled!"

So there was plenty to argue about for the rest of the journey.

Alicia lived in a charming terrace house in St. Germain, and I got a somewhat sentimental welcome from her. I knew that she was in her eighties and that the years had not been kind to her. Grannie had told me that she had been afflicted with arthritis for some years and now, and because of difficulty in walking she was more or less housebound. However, despite her problems her mind was as alert as ever, and she fairly fizzed with excitement.

At about six o'clock Philippe went off to fetch Michelle, and I soon found that she too had problems. "I've got to be careful now, Yvette, as my old ticker is unreliable. I've had a few operations, and I now have a pacemaker which lets me live an almost normal life, but I don't like going far from home. That's why, like Alicia, I can't come down with you to Mélitour much as I would like to."

She paused there before going on, "She and I are really a pair of old crocks, aren't we, and it really is a pity that we didn't do something about this affair long ago. I think that we all made a mistake back in 1956 when we agreed to do nothing. But thank goodness Alicia had the sense then to persuade us to keep the letters – even although the old Comtesse wanted us to tear them up. I can tell you that now I can hardly wait till it is time to open them!"

It was after dinner when we assembled in Alicia's salon, she and Michelle with their envelopes and me with Grannie's. Philippe looked at us, and produced an elegant paper knife, saying, "Here you are, you'll need this; you must open these famous envelopes in style."

"Let's do it by age," I said, "Michelle first, then Alicia, then me."

One after the other we slit the envelopes and removed the torn pieces, and I recognised the thick creamy writing paper as being the same as those other letters from Mélitour which I had seen. We then gave the pieces to Philippe, who neatly stuck them together with sticky tape, and this is what we saw, and I was surprised to see that it was written in English:

To Michelle, Alicia, and Hélène,
    My dears, if you are reading this, the war will
have been won and you hopefully you will have been
able to put to rest your memories our days in the
escape line under M. Ombre and M. Brume. Also, I
shall be dead, but with the knowledge that through
this letter I will be able stretch out a hand from
the grave and point a finger at the wicked man who
has betrayed us.
    I write this after I have just frantically cycled
back from Etourvy where it was confirmed that the
whole escape line in our region has been betrayed. I
was even told the identity of the traitor. Once I
have completed this letter, I will let you know most
of what I have learned, but I will keep the man's
name a secret because this knowledge is far too
dangerous for you at present. I will also tell you
about the package I received. My main purpose here is
to direct you to the spot where I have just I buried
it. As you leave Etourvy there is a graveyard on the
right. Look for small headstone with the inscription:
    Jean Duclos
    Né Juin 14 1865 - Morte Mai 16 1893
    Immortal dans nos coeurs
    Dig immediately in front and you should easily be

able unearth the package. It contains papers which
document the discovery of the bastard's identity and
a small metal canister, containing undeveloped film,
which provides the proof. So go ahead and put an end
to uncertainty!

Even with the precautions I am taking, I am afraid
to directly name the man in this letter. I just don't
know what the next few hours, or maybe minutes, may
bring. Possibly, with my hint you three already may
have guessed who he is. Anyway, it won't take you
long retrieve that package and then you will be in
full possession of the facts and the proof of his
guilt.

Goodbye my three good friends. I hope that you
never have to read this letter, but if you do that
please go after him for my sake.

Bless you; I could never have had better or more
loyal friends and helpers. It has been a privilege
both to know you and to love you.

P.S: Not many people in this area speak English,
but you have all learned some, so I have used this
language as the first defence for this letter.

It was so moving that I found myself with a lump in my
throat, and I wasn't surprised that both Alicia and Michelle
were crying. None of us felt like speaking. It was Philippe who
had the perfect Gallic solution to the problem.

"What we all need is some cognac. What an extraordinary
letter!" Soon he bustled back with four glasses containing very
substantial measures, and as he gave them to us, he said, "I'm
puzzled. What did she mean when she said that the three of
you may be able to guess the man's identity? Where is this hint
to which she refers?"

I was amused to see that both Michelle and Alicia were
also blank, but I had the advantage of having heard the story

just a few days ago, and also because English is my Mother tongue, and for them very much a second language.

"Come on," I said to them, "didn't she write down the code names of the British agent who worked with the escape line?"

Michelle looked blank, but Alicia suddenly brightened up, saying, "Of course, the original agent was M. Ombre (the shadow), and the second was M. Brume. That word can mean "mist" and we took it to mean that at the time, but in French it can also mean "uncertainty", so her phrase 'put an end to uncertainty' points straight at the new agent whom Hélène and Andrew suspect. Goodness! I was forgetting their suspense. We must phone them right away"

But before we could do so Philippe stood up, "You know, I am out of place here. You three have a job to do, and you are better off without me. Anyway, I have some work to do which I didn't finish before I went to pick up Yvette. So, if you don't mind, I'll just pop back to the office and finish it now; after that I'll head for home."

There were then tender salutations to the old ladies, and a rather more intimate one to me. This was uncalled for and I confess that I found myself not liking him very much.

We didn't talk for long after we phoned Grannie, who was as excited as we were to hear the news. I also phoned Mélitour to tell them that the letter was important, and I was glad to be put through to Comte Albert – the first time I had spoken to him. He seemed glad to receive my call, also to hear our news. He said that I would be most welcome to come and stay for a few days, and that I would be met at Troyes next morning if I took the train down.

That, in fact, was the end of the evening, as after all the excitement both Michelle and Alicia were getting tired, and we

decided to call it a day. We got a taxi for Michelle, and then
Alicia and I went off to bed – she no doubt to sleep – but I
managed to get in two good hours of university study. Maybe
because of that I slept till about eight o'clock, when Alicia
woke me with a cup of coffee. I was surprised to see that she
seemed to be distressed, and she whispered, "I'm so ashamed;
just look at this paper. How could Philippe have done this to
us?"

She handed me the morning copy of the *Paris Post*, and
what was all too obvious was a feature article with the banner
headline:

ENGLISH GIRL ON QUEST TO UNCOVER THE SECRET
OF WAR-TIME TREACHERY

And underneath was written, "From our special correspondent Philippe Duclos". I looked at Alicia with horror,
"This is dreadful; I'll have a posse of reporters following me
everywhere."

But as I read it I could see that it wasn't as bad as I had
feared, the article didn't mention any names or places, and in
particular it gave no indication of the District of France where
the events had taken place. It just said that a young English
girl had recently come to France, and that she had evidence
which could lead to the identification of a traitor who, in April
1944, had betrayed to the Germans the identities of members
of an important French escape operation. It then went on with
a long description of these organisations, and how they had
managed to smuggle large numbers of Allied aircrew through
France and into Spain, from where they went to Portugal, and
then to England. The end of the article was:

"She is almost sure of the identity of the traitor, who is
still alive and a very important political figure. If she is successful it will be an astonishing international scandal. We cannot yet name the person in question but further sensational

details may be expected very soon.

"Our readers will note that we have deliberately withheld any details of the Englishwoman as she must be allowed to pursue her quest without publicity. We shall be the first with news of any developments.

I tried to reassure Alicia that no serious harm had been done, but she was inconsolable. "To have this happen while you are a guest in my house is unforgivable. That boy has always been selfish, only two things are important to him – himself and money. I'll bet that he was paid well for this."

It occurred to me that maybe, after what he had said on the way back from the airport, the joy of seeing his words in print was really the most important thing in his life, but I decided that anything I said to Alicia would just make things worse. I also decided not to worry Grannie and Granddad with the news.

I did, however, ring Mélitour, as I felt I had to tell them about the article. I asked M. le Comte whether by any chance he had seen the *Paris Post* this morning. He said that he hadn't and could hear surprise in his voice at the very suggestion that he would read such a rag.

"Well, I'm sorry to tell you that Alicia's grandson, who knows all about the affair, has written an article about it for that paper this morning. He has not been very specific, and the article just talks of an English lady who hopes to expose a war-time traitor, but without mentioning any names or places. I don't really think it has done any harm, but it is unfortunate."

I heard him sigh deeply. "Certainly it is very unfortunate, and it is this sort of thing I have always been afraid of, right back to 1956 when my grandmother persuaded your grandmother and the other two to do nothing. But now we have gone too far to stop, so I shall look forward to seeing you this afternoon. As I said last night, I'll have a car to meet your train at Troyes, and I may say that I am very much looking forward to seeing you. We were very unkind to your grandmother, and I hope that you will now allow us to bury the past."

His kindness cheered me on my journey and, as the train neared Troyes, I remembered how my grandparents had been met by a large Hispano Suiza limousine and driver. I was still wondering what arrangements had been made for me when a tall young man came up to me, and said, "Excuse me. Are you Mlle. Dallachy?"

I confirmed that I was. He smiled and shook my hand, "Good, I'm very glad to welcome you. Let me introduce myself, I am Pierre, Albert's son. He is sorry that he couldn't come himself as he isn't very well today. You may know he is only just back from America, and I think he's going down with some kind of 'flu bug he picked up during his time in New York. I can tell you that I know a lot about you and your family, and I am very glad that you are here at last."

He stopped there and for a moment he looked thoughtfully at me, "And do you know, Yvette, now that I have met you I am even gladder!"

"Flattery, Sir," I smiled, "will get you anywhere! Can I ask if you have some Italian blood? Such talk is quite out of character for a dour Frenchman!"

He grabbed my bag with one hand, and my arm with his other, "We're going to get on well together, but come let's be on our way. We are too late for lunch at Mélitour, but I know a nice little restaurant where I can practice my Italian language."

Out in the car park there was no large limousine to be seen, but the open convertible XJ8 Jaguar to which he took me was much more to my taste. It was a bright sunny day, and with the hood down it looked wonderful. But then I saw him look at me doubtfully.

"Yvette, you don't mind the wind in your hair do you?"

There was only one answer to that, "Not a bit, but even if I did, I'd still come with you for a ride in this lovely car. I can also tell you that it is a big improvement on the vehicle which was sent from the Chateau to meet my grandparents, back in 1956, at a time when your great grandmother was still alive."

"And what car was that?"

"It was a Hispano-Suiza limousine which my grandmother remembers your grandfather driving back from the Paris Motor Show of 1938."

Suddenly Pierre was serious, "Now isn't that odd. Here you are, I've never seen you before and you've never been here before, yet you know something about my family that is new to me. I'd no idea where that old car came from. But it is still in the garage, and father takes it out sometimes for an airing, but really it is far too ostentatious."

I couldn't help smiling to myself, as obviously this beautiful Jag was not in any way considered to be ostentatious. We chatted as we drove, and I enquired about his name. "I was told that you were called Jean-Pierre, so why now just the plain Pierre?"

"I was of course, christened Jean-Pierre, but it was too long except for very formal occasions – so most of the time plain Pierre is my name."

I then asked if we could go back via Chaource, and explained that although Grannie had been born and brought up there I'd never seen it.

I could see that there was a question which he was too polite to ask, so I answered it for him. "It is in fact only in the last week – after the possibility arose of finding the traitor – that I have learned why she would never bring me here. Relations between our two families have been strained, and she didn't want to come to Chaource, or even visit this area. You no doubt know the story from your side; sometime I'll tell you ours."

He slowed the car down and turned to me, "Yvette, I do very much want to hear your story, and so does father, and we are both very glad that at last you are here."

For the rest of the journey we were quiet, and for lunch he took me to a little hotel-restaurant, Les Fontaines in Chaource. Maybe it didn't rate Michelin Stars, but our meal was just what I would have wanted, half a Charentais melon with smoked salmon, followed by an Assiette Anglais, washed down with a bottle of Chablis.

"Not a bad bottle of wine," he whispered to me, "but soon you'll be drinking some real Chablis from our own vineyard, it is classed as a Grand Cru. But now it is time that we got on our way, Father would have met you if he hadn't picked up this 'flu bug, and I know that he wants to get this meeting with you over as soon as he can."

That didn't sound too good, so I said, "What do you mean, Pierre, I thought that he wanted me to come?"

"Of course he does, and I'm sorry that I phrased it so badly. What I meant is that he knows that the rift between our two families is partly his fault. It will be difficult for him, but he wants to heal the breach as soon as he can."

"I'm glad, as I know that my grandmother, Hélène, will be delighted if we can all be friends."

He nodded, but then reached over and held my hand for just a moment, and a flash of what felt like electricity seemed to pass between us, and we looked at each other almost in

embarrassment. Then he laughed, and said, "This is an extraordinary day, isn't it, but let's get off cloud nine and get on
our way."

As we drove along, I couldn't help remembering that this
was the same road that Grannie had ridden along on her bike,
all these many years before, and – like her – I wondered what
my reception would be like at Mélitour.

Chapter Ten

Grannie had told me about the beautiful gardens at Méli-tour, but even her superlatives hadn't prepared me for the sheer beauty and perfection that I could see around me as we drove up to the Chateau. Pierre saw my wonderment, and said, "The grounds are beautiful, aren't they, but it needs a lot of hard work. In the old days they had six or more gardeners here, plus a lot of casual labour, but now we have only two. Fortunately I love to work here and do as much as I can find time for. Also, of course, we now have a lot of clever machinery to help us."

I remembered Grannie talking about her first visit to Mé-litour, how she was greeted by an elderly major-domo, and then taken in to see the Comtesse in a grand salon. For me, more than fifty years later, it was much the same. Pierre and I went up the steps to the front door where I was greeted by the present-day major-domo, who said to me, "Good afternoon, Mlle. Dallachy, do please come this way, the Comte is expecting you."

Then, just as Grannie had been, I was led over to one of the great doors, and ushered into a huge room. I was conscious of Pierre behind me and then a clunk as the door closed. Over by the window I saw an elderly man easing himself out of an arm chair, and I couldn't help thinking, "So this is the little Albert whom she raised till he was seven."

I went towards him, but he hadn't spoken, and I was puzzled by his silence. He was however looking intently at me, and suddenly he smiled. "Yvette, and I hope I may call you that, you must forgive my rudeness, but I was struck dumb. Maybe you don't realise that you are the reincarnation of my dear Hélène, and for a moment it was as if I were seven years old again."

"Am I so like her? I know that my grandfather mentions it sometimes, but I have never believed it."

"Oh, certainly it is true, but again please forgive me. The important thing now is to repeat what I said earlier, that I am so very glad to welcome you to Mélitour. I have been ashamed for a long time about how I felt about Hélène back in 1944, but I had an excuse then, I was only seven, and my childhood world had fallen around my ears, and I just blamed everybody. But I had little excuse for my coldness to her in 1956. I was nineteen then and should have admitted both to her and to myself that the disaster was in no way her fault. But I was a cocky young man, and couldn't bring myself to apologise."

He paused for a moment and then went on, "Do you think that she would forgive me now? I have spoken to her on the phone in these last days, but she seemed a little remote."

I could answer in complete certainty, "If you, Sir, were to stretch out a hand of friendship to her, you would make it one of the happiest days of her life. I know that you were as dear to her as if you had been her own child. I can tell you that she still grieves at the way she had to leave you – abandon you as it must have seemed – but she really had no alternative. I can tell you it has been a grief to her for all these long years that you turned your back on her. Why not phone her now?"

"You're right, Yvette, why the hell haven't I done so before? But before I do, I want to see my mother's letter." I handed it over and watched as he first scanned through it quickly, and then read it slowly for a second time. "The stress of that terrible day comes over so vividly. I see again how very brave my mother was, and how level-headed in the midst of such aguish. Oh dear God..." His voice trailed away and for a while his elderly face lost all expression. I waited and then with a shudder he said, "Sorry, my dear," and read the letter through yet again. "She alludes to the possibility that the three of you might have been able to guess the traitor's identity from something she said in the letter. Is there some cryptic message? Were you able to read through the lines?" I then explained how the used of the word "uncertainty" pointed to the British officer called Brume and went on to say, "We will find out for sure once we have the package, but in the meantime I really do think that you should speak to Hélène. It will be difficult, I know, but it will mean a great deal to her."

He nodded, and went over to the phone, but just before he was going to pick it up, I said, "I haven't told them about the article in the *Paris Post*, so please don't mention it, as it would only upset them. But do please tell them that we are now about to go off to the graveyard to find out what your mother hid."

"Regarding that, Yvette, I have a favour to ask you. I am sure that you and Pierre are all for getting in the car and going there right now. It would only take a quarter of an hour to get to Etourvy. But I would like to be there also. I have few links with my mother, and this would be an important one of them, but today I am feeling rotten, I think it is some bug I picked up in New York. So, will you be patient, and I'm sure I'll feel more like myself in the morning?"

I nodded my assent and, with a smile to me, he picked up the phone. Their conversation has no part in my narrative; suffice to say that it healed a wound which had festered far too long. As I listened I found that I had tears in my eyes, and I saw that Albert was the same. When the call was over he blew his nose, and said to me, "How stupid I've been not to do that long ago, but thank heavens that you've come now to act as a catalyst. I can hear Hélène hasn't changed much, and do you know, at the end I felt like a small child again, when she instructed me to phone the very minute that we had news."

He stopped there, and looked at me quizzically, "You know, Yvette, I was right when I said that she hasn't changed much. She still speaks with a pure local accent, one which is particular to this part of Yonne. What amuses me is the fact that you – who have never been here before – have picked up the same accent from her. Your French is of course, perfect…but it certainly isn't Parisian!

"But please don't think that I am making fun of you. I'm certainly not. My accent is just the same! You see, my grand-mother was devastated by the loss of her son in 1940, and then by mother's dreadful injury. As a result she became very protective of me. She kept me close by her side and wouldn't send me away to boarding school, so I went to primary school in Chaource, and a secondary school in Tonnere. By the time I went to university in Reims my accent was frozen – and still hasn't changed. On that subject I can tell you that it is a good accent to have if you live around here, and Pierre is working hard to forget the painfully posh accent he picked up from school in Paris and also university there before he was in Re-ims."

He stopped again, "But that's enough of that. Let's see this *Paris Post* article."

I had brought a copy with me, and handed it over to him, "Hm!" he said when he finished it, "there isn't much to worry about, but it is a nuisance. Obviously the young man expects you to tell Alicia all our news so that he can get an exclusive story, so we'll need to think carefully before we tell her anything. But now, you've got many things to explain to Pierre and me. I was too young at the time to understand much of what was really happening. And later…well…my mind was closed. I refused to talk of these things to Pierre so, to my shame, he knows virtually nothing."

I felt that I should go right back to the beginning and start with just a summary of the history which Grannie and Granddad had recently given me. When I had finishes, I said, "In fact I knew hardly any of these matters until last week. It was only when an article appeared in the *Daily Telegraph* which contained an old photograph of a young soldier who had been in France in 1944 that they realised that he was the traitor they had seen in the room with Major Kretzer. It was this that prompted them to involve me"

I knew that I had certainly hooked them, and they urged me to tell them about what had happened more recently. When I told of the astonishing fact that our suspect was now Lord Hempson, Albert broke in "This is incredible. Let us stop here and have a break after which I would like you to continue with a more thorough account. Yvette you must be dry with all this talking, so let's have a bottle of Chablis to drink"

Pierre laughed, "You will find, Yvette, that father is never at a loss for an excuse to drink our own wine. We have a saying in France…maybe you also have it in Britain…about being your own best customer, well it certainly is true for him!"

"You will observe, Yvette," said Albert, "how little respect children in France now seem to give their parents. I can only hope things are better in Britain. Anyway, Pierre, you needn't drink the Chablis if you don't want to, it will leave all the more for Yvette and for me!"

"Don't worry," said Pierre, "I'll join you in a little – just to be polite of course."

They both laughed, and I was glad to see how good their relationship was. Pierre then rang a bell, and when the major-domo came he had a few quite words with him. He returned a few minutes later with a silver tray, three glasses and a chilled bottle with a label which I now have come to know so well:

CHABLIS GRAND CRU de MELITOUR
(appellation Grand Cru Contrôlée)

It was magnificent wine and after the bottle was finished I went on to tell them the full story. Although I tried hard to be brief, it must have taken more than an hour, but I had a very attentive audience. When I finished, Albert looked at me, and shook his head. "What an amazing story, I hadn't before known just what adventures Hélène and Andrew had, nor about his heroism in getting the secrets of the flying bombs. It seems incredible that it was after that adventure that he happened to land up here, and what a good thing it was for us that he did. At the very best, I would certainly have remained in the custody of the Germans, and God knows what would have happened to Mother.

"And now it seems that our war is not over. What an extraordinary meeting you had at the Ministry of Defence; obviously somebody – very high up – is trying to hide things from us. Everything we know points to Lord Hempson, and maybe his son also, as the guilty parties. So there is no doubt that your quest is far more important than Pierre or I could have imagined yesterday. And I'm sure we are all impatient to see what is buried in the hiding place. I'm sorry we can't do it this afternoon, but right now I really must get off to bed, I'm feeling rotten, and must have a good rest and be fit for our expedition tomorrow morning."

He turned to go, but then paused and said "You'll appreciate that I've had so few links with my mother; for nearly sixty years I've never had a conversation with her. I feel I owe it to her to dig up her final legacy myself."

"Forgive me," I said, "but there is a question which I must ask before you go. How is your mother, and will I be able to see her?"

"Maybe sometime, but the trouble is that you are so very like a young Hélène that I wonder if we dare to let you see her, but I'll think about it. Sadly the years have brought no improvement in her condition, she seems happy enough, although in a world of her own. We have converted a small wing in the Chateau into her private quarters, and she lives there with a team of nurses who tend to her needs. It is awful but that is all we can do for her."

He stopped there, and shook his head, as if in despair, "I'd like to shake your grandfather's hand for killing that bastard, Major Kretzer. Maybe now we'll be able to shame his accomplice."

He went off to bed then, and for the rest of the afternoon and evening Pierre and I talked and talked...what about? Why about ourselves and each other. It was all quite astonishing and we both felt what only the French have a word for...a coup de foudre...a thunderbolt of love.

It had been a wonderful day, but rather a long one, and I was glad when it was time to get to bed, and I fell asleep as soon as my head touched the pillow. It was still dark when I was awakened by the sound of running feet, and then the voices of Pierre and a woman. I jumped out of bed and slipped on a wrap, looking at my watch as I did so; it was half past three in the morning. Just as I opened my door I saw Pierre coming out of his father's room. "Sorry you've been disturbed, Yvette, but father is quite ill – I'm going to phone the doctor now."

I saw him go into his own room, and then I heard snatches of the telephone conversation. "...we thought that he just had 'flu...yes, he's just back from New York...one of mother's nurses is with him now, and she suspects pneumonia, and she recommends oxygen...thank you, yes the sooner the better..."

He came back to me with a worried look, "Did you hear all that? My father's breathing is terribly laboured; he really is quite bad. It is fortunate that we have these nurses here, and I am told not to worry...but I'm afraid that I do. Anyway, the doctor will be here soon. Incidentally, he is the grandson of the Dr. Jeanfils who took in my father and my grandmother on that night in 1944. He'll be interested to meet you.

"I'm so sorry about this," I said, "if there is nothing else you'd like me to do; I suggest I make some coffee. I'm sure we are going to be awake for a long time."

"Good idea, none of the servants seem to have heard the commotion, and we might as well let them sleep. I can tell you, though, that old Jacques, our major-domo, will be cross in the morning as he reckons that nothing can be done here unless he arranges it. Come on, let's go to the kitchen."

When I got there I could see that it was unfashionably large, and much of the space was filled by a table which could easily have sat twelve people. As I looked at it I reckoned that it might well have been filled to overflowing in Grannie's time, what with six gardeners, the major-domo, the cook, plus housemaids, scullery maids, and assorted ladies' maids and valets. On a more down-to-earth basis, I was able to find some grounds for coffee which I made in the old fashioned way; lots of grounds into a pot; add a pinch of salt; fill with cold water; bring the pot to the boil and let it settle; bringing it to the boil again; add a dash of cold water to finally settle the grounds; pour and strain if you must.

Pierre took an appreciative sip. "This, Yvette, is the best coffee I've ever tasted!"

"Don't flatter me, young man, I certainly want compliments from you but they must have a basis in fact. This coffee is acceptable, but no more than that."

It wasn't long before we were brought back to the real world by the sound of the doctor's car. He came in carrying an oxygen cylinder, and he and Pierre rushed upstairs with it. But they weren't there for very long, and Pierre brought him downstairs again, introducing him to me as he said, "This is Dr. Jeanfils the third, who well knows that it was his grandfather who took Albert and my grandmother into his clinic, when they were brought in for treatment by your grandparents."

The young doctor smiled and then came over to me, "It is a privilege to meet you Mlle. Dallachy, my grandfather often spoke to me about that awful night. I can tell you that there wasn't much that a country doctor could do against the Germans, and he was quite proud of what he was able to do for them."

"He must have been," I said, "after all he just didn't help them that night, but also managed to hide them for the next few months until the Allies came."

"Yes, the old folks had their adventures, but for the present, Comte Albert is going to be fine. I have given him a shot of antibiotics and also some pills which the nurse can deal with. In addition there is oxygen, should it be necessary, but I don't think that it will be."

But then he turned to Pierre, "Please ensure that he stays in bed tomorrow. I'll look in at about eleven o'clock, just to make sure that all is going well. After that, though, he must stay indoors for at least two or three days – I don't want him catching another cold. But, being up and walking around the house should help to clear his lungs."

We went to bed soon after he left, and although it was then about five o'clock I still fell asleep again, waking at my usual time. I was down for breakfast not long after eight, to find that Pierre was ahead of me. "He's still asleep, but the nurse says that he is breathing easily, so that's good. Do you mind if we wait for a while before we go to the graveyard? I'm pretty sure now that he won't be able to come with us, but I think it would be nice if we spoke to him before going."

"Of course," I said, "and anyway, if you look outside you'll see that this wouldn't have been a good morning to go."

It was in fact pouring with rain and, just as I spoke, there was a tremendous flash of lightning and an almost immediate clap of thunder. So we had good reasons for staying in, which gave me another chance to get down to some work. Pierre was sympathetic to this, as he too had been a student not so long before. He also knew that my degree exams were early in June, just two months away, and that I was due back at St. Andrews on the following Wednesday, in just five days' time. So as it was now Friday I would have to leave on Monday at the latest.

"But you'll come back in the summer, won't you?" I just nodded.

"Good, I'll leave you now, and see you again when the doctor comes."

It was quite a while before he did come, and by then Albert had wakened, eaten his breakfast, and was demanding to know what all the fuss was about.

"The fuss," the doctor said when he came, "was because you were quite ill, and Pierre was right to treat it as an emergency. Thankfully that is now over, but you'll need to be careful for a few days. Pierre knows what I want you to do – you've got to stay indoors for a day or so, but you can get up as soon as you feel strong enough to do so. Please try to get some exercise by walking around the house, which will help to clear your lungs."

When he left Albert shook his head in disappointment. "Damn it, I did so want to dig it up myself, but I know, Yvette, that you have to get back for the start of your university term. So, unfortunately, since I can't be there, the sooner it is done the better, and you and Pierre can do it after lunch today – that is if you don't mind getting wet!"

So during the rest of the morning I was able to do some more work and fortunately the weather began to improve, so we could lower the hood of the car in readiness for our trip in the afternoon. We were both very excited as we drove off, but there was sadness too for Pierre as he imagined the desperation of his grandmother as she buried her secret in the graveyard and then pedalled back to the Chateau as quickly as she could to warn the three girls that all was lost.

Grannie had told me how very quiet the roads had been in her time, and I could see that they had changed surprisingly little. I had, though, noticed a motor cyclist fiddling with his bike near the entrance to the Chateau, and also a large Mercedes which seemed to follow us for a while before disappearing, but I wasn't that interested and didn't mention it to Pierre. Just outside Etourvy, Pierre pointed out the graveyard to me, on the left of the road, and then drove a little further on till he got to a place where he could turn the car. As he was doing so I saw the cyclist again, but he quickly passed our Jaguar without even turning his head.

Anyway, in all the excitement, I quite forgot about him, as Pierre parked the car by the graveyard entrance, and took my hand as we walked in. Almost at once we saw the little headstone for the young Jean Duclos, and it was only when I saw the name written down that I realised what an idiot I had been. "Pierre, I can't think why I didn't think of this earlier, as that young man who died over a hundred years ago is a relative of mine! You see my grandmother's maiden name was Duclos – so he was probably an uncle or more likely a greatuncle of hers – and I'm sure that your grandmother picked this grave deliberately as one which my grandmother would know!"

"Have you noticed," Pierre said, "that this affair is like an onion, you peel off layers, but then there are more and more. So let's peel off another one and see what we can find here."

He had brought a garden fork and trowel with him, and in fact it wasn't buried very deeply as, in a few minutes, he said excitedly, "Look, Yvette, here it is!" I suppose that I should have realised that after sixty odd years none of the papers would have survived, but still it was a disappointment to look at the rotten mess which Pierre had uncovered. "Look for the tin," I said hopefully; and sure enough – there it was. It didn't in fact look very promising; it was just a rusty old tin. I could just decipher some writing on it – Poudre de Moutard – but the rest was illegible. Pierre was about to prize off the lid, but I stopped him. "Don't do that! Remember that it contains an undeveloped film, and maybe it will have survived."

He smiled and nodded. "Thank goodness you stopped me! Let's get away from this depressing place." But before we did so he carefully tidied up the soil where he had dug, saying with a smile, "There, that should keep your great-great-great – or whatever – uncle happy!"

We ran back to the car and, as we drove along I suddenly had a frisson of unease as I looked in a mirror and saw that the same motorcyclist had turned around and was now quite close behind us. But before I had chance to speak we went round a bend and saw a large Mercedes at the side of the road, with a man beside it waving to us. Instinctively, Pierre pulled to a stop just beyond the Mercedes to find out what was the matter.

The owner was a tall bearded chap with dark glasses. He approached us saying, "I'm very sorry to bother you, but my…"

I was suddenly conscious that we were sitting there in an open car. The driver of the Mercedes was on Pierre's side, and the motorcyclist had come up at mine, and had stopped. It all happened so quickly as they each produced some kind of aerosol can, and sprayed what must have been nerve gas in our faces, and everything went blank.

When I opened my eyes I couldn't understand where I was. I was lying on a hard single bed in a small room, lit only by some chinks of light coming through cracks in the window shutters. Pierre I saw was lying on a similar bed to mine. It was all so very odd, but then everything suddenly came back to me, our stopping the car and the two men with the spray cans. I got up, and for a moment everything spun round, but I shook my head to clear it. I went over to Pierre's bed. He looked so peaceful that even as things were it seemed a shame to waken him – but a kiss seemed the most pleasant way to do it.

Well, maybe it was, but it didn't take him long to realise, as I did, how wrong things were. "What on earth can they want from us? Maybe they belong to a terrorist group. But surely we aren't important enough to them?"

"But darling," I said "isn't your father rather rich? Perhaps we've been kidnapped for ransom?"

We had only a few minutes together before the door opened and two men came in, switching on a light as they did so. There was a tall one, the driver of the Mercedes. In contrast, his companion was rather short, and presumable the fellow on the motorcycle. Something died in me as I saw they were both wearing silk stocking masks and each had a gun in his hand. It was the tall one who spoke, in good but accented French, and we were to find that he was always the spokesman. "Good, you are both awake, so let me first tell you that we have no wish to harm you, and you will be released – with our apologies for any inconvenience you have suffered – but only after the Comte de Mélitour does just one trifling thing for us. All we want is a single payment of five million francs which – as I am sure you will agree – is an insignificant sum for him to pay for the safe return of his son and heir, and of course also his charming girl friend."

I looked at Pierre and saw him, as I had done, shake his head to clear away the last traces of the drug they had used. He got to his feet, and rested a hand on my shoulder. "Look, your scheme involves using me as a lever to force my father's hand. Well, so be it, you have me here and you can try your luck with him. But Mlle. Dallachy has nothing to do with my family. She is British and is here just for a few days' holiday. Her only connection with us is that her grandmother worked for my grandmother some sixty years ago. Now, I am sure that it would be helpful for you, in your negotiations with my father, if you were to show him a token of good faith, and releasing her would be just that. He would then know that you are men of honour, and this could well make him believe that if you do get the money from him, you will in fact free me as well. So I can assure you that it is very much in your own interests to let her go."

As he spoke I was making up my own mind that I was damned if I were to go off and leave him here, but I would have wasted my time, as the tall man laughed and said to the other, "He's a persuasive chap, isn't he? But I think we'll be kind to him. After all he would be lonely here if we were to take his pretty girlfriend away. No, we'll let her stay; it will be better that way."

"Just look," he went on with a little giggle, "it would be a shame to part you when we have taken so much trouble to make you comfortable together. You will see that we have even arranged en-suite facilities. See there is a bucket in the corner of the room, and we shall even arrange to empty it every morning, just to keep the place clean and sweet smelling. But you can't be idle. You Mlle. Dallachy have a job to do. So come with me."

He gestured to Pierre that he should sit on one of the beds, and the smaller man sat on the other with his lethal looking gun covering him. I was then led out into a big room, and I could see that we were in some kind of holiday chalet, the walls were rough wood, and the steeply sloping roof was held up by exposed timber beans.

"Cosy, isn't it," the man said, "now here is a message which I require you to pass on to the Comte, and it would please me if you could sound just a little frightened."

He handed me a single A4 sheet with a neatly typed message:

```
Comte Albert: Pierre and I have been abducted. I
do not know where we are, but so far we have been
well treated. I have been told to say that if you are
```

sensible no harm will come to us. They require a
ransom of five million francs which you must collect
in small denomination notes of 100 Fr and 500 Fr.
They warn me that if any chemical or other traces are
put on them, then you will never see us again, and
the same will be true if you are foolish enough to
inform the police.

Today is Friday, and they will give you till noon
on Monday to obtain the money which should be packed
in ten parcels, each with half a million Francs.

They tell me that they will assume your agreement;
so there will be no further communication from them
until Monday morning when you will be informed how
the money is to be collected.

I have no knowledge as to how this second
communication will be made.

I read the sheet; it was like a nightmare. The man said,
"Now, Mlle. I want you to read that to the Comte, and it
would help if you could give the odd sob or two, and a break
in your voice would make it all the more convincing."

He pulled a mobile out of his pocket, and dialled the Mélitour number. It was Jacques, the major-domo who answered,
"Ah Mlle. Dallachy, we have been worried about you, do you
want to speak to Comte Albert?"

In a minute I heard his voice, and an urgent, "Where are
you, Yvette, Pierre's car was found by the roadside an hour
ago…"

But I broke in, "Please listen to me, Sir, here is a message
which I am now required to read to you…" And I read the
message over to him. I don't know if I sounded frightened,
but certainly I was. When I read the last word the man seized
the phone from me and cut the connection.

"That was well done, not so many breaks in your voice as

I would have liked, but it will do. You may have noticed that
our technique differs from that used by many of our friends in
this business. They tend to get involved with negotiations and
that is stupid. We believe in sticking to the basics. If your ransom is paid on Monday then you and Pierre will be freed immediately. If not, the outcome will just as sudden; but we
won't go into that, as I'm sure the Comte will do everything
we ask."

I was then bundled back into the room with Pierre, and I
quickly told him what had happened, and of the telephone call
that I had been forced to make to his father. We were then left
alone for over an hour until the two men came in again, the
short one stayed near the door, but he had a gun pointed at us.
But the tall one came over near to us, and my heart sank when
I saw what he was holding in his hand; it was the old rusty tin
can. He looked at us, and I could read his smile even through
that stocking mask, and said, "What on earth is this we found
in your car? An old tin mustard can is an odd thing to carry
around with you, so I am curious. What could be in it, I wonder?"

He shook it, and I could hear a rattle before he tugged off
the lid, "Well now, what have we here? It's a small aluminium
capsule, so again I have just the same question. What's inside?"

Before I could say anything he unscrewed the lid, then
shook out the reel of film, which I could see looked like normal 35mm, and peeled it out into the light. "Oh dear how unfortunate, it's a film. I do hope that nobody wanted it, as it is
useless now. Anyway, I'm a bit disappointed, as I thought it
might be something of interest."

And with that they both left the room, of course locking
the door behind them. We looked at each other in dismay, not

only were we captives, but we had now lost any chance of getting evidence against Hempson. We were a sad pair as we sat beside each other on one of the small beds.

But then Pierre mover a bit closer and put an arm round me, and I leaned against him and took his other hand in mine. I felt myself tremble, "Oh Pierre…oh dear Pierre".

"None of this really matters, darling Yvette. We have luckily found each other, and that is by far the most important thing."

Chapter Eleven

We were quiet for a while, but then Pierre said, "Do you remember, Yvette, how your grandparents passed the time when they were both cooped up in the back of that van among the wine boxes on their way to Spain and freedom?"

"You're a clever lad," I smiled, "are you suggesting that we tell each other our life stories?"

"Just that and I also suggest that now we become completely frank…are you game?"

It was ridiculous, I told myself, here I was with a man whom I had met just two days before and even if I weren't – yet – going to take off all my clothes, I was still being asked to bare my mind to him. Certainly we had talked a lot at Mélitour, but I had still a few secrets. However, I think I have mentioned before about making up my mind in a microsecond, and I'm afraid that on this occasion my nod came in no more than half that time.

So talk is what we did. At about seven o'clock the tall man returned, still covering us with his gun, and said, "Good news for you, it's dinner time." Then in came the small one with the meal, which turned out to be quite edible, brown bread sandwiches with some kind of meat filling, large slabs of a very rich cake, and also a litre plastic bottle of an anonymous red wine to be drunk out of paper cups – no cutlery or anything else which might be used as a tool. I thought that might be all, but no, as piping hot plastic mugs of coffee appeared about half an hour later, and the tall man said, "See what five-star service you are getting, you are bloody lucky to be picked up by two such charming men."

The coffee was strong and good but a little bitter, and soon after drinking it we both knew that we had been drugged. At first we found it difficult to keep our eyes open, but then we both collapsed in our beds, and a black cloud descended for the second time that day.

There was daylight coming through the chinks in the shutters when I woke, and with difficulty managed to focus my eyes to read the time on my watch. It was after eight o'clock, so I had slept round the clock. Pierre must have heard me stir, and I saw him give me a puzzled smile before he jumped up and put his feet to the ground as he remembered our predicament. "Good morning, darling," he said, "these bastards must have loaded our coffee with sleeping pills."

He came over and kissed me, or rather we kissed each other, but then he drew back, and said, "Now wife-of-mine-to-be – who goes first!"

"ME!" I said firmly, "that is a woman's privilege."

I went over and peed into the bucket, and made a resolution there and then that I was going to plead constipation until we got out. Pierre followed me; I have since learned that he made the same decision that morning. It wasn't long before the men came with our breakfast. They said nothing, just dumped it down, but again it wasn't too bad. Orange juice in paper cups was followed by slices of brown bread, already buttered – some with jam and others with meat paste – and a Golden Delicious apple for each of us. We looked doubtfully at the plastic mugs of coffee, but decided to risk it as it tasted fine without the bitterness of last night's.

The day seemed endless, as with the best will in the world

we couldn't spin out our respective life stories to any great extent. I remember being rather surprised at myself – and for Pierre too – as neither of us made any sexual approaches to the other, and I was glad that we felt the same, but most certainly I wanted it all to happen once we were free and all this nightmare was over.

But we did find one important link, and I was pleased to find that Pierre played golf – and played well – as he had a Class 1 handicap of 2. When he told me this, he went on, "I wonder, Yvette, if you play – after all you are at St. Andrews University?"

"Yes, I do sometimes – and that reminds me that I hope we get out soon, as I have a game arranged just next Saturday morning, a week from today."

"Have you now, who are you playing?"

"I'm not quite sure, but it will probably be a girl called Lydia Macpherson."

"I'm puzzled," he said, "why aren't you sure who you will be playing?"

"Well," I said with a rather smug smile, "there is a match that day between the St. Andrews University Ladies, and the Edinburgh University Ladies. She is their team Captain, and I am Captain of ours! It is of course usual for the Captains to play against each other."

"Glory be, don't tell me that I am going to marry a real golfer! What's your handicap?"

"I'm glad you mentioned that," I said very seriously, "because it does give rise to some difficulties in our relationship. You see, you tell me that you play off 2, but I don't know if I can live with that – it is such a poor handicap – at the moment I am off 1, but I expect to be down to scratch within the next month."

Even locked up as we were, Pierre could laugh. "I can tell that we are going to have fun, and as soon as we get out of here I am going to put you to the test. I play on a local course, the Club de Troyes-la-Cordelière, which is not far from Méli-tour. It is a jolly good golf course, and off the back tees it is as long as the Old Course in St. Andrews. I'll play you level, and I'll beat the daylights out of you, so there!"

I'm afraid that was the only bit of light relief we had that day; as whatever brave face we put on things we were in a frightening situation. Being locked up and not knowing what was in store for us was very unpleasant.

Lunch – a snack – came and went, and in the evening when it was time for dinner again, it was a repeat of the previous one, including two mugs of coffee about half an hour after the meal. We had had a whispered conversation during the afternoon, and had decided to empty our mugs into the bucket, and pretend to be asleep. We had no real plan of action, but we felt that we had to DO something. In fact it worked like a charm as we pretended to be asleep when they came in about an hour later, and we heard the tall man say, "Just look at them, aren't they sweet, like the babes in the wood. They won't stir till morning, so we're quite safe to get out of this bloody place and go for a drink."

A few minutes later we heard the sound of a car being started, and they drove off. We could hardly believe our good luck, but we realised that speed was of the essence in case they came back quickly. Fortunately Pierre is a pretty solid twelve stone, and at his third shoulder charge the door jamb split, and we were free, at least from our room. There was a low-power bulb lit in the living room, but we found that the very solid front door was locked. However we soon discovered the key to the back door.

Pierre was all for getting out at once, but I couldn't help wondering if the old tin was anywhere to be seen, and there it was on a table complete with the capsule and the ruined roll of film. I don't know why I bothered, but I did, and took it with me. It was dark outside with just a glimmer of moonlight and I could see masses of dark clouds in the sky, threatening a return of the thunderstorms of yesterday. I've said before how thinly populated the area is, and everything was dark except for some light in what looked like a farm house about half a kilometre away.

"Better keep clear of it," Pierre said, "you never know, they might be involved."

The track from the chalet went down quite a steep slope, and in about two hundred metres we came to a little road which we followed in the direction away from the farm. "I've no idea where we are," said Pierre, "trouble with all these clouds is that we don't know whether we are going, north, south, east or west...but surely soon we'll come to a sign post which will point the way to a town big enough to have a Gendarmerie."

Our prayers were soon answered, as we come to a crossroads and saw an encouraging sign pointing to a place called Sens 9 km away. "That's good," said Pierre, "Sens is a small town, and we'll be able to get help there."

But we still had our problems as just after we left the crossroads there was a blinding flash of lightning and the heavens opened. In a few minutes we were not just wet, but drenched right through, and I tried to laugh as I said to Pierre, "You know, darling, I really don't know if I am strong enough to live in France. I've been here for only three days and what with being abducted and now being well on the way to getting double pneumonia, I very much doubt if my delicate British constitution can stand it!"

Pierre put a soaking, but still comforting, arm round me and gave me a friendly squeeze. But then he suddenly turned to listen, "Hark, fair maiden, help is on the way – your fairy godmother must have heard you!"

Well, if the old girl had heard me I would have preferred a pumpkin coach to the vehicle which drew up beside us. It was an open truck of uncertain vintage, loaded with crates of milk, and the driver had seen Pierre's urgent signals. "Thank you for stopping," he said, "can you by any chance give us a lift to Sens?"

The driver's reply was in so thick a patois that I could hardly understand him. I gathered that the cab was full of chickens, but we could get in at the back, among the milk crates, if we didn't mind the wet.

We didn't!

Pierre arranged with him that we would be dropped off at the Gendarmerie – just saying that our car had broken down, and we wanted to tell them where it was. The driver just nodded, and after we climbed up and found seats on milk crates there was a jerk, and we were off – at a bone-shaking forty kilometres per hour on a vehicle which appeared to be devoid of any springs whatsoever, while the rain continued to stream down. Anyway, about a quarter of an hour later two drowned rats climbed down, and I saw Pierre have a word with the driver and a note changed hands which seemed to cheer him up, and he gave us a friendly wave as he drove off.

At first the duty officer in the Gendarmerie didn't look too pleased as we stood at the reception desk, dripping wet and leaving mud on the clean floor, but when Pierre told him who he was and what had happened things moved quickly. A bright young Inspector was summoned, who at once arranged for two vehicles. "We haven't a second to waste," he said. Pierre and I went with him in the lead car so that we could direct them to our prison. The second was a van into which piled several armed gendarmes. At high speed we retraced the route we had taken to reach Sens. Even in the dark, Pierre's was able to identify the turn-off leading up to the chalet. We bumped our way up the track and noticed at once that, while we had left the light on in the living room, now it was dark.

"Pity," said the Inspector, "that probably means that they have come back and found that you were missing. I doubt that they will have hung about, but let's see if we can find anything."

But the place was deserted, not a single thing had been left except a surprisingly well-stocked larder. "Nothing much here," he said, "so all we can hope for is that they have left some dabs somewhere. I'll get some print experts here as soon as I can. First, I'll need to get prints from you two for elimination purposes."

He instructed two of his armed policemen to remain behind, just in case the two kidnappers returned. He then took us, and the rest of his men, to the nearby farmhouse whose lights we had seen. It was now in darkness, but that didn't stop the Inspector taking precautions and he gave quick orders to two of his men, who drew their guns and covered both the back and front doors. This done, he told us to stay in the car, and went up and rang the front door bell. A light came on upstairs, and eventually the door opened and he spoke briefly to a woman and to a man who had also appeared. Fortunately he knew both her and her husband and soon we were invited into their living room. Pierre and I were still covered in mud and dripping wet, and apologised for the mess we were making.

They did offer to help us by way of dry clothes but Pierre insisted that we would just wait till we got home, and the quicker we got through things now the better. They couldn't help the police much with their enquiries. It turned out that they were the owners of the chalet which was often let for get-away holidays. It had, in fact, been rented just two days previously by a tall young man who had worn dark wrap-round glasses and who had paid cash in advance for a week's rent. She told us that he looked respectable and that he was driving a red Mercedes. At this point the husband suddenly looked up and said, "and I think it was a C Class Mercedes, probably a 2.0 200." So that was some help.

"Well that's the immediate matters settled," said the inspector to Pierre. "What, Sir, you need to do now is to call your father and let him know of your escape and that you are safe. You will, of course, have to come back with me to the station for some formalities. But after that he can either send a car for you to Sens, or I can arrange for one of my cars to take you home. The people here won't mind if you use their phone."

Whether from delayed shock of from the cold I had been shivering since our arrival at the farmhouse. When I started to sneeze as well, Pierre looked at me with sudden concern. "What you need, darling, is a hot bath and bed – and the sooner the better. There must be an hotel in Sens, so I'll phone Papa now and tell him that he has nothing more to worry about, but we are both soaked and will be staying the night. He can send a car for us in the morning." With that he went off with the lady of the house to make the call. He shortly returned, but did not hide his concern, "Papa was, of course, hugely relieved by my news. However, his breathing was laboured again. He has been distraught since he received that blackmail call through you, darling, and I fear that the stress on top of his illness has taken its toll. I think he was actually thankful that we would not be coming home tonight. He sends you his fond wishes. I'll tell you more later on."

Our drive back to Sens was more leisurely than the outward trip. On reaching the Gendarmerie the Inspector at once put out a call to trace the car, and gave a sadly limited description of the two men. I think we all knew that it was a forlorn hope. He then said to me, "Mlle. Dallachy, I'll get somebody to take you immediately to a hotel which is near here. I can assure you it is quite good. A police inspector is not without influence and I will make certain they have accommodation. You can then check in and get out of these wet clothes." Turning to Pierre, he continued, "I want you to stay behind, Sir, while you give your statement. For now I think that yours alone should be sufficient, although I may need one from Mlle. Dallachy later. It won't take long. One of my men will attend to that right away, after which he can drive you over to your hotel." He stopped there and gave both of us a smile of encouragement, "Thank you both for your cooperation. I must congratulate you on your level-headed behaviour throughout this ordeal. Please will you excuse me now? There are matters which require my attention."

When I got to the hotel I found that it was one of those increasingly rare family hotels, where everything was squeaky clean and nothing is too much trouble. And, when I went upstairs with Madame – and made some arrangements with her – I knew that we had been lucky. It was about half an hour later when Pierre came into the room, and looked thoughtfully at me, warm and cosy in a nice big double bed, after a hot bath. "Is there a mistake by the hotel, Yvette, the reservation would seem to be for a double room?"

"Surely you don't mind darling, although there is one problem. You see I have taken off all my clothes so that they can get dried, and I don't appear to have a nightdress!"

Pierre closed the door and for a moment just stood and looked seriously at me, very modestly covered as I was by the bedclothes right up to my neck. The he smiled and came over and was about to sit next to me on the bed, but I had more sense that he had.

"Don't you dare sit on this bed in your wet clothes; I've had enough trouble getting warm and dry without having a wet bed to worry about as well. But before doing anything else please tell me the details of your telephone call. What has your father done…and stop looking at me in that lecherous way, you can give me just one kiss, so long as you are careful and don't wet me or the bed…then on with your news please."

"So now, except for just one kiss, I can only look but not touch?"

"That's right, darling…for now!"

"And afterwards?"

"Well, that will be only after you've told me about the phone call, had a bath, and returned here without your wet clothes. Then, after that we can share this bottle of champagne which I have most thoughtfully got from the hotel. As we drink it I shall tell you a story!"

"Yvette, my beautiful, wonderful, and utterly exasperating girl, must we waste our time in story telling?"

"Yes," I smiled, "it is something I really must do, but I'll try to keep it short."

"And then?"

"That my dear will be up to you, but now tell me about your father."

"Well, obviously Papa was delighted to hear that we were

free. He had not in fact told the police because their threat frightened him. But I can tell you, although he is far from well, that he certainly has been busy. I confess that I'd lost track of the days, and didn't realise that this is Saturday. But despite the fact that tomorrow is Sunday, four banks were going to be involved in making up the parcels of money. Thankfully this can now be cancelled. He realises, of course, that there is bound to be some media interest in the affair, and has arranged a press conference at Mélitour at noon tomorrow. We'll be there in plenty of time as he is sending a car here for us at ten o'clock in the morning."

He stopped there, "Now, darling, I must go and have that bath, but there is a phone beside our bed, so why don't you phone Hélène now and tell her the good news?" He turned to go, but then came back and affectionately ruffled my hair, saying, "I must warn you that I'm going to hurry back!"

My call to Grannie was a mixture of laughter and tears. Albert had told them of our abduction and they had both been deeply concerned and had felt so helpless. Now, with relief she was able to shed the tears which had been bottled up. I told her the bad news about the film canister but she said firmly to me, "The idea that we might lose you has done wonders by way of concentrating our minds. Let the past go to hell, the only thing that matters is the present."

But she paused there, before going on, "Tell me about Jean-Pierre. What is he like?"

"Grannie, I hope that you are going to meet him very soon, and I can tell you that although I have only known him for three days, my feelings for him must be just about the same as yours were for Granddad on that very first day when you met him!"

She tried to get more out of me, but I wouldn't have it,

and the call ended with my saying that she would just need to be patient till I brought him to Henley. At least it didn't quite end there, as just then Pierre came back from the bathroom, with a towel very modestly tied round his waist. I thought I'd give her something to think about, and said, "Must stop now, Pierre is just back from having a bath!" and hung up the phone.

He was looking healthily rosy from a very hot bath, and I smiled at him before saying, "Pierre, I would never have thought that you were shy? What's with that towel wrapped round your middle?"

"Not at all, my dear, but you did tell me that we were going to drink champagne, and one must be dressed for that. But then when we finish it, I shall decide what clothes – if any – I shall wear!"

He lifted the bottle out of the ice bucket and skilfully eased out the cork with a most satisfying "pop", and without losing even a drop of the precious liquid. Then he filled our glasses using, I noticed, the old wine-waiter's trick of a little into the glass, let the bubbles subside and then glug in the rest. He gave me my glass, saying, "I suppose we have to have a toast, how about FREEDOM?"

We duly raised our glasses for the toast, and then he climbed into bed beside me but did so very modestly, hardly disturbing the bedclothes I had gathered round me, and he smiled at me and said, "Now, darling, what about this story you want to tell me?"

I snuggled closer to him, and said, "Put your arm round me. You may think that it is ridiculous, but I want to tell you what happened to my grandparents on that night after they met in Chaource and were involved in a minor war in which they killed eight Germans, wounded a ninth, and then freed your grandmother and your father, but unfortunately not soon enough to avoid the tragedy."

"But, darling," Pierre broke in, "you already told father and me about that the other day."

I smiled, "You've only had the expurgated version so far, and the truth is much more interesting. I'll tell you the story in detail sometime, but for now all you need to know is its conclusion, and their experience is one which must have been repeated many, many times during that awful war. You see, they spent the first night of their escape in small hut alone together miles from anywhere. My very proper grandmother, then a virgin of 23, found herself almost offering herself, by flaunting her nakedness, to a young man whom she had met only a few dreadful hours before.

"Grannie and Granddad first made love that night, and that love has lasted for nearly sixty years.

"Now here I am aged 21 and also a virgin. For the last two days I have been absolutely terrified. I have some idea how these two felt all these years ago. I find myself wanting to follow their example. Is that so wrong?"

He held me a little closer, "No, Yvette, it certainly is not, and I am so very glad that you have told me all this. You are, to use a hackneyed phrase, an old fashioned girl. I too am somewhat an old fashioned man.

"You see, as I told you this afternoon, I went to university when I was just eighteen and to begin with it seemed to be like an enchanted land. It was filled with pretty girls, very few of whom were maidens and most were, shall I say, available. My fellow students, I could see, seemed to change their partners as often as their underwear. But I soon found that there was a world of difference between having sex and making love. For me it never felt right in the morning, although there weren't

Gray Laidlaw 171

many of these incidents. So, my dear, although I am techni-
cally not a virgin – or whatever is the male equivalent of that –
I have never, as I see it, made love. I would like so very much
to make love with you tonight...but I'm afraid we can't..."

I had been happily listening to him and was leaning forward in eager anticipation to hear what was in store. But these
last few words – they came like a douche of cold water. All I
could think to do was interject, "But why not, darling?"

"Hold on! I was about to say that I wanted to ask some
questions." I was rapidly coming down off cloud nine. Questions and answers were a poor substitute for love-making, so I
said quietly, "Yes of course, ask me anything you like."

Pierre smiled, then brushed my lips with his and took my
face in his hands, "Please don't look so sad, my sweet, when
all I want is to ask you two questions. The first is, are you on
the pill? And the second is, when are we going to get married?"

"Jean-Pierre de Mélitour!" and I drew back a little so that I
could look him straight in the face, "Fancy asking a girl whom
you only met three days ago whether she in on the pill – of
course not! As for the second question, I suppose it counts as
a proposal of marriage. Don't you know that this is the most
romantic moment for any girl? There is no warm moonlight.
There is no orchestra playing softly in the background. This is
in a rather ordinary hotel room; and you aren't even on your
knees!"

"Yvette, my dear sweet wife-to-be, I love you when you
are serious; I love you when are not serious; I even love you
when I can't figure out whether you are one or the other. But
just to pursue my question, I was thinking that late June would
be a suitable time, just after your degree examinations and
your graduation. Now, if we were to pick that date and made

love tonight, would you still be a happy bride if you were to walk up the aisle when you were some two months pregnant?"

Talk about being serious, but now he certainly was. As for me I could climb right back up to cloud nine. "Poor Pierre, you really are a worrier, but I am happy to tell you that there is no problem. You see, before I went up to St. Andrews, three years ago, Grannie took me aside one day and talked very seriously about sex. I remember her saying 'Don't take the glitter for gold.' She hoped I would not feel I had to go onto the pill. But she did offer me a little box of these "morning after" pills, with a remark that she hoped I would not have to use them too often. Well, I can tell you that the box is still unopened and that it is in my toilet case back in Mélitour!"

He gave a contented sigh, and said, "You really are a wonderful girl, but you certainly aren't a patch on your grandmother!" I must have looked puzzled, but he laughed and said, "I seem to remember your telling me about that naughty virginal young lady flaunting her naked body to your grandfather. Damn it, look at you now, very modestly clutching the bedclothes right up to your neck."

As he spoke I realised that for some reason I was doing this, and I threw back the clothes, and found myself proud to see him looking lovingly at my nakedness. "You are beautiful," he whispered as he cupped my breast in his hand, but then he surprised me by saying, very seriously, "You know, I have always loved red hair, and I am delighted to see you don't need to dye yours!"

This puzzled me until I realised that as well as admiring my flaming red hair, now spread all over the pillow, he was also gently stroking my equally red pubic hair, and I couldn't help laughing as I said, "You're a rude man Pierre, and I'm sure I haven't known you long enough for you to be making such intimate remarks about my private parts."

"But they aren't private any more, my sweet, are they?" he laughed, "You see, they are now for my enjoyment as well as yours, and they are just about to make me that happiest man in the world."

And it wasn't long before I was quite certain that I was the happiest woman who had ever lived.

Chapter Twelve

It was daylight when I woke, utterly content and at peace with the world. Pierre was still asleep, looking just like an untidy boy with a lock of his hair falling over his face. I leaned over and brushed it aside so that I could kiss him, and he opened his eyes and stretched himself luxuriously as I said, "Good morning, darling, I hope that you don't mind my waking you?"

"Well, Yvette, my wonderful darling, I'm not so sure about that as what with one thing and another we didn't get too much sleep, did we?"

"No, darling, I am very glad to say that we got hardly any...but it was wonderful wasn't it?"

He turned and I found myself held tightly in his arms again. "It most certainly was. Are you sufficiently rested to try again?" Some wonderful minutes later there was a knock on the door (fortunately it was a self locking one) and I heard the voice of the proprietress, "M. de Mélitour, the police inspector has arrived and would like to see you as soon as possible."

I saw Pierre frown, "Merci Madame, tell him I'll be down as soon as I can."

I felt him move to – shall I say – detach himself from me, but I wasn't going to have any of it so I wound my legs even tighter around him. "To hell with the Inspector," I whispered, "we've both got some work to do here, and even if it were the blasted President of France himself who was waiting for us I'd still want to finish what…"

But I didn't get to end what I was saying, as Pierre closed my mouth with a kiss, and then went on, "I'll need to get used to this, Yvette, as you always seem to have more sense than me…now, where were we?"

It was after a most satisfactory conclusion that we were able to lie quietly in each other's arms for far too few minutes, after which we forced ourselves to get up. I gave myself a lick and a promise, and dressed. There had been hot pipes in the bathroom and both Pierre's clothes and mine were now dry if somewhat crumpled. But that didn't matter as jeans and tee shirts are often worn that way.

Pierre was taking longer than me to dress and I could see that he was having difficulty in scraping off the two days of stubble which he had grown during our captivity, and was finding the disposable razor, courtesy of the hotel, not quite up to the job.

So I was down first, and I hope that I managed to keep a straight face when I apologised to the Inspector for keeping him waiting. "You will appreciate that both M. de Mélitour and I were tired after our adventure, so it isn't surprising that we slept in."

"Of course, Mlle. Dallachy, I quite understand. Are you well this morning?"

And I could assure him I was – apart from a certain soreness…oh no, not there…it was my face that was the trouble, as my cheeks had been somewhat abraded by Pierre's stubble. But soon he appeared and with only a tiny nick on his chin to show what a struggle its removal had been.

As soon as the formalities of greetings were over the Inspector got straight down to business, and he had no good news to tell us. His finger-print people had worked all night at the chalet, and the only prints they could find were ours. They had, however, found the Mercedes in the railway station car-park at Fontainebleau, and it had been traced as having been hired on the Thursday afternoon, the day when I had got to Mélitour. And it too was a dead end as there were no prints in the car, and the hire people couldn't help. It had been rented by a tall young man wearing dark wrap-round glasses. He had paid in cash for five days, and had identified himself with a French driving licence. This turned out to be one which had been stolen while the owner had been in England, a few weeks ago. "It is obvious," he said, "that these two men are profes-sionals. The Sûreté are now involved, and I am hopeful that we'll be able to apprehend them, but it may take some time. On that subject, Mlle. Dallachy, how long are you going to be staying in France?"

"Well, Inspector, before all this came up I had hoped to travel back to England tomorrow. I am a student at St. An-drew's University in Scotland and the summer term begins on Wednesday." He looked disappointed, and I went on, "Why do you ask, would you like me to stay on for a few days?"

"Yes, I am afraid that we do, and we would greatly appre-ciate it if you were to give us a little time. You never know how some little bit of information can turn out to be very use-ful. There is in fact a colleague of mine from Paris who will soon be on his way to Mélitour, and he hopes to be able to see both of you early this afternoon." We both nodded our agreement, and he went on, "Good, so Mlle. Dallachy, per-haps you will be kind enough to talk to him, and arrange how long you should stay."

He was just about to take his leave when he paused, and said, "I know that your captors were well disguised, that they wore stocking masks at the chalet, and the small one wore motor cycling gear with a helmet and goggles, but is there anything at all you can think of which might help us to identify them?"

We both racked our brains and were about to give up when something suddenly struck me. Maybe French wasn't their home tongue. Indeed, the short one never even said a word, which was very odd. Maybe that was because he didn't speak French at all. I hesitantly told the Inspector my thoughts and suggested that they could have been British.

The inspector was a clever man, and he looked thoughtfully at me, "That's an interesting thought, but why do you say British; why not Dutch or German or Italian, or whatever?" I hesitated for a moment, and glanced at Pierre who was studiously avoiding eye contact. This made me wary and I realised that it would be unwise to suggest any connection between this affair and my quest. It would raise awkward questions. So I just shook my head. "Probably, Inspector, it was because I am British. You mustn't read any significance into my remark."

He left soon after that, but not before again remarking on the fact that the stolen driving licence had been lost in England.

After he had gone, there was about half-an-hour for breakfast before the Mélitour car came to fetch us. What with our limited meals at the chalet, and all that recent lovely exercise, we were both ravenously hungry. So we tucked in greedily to superb croissants and wonderful café a la crème. But it didn't stop us silently wondering about the possibility of a British involvement; but by common consent we abandoned such speculation, in favour of lovers' trivialities.

I wanted to forget everything except my love for Pierre, and as we finished our meal I felt quite weepy and sentimental.

I was so very happy. I said, "Darling, last night in room No. 7 upstairs was the most wonderful of my life, and I would very much like to come back sometime and spend another night with you in that same bed." He leaned over the table and squeezed my hand, "My wonderful Yvette, I was thinking the same thing. Let's make it a very private anniversary, and come back here every year, OK?"

The car arrived and we tried to settle up with Madame. But she would have none of it saying that it had been her privilege to help us. "But, if I am right, I think you will be returning as normal guests one of these days." Could our thoughts have been so obvious?

The drive back to Mélitour was without event. There we found Albert up and about, and obviously on the mend. He was overjoyed to see us safely back again, and it occurred to me that Pierre must be very special to him and the sole heir to the Mélitour line. There was a bottle of champagne waiting for us in an ice bucket, but first I begged to be excused as I wanted to get out of my grubby clothes which seemed to me still to have the smell of sweaty terrors. Pierre also changed, and he came into my room just as I finished dressing, "Chin up, darling," he smiled at me, "we're going to surprise father, aren't we! But don't you worry; nothing will make me change my mind."

It was as we went downstairs that I remembered that I hadn't taken my pill, but I saw Albert was waiting for us in the hall and decided to wait till after the champagne celebration. He took us into the saloon, which that morning was heated by a big log fire. It was all part, he said, of the arrangements for the Press Conference which would take place at noon, not much more than an hour and a half away. But as we sat round the fire Pierre was able to fill in the details of our adventure.

When he finished Albert stood up and extended a hand to both of us, saying, "I can't tell you how happy and relieved I am to see both of you back here safe and sound. That's the important thing; not the money I now don't have to pay. Let me propose a toast, 'to Yvette and Pierre, and their safe return'"

We drank the toast, and then Pierre gave me a wink, as if to say, "Wish me luck!"

I crossed my fingers, and hoped for the best as I wondered just what Pierre would say about it – about us. I saw him stand up and put his hand on his father's shoulder, and say, "Now, Papa there must be a second and much more important toast!"

My gaze switched from Pierre to Albert, and I saw him look puzzled, but Pierre was going on, "Yes, Papa, this toast is also to Yvette and to me, and it is because we are now engaged to be married!"

Albert looked thunder-struck, "Married! But you only met Yvette on Thursday and this is Sunday. To be engaged after such a short courtship is ridiculous!"

Suddenly my heart sank, and I realised that I had been living in a fool's paradise. He was right and indeed it was ridiculous. Here I was the granddaughter of a de Mélitour nursemaid presuming to marry the son and heir of this great old family, and that in just three days after we had met. It had all seemed so wonderful and easy, especially in bed last night, but now life was real again. I was ashamed to feel tears in my eyes, but then I realised that Pierre was arguing with his father.

"I am sorry you feel that way, Papa, but my mind is made up. Just look at her, she is a wonderful girl, and for both of us it has been a coup de foudre. In the last two days it has, of course, been inevitable that we have got to know each other very well. So I can tell you that I know, I am quite certain, that she is the only woman for me, and it is my personal miracle that she feels the same way about me."

Albert looked doubtfully at me, his forehead furrowed in thought, and I felt that I really had to say my piece. "I realise how difficult this may be for you, and I am sorry that the news upset you, but believe me when I say that I am as sure as Pierre, that we really are meant for each other, and I do hope you will come to believe us."

Suddenly his frown changed to a smile, "Yvette, I am sorry that I have been unkind to you, but you must agree that it was a surprise. At my age one doesn't like surprises. But now I can see that you would seem to be made for each other. What a very handsome couple you make! I am afraid that astonishment made me react without thought. I now I find myself both excited and delighted. Come and give me a kiss."

I went over and he embraced me, then there was a formal kiss on either cheek, and he smiled and said, "Now, do I get the other one?" I blinked away my tears, and kissed him on the lips. Those who have lived in France will understand this important step in French family relationships.

So it was with three happy people when Albert, having his arms round both of us, asked his next question. "And when are you planning to marry, maybe sometime next year?"

I looked at Pierre, and wondered how Albert would take the next shock.

"Oh no, Papa, much sooner than that. You see, Yvette hopes to graduate at St. Andrew's in June and we suggest that the wedding should be just after that, in the University Chapel there."

I think that Albert had by then decided that he had better give up on objections, but anyway Pierre was soft-talking him.

"Look at the advantages, Papa, we'll be able to go up to Scotland some days before the wedding. You've always talked of going there, and playing golf on the Old Course at St. Andrews."

Albert threw up his arms in mock surrender. "I can see that it is no use arguing. Anyway it is your wedding so it is up to the two of you to make the arrangements. Just tell me your plans, and I'll do anything which falls to me. As for you, Yvette, I am sure that you will be very happy with Pierre, he is a fine boy, and I am very proud of him. May I say that I hope you will give him both sons and daughters. Without them we are a dying family. I was, of course, an only child due to my father's death in the war, and although I was blessed with a daughter, as well as with Pierre, she cannot unfortunately have children because of an illness in her youth."

He stopped there and looked at me with a smile, "But you must feel like blushing, my dear, so again I must apologise. It is far too soon for me to talk about children when you are newly engaged."

At this point I really did blush, as I just remembered that damn pill which I still hadn't taken, so I excused myself with some remark about getting tidied up before the Press Conference.

I had got up to my room, and had just fished the box out of my toilet bag when Pierre came into the room, and smiled at me before he said, "What on earth are we going to do, darling? You see, the trouble is that there have been de Mélitours here for some five hundred years, and I am now the only possible heir. He worries to the point of paranoia that I might have no children. What would he think if you were to take that damn pill and, for all we know, kill one of them now?"

I shook my head, saying, "Actually, I don't think we need

to worry too much as I'm not in the most fertile period in my monthly cycle, so quite likely I am not pregnant."

"But you may be," and he paused and grinned, "Just remember how many chances I gave you!"

I was learning that Pierre could suddenly switch from frivolous to serious talk. He did that now, "Look darling, if you're feeling brave I think we should ask him to decide." I was totally bemused so I just followed him meekly back to the salon.

"Papa," said Pierre, "we want your advice!"

"Advice, Pierre? That will be a change…what about?"

"Well, Yvette and I have a confession to make. Well no, that's the wrong word because it isn't anything which we are ashamed of, rather the opposite. You will realise that we had a really terrifying time, not knowing what was going to happen to us. With the euphoria of getting free we weren't in an entirely normal frame of mind last night. So, I can tell you, Father, that in our hotel in Sens, we slept together."

I had expected that Albert would be displeased, but no. "Well now, I'm glad you told me, but there was really no need to do so. This is the twenty-first century, and it is a different world to the one in which I grew up. Anyway, Yvette, I presume that you are on the pill, but please throw them away after you get married."

I just stood there in an awkward silence while Pierre went on, "But no, Papa, she is not on the pill. Three years ago when she went up to St. Andrews, Hélène gave her a box of morning-after pills. She has the box in her hand now. I can tell you that the box is sealed, and she was in fact a virgin last night. Now, let me return to where I said that we wanted your advice. Does she take one of these pills now? Or, when she walks up the aisle in June, do we now accept the possibility that she may be two months pregnant with your first grand-child?"

I felt dreadful, as I could never have imagined such an intimate discussion with my father-in-law-to-be, especially one I still didn't know all that well. I could have sunk through the floor in embarrassment. But I needn't have worried, as Albert came over and put his arms round me, "Yvette, my dear, this must be very difficult for you, having your private life discussed with me, but I would like to thank both of you for your confidences. Is this the box that Hélène gave you…Yes?'

He smiled at me, took the box, turned it over thoughtfully in his hand, and then threw it into the heart of the fire.

"There!" he smiled, "Is that answer enough? I'm sorry to be so dramatic, but it will show you how I feel. I can also tell you that I'm sure you are going to be the very best thing that has happened to this old family of ours for a very long time. You have a saying in Britain, 'welcome aboard', and I say that to you now, most sincerely."

After that moment of high drama he suddenly turned into the successful business man who had so greatly expanded the family store business. "Now we shall all need to be quite clear what we are going to say at the Press Conference. It is now about eleven o'clock, and although it is timed for noon, you can bet that many of the reporters will come at least half an hour early to give them more time at the free food, and particularly the free booze, so we must get our stories straight."

He rang a bell and when the major-domo came in, said, "Jacques, please have coffee sent in to the library and we'll leave this room now so that you can get it set up. I can also tell you that I have had some very good news this morning, my son and Mlle. Dallachy have decided to get married. For them it was a case of love at first sight, and I have been pleased to give my blessing to the union."

Never a flicker of surprise passed over Jacques' face. I realised how well trained he must have been, and we had dignified congratulations from him before Albert hurried us
through to the library. When we were settled in chairs, he said,
"I have always dreaded any publicity regarding family matters.
With the tabloid press involved, I can just imagine the fanciful
stories that could be concocted for publication. This would be
even more unfortunate. I gather from Pierre that the film has
been rendered useless. It was our last chance of finding the
truth about those war days. Anyway, I do feel that to give any
suggestion now of there being a link between your search and
your abduction is absurd…agreed?"

Pierre gave an emphatic nod, and said, "That's correct,
Papa, to complicate things by mentioning our search would be
ridiculous, especially as now we'll never know what information your mother left for us in that film. It is tragic, but that
chapter is now closed for ever."

As for me, I was nearly convinced, but not quite. The behaviour of Mr. Butler at the MOD still worried me. However
this was not the time for me to say anything so I just nodded
my agreement.

"Good," said Albert, "that means that the conference
should be quite straightforward, but let's rehearse our answers
to the questions. First, Yvette, what reasons do we give for
your presence here?"

"That's easy; you can say that my grandmother was your
nursemaid and that we have kept in touch over the years. She
is now old and no longer fit to travel, and asked you to allow
me to spend a little time here so that I could see Mélitour and
her home district.

"Also," I went on, "my engagement to Pierre should perhaps be mentioned, and you can give a spiel about our romantic union that will occupy their attention for a while."

Albert nodded, and turned to Pierre, "Now, where were you taking Yvette on Friday afternoon when you were abducted?"

"Simple, I was taking her for a drive to show her the district, and some of the villages, and we were on our way back from Etourvy where Hélène was born when we were accosted."

Albert nodded his head, "You're right, keep it simple. Now, they are going to ask how you were treated, and I suggest that you paint a rosy picture, about how good the food was and so on. Remember that good news is not interesting news"

The Press Conference went as smoothly as Albert might have wished. No doubt the numbers had been reduced because it was Sunday, so it was short and there were no awkward questions. I could see that our having escaped unharmed had much reduced the media interest. The reporters who had come comprised a few local ones, several freelance stringers, and a few from national papers, including one from the *Paris Post*. I was glad to see though that he was not my bête noire, Philippe Dupont, so it looked as though a link had not been established. Albert was also right about the attraction of the food and drink, as although the actual conference was over by twelve thirty, we didn't see the last of them till nearly an hour later.

It was while we were thankfully sipping our aperitifs before lunch – elsewhere than in the salon which was a ruin of dirty plates and glasses – when Jacques came in. "Mlle. Dallachy, a gentleman has called who wishes to see you."

"To see me? Who is it?"

"He is a Mr. Philippe Dupont from Paris, who says that he knows you."

"Tell him to wait, and that I'll be out in a few minutes." I turned urgently to Albert, "Quick, I need help; this is Michelle's grandson, the young man who wrote that article in the *Paris Post* and who is on some kind of retainer from them. So, what do I say to him? He knows that I came here to find the old secret buried in the graveyard, and obviously he must suspect a link."

For a few moments he just looked worried, but then I could almost see an idea come to him. "Yvette," he said, "you'll have to admit to him that you did dig up the old can, and you can explain that the secret was in a film which was in it. However we have been able to check, and found that in the nearly sixty years which have gone by, with it buried in damp ground, the film is useless with the emulsion coming away from the celluloid. That can't be disproved, and it should wrap the whole thing up...no story...no connection...OK?

"I think that should do very well," he went on, "and what I suggest, Yvette, is that you talk to him in the hall and I'll stay behind the door here, listening to what is said. If things look like being awkward, then I may be able to help, but I'll need some time, so if you are in trouble, please try to spin things out as long as you can."

So I went, very apprehensively, out into the hall, leaving the door ajar behind me. Philippe came over and tried to kiss me, but I turned away. "Philippe, I can't say that I am glad to see you, both our grandmothers and Michelle were distressed to hear about your article in the *Paris Post*. Surely you realised that it was an affair which affected all our families, and you betrayed a confidence. Anyway, why are you here, the Press Conference is over?"

"You know very well why I am here, and I have the chance now for a real scoop! Don't try to do me out of it. I came down this morning with another reporter, who went to your precious conference, and a fine lot of pap you people dished out. Come to that, you've done very well for yourself, about to marry the son and heir! Jolly good…clever work…you're a girl after my own heart with your eye on the main chance. Now if you scratch my back, I'll scratch yours by painting a pretty picture of things here. In return I want the full story of what you have found. But if you don't, I can write a very different story. That drivel you gave out this morning was very touching, all about the devoted nursemaid and how she and Albert, her young charge, kept in touch for all these years. It's all balls. I know that there has been no contact whatsoever since 1956. We both know why you really came here, it was to solve a very pretty little mystery, and I want the exclusive."

As he had been talking I could hear Albert moving in the room, and I began to do what I could to spin out our conversation. "Philippe, you must know from speaking to your grandmother that none of us wants this affair to be blown up into a big news story. Just think of Marie-Claire, a heroine of the Resistance, who has been a simple-minded invalid since 1944. That surely is enough in itself to stay quiet for the sake of the family? Anyway there is no need for us to appeal to your finer feelings, since the story is dead!"

"What the hell do you mean dead?"

I mentally crossed my fingers and said, "It is dead, Philippe, because my fiancé and I, just as you thought, did go to the graveyard on the afternoon I got here. That was last Thursday. We did find a rusty old tin can there, buried where we were told to look. Inside was enclosed a capsule of 35 mm.

film. We took it to a photographic shop in Tonnere, and they told us that it was useless. The emulsion had come away from the celluloid base. It is very sad for us and now for you as well, as our quest is over. So Philippe, will you please go and leave us alone."

He looked at me hard, and his eyes narrowed, "I don't believe you; you're hiding something."

We argued to and fro for a while, and at last he said, "Well, if you won't play ball, I can still make up some kind of story about what I do know, and I think it will be sufficiently interesting to be published."

I heard a creak as the door behind me opened, and Albert came into the hall, and went up to Philippe. "M. Dupont isn't it? Let me introduce myself, I am the Comte de Mélitour, and there is a telephone call for you."

Philippe looked surprised, "For me? Do you know who it is?"

"Yes, it is a M. Maréchal who says that he knows you."

"Do you mean my editor?" he spluttered,

"I don't know," said Albert, "but he sounded impatient, so I suggest that you hurry."

I looked thoughtfully at Albert, but he just gave me a tiny shake of his head, and rapidly nipped off upstairs, obviously so that he wouldn't need to be involved again. It wasn't long before I heard the sounds of the end of a conversation, and Philippe was back, looking rather puzzled. "That was my editor," he said proudly, "an important story has broken which he wishes me to deal with personally, and he has decided not to run this one."

He stopped there and looked searchingly at me before going on, "It really is very odd…is it possible that the Comte has influenced him in some way?"

"Don't be absurd, Philippe, how could he possibly influence such an important man as the editor of a national newspaper? The days are long gone when the aristos had that much clout. Isn't it just as well that you have been recalled now that our story is dead?"

When I said that I crossed my fingers and hoped that Philippe didn't know where the Mélitour money now came from. Had he realised that the Comte was important and wealthy businessman he might have been less willing to accept the situation at face value. "Yes, you're right, and as things have turned out I am sorry that you had to be cross with me, but I did think that I was on to something. Anyway, that's all over now."

"I'll forgive you," I said, and I tried to smile as I spoke, "and I must say that I am very impressed about how important you have become in the *Paris Post* organisation. Fancy your editor wanting to speak with you personally; obviously you are going to go far."

He shrugged his shoulders, as if to say, "nothing out of the ordinary", and he certainly seemed to be in a very happy frame of mind as he prepared to leave, saying, "Can I have that kiss now that we have nothing to quarrel about?"

Well, I did kiss him, but I made a vow that I would never do so again. I was very pleased to see him go. A few minutes later Albert came downstairs and I said, "How on earth did you manage that?"

"Easy! You have a saying in Britain that it isn't what you know, but who you know, and while I have never met this Mr. Maréchal, he would love to know me. So I phoned, and explained to him how much my family dislikes publicity. I also mentioned that I was about to launch a major advertising campaign in connection with the launch of a new boutique in

Paris, and that my advertising agents were trying to persuade me to change our policy, and to use the tabloids, instead of the 'heavies' which we habitually use. This in fact is quite reasonable as the customers of *Jeunesse* are more likely to read them, than are our traditional Mélitour clients. So I was happy to assure M. Maréchal that I would take a centre page spread for the whole week, starting next Monday."

"You are a genius, and I am very much going to enjoy being a member of this wonderful family. But what about Philippe, won't he talk?"

"Not if he knows on which side his bread is buttered, as M. Maréchal will have told him to ring him back on his mobile phone, and right now will be telling him that if he breathes a word of it he'll never get a story printed in the *Paris Post* – so that's that!"

He stopped there, and put an arm round my shoulder, saying, "Come on now, Yvette, this is an awful day for you, and it's not over yet as we have this Inspector from the Paris Sûreté coming soon, so we'd better go now and have a quiet talk before lunch."

"One last conference, I hope," Albert said as we all sat down, and then went on. "So far we have lied to the police in Sens, again lied to the press, and now we haven't been entirely straight with the young reporter. We have deceived them all, so do we do the same with this Inspector from Sûreté who will be here in just over an hour?"

There was no argument about the decision, and we agreed unanimously to stick to the same lies. What was the point of complicating things, now that our quest was dead?

But although I agreed, I still had this tiny niggle of doubt which I couldn't explain to myself or put into words.

Chapter Thirteen

The policeman, Inspector Gaspard from Paris, duly arrived on time. We all said our pieces, very convincingly I thought, but when we had finished I got the impression that he had his doubts. I wondered if we were going to get away with it. He was a smooth and polished young man, maybe around thirty-five, and with a look of high intelligence which is hard to describe. He asked a few questions of Albert after which he turned to Pierre and me saying, "I'll address my remarks now to you two since you are chiefly involved. You'll forgive me, M. de Mélitour and Mlle. Dallachy for saying that this is a very strange case. It is a great mistake to think that criminals are stupid. They seldom are. In fact many of them are very clever indeed, which make the work of a detective more challenging that you might imagine.

"But having said that let's take your captors. They invested quite a lot of money in the enterprise. First of all they hired the Mercedes and maybe the motor cycle as well, which we haven't been able yet to trace. They paid in cash. Then they rented the chalet for a week; again they paid in cash. They also didn't waste any time. All these arrangements were made early last Thursday. The following day, on Friday afternoon you were abducted just outside Etourvy. They did all that very efficiently. The contact for ransom was highly professional and persuasive. I understand that M. le Comte arranged for all the money to be prepared today, in parcels of notes, ready to hand over tomorrow morning.

"But after that, for no apparent reason they chose to leave the two of you alone in the chalet in the belief that you were drugged. What puzzles me is what could have been of such over-riding importance that they risked leaving you? And remember also that whatever it was it can't have taken them long. When they returned to the chalet and found that you were missing, they had time to remove their things and clean off the prints, before you got back with the police from Sens. You told me that the coffee was drugged on the first night when you were captives, so why were they so naïve as to think you would drink it the next day? I understand that you made your escape after you actually heard them say that they were going out"

He stopped there, and looked very seriously at us. "So it is all very odd, and I do wonder whether by any chance you can think of anything – anything – which might explain these discrepancies."

Pierre indicated that he knew of nothing, and I said that I couldn't think of anything either. But it was a lie, as I had just realised what was probably the answer to the main question. But the Inspector accepted our assurances, and shrugged his shoulders, saying, "That's a pity as I did hope that you could come up with something, so there is now just one more thing to discuss."

And he turned to me, "Mlle. Dallachy, I understand that you are keen to get back to your university, but can I ask you to be so kind as to stay for a few days? I am hopeful that something will turn up, and if we manage to arrest suspects we would need you for an identification parade. I know that they wore stocking masks as long as you were in their hands, but you must have ideas about them, and before they picked you up, you did see them briefly."

I replied that neither of us had any clear recollection which we thought would help but that I would be willing extend my stay. Pierre continued, "Inspector, you may not have heard, but Yvette and I have just got engaged, and I want to go back to England with her so that I can meet her grandparents, with whom she lives. Would next Wednesday be a possible day for both of us to go?" The Inspector didn't look too pleased, but said that he thought that the date would be acceptable, and that he would let us know if anything came up.

And that was that. It certainly ended the interview, and Albert went to the door with him and I heard snatches of friendly conversation. When he came back he looked much happier, saying, "What a day this has been, beginning with excitement of your engagement, then that bloody Press Conference and that nuisance of a reporter, and this last interview with the Sûreté man from Paris. For God's sake let's talk trivialities from now on, I'm sure we are all tired and want some rest."

That was certainly true for me, especially considering how little sleep I'd had the previous night. However, I had just realised something important and I couldn't just leave things alone. I summoned up my courage and said, "I'm sorry Albert, but I'm afraid we have more to talk about. I'm pretty sure that I know why our captors did what they did. It was because they wanted us to escape!"

They both looked puzzled, and Albert said, "But why, Yvette, what's the sense in that?"

But, as he spoke Pierre slapped the table, "Papa, Yvette is right, how could we have been so stupid? They let us go because the whole affair was a charade. The only thing they wanted to do was to get from us whatever we dug up in the

graveyard, without our knowing that this was their only interest. You see if they had just stopped us and stolen the can it
would have shown us and everybody else how important it
was. But by staging our abduction they could make the loss of
the film seem to be just an unfortunate accident. The fact that
it was an old film was a bonus for them. All they needed to do
was just show us the film being exposed, and that was that, no
film and no evidence."

I could see that Albert was uncomfortable at the prospect
of more investigations, and he said ruefully to me, "You
know, Yvette, I could almost wish that you hadn't been so
clever. It is an ingenious idea, and one which may well be
right. However I am not quite sure. But what I do know is
that if we were to tell the police we would open a real can of
worms. They would be furious with us for not telling them the
background to the affair. And just think of the ramifications!
We would have to mention Lord Hempson, and the possibility
that he was guilty of treason in 1944. Then, damn it, the British police would be consulted and it would be inevitable that
both the French and British Governments would become involved. So, do we proceed? As I see it the tabloids would have
a field day and they would be the only people to benefit."

He paused and looked ruefully at me, "I know how keen
your grandparents are to bring the affair to a satisfactory conclusion, but sadly we have no clear evidence of Lord
Hempson's guilt. All we have is their recollection of a fleeting
look that they had at a young man escaping from that charnel
house, and being shot as he did so. There is also the reference
to 'uncertainty' in the old letter. You theorise a possible connection with M. Brume, but it's all very vague. Now, while I
find myself wishing that these suspicions were true, and damn
it I have every reason for trying to nail the bastard, I cannot

see that we have any case against him which would stand up in a court of law. Also, I know of your suspicions about Mr. Butler. Do you now think that he could have sent these two men after you? It does seem very unlikely."

He stopped again, and he reached over to hold my hand, "Let's pause for now, will you agree to leave it till we have had a little more time to consider things?"

I could not deny that, were I to be honest with the police, Albert's summary of the consequences would turn out to be completely accurate. It looked like his preferred course was to drop the matter altogether. I thought it best to say no more, and to change the subject I asked if he had come to any conclusion yet about my seeing Marie-Claire.

"I've been thinking about it. She hasn't been too well these last few days, but she is improving a little, and I hope you'll be able to see her tomorrow afternoon, that for her is the best time of day."

He then went on to talk about Pierre's visit to England with me and said how much he would have liked to come too, but that he had just got back from New York and was very busy. "I can tell you," he went on, "that as we have some three hours till dinner time I'm going off now to my study and catch up with some of my work. I suggest that you put your head down for a bit as the last two days have been very traumatic for you, apart altogether from stealing my son away from me!"

"Stealing?" I said, "I don't think so, as he certainly came to me quite enthusiastically!"

Pierre who had been sitting quietly, suddenly surfaced and said, "Enthusiastically? No, no, not at all…you see I am a polite chap and as you were so keen to have me, I just couldn't disappoint you! Anyway, do you want to change your mind now?"

I didn't say anything, just jumped up, then going over to plant myself down on his knees and gave him a smacking kiss. I think that bit of banter was good for all of us, and we all laughed before I said, "I've got to make two telephone calls before I have a rest. In the first I shall tell the truth, and in the second it will all be lies, but in both I'll tell some good news."

Albert looked doubtful a moment, but then said, "I think I can guess, you are going to tell the truth to Hélène, and tell lies to Alicia – right?"

I nodded, and then said to Pierre, "You'd better be beside me when I speak to Grannie."

The two of us sat together as I dialled England. Grannie answered, and when I told her that Pierre and I were engaged to be married, her reply was predictable. "But you've only known him for four days!"

"Yes, Grannie, that's true, but so far I am only engaged and, as I recollect, you and Granddad got yourselves not just engaged, but married, in about the same time."

"But things were different then – there was a war on."

"Don't try to make that an excuse, Grannie dear, remember that we too had our adventure when we were abducted. Anyway, if I have been too hasty it is due to two things, the first is this wonderful man here, and the second is your fault because of these naughty genes which I have inherited from you."

That silenced her for a moment, which gave me time to tell her that I had more news, but that she should first speak to Pierre. When he did so I was very pleased with him, as apart from saying all the right things, I could hear that he had adopted a pure Yonne accent, and I thought what a clever chap he was. After that I had to tell her of the press conference and the arrival of young Philippe Dupont, then how Albert got rid of him, and also tell her that she would soon meet Pierre as he proposed to drive me over on Wednesday and stay for couple of days till I went off to St. Andrew's at the weekend. I also asked her to mention to my favourite professor the reason for my late return, because I was staying some extra days in France. His subject was French literature, and any extra time in France would rank as a very good excuse. But, alas, all these careful arrangements were sadly to come to nothing.

After dinner, Albert, a forward planner I could see, suggested that we should have a kind of holiday next day, and that Pierre and I should go off in the morning and have a round of golf at the local Golf Club de Troyes-de-la-Cordelière. This seemed a splendid idea to me, and I was keen to see how well he played. I had no confidence in French golf handicaps, and felt that they might well be unreliable.

Chapter Fourteen

I slept late in the morning, and when I got down to break-fast I found Pierre on his own as Albert had already fin-ished and had retired to his office. He took me in his arms and kissed me saying, "Good morning darling, I hope that you slept well."

"Yes, I certainly did, as on this occasion I wasn't bothered by your keeping me awake. It was a most pleasant change!"

It was a beautiful spring day and I chased down my break-fast as quickly as I could so that we could get off to the golf course, because I had things to do before I could play. I had been promised a pair of shoes as Pierre's first present to me, and the clubs I could hire. The course was only a few miles beyond Chaource, and the clubhouse was a real surprise, as it could only be called magnificent. Pierre explained to me that it had been a chateau, and while we were having coffee prior to the game I told him about the old Comtesse back 1944, and how she had arranged jobs here for the two heroic old gar-deners.

As I explained this to Pierre he put his arm round my shoulders and smiled at me before saying, "Damn it, as I've already said, you've never been here before, but you know things I've never heard of. I can tell darling, that you are at home here already."

Right then I astonished myself by feeling that I really didn't want to play golf, but just to go off somewhere to be alone with my lover, but then sanity returned, and I told my-self not to be a fool, and concentrated on looking at the score card of the course. At once I saw a problem that Pierre would have in Britain, and I said to him, "Look at this card, darling; the lengths of all the holes are given in meters. Golf is one of the last bastions of the old Imperial Measurement, and 99% of British players and 100% of the Americans still think in yards.

"Now," I went on, "if I convert your meters into yards, I can see that off the Men's Championship White Tees it is about 6,700 yards, and off the Yellows it is nearly 6,300. I suggest that we both play off them. That should be quite long enough for a friendly game."

He looked at me with some surprise, "But darling, surely you don't want to play off the men's tees, the forward blues are for Ladies."

"Not for this one," I said bravely, "I said that I was going to play you and that is what we are going to do!"

He leaned over and squeezed my hand, "Well, that's OK by me, but you mentioned a few minutes ago something about the Yellow Tees being long enough for a friendly game. What on earth gave you the idea that it was going to be friendly? Come on darling, the moment of truth is upon us!"

So we repaired to the golf shop where he bought me a very elegant pair of shoes with soft studs, and I was able to hire a set of golf clubs which were very similar to my own. It was while I was changing into these new shoes that an odd thought came to me. Did I really want to win? Would his masculine pride be dented if I were to beat him? I had still not made up my mind when we got to the first tee, and I saw that it was an inviting hole of about 410 yards with a slight dog-leg to the right. Pierre had won the toss, and so drove off first, hitting a long drive straight up the middle, and opening up an casy shot to the green. Suddenly my competitive spirit rose to the surface, and I muttered an ungracious, "Good shot!"

I hadn't hit a ball with these hired clubs before, but they felt right and after a couple of practice swings I proceeded to hit one of my better efforts. His "Good shot!" was rather more convincing than mine, but he was hard put to it when I hit a perfect 5 wood shot to the green, and parked the ball no more than a yard from the pin, good enough for a birdie, to go one up.

I confess that my reservations about the French handicap system were, at least in Pierre's case, unfounded. By the time we reached the 18th tee we had both played out of our skins and were all square. This was testing par 5 hole of about 500 yards. It was his honour and his drive, as usual, was inch perfect and very long. Mine wasn't and I ending up in the rough from where I had to hack out to a point no more than 50 yards past his drive. My only hope seemed to be that I could squeeze a half in five, but he then opened his shoulders and hit a beautiful 3 wood shot which took him to the front edge of the green.

"Well done!" I said ruefully, but then I saw him frown, and he came over to me, "Come on, darling, you can easily reach the green from here, put it near the hole just like you did on first!"

As he said that, I realised that he too had a problem with the game, a similar problem to mine, which I had entirely forgotten since I'd been on the first tee. He couldn't LET me win, or even let me win half the game, but for now he was on my side. Anyway I decided that again a 5 wood would be the right club, and I hit it right on the sweet spot. I was just admiring it landing on the green and finishing up near the hole when he seized me in his arms, "Bloody good shot, darling...I

do love you!" And his kisses certainly seemed to indicate that
he did.

Our good shots, and our embrace, had not gone unno-
ticed and there were about half a dozen people round the
green to see us finish off. Pierre certainly had a putt to win the
match, but it was a long one, all of 20 yards, and it finished up
at about the same short distance from the hole as mine. For a
few moments we both looked at the balls, and then almost in
unison said, "CALL IT HALF, DARLING!"

He bent down and picked up my ball, and I did the same
for his, and then we solemnly exchanged them. It was I realised, quite an important moment in our lives together. Although it was just a golf game, and we would play many more
in our lives together, to have finished all square on our first
game seemed to be a good omen.

We must have looked an odd pair, standing there with the
balls in our hands, but then Pierre laughed, "Come on, darling
it is time for us to shake hands – for the very first time I think
– and then there are some friends of mine over there I'd like
you to meet. But after that handshake give me a kiss just to
surprise them!"

I wondered what his friends would think of me, but
maybe because of my shot to the green they couldn't have
been nicer, despite the fact that I had seen some surprised
glances when we kissed. Pierre had to confess that we had just
got engaged and we were submerged in a flood of congratulations. Nobody was direct enough to ask where I lived, but one
lady asked how long he had known me, and his reply was a
masterpiece of truthful deception. "Oh, Yvette's family and
mine have known each other for nearly sixty years."

Then there were congratulations about our escape from
the kidnappers, but none of them were awkward, and I know

that we were both happy to find that they hadn't seen anything suspicious regarding the story as it had been reported in
the press. I had expected that we would have lunch in the
clubhouse, but when Pierre was asked if we would join them
he surprised me by saying, "Not today, Yvette and I have a
lunch engagement, some other time perhaps."

I had more sense than to query this, and when we were
driving off I asked him where we were going. "Why, anywhere
where we can be on our own. I was damned if I was going to
share your company with anybody. You are my own special
woman, and I'm selfish enough to want to keep you to myself."

"Ditto!" I smiled, "so let's go back to Chaource, and that
restaurant where we had our first meal together. I think that is
where and when I fell in love with you."

"Only then?" Pierre said with a frown, "Damn it, I'd fallen
for you before we left the station at Troyes!"

It was after 3 o'clock when we got back to Mélitour and
Albert seemed genuinely interested in our game. I thought that
maybe was he just being polite as he attentively settled down
while Pierre began to go through our game almost shot by
shot. But he was an enthusiastic listener and I learned that he
played quite a lot of golf himself. He had a handicap of 12,
which is quite reasonable for his age. As I listened to Pierre I
realised with delight that he was proud of me, which made me
feel very humble, and I found myself overcome with joy at my
good fortune in finding such a wonderful man for my mate.

It was then my turn to say some nice things about him
but, as I started, there was a knock on the door and a nursing
sister came in. Albert smiled at her, and said, "Sister le Blanc,
let me introduce you to my son's fiancée, Mlle. Dallachy."

He then turned to me, "I should explain to you, Yvette,

that Sister le Blanc is in charge of the nursing, and everything that my mother needs. There are also two other nurses, so that she can have round the clock attention."

I took an immediate liking to the sister; she had a most pleasant manner, and looked utterly competent. She gave me a warm smile as we shook hands, and then she turned to Albert, "I think this is as good a time as any for Mlle. Dallachy to come and see your mother, she is awake now but that may not last long."

Albert came over and put an arm round my shoulders. "You must realise that her condition has been heartbreaking to us all, but it will do no harm to remind you of that. The pity of it is that physically she has remained healthy, and is a fit woman for her age, but she has the mind of a young child. Very occasionally she says the odd word, but it is never more than that. Now, of course, she is over eighty years old and her physique is failing her, and she has taken to spending most of her time in bed where she sleeps for much of the day. Anyway come and see her now and try to remember the brave and lovely girl she once was.

There was a chill in the room, and it was a shock to be talking like this after our light-hearted chatter about golf. I felt a prickle of tears at the thought of the shadow which for so long had hung over the Mélitour family. But then an idea came to me, and I said, "Before I go, I wonder if it might be a good thing if I were to bring the old tin with me?"

Albert shook his head, "I shouldn't think it will mean anything to her, she really isn't in our world now, but bring it if you want to,"

I ran upstairs and got the tin, then went into the bathroom and smeared a little cold cream round the top, so that the lid would slide on and off easily. Inside there was just the capsule with the now useless film.

As soon as I rejoined them Pierre took my hand and the sister led the three of us through the hall into the East Wing of the chateau, which I knew had been converted into a luxurious nursing home. On the ground floor there were three en suite bedrooms, one for each nurse, then upstairs just two big rooms, a salon flooded with light from huge windows, and a big bedroom with bathroom to the rear. I had heard so much about Marie-Claire, the beautiful Comtesse as she had been, and I was prepared for the worst as I went in. The room was sparsely furnished, and she was reclining on the big bed, propped up on pillows, with a nurse beside her, who stood aside as we came in.

As I walked over to the bed I was astonished to see that she didn't look old, there was hardly a line on her face, and I could see how lovely she must have been. Her eyes were wide open, clear and blue, but they were the eyes of a doll, with nothing behind them. But then, I saw a spark in them as she looked at me, then down to the tin, and back to me again. Suddenly, it was as if a light had come into them, and she raised herself from the pillows and stretched out a hand to me. Albert and Pierre were on the other side of the bed, and I saw their surprise at her movement. As for the Sister, she was about to speak but Albert silenced her with a gesture. I took Marie-Claire's hand, and there was a ghost of a smile on her face, and she whispered faintly but quite clearly, "Hélène…Je suis…très heureux de te voir."

For a moment I didn't know what to do, and what followed was so surprising that I must tell you in the original French. I had often been told how like Grannie I was, and so I realised that I had to pretend to be her. I knelt down beside the bed with the tin in my hand and kissed her cheek, saying

"Marie-Claire...ma chere amie... Je l'ai découvert."

She reached up towards me and to the tin, so I closed her hand round it. She stroked it for a moment as if it were a precious object before easing off the lid and gave a satisfied sigh as she saw the closed capsule of film inside. She picked it out carefully, then handed it to me, whispering, "ICI..." and it was so soft that I found it difficult to make out, but it sounded like, "Regarde ici ... Voici l'évidence contre le Bâtard!"

I wondered then if I dared take a chance, and I decided to risk it as it might be the only chance I would ever have, so I kissed her cheek again and said, "Marie-Claire...le Bâtard, est il M. Brume?"

And this time her whisper was crystal clear, "Oui, tu a deviné juste...Venge-moi, Hélène... La mort à lui!"

I saw the light begin to fade from her eyes, so I leaned forward and kissed her cheek again. For a moment I saw a flicker and she smiled at me before her eyes closed. She looked so peaceful, but I noticed that she was still holding the old tin in her hands as if to protect it. But for me the film capsule was a reminder to me that her dream of vengeance was now impossible. She had done all that she could, but we had failed her.

In a little while I stood up and joined the others, none of us saying a word, as we tip-toed out of the bedroom and into the salon, so garishly bright after the shadowed sick room. I saw from the faces of the others how different our reactions had been. Albert was most moved and he sat down on one of the armchairs with a muttered "Excuse me," and mopped his eyes as he struggled to recover himself. I could sympathise with him as I too felt grief, but to me it was more a sense of shame after the fiasco of the film. But the sister was excited by this medical miracle.

"M. le Comte. We must get Dr. Jeanfils round at once. To have spoken again after more than fifty years of silence is incredible…can she be recovering?"

But Albert, the layman, had more sense than she, "No, Sister, time enough for that tomorrow if we then see any change. I am sure that this flash of sanity will be a fleeting one, and I would ask you to treat what you have just seen in the strictest professional confidence. To let you understand, I would remind you that my mother's injury was due to her Resistance Group being betrayed to the Germans, back in 1944. What you do not know is that just prior to her capture she discovered who had betrayed them. We have known for some forty years that she buried something which could identify the traitor, and it is only in the last few days that my son and his fiancé discovered the location and dug up that old tin which you have just seen. Now Yvette is very much like Hélène, her grandmother, who was my mother's closest friend and her colleague in the Resistance. That lucid flicker today was triggered when she saw Yvette holding that tin, and took her right back to 1944. You also saw a capsule of film. Sadly, the evidence that was so important to my mother has not survived the years. The film is ruined and its secrets lost.

"What I am sure we saw this afternoon was the survival of one of the strongest human emotions – vengeance – and I am glad that she will never know that we are impotent, and can do nothing further. The important thing is, in whatever part of her mind that is still there, she believes that we now have the evidence on which to act, and which will avenge her. I find it hard to say, but I now believe that she will die very soon, but at least she will die happy. Because of this, Sister, you will understand why I ask you to say nothing. We have already had an invasion of the Press yesterday, and the last thing we want is another story about our family. "

Her reply was brief, "Of course, M. le Comte, you have my word...and my sincere sympathy."

We left her there, and went back to the salon in the main part of the chateau, and as we went in, Albert took my hand. "Come and sit beside me, Yvette. Over the last few days since you came here we have gone through a whole gamut of emotions, haven't we? For me it began with the curiosity about what you would be like, then a pleasant surprise as I found how nice you are and astonishment at your likeness to Hélène. Then the next day you and Pierre were abducted. Two days later you returned with Pierre who tells me that you are engaged to be married! I can tell you that my surprise and worry that you had so quickly won his heart soon changed to pride that my son had managed to win yours. Now you have brought about this wonder with my mother. It was so intuitively correct of you to realise at once that you had to pretend to be your grandmother. You did it so beautifully. For me it was miracle to see her come alive in your presence. For a brief moment she was rational and even passionate."

He paused there, wiped some tears from his eyes, "However, as I said to the Sister, I am a realist, and I do not think that it is likely to happen again. And one burden which I shall have to carry for the rest of my life is the thought that we should have got together sooner and assembled the pieces of that letter, perhaps at once after the war was over, and if not then certainly in 1956. We could have identified the traitor, and maybe...just maybe...the ensuing drama would have acted like shock therapy. After all, she was then less than forty years old. Would she have recovered? Probably not, but the thought remains.

"The fact that mother identified M. Brume as the traitor

really doesn't help. You have told us that the Ministry of Defence couldn't – or wouldn't – identify the people behind the code names. Even if they did we would still have no proof. All we have to rely on is a fleeting glimpse which your grandparents had in 1944. As for me I was too young and distressed to remember anything, and this whispered identification of my mother would be laughed at if we were to go to court. Just think what would happen if we were to make any accusation against Lord Hempson, he could sue us for a vast sum."

He paused again, and shook his head sadly. "So, Yvette, and you too Pierre, we have come to the end of the road. For God's sake let's forget it, and get on with living!"

For me, that too was enough, "You're right, Albert, after this afternoon we at least know who was guilty. The rest of the world can live in ignorance. What do they care? I can only hope that Grannie and Granddad will also accept that things are best left as they are."

Then it was my turn to pause, "I'll be home the day after tomorrow, so I think I'll not tell them about this afternoon till I see them, OK, Albert?"

And that was agreed to. We were a quiet trio at dinner, and it was as the sweet was being served when the nursing sister came rushing in. "M. le Comte, come at once, I'm afraid that your mother may be dying!"

He and Pierre ran off with her, but I stayed where I was as I felt that a bogus Hélène had no place at her death bed. It wasn't long till they came back, and Pierre took me in his arms, "It's over darling, she never woke up after this afternoon and in fact she just went peacefully from sleep to death. Don't be sad as thanks to you these last few hours have, for her, been the happiest she has had for many years."

Albert then came over and took my hand, "Pierre is right,

and we all must thank you again. But now I would like you to come with me, as I would like you to be able to tell Hélène how her old friend looked in death…come now."

I had never before seen a dead person, so it was with some reluctance that I followed him into the bedroom. But I needn't have worried as she was lying just as we'd left her, her eyes closed and a look of serene happiness on her face.

Albert struggled to speak, but then managed, through his tears, to say, "Tell Hélène how happy she looked!"

And he lifted the sheet to cover her face.

Chapter Fifteen

Quite a lot was to happen in the next few days, but I'll try to be brief. The funeral was arranged for Thursday. I had of course to phone Grannie to tell her the news, and we arranged that instead of Wednesday, Pierre and I would come on Sunday, and that I would continue to St. Andrew's on the following Wednesday. But I still kept back from her the details of my conversation with Marie-Claire, as I reckoned it was something we should talk about face to face. She also promised to tell my Professor the reason for my arrival being delayed again. I told her that he was somewhat of a snob, so to have got myself engaged to a real live Frenchman, heir to the de Mélitour title, was the best of all excuses. Just as all these arrangements had been made we got a useless call from the police to tell us that nothing had emerged, and so we were free to leave on Wednesday.

Next day Pierre's sister, Marie de Valois, and her husband Henri came down from Paris, and thank heavens, they seemed to approve of me. She was a dark-haired beauty, very much a smart and elegant Parisienne. He looked a bit older, maybe in his late 30's, a suave business man who ran the Maison d'Argent store in Paris. However I could see a twinkle in his eyes, despite the sadness of the day.

Soon after they arrived Marie took me aside, "Yvette, it won't surprise you that Henri and I were somewhat taken aback, and indeed worried, at the speed of your romance with

Pierre. We were especially perplexed because, as I'm sure you have already guessed, my dear brother has been playing hard to get and leaving a few broken hearts along the way. But now that we've met I can quite understand his haste and I'm sure that you will be very happy together."

"That's very kind of you," I smiled, "but perhaps, knowing your brother, you can see why I was in a hurry too!"

We talked trivialities for a while, but then she said, "But we must now get down to work. I knew that you wouldn't have any black clothes, so I got Henri to bring a selection of dresses and accessories from La Maison d'Argent with him, and I can tell you that Pierre seemed to be able to tell me exactly what your measurements were!"

One of my failings is that I blush easily, and I certainly did then. "You must think me a fool Marie, but with all the excitement here the question of clothes hadn't crossed my mind! You are an angel to look after me."

She smiled and leaned over to kiss my cheek, "I can tell you that it is time you started to wear clothes from the store, and you are going to be condemned to a lifetime of doing so! But don't worry as they have an excellent Haute Couture department, and I love their clothes. Anyway, Yvette, I am sure that we are going to be good friends, and if ever I can help you…just ask. But now let's go and try on clothes."

Wednesday was quiet, but Marie and I found work to do in helping the staff to prepare the chateau for the reception after the funeral. Not that there would be a large number as Albert decided, because of his Mother's long illness, that the attendance would be by invitation only. So, apart from the five of us, there were only another twenty of the oldest friends of the family.

Thursday dawned, a beautiful spring day, and it was as a

family group that we walked out through the grounds to the
little chapel at the edge of the woods. The other mourners
were waiting outside, and I was conscious of the fact that despite the occasion I was the focus for all their eyes. But I could
hold my head up high, as I had Pierre beside me, and thanks
to Marie's foresight, I knew that I was most elegantly and correctly dressed. The service was a short one, but the priest
spoke most eloquently and seriously about Marie-Claire's
heroism, and the terrible price which she paid for it. It was a
strange time for me to meet these family friends, but they all
knew of my engagement to Pierre and were very kind. I did
notice, however, that one or two of the ladies seemed to be
taking a very close look at my figure, no doubt to decide
whether there could be a particular reason for the suddenness
of the engagement.

It was after dinner that night, when we were on our own
again, that Albert asked us all to come into his study, and he
sat down with a plain square leather box in front of him. He
smiled at the four of us before speaking. "This is family business, but I feel, Yvette, that for all practical purposes you too
are now family, and I can tell you that both Marie and Pierre
approve of your being present. They both know what is in
their Grandmother's will and she was, of course, classified
over fifty years ago as unfit to look after her own affairs, so
her will was written by me. It is very simple, and her monies
and her effects will be divided equally between them, as they
may arrange. But her jewels are not part of this arrangement,
and none of them have seen the light of day for nearly sixty
years. My wife, you see, would not wear them while Marie-
Claire was still alive, and Marie has followed her example. As
regards them it was understood that Marie and Pierre – or his
wife should he have married – would agree an equitable divi-

sion. Yvette, they also agreed today that you should have a hand in the selection."

He stopped there, and both Marie and Pierre nodded their agreement, but I felt that it was really ridiculous, and far too soon for me, who had only known the family for a week. I said, "No, you are all so kind, but much as I look forward to being a family member, I still am not. It is very sweet of you, Marie, to be so generous, but it must be left to you and Pierre."

But she would have none of it, "Papa, don't listen to her, Pierre and I agreed this afternoon that she was already family, so she must be with Pierre when the selections are made, that's enough talk so let's get on with it!"

As she spoke Albert opened the box and tipped out a glittering cascade of the most magnificent jewellery, and for a moment I just gazed in astonishment, and probably greed too, but then some common sense returned to me.

"These jewels are beyond anything which I could have dreamed of. It will be wonderful to wear some of them, sometime, but not before Pierre and I are married."

"That," said Albert, "is what I hoped you would say, but Pierre and Marie and I have had a talk today and there is one matter which must be arranged now."

He carefully spread the jewels on his desk, and then picked up a small box and opened it to show a gorgeous emerald and diamond ring, "This, Yvette, was my dear mother's engagement ring, and Pierre hopes that you would like to have it for yours?"

It was so magnificent that in truth it took my breath away, and I saw Albert hand the ring to Pierre who came over, "Yvette, my darling, may I put this ring on your finger, as a token of my love for you?"

All my instincts told me that it was ridiculous for a twenty-one year old to wear a ring like this, but that didn't stop me holding out my hand and, when he slipped it on to my finger, the fit was perfect.

"There now," he smiled, "the fit is perfect, it might even have been made for you."

But then a little sanity came back to me, "But, Pierre, how can I wear this ring, it must be worth a fortune?"

It was Albert who answered, very much the clever business man.

"Don't worry about that, Yvette, it certainly is valuable, but I'll have all the insurance tied up before you leave. And as for you wearing it, just remember that when it was given to my mother she was even younger than you now are."

I was then surprised to see him looking rather intently at the ring on my finger, and he said, "It may surprise you to know that I have never seen this ring worn before tonight!"

"Never? But surely your mother must have worn it sometimes when you were a little chap?"

"No, never. Very soon after the war stared she paid a visit to Paris. I'm sure Hélène will remember the occasion. When she came back she put this ring into our bank for safe keeping, where it has remained until now and nobody guessed that it was there."

It all seemed rather improbable, and all I could say was, "But why?"

"Because," he laughed, "she wore this other ring!"

And he produced another one which looked exactly like the first.

"You see," he went on, "she worried about what the conditions would be during the war, so she had a costume jewellery copy made, and it was this ring which she wore. Actually it is quite a good ring in its own right. The fake diamonds are zircons, and it will fool anyone but an expert. Please take this copy ring as well; it should come in handy for everyday wear."

He paused again for a moment, and then went on, "But you mustn't spoil your enjoyment in wearing the ring by worrying about the value. Its real value is a token of Pierre's love for you, a love which I share, so never be afraid to wear the real one. "Jewellery is nothing if one cannot take pleasure in putting it on."

But I was still unhappy, "Albert, and you too Pierre, I don't need to tell you how much I appreciate your entrusting me with this wonderful ring, but I really must have some idea as to its worth. A few minutes ago we talked of it being valuable. But how valuable? Please don't think, Pierre, that I am trying to put a price on our love, and it would never have occurred to me to ask the question if the ring had been anything which I might have imagined seeing in our local jeweller's window. It is only because it is so amazing that I have these fears…insurance or no insurance."

It was Pierre who put an arm round my shoulders, and said, "Yvette, my dear, do please wear it. I shall be so proud to see you with this family ring. If it is lost, well that is what insurance is for. But since you ask the question, I know that Albert had valuations made yesterday, and the real one is being insured for a hundred and forty thousand Euros, and the fake one for fourteen thousand."

I did some quite easy mental arithmetic and came up with a hundred thousand pounds for the real one, and ten thousand pounds for the fake. Marie, who must have seen my bewilderment, came over. "Yvette, please don't have any reservations about the ring. Wear it and be happy. I can tell you that I have always known that the ring would never be mine. It was always going to belong to Pierre's wife. I am sure that my dear grandmother is now happy that it will be yours. By rights you must inherit it, my dear, and Henri and I are sure that by wearing it on your finger you will make Pierre very proud."

"That's not exactly right," Pierre broke in, "I am proud of her already whatever she may be wearing," and he gave me a blatantly lascivious grin, "or not wearing, as the case may be."

I have already mentioned that I blush easily, and also tend to cry when I am happy, so what could I do then but both blush and cry while I distributed moist kisses around the three of them.

I sat quietly for a little while, and watched Marie and Pierre turning over the pile of jewels, but then a thought suddenly came to me, and I excused myself and went up to my room, still wearing my wonderful ring.

What I had remembered was the necklace which Albert's grandmother had given to Hélène back in 1954 which she had given to me just before I left for France. Grannie had told me to put it on when I came to Mélitour but I had felt uncomfortable about wearing it while Marie-Claire was alive. However now with her ring on my finger it somehow felt right. When I went downstairs I was surprised to see that they were all sitting down in armchairs, and that there was no sign of the jewels, and the old leather box was closed.

It was Pierre who explained things to me, saying, "You know, Yvette, that sister of mine can be very sensible sometimes, and she has solved the problem about how we deal with jewels. You will remember that you said that you didn't want to help in the selection of the jewels, as you were not married to me? Well she just pointed out that the best thing for now is that we should do nothing, but that we meet up again the four of us, Marie and Henri, and you and me after we get married.

And a convenient time might be after we come back here from our honeymoon."

I didn't get a chance then to say to Marie how kind she was, as Albert suddenly exclaimed, "Yvette, is that necklace which you now are wearing, what I think it is?" And that led to my telling the others about that meeting nearly fifty years ago when the old Dowager Comtesse gave it to Grannie as a kind of apology for her unkindness back in 1944.

When I finished, Albert took my hand, and led me out of the room and into his study which I had never before seen. He smiled at me, and said, "Yvette, my dear, it is wonderful that already you are so much a part of the family, just look at that picture." It was a beautiful oil painting of a young Marie-Claire, and round her neck was the necklace.

So after that we all settled down to chat, and they were all so nice to me that and I found myself, for the first time in my life, feeling part of a family of people of my own generation.

In my room that night I could hardly bear to take my ring off, and despite all that had been said I wondered if I would ever dare to wear it in St. Andrew's. But then I realised that I would certainly wear it at least once, as if that dear old French professor of mine were to see it, he would never dare to fail the wearer of such a jewel.

We still had Friday and Saturday before Pierre and I were due to leave, and he and Marie decided that I had better see, and understand, something about the estate and their other local interests. They all took me off next morning on a conducted tour. I had known that there were farms around the estate, but I hadn't realised that, over the years, Albert had managed to buy back the tenancies. Now they all worked together as a big cooperative, with the various farm managers getting a share of the profits, and these profits were considerable because of Albert's marketing skills. What he had done was to jump on the "Green" bandwagon, and most of the estate produce was sold in elegant parcels, sacks or bags labelled, "Organically grown on the Mélitour Estate."

They had even brought back into service an old water mill, after nearly a hundred years of idleness, and the estate flour was marked, "Stone ground by an 18th Century water mill on the Mélitour Estate."

That was Friday, and on Saturday I was taken to Chablis to see the magnificent vineyard which was responsible for producing one of the most famous *Grand Crû* wines of the district. We got back to Mélitour in time for dinner which was to be served an hour earlier than usual. The idea was that Pierre and I would make and early night of it and get off for England at dawn the next day. But that was not to be.

After dinner Marie asked me if I would show her the tin which we had dug up. I went up to my room and brought it down, complete with the capsule of film inside. I saw her turn it over thoughtfully, then open the tin and take out the capsule. "It's a damn shame," she said, "We'll always wonder just what the photographs on this film would have shown. Maybe we would have seen pictures of the young Lord Hempson on obviously good terms with Germans. It is so frustrating, isn't it, to think that this evidence was just along the road, waiting to be discovered ever since 1944."

I saw Henri lean over to take the capsule, and then, just as our captors had done, he took the film out and unreeled it. I saw a look of surprise on his face as he reeled the film up again and put it back in the capsule. Then, as if he couldn't believe what he had seen, he got it out again for another look, before saying, "Look, Pierre, and you too Yvette, are you quite sure that this is the film that these two men showed you as being the one which had been in the capsule?"

That was easy, and we both agreed that it was.

"Well, my children, I have some news for you. Pierre will remember that my hobby is photography. I can, therefore, say with absolute certainty this cannot be the film which Marie-Claire buried in 1944. Why not? Because this particular brand of film has only been in production for the last five years or there about. So where is the original film?"

That certainly put the cat amongst the pigeons, and I won't try to put things down as they were said, because we all spoke at once.

In the end we agreed that our previous conclusions regarding the purpose behind our abduction were still valid. We were intended to think that the film had been destroyed by a silly act of vandalism while we were being held hostage. We now knew the deception went further and that our captors had actually stolen the film. But why had they done that?

Our scenario went like this. The sequence of events had been triggered by my visit to Mr Butler at the Ministry of Defence. I sorely regretted the revelations that I made to him in my anger over his deceptive behaviour. Either Butler was loyal to his old political master, Lord Hempson, or was in some way obliged to him. Between the two of them they must have decided that the evidence I might discover had to be destroyed. Maybe they had even involved the new Minister of Defence, Michael Marshall, who was after all Lord Hempson's son. Whatever, all three were perfectly positioned to tap into resources of the British military. Somehow our two abductors where recruited; possibly they were ex-members of the SAS or similar units who would welcome some excitement in return for a large fee. They could have been spun some yarn about National Security.

We were almost certain that their mandate was to ensure that the evidence was destroyed but in such a way that we would believe that its destruction was an unfortunate coincidence and not a planned action. Try as we might, we were unable to convince ourselves that Lord Hempson would have wanted the evidence returned to him. Putting ourselves in his shoes, the sooner the damming evidence was disposed of the better. It was inconceivable that a traitor would want a souvenir of his misdeeds. We surmised that the briefing of our two captors was overly emphatic when they were instructed to physically destroy whatever I may discover.

These were two clearly intelligent men. They must have wondered what could have been so terribly important to the powerful men who had employed them. We concluded that they were unable to resist the temptation to learn for themselves what the film contained. The theft of the film was thus not a part of Hempson's plan but rather an independent and unauthorised action.

There we became stuck. We did not know if the film was in a sufficiently good condition for it to be properly developed. Even if it was, would our two men be able to understand the meaning of the pictures? We did talk for a while about the possibility that our abductors may have hatched a plan to blackmail their employers. In this connection Pierre wondered if we should do some advertising, but as to what we had no ideas.

The wonderful thing was that the film probably still existed. The possibility that we might find out the truth had been rekindled. But where was the film? Who had it now? And how on earth might we recover it?

Finally it was Albert who summed up what we were all thinking, "The obvious thing is that we made a serious mistake in not taking the police into our confidence right from the beginning. Had we mentioned the possibility of a British interest we might even have got the two men arrested before they left France. But now I am afraid that any future action is entirely up to us. We daren't speak to the police after deceiving them to begin with. Anyway, apart from being very cross with us, there is nothing they can do. All the players in this drama are, I am sure, now in England."

"So Pierre and Yvette," he went on, "I suggest that you discuss the whole affair with Hélène and Brigadier Dallachy when you get there tomorrow. Probably the first useful step will be a new approach to the Ministry of Defence. I hope that the Brigadier will be fit enough to tackle that in person. I'm certain that the British military works the same way as it does here. Influence and the loyalty old friends are powerful forces. Mr. Butler may find that he is circumvented and unable to fob your grandfather off with stories about information being lost or not available.

"I would hope that he can unearth the identity of the illusive M. Brume and retrieve the records of his service in wartime France. Let us wait until we see the outcome this direct approach before we decide on what further action to take. Are we agreed?"

We were.

Chapter Sixteen

Although I usually enjoy holidays, I often find that when setting off I am reluctant to leave home. I felt just like that when we left Mélitour next morning. When we got to the entrance gates I found myself looking back with affection at the Chateau, and Pierre saw me doing so. "What are you looking at, darling?"

"I'm looking back," I said happily, "not just at Mélitour, but at what is going to be my home. From now on, you see, wherever you are will be home to me."

But that was the only bit of sentiment for a while, as we began again to talk about the affair, and suddenly I'd had enough of it. "Look, we've been thinking about this and talking about it for most of the time these last few days, and I'm full right up to here. So let's give it a rest now, as we'll be right back into it again when we get to Grannie and Granddad."

For the rest of the journey we talked the inconsequential nonsense which is part of getting to know your loved one. The Jaguar ate up the 250 odd miles to Calais, and after a sandwich on the boat – we preferred a boat to the Tunnel – we rolled into Henley in the late afternoon.

They must have been looking out for us, as the car had hardly stopped before they were out to greet us, and there was almost embarrassment in their very formal greetings, which didn't please me at all. "Come on, Grannie," I said, "surely you can do better than that? You changed his father's nappies, so why not give him a proper kiss!"

That seemed to break the ice, and I was relieved to find us a much more congenial group when we sat down in the garden to drink some celebratory champagne. For safety reasons I had travelled in thin gloves to hide my ring, and when I slipped them off I saw Grannie look at it in astonishment. "But that must be Marie-Claire's ring…is it now yours?"

I nodded, "Yes, it's wonderful isn't it? After Marie-Claire's funeral Albert got her jewels from the bank where they had been since early in the war. It had been arranged long ago that although all her effects – including the jewels – were to be divided equally between Pierre and his sister Marie, this ring was different and it had to go to Pierre's wife."

I stopped there and smiled at Grannie, "I can tell you that Albert paid me the compliment of suggesting that I should have it as my engagement ring. What could I do Grannie? It was so wonderful that I just couldn't stop Pierre putting it on my finger…"

"And there it stays," Pierre broke in, "and I am very proud to see it on Yvette's finger."

As we were speaking I saw her looking doubtfully at it, and I could read her thoughts. "Yes, this is the real one; the other ring is upstairs in my bag."

Grannie nodded her head, and smiled at me, "I wondered, you see, as I well remember Marie-Claire going up to Paris in the autumn of 1939 and having it copied, and she never wore the real one after that."

She called Granddad over to admire it, and although he said all the right things I could see him wondering just how many zeros there were in its price.

"Don't worry," I smiled, "Albert arranged to have it covered for insurance. I hate to tell you how very valuable it is…about a hundred thousand pounds!"

That was a real conversation stopper and I said, "How about Pierre and me telling you about all our adventures now, and I can tell you that we have some interesting news."

But, typical of Grannie, she said, "No, not yet, we are having a simple cold meal, so let's have that now and we'll get down to the serious stuff after we have eaten."

I couldn't help laughing, and I turned to Pierre, "You'll find that these two always do this. Anything important has to be left till after the evening meal. This gives Grannie an excuse to have a large digestif with her coffee."

Grannie frowned at me, "You are talking nonsense, Yvette, because as I am sure Pierre knows, no French woman needs any excuse for that, since to do so is just normal."

"Of course," said Pierre, "I really can't think how Yvette could be so ignorant. I think she should apologise at once!"

We could laugh at that and then we talked generalities for a little while longer. As we did so I was glad to see how well Pierre and Grannie were getting on, but I wondered about Granddad. He had, of course, lived in Alsace until he was a teenager and had been married to a French woman for more than fifty years. However, in other respects, his years in the army had made him very much a caricature of the old guard "true Brit". It amused me to see him blame the many absurdities from Brussels on the French and listen to him ranting on about these "damnable, stupid Frogs". He was suspicious of all Europeans. Understandably, the war had left him with an irreconcilable loathing of anything German. Less excusable was his conviction that all Frenchmen were ineffective nincompoops whom he held accountable for most of the failings of the EC. Grannie, inevitably, shared his view regarding Germans and had come over the years to accept his other prejudices with a smile. Love has a wonderfully illogical way of reconciling contradictions and I suspect that she understood that she had been promoted, in his mind, to the exclusive category of "Honorary Brit". I had my fingers crossed that Granddad would apply the same mental gymnastics in forming his attitude towards Pierre. At this stage I was cautiously optimistic that things would work out well.

We had of course been talking in French, and I thought it was a bit awkward that here in England we had to speak French because Pierre's English wasn't very good. I expressed this thought out loud, and said, "You know, Pierre, we really must bring our children up to be perfectly bi-lingual. Grannie and Granddad were so good to me in this regard, and I would like us to follow their example. In the first place, though, I am going to work hard on your English."

Grannie I saw looked a trifle disapproving at this talk of children when we had just got engaged, and she said, "I think, Andrew, that it is time for a pre-dinner drink. You and Yvette can have your ghastly sherry, but I'm sure that Pierre will prefer something French."

I knew that he too liked sherry, but he had more sense than to say so, and he asked for a gin and dry Martini, giving me a surreptitious wink as he did so.

One thing of interest did come up at dinner time, as when I was eating a beautiful dish of cold salmon, I asked Granddad, "Tell me, did this wonderful fish come from the Dee, and John Brand?"

"Yes, as soon as I knew you were coming I phoned him and he said he'd send one down if he were lucky enough to catch one. Well, he did, and this one arrived yesterday by Data Post.

I could see that Pierre was puzzled by the conversation, so

I said, "Remember the story I told you about Granddad's adventure when he was driven up to V1 Flying Bombs Control Centre in the Pas de Calais by a German driver. Well, after that affair, the driver joined the French Resistance and came to Britain after the war as an honoured immigrant. He has prospered extraordinarily well. One of his houses is a large one on the river Dee in Scotland which is one of the finest salmon rivers in the country. I can also remind you that although he was German, he couldn't stomach the Nazis. It was thanks to his bravery that Granddad was able to steal the V1 secrets.

Pierre shook his head in surprise, "Andrew, you'll have to tell me all about your adventures sometime soon, so far Yvette has only covered the highlights. One thing which she and I have in common is that we have remarkable grandparents. You know all about my courageous grandmother, but did Hélène tell that my grandfather was killed in 1940 in a heroic but hopeless last-ditch battle to counter the German invasion of France?"

After dinner we went back out in the garden again, and Grannie started the ball rolling by saying, "We've got a lot to hear from you, but let's leave the serious bit till you've told us how the two of you, Pierre and Yvette, came to fall in love and get engaged so very quickly."

"Quickly, Grannie," I said, "I don't think it was. It must have been at least ten minutes after I met Pierre before I decided that he was the man for me."

"Quite right," said Pierre, "I would never have liked a girl who was too hasty, so nice and slow like Yvette suited me fine. Now, as for me, I'm not a man to rush things, I like to ponder and to think carefully before I make up my mind, so I was a lot slower than Yvette – it must have taken me all of a quarter of an hour to make my decision."

But Grannie wasn't going to let things go as easily as that. "That's all very well, but you did get engaged in only three days and..."

"Darn it!" I broke in, "we were slow coaches compared to you two. If I am counting the days correctly, it was only four days after you met when you got married, and my dear Father was born about forty weeks later...so don't lecture us!"

Grannie began to talk of things being different then because of the war, but Granddad laughed, and said to her, "Hélène, my dear, I'm afraid for the very first time you are showing your age. You seem to be forgetting how we once were, at the time when you were just Yvette's age. And as for me I can tell you that if I had met you in the most peaceful surroundings I'd still have fallen in love with you just as quickly – or even quicker – than Pierre tells us he did. Also, unless you are a consummate actress, don't tell me that it wouldn't have been the same for you."

"I give in!" she laughed, "but I hope they haven't been as quick as..."

She suddenly stopped, as I wondered if she really were blushing, but anyway she cleared her throat and changed the subject, saying, "Enough of this, Andrew, how about topping up our glasses?"

When no one was looking, Pierre gave me a wink, but I was in no mood for more confidences, telling Albert had been bad enough.

For a few minutes we all seemed to run out of conversation, but then Grannie reached over and took Pierre's hand, "I must apologise, here we are asking all these questions, and neither of us has yet said how very glad we are that Yvette has found such happiness with you. She is a lucky girl, and I'm sure you know that you are a very lucky man, so how about giving your Grandmother-in-law-to-be a kiss?"

He duly did so, and she smiled, saying, "That was nice, but now tell us about your adventure and what about your plans for the wedding?"

Before Pierre could answer I broke in, "Grannie and Granddad, Pierre and I haven't even got our bags upstairs, so give us a few minutes to get organised, and we'll be back down in a few minutes." I saw Pierre look at me strangely, but there was something that I urgently needed to discuss with him. In France, the idea of a wedding in the University Chapel at St. Andrews had seemed wonderfully romantic. Now, watching Granddad I realised how frail he looked and how heavily his more than eighty years was were bearing down on him. I had only been away from Henley for about ten days, but I imagined I could see a further decline.

I led Pierre upstairs and then shared my thoughts with him, "Darling I'm worried. Granddad doesn't look too well, and I wonder if we shouldn't scrub the idea of getting married in St. Andrew's? He seems to have worsened in the few days since I last saw him, and I wonder whether the journey and all the hassle there might be too much for him. Would you mind very much if we had just a quiet family wedding here, and then after the honeymoon I'm sure that Albert will want to arrange some kind of party at Mélitour?"

For a moment Pierre didn't say anything, he just took me in his arms and held me close, then, "Yvette, my sweet, anywhere in the whole world is OK by me. All I want is to get that wedding ring on to your finger as soon as possible. Is that a sufficient answer?"

His kiss was my answer, so thankfully I said, "Let's go downstairs and tell them this new plan, without, of course giving them the actual reason."

Our suggestion went down very well, and we arranged a provisional date, subject to Albert's approval, of the 5th of July, a Saturday. The guest list was easy, just the four of us here, Pierre's immediate family Albert, Henri and Marie, plus another dozen or so of our close friends in Henley.

"That's all right, so far as it goes," said Grannie, "but what about your University friends, won't they feel out of things?"

I hadn't thought about that, but Pierre had the perfect answer, "That, Hélène is a very good point, and it gives me an excellent excuse to go up to St. Andrews and play some golf. How about it if I were to go up at the end of term? I could then see Yvette's graduation, and also arrange a little party for her friends..." He stopped there with a frown, "But kindly, Yvette, do not parade all those handsome boy-friends of yours you've got up there...or I'll be jealous." On that note we reach a happy conclusion to the marriage arrangements.

There followed a pause in the conversation, but shortly Grannie said very hesitantly to me, "You'll be wondering, Yvette, why I haven't as yet pressed you to tell us about your stay in Mélitour. I have been distressed about Marie-Claire's death. The fact is that I was so upset about it that I have been avoiding the subject. We have already learned from your phone calls about the failure of your mission, so tell me now about my very dear old friend. Did you see her before she died?"

"Yes I did, and she died happy, but first I think I had better say just a few things about our adventures, because it will surprise you to know that our mission, as you called it, may not be over!"

That certainly woke Grannie up, and she burst out with, "That's wonderful, tell me quick!"

I couldn't help laughing, and I said, "Pardon my language, but not bloody likely! Just remember that I listened to you and Granddad for several days while you spun your wonderful stories, so allow me to do a little of the same!"

In fact I didn't take very long about it, just the main items, my time in Paris, meeting Pierre, Albert's illness, our finding the old tin, our abduction, seeing the film exposed, our escape, the Press Conference and the awkwardness of Alicia's grandson Philippe Dupont. Then, after all that, our reluctant conclusion seemed to be that our quest was over, and although we couldn't hope to prove the name of the traitor, we did suspect Lord Hempson.

I could see that Grannie was about to break into my story, so I said, "Just be patient, there is yet more to tell you…"

And I went on to explain how I had been able to see Marie-Claire, and how I had taken the old tin, containing the capsule of useless film with me. How she was lying there, still looking beautiful but with empty eyes, how she thought I was Hélène, and the extraordinary moment when, with the old tin clutched in her hands, she was briefly jerked back into reality to confirm that M. Brume was the traitor with the words, "Oui, tu a deviné juste…Venge-moi, Hélène… La mort à lui!"

"And that, Grannie," I went on, "was the last thing she said, before she died just a few hours later. But when Pierre took me up to her room I could see her eyes were closed as if in sleep, but there was a look of serene happiness on her face."

I stopped there as Grannie was crying unashamedly, and through her tears she managed to say, "It's awful, isn't it, I can't bear to think of her lying there, imagining that you, Yvette, were me. But thank God you were there to give her some last comfort. What I find the most distressing is that she thought we had the evidence to expose the man she called 'le Bâtard'. But now that vital evidence in the film is destroyed...at least she never knew that!"

"But, Hélène," Granddad said, "Yvette mentioned that maybe our quest is not yet over. Come on, Yvette, what else have you got to tell us?"

And I went on to explain about Henri's discovery that the film which we had seen exposed could not have been the original one, and our belief that the old film must somehow still exit. I finished by explaining what Albert had proposed for our immediate course of action. I was interested to see that Granddad seemed to shed years at the prospect that he could now DO something. He said, "All this is fascinating, and there is no doubt that we must do everything we can. I agree with Albert. First of all we must see this Mr. Butler at the Ministry of Defence. If we all go as a party of four, it will be harder for him to be evasive. So, could you, Pierre, drive us down on Tuesday morning? I may say that fully I intend to go, and to hell with my doctor's advice about not travelling. If that's agreed, I'll phone Butler tomorrow morning, and I'll take no excuses from him."

"You're a clever chap, Granddad," I smiled, "how can we fail with Pierre, the grandson of Marie-Claire a heroine of the Resistance, and you, Grannie also a heroine and her chief aide, not to mention you, Granddad, the chap who won the war for us by getting the secrets of the V1 bombs!"

It all sounded so easy, but I did wonder if Mr. Butler really would be any more helpful to them than he had been to me. And, with that thought, I suddenly felt tired. It had been a long day, and I yawned. I saw Granddad look at me, and then shake his head as he turned to Pierre,

"Probably you haven't yet learned that Yvette is a first

cousin to a dormouse. She can be perfectly alert one minute, and fast asleep the next; in fact the only way to deal with it is to pack her off to bed while she is still conscious."

"Granddad," and I shook my head at him, "you really mustn't tell Pierre all my faults or you'll find that I am back on your hands again, because he'll make good his escape. But yes, it has been a long day, and it probably is time for us to make a move."

Pierre and Granddad seemed to agree with me, as we all stood up, but then I saw that Grannie had been oblivious to our conversation, and was deep in thought. But then she straightened up, and while there were tears on her cheeks, there was steel in her backbone and in her voice, as she said, "You heard Marie-Claire's words. In those brief moments of clarity just before her death she instructed me to kill 'le Bâtard'. Oh yes, there is no denying it. Those were her instructions and they were intended for me. I am spurred on to avenge her tragic life. The fact that there may be a chance of getting the old film is wonderful news. I just refuse to believe that we can't somehow manage to prove his identity. Then we can act!" Granddad was looking startled, "Look here, old girl…" Grannie softened, "Oh, I know the war has been over for a long time. Even if we can't actually kill him these days, we can still see justice done. Let's hope that we can make some progress at the MOD on Tuesday. But progress or not, I'll still find some way to nail him."

She paused there and looked straight at me, "Over the last few weeks, Yvette, I've tried to unload my responsibilities onto you, but that was wrong, reaching for the truth remains my duty. I can tell you that I won't let Marie-Claire down, and I don't care how much it costs either in time, money or my own hardship."

We all nodded, and made what we felt were suitable comments, but I for one really didn't pay sufficient attention to the imperative in her statement, an imperative which was to send her on the road to disaster.

The following morning, according to plan, Granddad phoned the MOD and asked to speak to Mr. Butler. There was no hint of unpleasantness. Mr Butler said that he was delighted to hear from Granddad, and that he would, with pleasure, set aside some of his time to meet with the four of us. A time at twelve noon the next day was arranged and he invited all of us to have lunch with him. Rather surprisingly he then went on to say that he had been working on the case and hoped to have news for us when we came. Granddad tried to get him to tell him more, but he laughed and said that he would keep it as a surprise.

However I wondered how pleased he was going to be when we put our cards on the table and asked him to give us access to the records of what young Lieutenant Henry Marshall had done in France in April 1944. If they showed him as being in charge of escape lines in the Troyes-Auxerre area then we were nearly home and dry.

When the call ended we discussed whether we should talk to him about the events related to our capture. Even if he were innocent, it would be natural that he would have been informed about the abduction, the ransom demand and our subsequent escape. If our suspicions were correct then he would certainly know a great deal more. We were unanimous that, if the matter came up, we should behave just as two people would who had suffered through a failed ransom attempt. If he were guilty, then he would be encouraged to believe that the charade had been a success.

That done Pierre phoned his father to tell him about the

new arrangements for the wedding, and to ask if the suggested
new date of Saturday the 5th of July was convenient. Albert
confirmed that it that was perfectly fine. He told Pierre that
the police had been in touch with him to say that they had
made progress. They had found an attendant at a petrol station on the A6 who remembered the two men in a red Mercedes. Furthermore, he had heard them talking together in
English. This confirmed our suspicion that the reason the
shorter man remained silent with us was because he didn't
speak French.

With all the telephone calls out of the way, I said to Pierre,
"Right, my lad, now you are a client of Dallachy Cultural
Tours! I'm sure those French schools of yours did not pay
sufficient attention to the Immortal Bard, so I'm taking you
off now to Stratford-Upon-Avon to repair this gap in your
education!"

Well, we did have our day in Stratford, but I'm afraid that
I was not very successful at turning Pierre into a fan of Wil-
liam Shakespeare. What I do remember, though, is a very
good bar lunch which we had in the White Swan Hotel' and
the happy smile on his face when he espied a sign pointing to
the Stratford Motor Museum.

That evening Granddad and I felt rather out of things as
Pierre tried to bring Grannie up to date with the gossip of
Chaource and its area. She found, rather to her surprise, that
there were still families there, and even schoolgirls of some
sixty years ago, who would probably remember her. Pierre said
something about hoping that she could come to Mélitour
sometime, however she just shook her head, saying she didn't
feel up to making the journey.

For once Granddad dared to argue with her, "I don't care
what you say, Hélène, I know that I can't make the journey

but I am not senile yet, and am perfectly fit enough to look after myself for a little while, so please go. Not only will Albert be glad to see you, but you can renew old friendships. It will be good for you."

Grannie smiled and said, "I'll think about it, dear." But I knew perfectly well that she would never leave him, not even in my care. Her priorities always made him very much "Number One".

Chapter Seventeen

We had quite a pleasant run down to London the next morning, with no major traffic problems, and when we got to the Ministry there was even a parking place reserved for us. I had told them all about Mr. Butler's luxurious office, and his welcome was friendly, especially to Grannie and Granddad, as he said all the right things to them about it being both a privilege and a pleasure to meet them. Then he turned to me and congratulated me on my engagement to Pierre. Finally it was Pierre's turn, and he expressed his sadness to him at the death of Marie-Claire. He concluded all these pleasantries by saying how thankful he was to learn that we had managed to escape without harm from our abductors.

It was all done with convincing sincerity, but it occurred to me that he must have been keeping a pretty close eye on our activities. So far as I knew, the abduction, our engagement and the death of Marie-Claire had not been reported in the British press. He then asked me, quite ingenuously, whether I had found anything of interest during my visit to France. I managed to answer that very easily by saying, "Why on earth do you ask that, surely you can see my handsome fiancé here, wasn't that enough?"

That gave him the opportunity of paying both of us some more compliments. Finally he beamed at me, saying that his curiosity had been arouse by my visit, and that he had now managed to find some information which might be of interest to us. "But," he went on with a smile, "you have come here just a little too early. I've arranged for you to see some new documents from Germany and they should be ready very soon. In the meantime, let's go off for lunch. I have arranged a driver to take us to the restaurant and bring us back. I'll deal with all your questions after you've seen these new papers"

What could we do but to go along with the arrangement and it was nearly half past two before we were back in his office again. It was Granddad who took up the cudgels when he said, "As you know Yvette here was at the Chateau de Mélitour last week, and she was there when Pierre's grandmother died. Now, when Yvette saw you, she mentioned the two code-names, M. Ombre and M. Brume. On her death bed, Marie-Claire identified M. Brume as the traitor who betrayed the escape line, so it really is imperative that we find who he is. I feel that it is not too much to ask that a full-scale search be instituted. The records on this man must exist somewhere in the Archives."

But Butler shook his head sadly, "Brigadier, I can tell you that I was very conscious when Yvette was here two weeks ago that I was not giving her as much help as I would have wished. So what I did was to commission a full search, just as you have now suggested, for those code names. I can assure you that although some of the code names are identified there is nothing whatsoever about Ombre or Brume. But after that disappointment I had an idea and contacted a colleague of mine in the British Embassy in Berlin, just on the off-chance that he could help. I am very glad to tell you that he phoned on Friday and told me that he had found some papers in German army archives which he felt might be of interest. Getting copies took some time, and it was only this morning that he was able to send them to me on a secure Internet line. The papers, in fact, arrived just before you came, so I haven't yet seen them myself, but they have now been translated into English and also copied. I think my secretary will be able to give them to us within just a few minutes."

Almost as he spoke, in she came, and handed him two sets, each consisting of two A4 sheets clipped together and, after just a quick glance at them, he handed one set to Grand-dad, saying, "Here you are, Brigadier, I haven't read them yet and I am looking forward to doing so. Let's hope that you find something of interest in them. I know that they deal with several operations, but I believe that there is something about the Troyes to Auxerre part of the line. One of the sheets shows a copy of the original hand-written report, and the other is the English translation."

Pierre and I sat together on adjoining chairs, and I saw my grandparents avidly reading the two sheets, and then Grand-dad carefully checking the translation of the original German, and then giving a quick nod to Grannie as he finished it. But it was soon obvious that the papers weren't of any help, as after a few minutes he handed the papers to me, saying rather sadly, "They are certainly very interesting."

I took the sheets from him and leaving out the formal German Army language, this is the relevant portion of the English translation which Pierre and I read, with the heading:

```
1944 - Early April - Operations against
French Resistance Groups.
```

The paper began by mentioning that increased German activity was now being made against French resistance Groups and some recent operations included:

```
14th. April: The successful night actions
of a Platoon who discovered a resistance
```

group planting bombs on a railway line
near Troyes.

Initially they met gun fire, from a man
whom they discovered to be a British officer. His action allowed the remaining
saboteurs to escape, but fortunately another platoon caught them soon afterwards, and they were all killed. The
British Officer was quite badly wounded
and in order to save his life, he was
sent to hospital in Cologne on 16th.
April.

17th April: Successful operation against
French resistance line in area of Auxerre
in which eleven French traitors were captured, and an old French General M. Mat-
thia was shot while resisting arrest.

18th. April: Endeavours were made in Cologne to interrogate the wounded British
officer, now identified as Lieutenant
Henry Marshall, but because of the severity of his injuries this was still not
possible and in any case his information
was no longer of any importance locally.
It was confirmed therefore to the Cologne
authorities that on his discharge he
could be sent direct from the hospital to
a POW camp in Germany.

19th. April: Successful operation against
French resistance line in the area of
Troyes in which twelve French traitors
were captured. The Leader of the group, a
M. Andre Chapelle, managed to escape, but
was arrested in Etourvy later that day
and was subsequently shot while trying to
escape.

That evening there was an unfortunate
event when the French resistance group in

the Tonnere area, aided we believe by another British Officer, managed to intercept and then to kill a Corporal and a
Private soldier who were on a security
patrol, after which they stormed the HQ
near Tonnere killing Major Hermann Kretzer and wounding his Lieutenant, which
allowed the Comtesse de Mélitour, the
leader of the resistance group in that
area, to escape.

Pierre and I looked at each other in dismay, but we didn't
get round to saying anything as Mr. Butler suddenly slapped
his hand on the desk, "I am enormously indebted to you people. I haven't seen these papers before and I wonder if you
noticed the name of the captured British soldier, Lieutenant
Henry Marshall. For me this news is something quite extraordinary. You see, after the war he entered politics where he had
a brilliant career. I sure the Brigadier and his wife will recall
that Henry Marshall was the Minister of Defence for some
years in the 1960s. But, of course, you would, Sir. You were a
serving officer at the time and I myself had just joined the
Ministry. The young couple will probably know him better as
Lord Hempson. He will be fascinated to read this. It had
never occurred to us to check whether there was any mention
of his heroism in German Army records. I'll certainly send
him a copy of this paper as am sure he will find it most interesting."

He then shook his head sadly, and turned to Pierre, "I'm
sorry, though, that it deals with your grandmother so casually,
but that, I am afraid, is war…"

It was obvious that there was nothing much more we
could do or say at our meeting and we were all bitterly disappointed. Not only had we failed to prove that the young Lord
Hempson had been our traitor; we now had proof that he

couldn't have been. The day that Marie-Claire was captured
was 19th. April. The document showed that Lieutenant Henry
Marshall, as he then was, had been sent to a hospital in Cologne three days before as a German prisoner. But still there
were two things which jarred. I could certainly excuse Mr.
Butler for being pleased at getting this paper, which dealt in
part with his friend Lord Hempson. But he wasn't just pleased
– he was delighted. Then there was his reaction when he first
read the document. I have said that he wouldn't have made a
good poker player. His surprise was too sudden. The normal
reaction would have been bewilderment yielding to astonishment as the significance of the words dawned. His behaviour
just seemed too contrived. Maybe the whole afternoon had
been another charade.

Obviously I couldn't call him a liar and couldn't think of
anything else to say. At last Grannie did ask him to try again to
see if he could identify the name of either M. Ombre or M.
Brume, but he just shook his head and said that everything
possible had already been done. It was all so very polite, but
his body language now indicated that we had out-stayed our
welcome, as he began to fidget rather awkwardly. I suspect he
realised that he wasn't behaving well and, just as we were leaving, he tried to lighten the atmosphere by sympathising with
Pierre at having got engaged to a girl who played such good
golf, and wondered how he could enjoy playing with me, and
losing the game.

But Pierre had the perfect answer when he mentioned that
in our only game, so far, we had ended all square.

Back home again we were a pretty miserable bunch as it
seemed that this time we really had come to the end of the
road. On this question, Granddad said, "I'm certain that these
German papers we saw today are genuine. Far too many peo-

ple in the MOD would have to have been involved for them to be false. So we now know that our suspect cannot be Lord Hempson, and there are no pointers to anybody else."

It was not long afterwards that Grannie got up to go to bed. This was unusually early for her but as she left the room she turned back and said, "I'm afraid, as Andrew said, that those papers must be genuine, but – and it is a very big BUT – I feel sure that Mr. Butler was hiding something. He was as nice as ninepence, but I certainly wouldn't buy a used car from him. Think about it, Yvette, I certainly shall!" She paused for a moment and said to Granddad, "Don't forget to speak to these two about tonight."

I wondered what she was talking about, but I hadn't long to wait as he looked thoughtfully at the two of us, and said, "It is going to be some two months before you two meet up again, and Hélène and I have had a talk and we wondered, Yvette, if you would mind very much if tonight Pierre squashed in beside you in your bed, as it isn't very large!"

I reckon that I had the perfect answer to that, when I said, "I think I can put up with him, and anyway I'll bet that it wasn't as narrow as that couch by the dam which you shared with Grannie!"

So we did get to sleep together that night, but I had something to tell Pierre, "I'm afraid that I have both bad news and good news to tell you. My period has started today, so we can't have any love-making, but the good news is that this means that I'm not pregnant so you won't have a bride with a bump on her tummy come July!"

We were a quiet group at breakfast next morning, and we talked trivialities, but as we were finishing Granddad said, "We seem to have reached a dead end in our quest, and I'm afraid that there is nothing more Hélène and I can do. Certainly we have no ideas now as to how we can find the identities of your abductors, and so we can't think how to trace the missing film. But for now I do mean to do one thing, I have some army friends in Germany so I'm going to ask them to get copies of those damn papers we got yesterday. I can hardly believe that they were faked by the MOD, but let's make sure."

He then turned to Pierre with a smile, and changed from French to English "Now my lad, Yvette has said that she wants to improve your English, well I'm going to teach you a Scottish phrase. Just now I said 'make sure', but a much better expression is 'mak siccar', so just remember it!"

It was afterwards when I was packing up my things that I was suddenly sad when I realised that – for the very first time – I was going to say "adieu" to Pierre, and I hated it. However we arranged our departures as a joint event, and he went off in a rather macho fashion leaving a smear of rubber on the road from his rear tyres. Obviously my departure in the Fiesta was not so dramatic, and that added fuel to the fire of my indignation against Pierre, which had just arisen in the last few minutes. You see, just before he left, he had dared to belittle my Fiesta when he looked at it rather contemptuously, saying, "But surely you can't think of driving all the way to St. Andrew's in a day in that little thing? Damn it, it must be nearly six hundred kilometres!"

And he hadn't been best pleased by my indignant defence of my prized possession. One's first car is always very special, and I wondered just what staid, and larger, French model he would consider suitable for my use at Mélitour. So I was still not too happy with life when I ran straight into the morning rush-hour traffic as I skirted Birmingham. But this gave me time to get round to thinking some more pleasant thoughts, and how much I had enjoyed being in bed with Pierre, even although we couldn't make love.

What we had done was to lie naked in each others' arms and be blissfully happy with our nearness. Also there seemed to be no barriers whatsoever as we whispered our most intimate thoughts to each other, and I knew that I was extremely blessed at having found such a wonderful man as my lifetime mate. I remembered a phrase in a love story which I had read: "they were meant for each other" and I was sure that Pierre was meant for me.

There must have been a good fairy watching over me, because as soon as my thoughts became happy ones, the traffic miraculously cleared and I found myself on the M6, leaving Birmingham behind me. So, despite Pierre's fears, I was in St. Andrew's in time for afternoon tea with my friends in Macintosh Hall, a student residence in the town, just the distance of a nice 6 iron shot to the First Tee of the Old Course.

I had driven up wearing thin gloves, so it was only when I joined my friends in the common room that they could see my wonderful ring. It was the real one as I felt I'd wear it for the first few days. It certainly produced a myriad of questions about what had happened to me and about my love-life, both of which I could answer by saying that I had found the most wonderful man in the whole world.

Just one of my friends was rather nasty to me when she said, "Fancy you, Yvette, marrying into the aristocracy, I didn't think you were a social climber!"

I've mentioned earlier my rather nice but snobby Professor, and I still wore my real ring when I went to see him and to apologise for my late return. As we talked I noticed that his eyes kept on flickering back to it, and I knew that he would love to have known what it was worth.

But that's enough about my university life which has nothing to do with my adventure, suffice to say that for the next two and a half months I really did work very hard. I would hate to have made a fool of myself at my Finals.

Chapter Eighteen

So April went by, then May, during which I for one seemed to forget the quest, especially after Granddad was able to check the German records and to find them just as we had seen. Then, far too soon, it was early June and time for the final examinations. I really cannot remember much of those weeks when I tried to write down what little I could dredge up from my poor memory. Oddly enough the only thing I do remember is how I always had to dash off for a last minute pee before going into the examination hall.

But if my memory has drawn a veil over much of that time I well remember the day when I looked anxiously at the Lists and saw:

    Miss Yvette Duclos Dallachy: Master of
    Arts

I also remember a few days later, when one Monday morning I drove over to Edinburgh to pick up Pierre from the airport. It was a beautiful day, and Scotland was going to look its best for him. I had missed him so much, and it was bliss to be held in his arms again. Unfortunately, though, I felt rather less loving as we drove the few miles out of the airport and over the Forth Bridge. I couldn't help noticing that he was driving every yard, or metre, of journey along with me, pushing his foot hard down when I braked, and looking around apprehensively all the time. So I pulled into a lay-by and said to him, "My sweet, if we are going to have a happy marriage you really must learn, and come to believe, that I am not a maniac when I get behind the wheel of a car. I am probably just as good a driver as you are…so there! Now, will you please relax and enjoy the run. For your information, we're now in the Kingdom of Fife and it is worth looking at."

Trust Pierre to come up with a tactful reply. "But Yvette, I have every confidence in your driving, it is only because, from my point of view, you are driving on the wrong side of the road!"

"Good try, darling," I smiled, "you almost convinced me. Anyway, can I please drive on now without you trying to push a hole in the floor every time I have to brake?"

Our journey wasn't in fact very long as we didn't have to go as far as St. Andrew's. I had felt oddly embarrassed at the thought of sharing a room – and a bed – with Pierre in the town which I knew so well, so I'd booked us in at the Lethan Grange Hotel near Cupar, a pleasant country hotel where I was sure that the food would satisfy even Pierre's fastidious palate. The next days were magical; we spent many of our waking hours in mortal combat on the wonderful golf courses, the Old, The New and even the Jubilee, plus some of the new ones, and then spent the night in each other's arms. On our last night I'd arranged a dinner party in Russack's Hotel for ten of my university friends. We enjoyed a very convivial evening with them. There had been considerable curiosity about my French fiancé, but I could see that they all thought that I'd done very well for myself.

On occasions like this there is, inevitably, a lot of talk about keeping in touch and meeting up again, and Pierre surprised me with the warmth of his invitations to visit us as at Mélitour. He also surprised me by the fluency of his English which had much improved since April. When he saw me look-ing puzzled he whispered, "Don't worry, darling, I haven't been having pillow talk with any beautiful visiting British girls. I was so ashamed about my bad English that I've been having lessons from the English teacher of our local school."

He stopped there and laughed, "But I have made a deci-sion that we'll always speak English when we are in bed to-gether, and as I intend to spend a great deal of my life there, I'm sure that you'll soon have no cause for complaint at my linguistic failings."

Then came the morning when it was time for me to head back to Henley to help with the preparations for our wedding. On my way I could deviate to Edinburgh and drop Pierre off at the airport to fly back to France. He and his family were coming together on the day before the wedding, and Albert, Marie and Henri planned to stay on for a couple of days after it, just to get to know Grannie and Granddad.

Looking back on the events of the next few months is rather like seeing one of those black and white films where everything goes too fast. Our wedding went off very well, at least we enjoyed it, and Granddad had arranged things with the local vicar who was broad-minded enough to marry two people who had strayed from the fold. The ceremony was at eleven o'clock, and by three the lunch and speeches were over and it was time for Pierre and me to experience a very tradi-tional and enthusiastic send off. Had our honeymoon hotel any doubts about our status, these would certainly have been dispelled by the continuing appearance of rice and confetti from our cases and our clothes.

I suppose that all honeymoons are special but ours, I am quite sure, was the very best. A hired car took us to Birming-ham airport and by late that evening we were arriving at Reid's

Hotel in Madeira. I'll never forget those warm nights of love followed by elegant breakfasts on our balcony, served with exotic locally grown fruits such as mangoes and papayas. After that, a lazy morning in the sunshine beside one or other of the pools, then maybe a swim followed by a walk in the shady garden as a change from the sun. By midday we were ready for a little lunch and a siesta…but perhaps that was usually not the right word in our case. We had been warned that formal dress was preferred in the dining room, and we were old fashioned enough to like dressing up. It was magical to sit down for dinner – sometimes out on the terrace – and look at my handsome husband, immaculate in a white dinner jacket with a flower in his button-hole.

But honeymoons can't last forever and three weeks later we were back in Mélitour, which had seen considerable changes since I'd been there in April. Pierre had said nothing about them as he wanted to produce a surprise for me. Marie-Claire's suite of rooms had, of course, been closed, but Albert had turned another wing of the chateau, including a part of the old servants' quarters, into a self-contained house. This left Pierre and me with the principal part of the chateau to ourselves. I think Albert saw my doubts about the new arrangement, and said, "Yvette, my dear, that is what I want. I'm nearly seventy now and although I hope to see a lot of you, I do want privacy whenever I feel I need it, and I certainly shall not miss the old house. Fact is that I've been rattling around in it for far too long, and I'm tired of it. Anyway it is time for you to hurry up and get some kids to help fill it!"

That was at the beginning of August, and just over a month later I could tell him that if all went well he'd be a grandfather by next May.

September and October were very busy months for those

concerned with making wine. For about six weeks Pierre spent most days down in Chablis while the grapes were picked, then crushed and put into fermenting vats. It had been an above average harvest, the grapes had ripened to just the right degree, and all the signs were that this year's *Chablis Grand Cru de Mélitour* would be an excellent vintage.

It was on the first Saturday in November when Pierre and I, for the first time in many weeks, were enjoying a leisurely and late breakfast, when the phone rang. I answered it and as soon as I heard Grannie's voice I knew that it was bad news. She told me that Granddad had been more tired than usual the previous evening and had gone to bed early. He had awakened in the middle of the night and said that he was fine but would like a hot drink. She had gone downstairs to make some tea, but when she got back with it he was dead. It was as quick and easy as that.

She was quite adamant that we should not come immediately. "There is no need for that. I'd like to make all the arrangements for the funeral myself, and it will be next Thursday afternoon. So if you come on the day before that it will be early enough."

We did as we were told, and Pierre and Albert flew with me to Heathrow on Wednesday morning and we hired a car there. When we got to Henley I could see that Grannie had come to terms with Granddad's death, and I was sure that she had been right not to ask us to come any earlier. She had been kept busy making all the arrangements, and this had been the best therapy.

The funeral, however, has no part in this narrative, but what happened after it certainly does. The service was at two o'clock, after which the mourners were invited to a little function in a village hotel, and I was glad that Grannie had booked the ball room as there were an astonishingly large number of people. I hadn't before realised just how famous he was. But I could be very proud of him, and was glad that Albert and Pierre were also there to see it. I was also glad to see that the mourners were a good-mannered lot and didn't stay long, so we were back at the house before four o'clock, accompanied by John Carson, our family lawyer, whom I had known all my life.

When we were all settled, Grannie surprised me when she looked across at Albert and Pierre, and said, "Yvette well knows my habit of leaving serious discussions until after dinner, but today we have a lot to talk about. I'd like to start now in regard to my future plans, and we can finish things off after we've eaten."

But she had to stop there, as Albert interrupted her, "Hélène, before you talk about your plans, can I tell you what we – all of us Yvette, Pierre and I – suggest? Mélitour is a large house. As you know I have taken myself off to the west wing, and Marie-Claire's old apartments are closed off and empty, but they could easily be converted into a pleasant little house for you. So why not sell up here and come to live with us, and put your roots down in France again? We would be very happy if you would come, and remember too that, by next May, you'll have a great-grandchild to look after."

She looked round at us, and I could see her blinking away her tears, "That is a wonderful offer, Albert, and if I could only accept it my life would be very much easier than it is going to be. I can't tell you how very happy I would be to take up your offer, it would be a delightful privilege to live near you young people, and to have great-grandchildren to play with would be a wonderful bonus…"

She suddenly stopped there, and a shadow came over her

face, "But, unfortunately, I can't make the move for some time, and by then I'll probably be so notorious that you won't want me to come!"

We all broke in with an assortment of "whys" and "what do you means" But she didn't answer our questions, saying quietly, "Just wait. First of all I would like John to read Andrew's will, and do please remember that its terms are exactly as he and I very recently decided they should be. So just listen."

John Carson zipped open his brief case and produced just a single sheet of stiff white paper. "This," he said, "is the last will and testament of my friend Andrew Dallachy, and it was drawn up just six weeks ago. As you can see it is short and if you allow me I'll explain it in simple language…agreed?"

He sat up in his chair and, as he spoke, he numbered off the items on his fingers:

"First: Let me say that Andrew was not a rich man, but he was comfortably off with a generous army pension of which two thirds will continue to be paid to Hélène.

"Second: His principal asset is a half share in this house which is worth about a quarter of a million pounds, so his half share will be worth about a hundred and twenty five thousand pounds. That, Yvette, he has passed to you free of estate duty."

I was about to break in, but Grannie held up her hand, "Be quiet, Yvette, we can talk at the end."

He went on, "Third: Andrew held shares and several other items which amount in value to a total of approximately a hundred thousand pounds. These also are passed to you, Yvette. I think that the sum of these items will be just under the estate duty limit, so there will probably be no duty to pay."

He stopped abruptly there and said to me, "Perhaps,

Yvette, you could come round to my office before going back to France; there are a few papers which you will need to sign."

But I was having none of this, and turned to Grannie, "Just wait a minute, this is absurd, why should Granddad cut you out of his will and leave everything to me. I can't take it!"

"Oh yes you can," she smiled, "you see there is a very good reason for it as within a few months I am almost certainly going to be declared bankrupt, and so the less I have to pass to my creditors the better!"

That certainly woke up Albert, "Hélène, I don't know what sort of trouble you are in, but I can certainly look after things for you. Money will be no problem as I've got lots of it doing nothing."

"Albert, my dear boy, that is very sweet of you, but right now I am in no sort of trouble whatsoever! Quite soon, however, I am going to dig a great big financial black hole and jump straight into it."

I didn't know whether to laugh or cry as I turned to her, "Grannie, stop it at once! This is your old technique, so don't tease us, what on earth are you up to?"

"All right, Yvette, but you do know how much I like my fun, and what I am now going to tell you is very serious. You see, I absolutely refuse to let Lord Hempson off the hook. I do know that the German papers appear to show him as being in the clear, but I distrust them. This is despite the fact that a few months ago Andrew got one of his army friends to check them and he found that, indeed, there they were in the German archives. However I am not convinced. Think of all the other arrows which do point in his direction."

It was then her turn to number off the items:

"First: Andrew and I saw the traitor clearly in that terrible room where Marie-Claire and Albert were being held captive.

Contemporary photographs of Lieutenant Marshall convince us that he was that man.

"Second: When he escaped by diving out of the window, I'm pretty sure that we then shot him in the shoulder. Lieutenant Marshall is reported to have been wounded there too.

"Third: We know that there was a British Officer involved in our section of the Escape Line and his code name was Brume. There must have been record kept of his activities in the MOD archives. The relevant papers would seem to have disappeared in 1964. This was when Henry Marshall, now Lord Hempson, was the Minister of Defence.

"Fourth: This is something which only occurred to Andrew and me recently. What we remembered was that when we went into the torture chamber, Kretzer was taunting Marie-Claire, by saying something like, 'That precious pill of yours wasn't much good, was it? It was changed to a useless one!' You'll recall, Yvette, I told you that M. Brume had promised to give her a cyanide capsule. So why didn't it work? The conclusion is obvious. M. Brume had turned traitor before he handed over the capsule – a harmless one.

"Fifth: Marie-Claire confirmed that M. Brume was the traitor shortly before her death. She also confirmed, what she said in her letter, that the buried film which you retrieved contained the proof of M. Brumes guilt and identity.

"Sixth: That film was deliberately destroyed. The business of your abduction was a professionally executed plan to avert your suspicions of deliberate intent. Who would want to do this and why? Apart from us only Mr. Butler at the MOD knew where you were going and what you were going to try to do. Thus the plan to destroy the film originated from with the MOD. This does not directly implicate Lord Hempson, but if he were the traitor, then this is exactly the sort of cover-up operation that you would expect.

"There is still, of course, the tantalising possibility that the film may yet exist. It seems likely that your two captors went against their instructions and decided to keep the film for their own purpose, whatever that might be. But for me these six points of mine are sufficient. Lord Hempson is damned in my eyes."

She stopped there and turned to me, "Please make yourself useful dear; I need a drink. In fact is I'm sure we all do, and we still have plenty of time before dinner."

"Grannie," I said, "your technique is as exasperating as always. I'll bet that we are now coming to the point, and you are teasing us by making us wait! However I'll get the drinks, but please don't keep us waiting any longer!"

None of us could think of anything else to say while I got the drinks, but when she had a full glass in her hands she began to talk very briskly, "I can tell you that in recent months Andrew and I spent a lot of time talking about the affair, and it was good that he had this puzzle to think about. You see, shortly after your wedding our doctor told us that Andrew had only a few months to live, and it was unlikely that he would see the year out. I may say that he insisted that you, Yvette, were not to be told as he said that nothing should spoil these early days of your marriage. It was then in these sad final days that we hatched a plan. It was a plan which I only could initiate. Your grandfather had to die first if we were to protect your inheritance.

"You see, what I intend to do is to challenge Lord Hempson. The unfortunate thing for me is I doubt that my charges will stick. The cover-up operation has been far too thorough. However, in order to clear his name, he will have to sue me for libel. I shall defend myself as best I can, but in all likelihood I shall fail. The damages he will be awarded will be far in excess of anything I'll be able to pay, so I shall have to declare myself bankrupt. John tells me, though, that my pension will probably not be affected, so I shall still have something to live on. And, of course, Yvette, your inheritance would be out of reach. The important thing for me is that my charges will have been heard. For some people at least the thought may remain – could they be true?

"Unfortunately, though, I am already beginning to pay a price, because since Andrew and I thought about it we have been in touch with my old friends in Paris, Michelle and Alicia, and we have had a falling out. They are concerned lest people think that they are involved in some way – and want nothing more to do with me – so we are no longer even on speaking terms. It is a great pity…but I can't help it."

She got up and went over to her desk, then came back with a clip of papers. "See, here are some copies of a draft letter which Andrew and I had great fun writing. As you see I intend sending it to the editors of all the national papers, and also to all Members of Parliament and the House of Lords. I reckon that should give it quite a fair bit of publicity, shouldn't it!"

And she sat back in her chair with a happy smile, like a cat that has swallowed the cream. "You will see," she went on, "that I have kept it simple. I have just put forward my accusation and nothing else. I don't want to show my whole hand now, so we can keep all these pointers I have mentioned until the case comes to court. I certainly don't want to give them the opportunity to blunt my attack. So go on and read it." And this is what we read:

Gairloch
Henley in Arden
West Midlands

Address list:
Editors of National Newspapers
Members of Parliament
Members of the House of Lords

J'ACCUSE!

I, Hélène Dallachy (nee Hélène Duclos), the widow
of Brigadier Andrew Dallachy DSO, do hereby accuse
Lord Hempson - Lieutenant Henry Marshall as he was in
1944 - of treachery whereas in April of that year he
collaborated with the German authorities in France,
in the Department of Yonne.

Because of his treachery an important escape line
for Allied Servicemen was penetrated and many brave
French citizens were captured, tortured or killed.
One of his victims was a twenty-eight year old
female, Marie-Claire, Comtesse de Mélitour. She was
the Section Head of a portion of the escape line. On
the night of the 19th of April 1944 she was captured
and taken with her seven-year-old son to a house used
by the German military. There she and her son were
tortured by a German officer, Major Kretzer, in the
presence of Lieutenant Marshall. The house was
attacked by a French resistance group lead by a
British officer and the Comtesse and her son were
rescued. Unfortunately, the Comtesse had been
severely brain-damaged and spent the remainder of her
life in a child-like state. She died only a few
months ago. The young boy lived and is now Albert,
Comte de Mélitour.

I know this to be true because my husband, then
Major Dallachy, was the British officer leading that
French resistance group, and I was one of its
members. We witnessed the torture in progress. My
husband shot and killed Major Kretzer. Lieutenant
Marshall managed to escape through a window, but not

before we managed to shoot and wound him in the
shoulder.
    Although the Comtesse subsequently lived in a
twilight world, she had moments of lucidity. Shortly
before she died, she was able to confirm the facts of
my accusation before witnesses. It is only now, after
her death, that the Comte de Mélitour and his family
both allow, and welcome, the fact that I make this
accusation.

I am,
Yours faithfully
Hélène Dallachy

I read Grannie's letter with increasing dismay. She was
over eighty, and here she was taking on a pillar of the establishment, and with no real evidence to prove his guilt. To say
that she would be notorious would certainly be an under-
statement. Lord Hempson would obviously have no option
but to sue. But before that she would be besieged by the media and her life would be made a torment. I looked over at
Pierre and Albert, and I could easily read their similar consternation.
    "Grannie," I said, "you really must not do this. We all
know how deeply you feel, but it all happened so long ago.
You said that you were jumping into a black hole, but you
won't be, you'll be centre stage in a blaze of media attention. I
care far too much for you to see you ruining your life in this
way. So please, please, forget it, pack up here and now, and
come to live with us at Mélitour. I know very well that the past
is painful, and even though you can never forgive, I beg you to
put the past to rest"
    I saw her shake her head, but before she could speak Al-
bert said, "Hélène my dear, I agree with everything that Yvette

has said. Even though you cannot agree with us now, why not give yourself a little more time? With your dear husband now dead you are about to start a new life, and we all hope that you will be happy living with us...living at Mélitour. It will take you a little time to get packed up here, and I'm sure that Yvette will be glad to help you. For my part I'll get the necessary work at Mélitour put in hand right away.

"Let's make a pact. You do what has to be done here, and I'll get your little home ready for you. I'll make sure that we'll all be organised before Christmas. You will have the time for a quiet think over things. I hope that you may change your mind, but whatever you decide, that decision will still be yours."

But she shook her head as she spoke sadly to Albert, "I'm very sorry, but I can't say yes. I can see that you all think that I may be mad; certainly John does His tidy legal mind can't make any sense out of it. But, as for what will happen to me, I can easily see that the media could make my life a misery. With John's help it shouldn't be too bad. Wait a bit; I want to show you something."

She stopped there, and there was a rather guilty smile on her face, one that I knew well, when she was going to do or say something rather naughty. She was away for about five minutes and, when she came back, I didn't know whether to laugh or cry. She was almost unrecognisable. To describe her appearance from top to toe, she was wearing a blonde wig which contrived to look unwashed and which hid her shining white hair; she who never wore mascara now wore it to excess; her normal peachy lipstick had been replaced by a vermillion one; and her simple below the knee grey dress had changed to one which could only be called a tart's dress — flaming orange and above the knee.

I think for a little while we were too astonished to say any-thing, and she laughed and said, "Bit of a change, isn't it! You see, Hélène Dallachy is going to disappear. In the last few days I've rented a little house in Grassmere, up in the Lakes, in the name of Amelia Ballantyne. With the background I've in-vented for her I can play her very well.

"She also is going to be French and the widow of a Scotsman. I needn't depart too far from the truth; how else would I explain my accent. For a while she has lived in the Highlands, near Gairloch, which I know well. As you know I dabble in water colours and my cover story is that over the winter I've decided to paint the lakes and hills. I hope these ridiculous clothes will fit the part of an eccentric elderly artist.

"I intend to move into my new identity about two weeks before the letters go out. Who will associate the notorious Hélène Dallachy with a batty old bird who paints insipid water colours? Obviously, once I have disappeared, I cannot have any direct influence on the course of events. John here has agreed to act on my behalf, which I think is rather splendid of him, don't you?"

She then turned to me, "Now, I'm not going to have din-ner dressed like this, so while I change, you can freshen up the drinks and do what has to be done in the kitchen."

Chapter Nineteen

It was a beautiful evening, and it was like old times as we assembled after dinner and settled ourselves round a large fire. Only this time it wasn't Grannie telling me a fascinating story, instead she was horrifying us with her mad scheme to disgrace Lord Hempson. She began by speaking about the details of her plans, saying, "John is the real hero, apart from sending out the letters, he has promised to field all the media wolves. No doubt, in due course, he will have deal with the legal procedures when Hempson sues. You see, I plan to hide away and not to surface until just before the case comes to court. I may say that John tells me that, because of the serious nature of my accusations, it is likely to be heard quickly."

None of us quite knew what to say except Albert. That facet of his character which made him a successful business man recognised that she had made up her mind, so he didn't waste any more time in useless argument. He just accepted her scheme as a fait accompli, and tried to make the best of it. "Maybe you are a bit mad, Hélène," he smiled, "but I am sure that I know the reason, and can sympathise. It was these last words of my Mother, wasn't it? Well, I can't say that I look forward to the next few months. We in Mélitour are sure to get involved with the media. I accept that you had to mention my name in your letter. There is also the family tie-up with Yvette now married to the grandson of Marie-Claire. So, what are your plans for us?"

She shook her head sadly, "I'm sorry, but I haven't given much thought as yet to that, and I'm sorry to drag the affair to your door. I would suggest, however, that you stick to very simple lines, for example:

"We haven't seen Mrs. Dallachy since the funeral of her husband," or "No, we do not know her address," or "We are, of course, aware of her opinion regarding Lord Hempson, but because of the possibility of legal proceedings it would be inappropriate for us to comment further."

All of the above would be true; we would not see her; we would not know her address, and all our letters would be sent to John Carson who would forward them to her. Only in case of an emergency would he tell us how to contact her directly. I think that Albert and Pierre were upset at her keeping her address to herself, but I knew well why she had done so. Dear old Granddad had been taught how to keep secrets during his time in the SAS, and he had often said to me, "Just remember, Yvette, that a secret shared is no longer a secret!"

Soon after that Albert turned to John Carson, and asked the 64,000 dollar question, "What do you think will be the outcome of the case?"

"I wish," he said, "that I could give you any hope whatsoever of a favourable outcome. I have to tell you that when – it would be absurd to say if – Lord Hempson sues, he will win the case. I can't put a figure on the damages, juries and the courts are so unpredictable, but certainly they will be enormous. You can also bet that he will employ the best legal team. These people won't come cheaply either, and costs will be awarded against her. The thing that kills our case is these damn German army records. We've tested them, and they are certainly genuine. I confess that, despite what Hélène hopes, he really is in the clear." He paused for a moment, "But there it is, she won't change her mind, so all I can do is to make things as easy for her as I possibly can."

I thought that would be the end of the matter, but then Albert produced the most sensible proposal of the evening. "Look, Hélène, I have had an idea, and I think that you will find my suggestion useful. Before issuing your letter, why not write to Lord Hempson?"

"Write to him!" she exploded, "What I would like to say to him is far too crude to be written down."

"But just wait a minute," he said, "I propose that you write a very simple and correct letter. You see, it may be interesting, and helpful to us, to see how he replies. Give me a few minutes and I'll jot down my suggestions as to what you should say." And this is what he wrote:

> Gairloch
> Henley-in-Arden
> West Midlands
> 9th. November

Dear Lord Hempson,

I am taking the liberty of writing to you as I have recently learned that you served in France during April of 1944.

You may have been aware of, or involved in, the escape line for Allied servicemen which existed at that time. I am particularly interested in the section of the line from Troyes to Auxerre. That area was headed by Marie-Claire, Comtesse de Mélitour and I had the privilege of being her chief assistant.

She died this year after a lifetime of illness following torture by the Germans.

What has led me to write is that my granddaughter, Yvette Dallachy, has recently become engaged to Marie-Claire's grandson. We are, as a matter of family history, trying to record what we can about her remarkable career in the resistance, and its tragic end.

With the help of Mr Butler in the Ministry of Defence, whom you may know, we have consulted the archives there. Unfortunately the records were not very helpful. Apparently the original papers were lost some time in the 1960's when you were the Minister. They did show, however, that during the war you were active just to the north of where we were. It seems quite possible that you may have met Marie-Claire or knew something of her work. Any information you have about her be most welcome.

I realise, of course, that I am asking you to dredge up memories of nearly sixty years ago, but it would be wonderful if you could help me.
Yours sincerely,
Hélène Dallachy

I needn't go into all the discussions regarding the letter, but I for one kept out of it. I really couldn't see how it would help, unless as a ploy to delay Grannie and give her more time to think. Anyway, in the end Albert got his way and she reluctantly agreed to send the letter, and do nothing further until she got a reply.

Our plans had always been that I would stay on for some days to help Grannie by way of sorting things out in the house and getting rid of Granddad's clothes and the various things which she didn't want to keep. Pierre and his father had to get off home as it was a busy time for them, although in quite different ways. Pierre had to supervise the progress of the fermentation period of the new wine, and also to start bottling the previous year's wine, which so far had been resting quietly in barrels. By this time I had learned that there is never a month when a vintner can rest. Albert's programme involved the last stage of preparations for the Christmas season in the store, and December produced no less than a fifth of the year's sales.

Grannie duly posted her letter on the morning which saw Pierre and Albert heading off back to Mélitour. As soon as we had waved them off, Grannie said to me, "Now Yvette, as I am sure you can see, I am finding it very hard to get used to the idea that Andrew is no longer by my side. Also, I am sure that already you are missing Pierre; so let's keep ourselves busy. There is a lot to do in getting this house cleared up, as I'll be away for some months. It's Friday, let's see if we can get everything done by Monday." ·

Well, in the event we did better, and by Sunday evening everything was finished. We had a mountain of stuff to dispose which we managed to get neatly packed away in the tea chests, labelled either to Oxfam or to our local church. For the next couple of days we did nothing at all – that is no work at all. I could see Grannie was tired and I managed to get her to rest and also to leave the cooking and housework to me. But on the Wednesday morning I slept late and Grannie had already finished breakfast before I got down. She was, however, still drinking coffee, and there was an opened envelope beside her plate.

"Yvette," she said, "This is Hempson's reply." And here is what I read:

                                        Hempson Grange
                                        By Kenilworth
                                        West Midlands
                                        14th. November
My dear Mrs. Dallachy,
    I was most interested to receive your letter, and
let me first say how sorry I was to hear of the

recent death of your husband, Brigadier Dallachy. His
bravery and remarkable success in obtaining the
secrets of the V1 Flying Bombs are known to me. The
country owes him a continuing debt of gratitude.

You mention the name Marie-Claire, Comtesse de
Mélitour. I am afraid that I never had the privilege
of meeting her, although her name was mentioned to me
as one of the principals in the escape lines south of
Troyes.

At the time when I came to France, late in March
1944, the top priority had become working with the
resistance, prior to the invasion, by way of
disrupting road and rail communications. That was my
job. I was responsible for giving advice and working
with the French regarding suitable targets, and also
for arranging air-drops of arms and explosives. I was
in the area north of Troyes only for a short time.
Important as the escape lines were, I was not
involved with them at all.

There was however an active Resistance unit in
that area with whom I worked closely, and on the
night of the 14th of April, things went sadly wrong.
We were trying to blow up a railway bridge when we
were surprised by a platoon of German soldiers. It
was quite a fight, and although my men did manage to
get away in the first instance, they were soon
afterwards caught in a second gun fight and all of
them were killed. As for me I was severely wounded
while still at the bridge. I was lucky enough to be
well treated by the Germans and I was transferred to
a hospital in Cologne some thirty-six hours later.

You mentioned in your letter that you are writing
a family history, including Marie-Claire's tragic
life, and I would be most interested if you could let
me have a copy to put with my own papers.

I may say that I found yesterday that you are
going about things in the right way, and making a

thorough job of it. You mentioned in your letter that
you had been in touch with the Ministry of Defence,
and I phoned them yesterday to check on my own dates.
The man I spoke to was Mr. James Butler. You were
correct; I do know him, and he is, in fact, an old
friend of mine.

It is unfortunate that some of the records
regarding your activities in France have gone astray,
but I can assure you that every effort was made to
trace them, without success.

It was tragic that the escape line you were
involved in was penetrated and destroyed. I am sure
that you often wonder who it was that betrayed it. I
can tell you that I too have had these personal
concerns. In my case it was surprisingly opportune
when that German platoon caught us at the bridge just
as we were laying the explosive charges. Had someone
told them that we were going to be there?

But I am afraid that neither of us will ever know.
It all happened so long ago, and there aren't many of
us now who remember those days.

Again, let me express my thanks for your letter. A
reminder of those old times is bitter-sweet, but I
hope that for you they may be more sweet than bitter.
Yours very sincerely,
Hempson

My first reaction was "what a nice letter", but then I began
to have second thoughts, and I could see that Grannie had no
illusions. "He's clever, isn't he? On the surface it seems just a
pleasant reply to my letter, and politely says that he can't help
me. But, looking at it from my point of view, from the belief
that he is guilty, it reads quite different. He begins by explaining that he had nothing to do with the escape lines, so it is no
use my asking him about them. Then he establishes his alibi

about being wounded on the 14th of April and being carted off to a German hospital. Next he tries to explain away the failings of the Ministry. Finally, to allay any suspicions I may have about the betrayal of the escape line being something special, he speculates about his own resistance group also having been betrayed. This is a very well thought-out reply by an astute politician."

I confess that I was torn two ways; I could wish with all my heart that she would succeed, but how could she? So, obviously I should have one last try to get her to change her mind, but I soon realized that I was wasting my time, and the only thing I could do was to shut up and just try to help her. We went round to John Carson's office that afternoon, and when we went in he looked ruefully at her, "I'm very sorry Hélène that despite all our advice you are still going on with your scheme, but I did promise you that I would help, and so I shall."

Soon we got down to details, and I found that his help was going to be invaluable. John had already done the ground work and had compiled a mailing list of the people Grannie wanted to reach. "That's nearly a thousand names and address, Hélène. It wasn't as difficult as you might think. Businessmen could have been trickier, but politicians seem especially eager to make their contact details public." Grannie was keen to make the letter look as personal as possible, and fortunately John had a friend in the mail-order business. With his fancy computer all that was needed was to enter the mailing list, and it would produce the letters duly addressed and with the appropriate "Dear so and so," plus an addressed envelope. John told her that the machine could even replicate her signature in blue ink. Grannie wasn't having any of that, "I fully intend to sign each and every one of them myself."

We left him to get on with the arrangements, and he promised to get back in a couple of days. So there it was, the explosives were being prepared, and soon the fuse would be ready to light. I stayed on with Grannie helping her to get the house ready for it being left empty for the winter. Grannie asked me to drive to a post office that was twenty miles away and buy the First Class stamps. I rather thought that she was beginning to enjoy the clandestine parts of this exercise. Two days after our meeting, John came round with letters and envelopes. We did a combined operation on them – she signing and me putting them into the envelopes and affixing the stamps. It made quite a pile and it took us most of the day to finish the job.

Her plan was to depart immediately for her Lakeland hideaway. She had agreed with John that she would post the letters in five days time. "I'll drive down to some busy Post Office in Birmingham where nobody will remember me. And then," she said with a gleeful smile, "I'll sit back and wait for the fireworks!"

So we left Henley on the same day – she for the Lakes, and me for Mélitour – and all I could do was to give her a tight hug and remind her that, if ever she wanted a bolt-hole, Mélitour was ready and waiting. And, back home, that was what we had to do – wait.

Normally only a few British papers come to Tonnere. Pierre had surprised our local newsagent by ordering a copy of every national paper for the next week. Well the day came, and Grannie certainly couldn't complain about the extent of the Press coverage. It was front page news in every paper from the tabloids to the "heavies". It was obvious, though, that every editor had the same problem; how to deal with accusation? Here was an elderly lady accusing one of Britain's most senior politicians of treachery. It was a particularly dreadful condemnation considering his long association with the Ministry of Defence; and doubly so because his son, the Right Honourable Michael Marshall, had followed him as Secretary of State for Defence.

The newspapers had to write their stories quickly, but the TV news people had more time. We could now, thanks to modern technology, get British programmes, and the BBC had managed to get an interview with the young Minister. As we watched it I realized that he had been well-trained in TV skills, and his technique was superb. He began by saying how sad it was for an old lady to make such a fool of herself, particularly since she herself had been something of a war heroine and had married the late Brigadier Dallachy, a man who had done probably more than anybody else to blunt the potentially fatal V1 attacks. He then went on to say, "My father and I are naturally most distressed by this ridiculous allegation, but we wish her no ill. We know that she has recently lost her husband after nearly sixty happy years of marriage, and so it is a difficult time for her. We can only hope that her family can find ways to alleviate the mental stress which has caused her to issue such an absurd document."

The reporter was obviously not too happy about such a bland denial of everything, so he said, "But Minister, I must put this question to you…is there absolute proof that the allegation is false?"

Marshall's expression of surprise was beautifully done. "Oh, I'm sorry; I thought by this time that you would have heard. It has now been shown, beyond any possible doubt, that the allegation is false – not just unlikely – but quite impossible."

"And what evidence is there, Minister, to show this?"

"Just a moment," and he made a great show of fumbling in his pockets, as if unsure what he was looking for. "Ah yes, here we are, I wondered if I might have left them in my office. These are papers which I have obtained from the archives of the Ministry of Defence, and they are authentic copies of original German army records which cover actions against the French resistance during the period of April 1944. Copies of these are now being made available and as you will see they begin with the actions on the night of the 14th of April 1944 when the Germans surprised a resistance group who were laying explosives on a railway bridge near Troyes, about fifty miles south of Reims. All this will I am sure soon be reported in the papers, but briefly, they relate how the British officer in charge of the Group fought a desperate action in a brave, but sadly vain, attempt to save the Frenchmen, and was severely wounded in the engagement...And who was he?...He was none other than my father, Lieutenant Marshall as he was then. Far from being a traitor, he was a hero, which makes the present nonsense all the more painful."

But the interviewer had done his homework. "I'm sorry, Minister, but I don't quite follow you. This engagement was on the 14th of April, but Mrs. Dallachy's allegation is centred on an event that took place on 19th April, so...?"

But he was interrupted, "Just let me finish, these German records go on to praise my father's bravery, and then tell us that because of the severity of his wounds he was sent to a hospital in Cologne on the 16th of April. So Mrs. Dallachy's assertion that he was involved with an action with the Germans on the 19th of April is plain nonsense. This is, of course, the only specific allegation which she makes, and it is all the delusions of a confused old lady."

He paused for a moment, but then went on before the interviewer could speak, "I may say it gives neither my father nor me any pleasure to see her making such a fool of herself."

"And will your father, Lord Hempson, raise an action for libel?"

"He can, of course, do so, but it would be with reluctance. He could not fail to win the case and the damages and costs which Mrs. Dallachy would face would be horrendous. Despite her actions, we would certainly take no pleasure in seeing an old lady ruined. Her only course now is to come to her senses, and to apologise. My father too is old, and I am sure that he would agree to let bygones be bygones, subject of course to his receiving a full apology."

As I have said, it was all superbly done, and I confess that I really was convinced, and hoped that Grannie would see reason. But, oddly enough, Pierre had his doubts, just based on it having been such a bravura performance. "He was clever, but indeed too clever for my book. Just remember that he must also have given interviews to SKY and ITV before this one, and I'll bet that he also went through the same palaver of hunting in his pockets for the papers. A likely tale isn't it?"

So there we left it, but I felt that I had to phone Alicia and Michelle in Paris, and my conversations with them were not pleasant. Both of them had seen references in French papers to the case, and they were displeased at the prospect of journalists tracing their connection with it. The only bright bit of news was that the nasty Phillipe Dupont was just off on his honeymoon and wouldn't be back in France for several weeks, by which time the affair should be out of the papers. Later in the day, however, Alicia did call me back, and apologised for her brusqueness, saying that it was because of her aversion to publicity, and she went on to congratulate me on my marriage saying, "Do please ask Hélène to come to see us when all this business is over, our friendship is too old to lose touch again."

I'll draw a veil over the next few days – they were hell. We had press-men and TV caravans camped all round Mélitour, and we could see them getting more and more frustrated by the replies which we'd agreed to give, such as: "No, we do not know where Mrs. Dallachy is," or, "Because of the possibility of legal action we cannot comment on the matter."

To begin with they had, in the main, been friendly, but soon their treatment of us began to change, and headlines in the papers began to appear, like: "What are they afraid of?" or "What are they hiding?"

But we stuck it out, and at last they struck their tents and departed, leaving just a few in Chaource and Tonnere in the hope that something would turn up. However, at last, they too left.

During all this time, however, there had been some developments in England. First of all Lord Hempson had issued a Press Statement which read:

```
I have been astonished by the bizarre letter
issued by Mrs. Hélène Dallachy which accuses me of
treachery during my time in France in the spring of
1944. I have always thought that my war record spoke
for itself, and it has been very painful for me to
read these absurd allegations. It is a matter of
plain fact that the accusations are untrue. The
official documents which have been issued by the
Ministry of Defence make that quite clear.
    Had the authoress of these letters been other than
an old lady, living in the shadow of her husband's
recent death, I should at once have issued writs for
libel. I too am old, and I have no wish to cause
further distress. All I ask is that she should
retract her accusation and give me an apology.
```

For once the editors of papers of every persuasion were unanimous in their treatment, and that of the *Daily Telegraph* is perhaps typical:

Public figures must, unfortunately, find
themselves to be the target of cranks. It is Lord
Hempson's misfortune to find himself in such a
situation. At a time when the knee jerk reaction of
too many people is to make a dash to the courts it
does him great credit to make such a dignified and
generous response.
It appears that Mrs. Dallachy has gone into
hiding. Wherever she is, common sense should prevail.
She should make her apology, and let this distressing
matter be put to rest.

However, on the very next day Grannie issued her own press release through John Carson:

I have read Lord Hempson's statement regarding a
letter which I circulated in which I accuse him of
treachery while in France in the spring of 1944. I
wish now to state categorically that I do not agree
that my accusations are without foundation.
His defence would seem to be based on German Army
reports, but I prefer my own evidence. I am, of
course, prepared to defend my beliefs in courts if he
so wishes.

So, Grannie had burned her boats for the second time. There could be no turning back now.

Chapter Twenty

In those early days we had no contact with her. She'd decided to keep her own counsel lest we tried to influence her. She did phone the day after the Press Releases and sounded surprisingly cheerful. She told us that she was enjoying what she called "her holiday in the lakes" and that she intended to remain incommunicado until the case was called. And called it was for 5th March, just a little over three months later, a very expedited time no doubt due to the many strings that Lord Hempson could pull.

Down in Mélitour, some seven hundred miles away, all we could do was to wait and worry. It was a relief when finally it was time to make tracks to London, and to meet her prior to the case. We wanted a big comfortable hotel where we could hope to be anonymous. Albert had booked one of the larger apartments in Grosvenor House, where we could stay and keep to ourselves. He also booked a room in the hotel for John Carson, as we would need to make arrangements with him. All in all, we thought, it would be a very safe bolt-hole, and nobody would know that we were there. How wrong we were.

Grannie came down by train in the early evening of the day after we arrived, and just two days before the case was called. We all decided, foolishly as it turned out, to meet her at Euston. We had expected her still to be in her disguise, but no, she was herself again. After the somewhat sentimental greetings were over she said, "I decided that it was time for me to face the world again. Damn it, I'll be in court the day after tomorrow, and I can't hide there."

We had a hire car waiting at the station and I didn't see any problems about getting into our apartment without being recognised. Unfortunately, as we were leaving the station, I looked back and saw a young man waving what looked like a twenty pound note at a taxi driver and pointing to our car. There was nothing our driver could do, as there was no way our limousine could out-run a taxi in London traffic. So, when we got to Grosvenor House, there he was. He jumped out of the cab in a flash and started snapping our pictures. I suppose that he was good at his job, for later I discovered that he got an excellent shot of me when I went round the back of the car to fetch Grannie's luggage. The hotel staff were very efficient at keeping him well away from us, but he had his pictures.

It was by then too late for our photographer to catch the evening papers. The damage came the following morning. He must have been operating on a free-lance basis as every national newspaper had the photographs which they treated as a welcome lead-in to the court case on the following day. The "heavies" all expressed sympathy for Lord Hempson writing that it was unpleasant for such a dignified old man to be dragged down by this sordid accusation; but they stopped short of calling Grannie a liar. The tabloids were not so restrained. For example, the Sun had a bold-type caption to our picture, "A FAMILY IN TREACHEROUS TROUBLE".

This was followed by an article which skated perilously close to calling Grannie a silly old bag. There was a lot of stuff about how sad it was for the name of a distinguished French family like the de Mélitours to be tarnished by her stubborn foolishness. They used that good picture they had of me to attack my marriage to Pierre. While they didn't quite call me a gold digger, their readers were left in little doubt.

All this was very upsetting to Grannie and we thought that maybe at last she was beginning to regret what she had done. "I've been very selfish," she said, "I see that all I've done is to cause all of you much distress, and there is still a lot more to come. I'm also afraid that as the case comes nearer, I begin to realise what a silly old woman I am going to look. All these 'pointers' I was so proud of mean nothing compared to these damn German documents which show that he couldn't have been with Major Kretzer that night. If only they didn't exist we would be fine."

There was not a lot to do that day except, late in the afternoon, to have a very sombre conference with John Carson and the leading Barrister, a Mr. Jonathan Harkness, who was acting for us. He spelled things out very clearly, "I must tell you again, Mrs Dallachy, that I have never appeared in a case where I felt more helpless. A child could take on Lord Hempson's case and win. The whole of your case stands or falls on your assertion that he was present when the Comtesse de Mélitour was tortured. We have no defence against the German papers. I understand, just to hammer home the point, that they are bringing an official from the German Army Records office to confirm that they are authentic."

We had stayed all that day in the privacy of our apartment, secure in our knowledge that the press would be kept away. So I wasn't too pleased when, just as we finished dinner, the phone rang and the hotel receptionist told me that a German gentleman, Herr Willi Heldorff, wished to talk to Grannie. The girl I spoke to seemed convinced that he was not a reporter. When I spoke to Grannie she looked puzzled, saying, "I'm sure I've seen that name somewhere, but I can't remember. You'd better bring him up."

So, off I went to the reception desk where they pointed me towards an elderly white-haired man sitting at one of the tables. I went over to him, and I'm afraid that I wasn't too polite, saying, "I understand that you wish to speak to Mrs. Dallachy, what do you want with her?"

He looked up at me, and I could see a flicker of surprise on his face. "Ah, you must be Madame de Mélitour, you are so very like your grandmother!"

But I wasn't going to fall for talk like that, "Herr Heldorff, I have spoken to my grandmother, and she tells me that she does not know you."

"Does she now? Well I can tell you that she is mistaken, and I can also tell you that I am here to help her in this unfortunate court case she is involved in."

He wouldn't say anything more, but he did seem genuine and so – hoping that I was right – I took him to our apartment. When he got there I was surprised that he ignored Grannie, instead bowing to Albert and Pierre and saying in his accented but very precise English, "Good evening, M. le Comte…good evening M. de Mélitour."

And only then did he turn to Grannie, and this time all formality was gone, "May I say, Hélène Duclos, that I am very glad to see you again!" Grannie, I could see, was looking as puzzled as we were, "I'm sorry, but I don't remember you…"

He smiled at her, but didn't speak, just turned back to Albert, "M. le Comte, I hope that your broken leg has healed up well, as for me, my shoulder wound only bothers me occasionally if the weather is very cold!"

He turned back to Grannie, and I saw a look of astonishment on her face, "You…are that German lieutenant whom I…"

"That's right!" he laughed, "I'm the man whom you shot on the night of the 19th of April 1944, getting on for sixty years ago, the man whose life you spared , so maybe it is now possible for me to repay that debt!"

Suddenly it was all clear to me. I could see that Hélène and Albert had also realised who this stranger was. Pierre just looked bewildered, so I said to Herr Heldorff, "I'm truly delighted to meet you. This is an astonishing moment. But please excuse me briefly while I explain things to my husband who has no idea what is happening."

I took Pierre aside while the others talked together, and said, "I'm afraid this concerns a part of Grannie's story which you may not have been told about. You see on that night when my grandfather shot Major Kretzer, there was a second German officer in the room. It was Grannie who shot him and they both believed that he too was dead. However, before they left she found that he was still alive. She was about to shoot him again, but he begged for his life and promised silence if she spared him. So she didn't shoot; and Herr Heldorff is that man."

Pierre put his arms round me and whispered, "Aren't you glad, darling, that we live in the world as it is now. These were awful decisions that the old folks had to make."

I smiled my assent, and then looked over at Grannie who had shed twenty years. She was embracing Herr Heldorff, and saying, "Tell me…You must know…The other man in the room…The civilian who made his escape. Who was he?"

"Why do you ask? It was Lieutenant Henry Marshall, of course, just as you are claiming!"

"But what about those German army records which say that he was in hospital in Cologne?"

"They do say that don't they? If fact, I know exactly what

they say. I should, because I wrote the words myself. They are a complete fabrication."

There was a confusion of questions from Grannie and from Albert, but I managed to over-ride them. "Look, all this is incredible, but at this eleventh hour it concerns our lawyers more than us. I know that John is having dinner in the hotel with Mr. Harkness, so let me go and see if I can page them if necessary, and bring them back here."

Fortunately I did find them just as they were finishing dinner, and when I told them of the development Mr. Harkness gave a little whoop of excitement, "Thank God for that – lead me to him!"

Back in the apartment I found that Albert had organised things as if for a formal meeting. There was a small dining room off the sitting room, and we sat round the table with Herr Heldorff at the head. We were all in a state of suppressed excitement, especially Grannie, and I could see that she was hanging on every word.

But just as he started, she suddenly said, "Just wait a minute, Herr Heldorff, I've got something in my room which will interest you and the others."

She was back in just a minute with a clip of two A4 sheets of paper, and laid it on the table, saying "You see, Andrew wrote to a friend in Germany to get a copy of the report, just to check that our Ministry of Defence had given us the right one. Well here they both are. The one on top is the copy obtained from Germany and other is the MOD copy. You can see that they are both the same except for one small detail. The slight difference between them was that the one from the Ministry doesn't have what is at the bottom of other"

And she passed the two sheets round to us. When you knew where to look, the difference was obvious. The sheet from Germany ended with a signature, and a name, "Hauptmann Willi Heldorff."

"I can tell you," she went on, "that Andrew and I discussed whether or not it would be worth while trying to find this man, but decided that it wouldn't. How wrong we were! Now it occurs to me that the Ministry must have decided to play it safe. They cut off your name from the sheets which they showed us, just in case we followed up that lead."

Herr Heldorff smiled at her, and said, "Well, if you had done it would certainly have been less dramatic than this. You see, just this morning I was reading the papers after breakfast in my house in Berlin, and I saw an item about a libel case coming to court tomorrow, involving Lord Hempson. I also read that it related to an affair in France in April 1944. That grabbed my attention, and I then saw a photograph of you, Yvette. I couldn't believe it. To me it was that of my saviour, Mrs. Dallachy here. Now I have a friend in the office of that paper, so I phoned him to get more details. He could even tell me where you are staying, so I decided immediately that I just had to come to London in order to repay the biggest possible debt that one can have…and so here I am!"

It is difficult to know how best to record what he told us that night, as he tended to be somewhat long-winded. Listening to him, and at the same time remembering Grannie's story, it was often like seeing a mirror image of the events. He began by telling us that he had been sent to France in late March 1944, after having been wounded in Russia. This was at the time when General Rommel had taken over command of all the German forces on their western front. The General's main job was to make preparations to repel the invasion when it came, and to this end good intelligence was vital.

"Unfortunately," he went on, "although quite a number of

Allied officers and Special Operations people had been captured in France, Rommel was unhappy with the quality of information obtained from them. Torture, he began to think,
might not be the most effective method of extracting information. Sometime in March he decided to try an experiment. He
instructed that Allied prisoners were, immediately on capture,
to be given an attractive proposition to encourage their col-
laboration. They were to be offered a guarantee that, if they
cooperated, the Germans would do a deal with them, and the
army official records would show that they had shown great
bravery and had not given away any information. Rommel laid
great stress on the fact we had to play fair with such men. The
records had to be convincing and assure the captive that he
could return home as a hero after the war was over. From
Rommel's point of view there was no downside to this experiment because, if the captive rejected the offer, then he was
to be handed over and subjected to our standard methods of
interrogation.

As it turned out, your Lieutenant Henry Marshall was one
of the first to be captured in the area where I was. I may say
that he was picked up because of his own stupidity. He was
drinking on the morning of the 14th of April in an estaminet
near Troyes. There he was overheard by a member of the
Milice making the remark to his companions that they all had
to meet that night beside the railway bridge at eleven o'clock.

"Soon after that," said Heldorff with a happy smile, "it
was a complete vindication of Rommel's idea. When we pulled
him in and he had the offer explained to him, the information
about the planned attack poured out of him. He was instructed to fake an illness so that he didn't have to go to the
bridge that night with his men. It was a very successful operation," He paused for a moment then said, "I can tell you that

it was just like shooting tame rabbits when we went to the railway bridge!"

It was awful to hear him speak so happily about the death of those Frenchmen, and yet here he was about to be of enormous help to us. However, I couldn't pursue these thoughts as he was going on to tell us that the German HQ had congratulated them, and told Kretzer to play fair by Marshall. He, Heldorff, had accordingly been instructed to arrange a cover story.

"From then on he was comfortable and safe in our hands. Soon he was telling us all that he knew. In fact he was so cooperative that Kretzer decided to take Marshall along with him on our counter-resistance actions." He then went on to be more specific:

"On the night of the 16th of April a signal was sent to every German unit in France. It said that a British officer, probably part of the Special Operations Executive, was in possession of top secret information and that it was imperative that he either be captured or killed. The signal also gave a description of him as being a tall young man with red hair who spoke German with an Alsace accent. It ended by saying that it was suspected that he was heading south, probably towards Spain."

I could see that Grannie was fascinated by all this, and no doubt was remembering just what she had been doing at the same time. But there was a sudden silence, and Heldorff said to Grannie, "I wonder, Mrs Dallachy, if you want me to tell you the rest. You know how the events unfolded and particularly how they came to a tragic end."

I saw her reach over and take his hand, "Let me hear it all from your side. I'd never forgive myself if I chickened out now. And do please call me Hélène. I think that, as I shot you, we should be on Christian name terms!"

It was then his turn to hold her hand, saying, "Life is strange, isn't it; to think that we might both have killed each other. But let's get on. Marshall was a real plum. He was the British liaison officer for all the French resistance groups in the region. Not only was he organising the sabotage efforts but he was coordinating the chain of cells which formed the Allied escape routes.

"You may have heard that Kretzer had lost his foot during an attack in 1940 by a British fighter plane. He had good reason to hate British but he was also aggressively ambitious. When that signal from Rommel arrived he saw that, through Marshall, he had a golden opportunity. He swallowed his animosity and treated Marshall as a respected advisor. Your man, I may say, was not only a coward but had hugely exaggerated view of his own importance. I have, in later life, often observed that these two personally weaknesses go hand in hand. Kretzer played Marshall brilliantly and manipulated him from the role of a collaborator to that of an eager participant.

"First, on the night of the 17th of April, they went to eliminate the most southerly part of the escape line, near Auxerre. Then they began to organise a rather small force to deal with Troyes.

"However, on the morning of the 19th of April another priority signal was received. This one said that a Frenchman in Reims had been interrogated, and before he died, had said that the very-much-wanted British soldier had already left Reims, and was heading south. With this news Kretzer had to take action at once, so he decided to proceed immediately with the liquidation of the Reims/Troyes section. But the Troyes operation was not a complete success as the Controller had made his escape. Kretzer and Marshall went into the town and Marshall pointed out the houses where the members of the escape line lived."

At this point I can remember that Herr Heldorff's voice almost broke with emotion, "It was a terrible day, one that I shall never forget. We arrested six Frenchmen in Troyes and they were taken to our base in the town for interrogation. I very much doubt they knew anything of the whereabouts of the British soldier. All the torture they suffered was pointless. None of them survived.

"It was then that Kretzer decided that he must move against the Comtesse. It took a little time to organise and we didn't get to the Chateau till about six o'clock. That, Hélène, as you will remember was on the night of the 19th of April. Kretzer arrested the Comtesse and took her to our Tonnere HQ. He also took her young son and I can only think that this was a measure of his desperation to get information about this British soldier.

"It was," he went on as he turned to Albert, "a shameful act to take you with your mother, and one which is a stain on my country's honour. What could I do? I was only a Lieutenant and Kretzer was a Major and my commanding officer."

He paused again, before telling us there had been another development that evening, "We had learned that the Controller in Troyes, a M. Chapelle, who had escaped that morning, had gone into hiding in Etourvy. A team had had been dispatched to arrest him and Kretzer had decided to delay the interrogation of the Comtesse until they returned. I suppose that his intention had been to play one off against the other.

"However, when our team arrived back at the Tonnere HQ, the brave M. Chapelle somehow managed to swallow a suicide pill before we could get any information out of him. That, Hélène, left just the Comtesse whom Kretzer believed knew where the British soldier was. The rest is a nightmare which I cannot forget. His treatment of her was awful, and that of her young son was even worse. All that can be said is that he met his just deserts when your husband's shots almost cut him in half.

"As for your shots," he smiled, "they were pretty good for a beginner! Both you and your husband got me in the shoulder causing me to fall. As I did so, I hit my head which gave me a good excuse to play possum. Marshall, of course, made his escape but was wounded as he dived through the window. Letting him escape was the only mistake your husband made. I can't really blame him for shooting the four soldiers in the kitchen. They had seen both of you and the two older men who were with you.

"But, just as you were about to leave, you came back into the room and found me alive. I thanked you then for sparing me, and now I can thank you again. Anyway, I played fair by you. When Marshall decided the coast was clear, which was about half an hour later, he came back in considerable pain with two bullets in his shoulder. I feigned unconsciousness as long as I could. He must have lost consciousness himself because it was over an hour before the alarm was raised, by which time I presume that you were well away."

Grannie nodded, and said, "And what about Marshall?"

"Well, his usefulness to us was over. My wounds were not serious and I made a fast recovery. With my shoulder dressed and with my arm in a sling, I was fit for duty. I assumed temporary command and my first decision was to get rid of him. The next morning, which would have been on the 20th of April, I sent him to hospital in Cologne and arranged for him to be transferred to a POW camp as soon as he was fit.

"But what about those German army records? They show

that he was admitted to hospital on 16th April?"

"Oh, as I said, I wrote them myself, in terms of General Rommel's orders to conceal his treachery. And he certainly had been very useful to us. Had he been on our side we should have given him a medal. So I turned him into a hero, single-handedly fighting off a German unit and risking death to save his comrades. I personally had reason to be grateful to him. We may not have captured that British soldier but, thanks to Marshall, the Allied escape route in my district had been smashed. As a result, my superiors were pleased to promote me immediately from Lieutenant to Captain. That rank is 'Hauptmann' in the German army and, as you would have noticed, that was how I signed my report."

"That's it!" he smiled, "anything else?"

We did have a few questions, but none of importance. As we were talking I saw that Mr. Harkness and John Carson had been having a quiet chat together. It was Mr. Harkness who spoke, "Herr Heldorff, yours is a remarkable story, and it turns what was an impossible case into a much more attractive one. It will be a cause célèbre whichever way it goes. There remains an element of doubt because your information, valuable though it is, still doesn't go far enough. The trouble is that, after all this time, most of the characters in the case are dead."

He turned to Grannie, "I am sorry to tell you that there is a major weakness in Herr Heldorff's account. You see, according to both your stories, he owed you an enormous debt of gratitude for sparing his life. Lord Hempson's defence team is sure to exploit that fact. They will claim that, after all these years of silence, Herr Heldorff only now comes forward with this altered version of the events in order to help you to win your case. They will suggest, and the jury may easily believe, that his new account is no more than a pay-back. I ask you to put yourself in the position of a juror; can you think of anything else which would help?"

I could see however that Herr Heldorff was still looking happy, "Well, you will be glad to know that there is something. I too know about evidence in court as my subsequent career after the war was in the police. My last rank was equivalent to your Chief Superintendent. Consequently, I knew that my word alone would not be sufficient. Before I left the house this morning, I phoned a young colleague in Cologne and asked him to check if, by any chance, the hospital there still had records going back to 1944. I was still there an hour later, when I got a fax and also a telephone call back from him. Unfortunately, he had found that due to the confusion of those war-time days all of their records prior to 1945 were missing. But all was not lost. The hospital, as part of its retirement benefits, makes hospital beds available to their elderly ex-employees in the geriatric unit. There he found a frail old man who had been one of the admissions officers in back 1944. Apparently he remembers a British soldier being admitted on the 20th of April. My friend told me that he would interview the old man later in the day and promised to send me another fax here with the result."

I saw Mr. Harkness shake his head doubtfully, "Well, every little helps, I suppose, but a conversation with an old man in Cologne won't get us very far. It will just be hearsay at the second or third hand, and won't be very persuasive."

"Not quite," said Heldorff, "my colleague isn't a policeman for nothing. If anything of interest arises he will arrange a formal interview and everything will be signed and witnessed."

"Well," said Mr. Harkness, without much confidence, "we can but wait." But, just as he finished speaking and had assumed a patient posture, there was a knock at the door. It was hotel porter, and he came bearing a fax addressed to Herr Heldorff. As he read it I could see him looking rather pleased, "Just listen to this, and I'll translate it from the German."

It was quite a lengthy document but in essence it confirmed:

That he, Adolph Brandt, had been one of the admissions officers of the hospital in April 1944.

That on the 20th of April he remembered a rather unusual occurrence when a young British officer was delivered to the hospital by armed escort.

He remembered that the officer's name was Lieutenant Marshall. He said that he was able to recall the name because he found it peculiar that it consisted of two military ranks, "Lieutenant" and "Marshall".

The officer was treated for a shoulder wound for a few days before being sent off to a POW camp.

He clearly remembered the date because it was his fifth wedding anniversary. There was a bottle of French perfume in the prisoner's bag which he purloined to give to his wife as a present.

"Certainly that is helpful, said Mr. Harkness, "but a fax message isn't going to impress the court very much. In Britain such evidence is treated as hearsay."

I was beginning to get quite irritated with Mr. Harkness and his gloomy pronouncements on each breath of new life that Herr Heldorff had brought into Grannie's case. But looking across I could see that Herr Heldorff still was enjoying himself as he said, "Mr. Harkness, don't you remember that I said a few minutes ago that I know all about evidence in court. Our courts in Germany are no different from yours. So I knew that a fax message is open to question. Because of this I pulled some strings with Lufthansa before my departure. I can tell you that the original document which has been signed and witnessed will being sent to Heathrow on a late night flight. One of their people will bring it to me here, and I expect it not long after midnight."

He stopped there and looked at Grannie, "How's that, Hélène, have I now repaid my debt in full?"

Chapter Twenty-One

In bed that night I looked enviously at Pierre as he slumbered peacefully beside me. He is one of the lucky ones who can just turn over, shut his eyes and...Bingo!...He's off. Usually I'm not too bad myself, especially after love-making, but now I was in the seventh month of my pregnancy and turn as I might, I just couldn't get comfortable.

Also, of course, it had been such an exciting evening, and I couldn't stop my mind going round and round in circles. Herr Heldorff's arrival had been a miracle, and now it really looked likely that Grannie would win her case, but one thought surfaced, and wouldn't go away. I just didn't like the man! We did, of course, owe him an enormous debt of gratitude. Here he was, an elderly man in his eighties, reading an article over breakfast and then taking the trouble to fly from Berlin to London that same day, so that he could give evidence in court to help a lady who had shot him many years ago. It was all very noble. But what bugged me was the manner in which he had told some parts of his story; his obvious satisfaction with how they had turned the young Henry Marshall; his equal pride at the efficiency of his soldiers when they had killed all the French resistance people at the bridge; and his apparent regret that the Tonnere Controller had managed to swallow a suicide pill before he could be interrogated. Maybe he really had meant his apology to Albert, and maybe his regret about the way in which Marie-Claire had been treated was genuine, but, nevertheless, there were two sides to his character.

My thoughts then turned to my dear Grannie, and I realised that this was also true of her. In her story she had told me, almost with pride, of the German blood and guts on her face, and how she had calmly discussed with Granddad how best to cut the throat of the German sentry. It came to me then that nobody of my generation should dare to judge those who had fought in the war. They could not help the way that circumstances had moulded them. But then a thought came which kept me awake even longer. Were we right, after so many of these long years, to try to judge Lord Hempson?

However, next morning I put aside all these reservations. I could see that Grannie had no second thoughts. She positively fizzed with excitement as she said, "I just can't wait to see Hempson's face when Heldorff gets into the witness box."

The four of us, that is Grannie, Albert, Pierre and I. set of for the court in a taxi. For good reason, it had been decided that Herr Heldorff should be smuggled into the court by one of Mr. Harkness's staff and kept on his own and out of sight until he was called to give evidence.

The grim formality of the court was rather frightening, with the four of us sitting behind our counsel's table. This was occupied by Mr. Harkness and his junior, with John Carson sitting beside them. The seats behind the opposing counsel's table were empty until just a few moments before the Judge entered. Then in they came and for the first time I saw Lord Hempson in the flesh, a kindly-looking elderly gentleman who studiously avoided looking at us. He was accompanied by a younger man whom I recognised as being his son, Michael Marshall the Secretary of State for Defence, and a woman whom I took to be his wife. I glanced sideways at Grannie, and I saw her looking at Hempson as if he had horns and a tail. I hadn't time to speak to her because the Judge then entered and everybody had to rise. I've often heard how long-winded court proceedings are, and I'll skip the bit about the jury being sworn in, and certainly not try to quote the speeches verbatim, so all that follows is much abbreviated.

Lord Hempson's man, Sir Thomas Carrington, led off by suggesting that despite his client having been maliciously defamed in a ridiculous letter by Mrs. Hélène Dallachy which had been given a wide circulation, the whole affair could, this morning, be disposed of quickly and her allegations proved to be false. He started by outlining how things were in 1944 and about the bravery of Lord Hempson, as was fully documented in official German army records. He pointed out that the only specific allegation which she made was that the young Lieutenant Henry Marshall had been present when the Comtesse de Mélitour had been tortured by a German officer on the night of the 19th of April 1944. All the rest, he indicated, was just a number of unsupported statements which had no significance whatsoever once the main accusation had been proved to be false.

Having said all that, Sir Thomas sat back with a satisfied smile on his face. It was now our Mr. Harkness's turn. He electrified that court by saying that while he hoped to show to the satisfaction of the court that his client's statements were correct, he could nevertheless agree with much that the Learned Opposing Counsel had said. He would concede that everything did hang on the simple question, "Was Lieutenant Henry Marshall present when the Comtesse was being tortured on the night of the 19th of April 1944?" If he had been there, it proved his guilt, if not then he could be adjudged innocent of the allegations.

It was an odd statement for the Defending Counsel to make, and I could see that the Judge was looking at him with some surprise, as was Sir Thomas, his opponent. I am afraid then that all my reservations of the previous night had vanished and I was looking forward with unholy pleasure to the appearance of our star witness.

Things proceeded with considerable formality when Sir Thomas produced copies of the German army record which were validated by a very proper Mr. James Butler of the Ministry of Defence. I noticed that he took great care not to look at us. Anyway he hadn't much to say, and just confirmed that they were indeed taken from the official records kept in the Ministry and originated from the archives of the German army.

It was now our Mr. Harkness's turn, and all he said was, "No questions!" Only then did I see a slight frown on Sir Thomas's face, as he obviously wondered what we were up to, and I saw Lord Hempson lean forward to have an urgent word with him.

Sir Thomas went on, obviously hoping to drive a final nail into our coffin, by calling the next witness. He began by saying, "You will of course all be aware that my client was at one time the Secretary of State for Defence, a position now held by his son, so lest there can be any suspicion that the papers could have been tampered with, my next witness is Herr Heller of Berlin, a senior official of the German Defence Ministry, who is in a similar position there to that of Mr. Butler in our Ministry."

Herr Heller duly appeared in the witness box, and confirmed that the papers, obtained from the British Ministry of Defence and which had been presented to the court, were in fact authentic copies.

Only then did our man ask a question, "Herr Heller, it is very kind of you to come here today, and I wonder if by any chance you brought your own copy of these army reports with you?"

He indicated that he had done so, and Mr. Harkness then asked if he might see them. I could guess the reason for his smile when they were handed to him, and he then surprised the court by asking if this copy could be substituted for the one which had come from the Defence Ministry.

Obviously Sir Thomas didn't know what this was about so he strongly objected, saying that it was absurd to question the original papers which had been validated just this morning.

Mr. Harkness was all politeness, as he said that he had no doubt that the original papers from the MOD were correct, but he paused there before continuing, "…as far as they go."

I heard a buzz of questions from the body of the court, and the Judge said, "I do not understand your statement, please explain."

"The difference, your Lordship, is a very simple one. The report from Germany includes at the end the signature of the German officer who wrote them, and his name, Hauptmann Willi Heldorff."

"And is that relevant to the case?"

"Yes, your Lordship, it is."

He just stopped there and sat down without explaining his reason. After quite a long pause, the Judge said to Sir Thomas, "I presume that since Herr Heller is here at your request you have no objection to this?"

Sir Thomas obviously smelt a rat, but couldn't think of any reason to object, so he just talked about how stupid it was to waste the time of the court on such a triviality. I think that the Judge was becoming interested and waved the complaints away, and the German papers were accepted by the court.

I was pleased to see that Lord Hempson was suddenly looking rather worried.

It was now time for Sir Thomas to give a very polished speech to the Jury in which he paid tribute to the German ability for producing good accurate records, and emphasised that they gave conclusive proof that his client could not have been present during the unfortunate events of the 19th of April 1944, as he was then lying on a sick bed in Cologne. He also pointed out that since this allegation was false, the other allegations in Grannie's letter were also absurd and could be ignored.

He ended his speech by saying, "I am asked by my client to say that it gives him no pleasure to see an elderly lady, a re-spected heroine of France, make such a fool of herself. It baf-fles him that she has gone so far without admitting that this nonsensical story is a tissue of lies."

When at last he finished and sat down there was a buzz of subdued conversation round the court, despite the Judge call-ing for silence. I could see that most of those present, includ-ing no doubt the Jury, had already made up their minds. The sound died away when Mr. Harkness got to his feet.

He began in a quiet, almost conversational tone, "This is rather an odd case as both sides would seem to agree that eve-rything stands on what is written in that old German army re-port of April 1944. You will remember that an official of the German Defence Ministry was kind enough to give evidence here today, and his own copy of the German Army report is now lodged in court as a true record. However, unlike the copies of the report provided by our own Ministry this one included the name of the officer who wrote it – Hauptmann Willi Heldorff, as he was in 1944. It was my client's good fortune that Herr Heldorff, who now lives in Berlin, read about this case in yesterday morning's newspaper, and realised that, because he wrote the report at the centre of this case, he was the best person in the whole world to explain its content. So he at once flew to Britain, and my client and I saw him yesterday evening. I have also been able to arrange to have an official from the German embassy to be available. He will confirm that Herr Heldorff whom I now wish to bring before the court is the Hauptmann Heldorff of 1944.

I saw Sir Thomas turn to Lord Hempson for guidance, and quickly turn away again recognising that any question would be pointless. The genial senior politician had evaporated. He had been replaced by a scraggy old man with a look of horror on his face. Sir Thomas could not have got where he was without being able to think on his feet. Although he must have known that something had gone very wrong, he started a skilful attack, saying that it was ridiculous to spring a surprise witness on the court, especially now when the case was nearly over, and the German papers had been authenticated both by British and by German officials.

I am sure, though, that the Judge was beginning to be interested in the case, and gave his ruling that, since both sides placed such importance on the German papers, the new witness could be called. He then gave a little twist as he said to him, "Just remember, Sir Thomas, that it was you who called Herr Heller so surely you can't ask me to exclude Herr Heldorff."

I needn't describe in detail what happened, but Herr Heldorff was magnificent, no doubt because he'd had a lifetime of giving evidence in court. Mr. Harkness led him through the points which he had made the previous night, right up to when he was explaining about General Rommel's plan to persuade Allied soldiers to give them information in exchange for a promise to paint them as whiter than white in the official records. He then went on to say that Lieutenant Marshall was captured on the 16th of April, and then agreed to cooperate with the Germans. He then explained that he was present, with a Major Kretzer, when the Comtesse de Mélitour was tortured on April the 19th. And how he came to write the false records, and why the dates of admission to the hospital were wrong.

But, just then, I saw Sir Thomas jump to his feet, "Your Lordship, this is absurd, the witness is making more of the same unsubstantiated allegations as the Defendant. There isn't a shred of proof for all this nonsense."

The Judge looked over at Mr. Harkness, "Have you any observations which you would like to make?"

"I have, your Lordship. I have not finished with my witness, and the proof of his allegations is still to come."

He turned back to Heldorff, and said, "Will you please tell the court what you did yesterday morning before you left Germany."

Heldorff then explained how he had spoken to a colleague in Cologne and got him to check with the hospital, only to find that the records for 1944 were missing. Before he could go on Sir Thomas was on his feet again to complain that if these records were missing then the whole things was a waste of the court's time, but the Judge would have none of it.

"Let us hear what Herr Heldorff has to say, Sir Thomas, he has come a long way to be here." Then there was a nod to Heldorff and he said, "Carry on please."

Heldorff explained about his colleague's interview with the old admissions officer, and mentioned that he had with him the original record of this interview of yesterday.

"It begins," he said, "with the arrival at the hospital on the 20th of April 1944 of the young British soldier, Lieutenant Henry Marshall, with a shoulder wound."

I was surprised then that he did not mention why the old man could be certain about the date, but in fact he had omitted this just to leave a trip-wire for Sir Thomas, who jumped to his feet again, "This is absurd! How can an old man remember a specific date after nearly sixty years…the very idea beggars belief!"

There was a murmur of agreement round the court, and Mr. Harkness waited for silence before going on, "Please tell the court, Herr Heldorff, why this old man can be so certain about the date."

"That is easily explained," he went on, "you see, he was married on the 20th of April 1939, so it was his fifth wedding anniversary. At that time there were no luxuries available in Cologne. I'm afraid that he purloined a bottle of French perfume from Lieutenant's Marshall's bag, and gave it to his wife as an anniversary present. I have here a notarised and witnessed document, giving details of the interview."

I do not know what would have happened after that because suddenly the proceedings were interrupted by a shout from Lord Hempson's son, "Sir Thomas, you must ask for an adjournment, my father is ill!"

Like everyone in court I looked over and saw that Lord Hempson had slumped in his seat and was obviously in considerable distress. Things were handled most efficiently. Two attendants appeared with a stretcher along with two tall young men, plain-clothes policemen I afterwards learned. Hempson and the rest of his party were escorted out of the court through the side door.

There was a brief exchange between the judge and the two

counsels, and an adjournment until three o'clock was agreed. Our man, Mr. Harkness, knew London well and took all of us to a quiet little restaurant in a back street, all of us that is to say, except poor Herr Heldorff who had to be held incommunicado in court since he was in the middle of giving evidence. I can't now remember what I, or the others, ate or drank, and I for one, felt as if I were in limbo. We'd been prepared for all sorts of drama. But what was going to happen now?

Mr. Harkness, however, was cheerful. "That was a bit of good luck for us! It will certainly damage Hempson's credibility with the jury, now that they have seen how much Heldorff's evidence has upset him."

But in Grannie's book, it was the wrong thing to say. "Mr. Harkness, I am ashamed of you. How can you take any pleasure in seeing someone, even an adversary, look as bad as he did? I have every reason to hate him, but his illness distresses me, especially as I very much fear that it is my action which has brought it on." After that we became a very quiet party.

When the court reassembled at three o'clock I was surprised to see that Sir Thomas was the only person on the opposing benches and his speech was short and to the point, "Your Lordship, as we all know, Lord Hempson took ill this morning. The doctor who examined him found that he had suffered a mild heart attack. I am glad to say he is now resting comfortably and may be expected to make a full recovery. Unfortunately, however, his medical advisors recommend that he avoids any excitement during the period of his convalescence. At this early stage, they cannot say how long this will take. I have, therefore, been instructed to abandon this action. My client and I deeply regret that we cannot see this case to a conclusion, but his health is more important than any other consideration."

There was another of those sudden murmurs round the court and, to my horror, I suddenly realised that to most of the people here it was Grannie had horns and a tail. It was her action that had caused so much distress to a well-liked national figure. Anyway, after that things didn't take long. The Judge expressed his condolences to Lord Hempson and hoped that he would soon be restored to good health, the jury were discharged, and costs were awarded to Grannie. But I am afraid that he made no effort to hide the fact that his condolences to Lord Hempson were more sincere than any pleasure he might have had in awarding costs to Grannie.

There was no protection for us as we left the building, where a swarm of reporters and camera crews were waiting. Fortunately, however, Mr. Harkness had made his preparations and one of his staff had a statement ready to be handed out. I still have one of them, and it reads:

Mrs. Hélène Dallachy has asked me to make a statement on her behalf. You will appreciate that, as a lady of over eighty, the recent days have been very stressful and exhausting for her. She did not make her accusations lightly, and took this course only because of the dreadful consequences of Lord Hempson's treachery during the Second World War.

She wishes to pay tribute to the generosity of Herr Heldorff who took the trouble to fly here from Berlin in order to give evidence on her behalf. Despite the fact that Mrs. Dallachy shot and wounded him back in 1944 he still felt impelled to bring the truth before the court.

Mrs. Dallachy believes that her accusations against Lord Hempson were fully vindicated in court today. Lord Hempson did betray his country. He did collaborate with the Germans. He was present in the room while her friend was being tortured.

His only defence was a German army report which allegedly showed that he was not in France when the atrocities were committed. That report was a cover-up written by Herr Heldorff to conceal Lord Hempson's guilt.

In conclusion she wishes to say that, despite everything, she regrets that Lord Hempson has taken ill. She is sorry that her actions to bring the truth into the open have had this result.

We had all been warned not to say anything at all in reply to the barrage of questions, and at last we made it to the safety of our taxi, with Heldorff and our legal team in another. It was so quiet and peaceful when the doors were closed after the struggle and confusion outside the court. Grannie was clearly still distressed by the way the reporters had behaved. One had hurled at her, "Sorry for Lord Hempson, Mrs. Dallachy...pull the other one dear!"

The evening papers were somewhat of a disappointment. We had hoped that they would portray Grannie as something of a heroine and write that she had, against all the odds, exposed the treachery of a public figure. But they didn't. Instead their feature stories went on about how long ago it was, and the difficulty of getting reliable evidence after so many years had passed. And, of course, they made much of the fact that the case had come to a premature end because of Lord Hempson's illness.

To cheer us up Albert had arranged for us to have dinner in the hotel dining room as we were getting tired of hiding in the apartment, and after a few glasses of wine Herr Heldorff became a most congenial companion, as we talked trivialities about anything but the case, until Grannie said to him, "Tell me, Willi, where did you go to get your shoulder treated, and how long did you stay in France after the affair?"

"As for my shoulder I only had to use a sling for a few weeks, so I was never off duty. It did in fact give me an immediate advantage as I was promoted to Captain and put in charge of the area. That lasted for about three months, until the Allies broke out of the landing beaches, and every fit German soldier had to be drafted to fighting units. You will notice that I said "fit", well, that didn't apply to me, as although my shoulder had healed I was still troubled with my Russian wounds and so was returned to administrative duties in Germany."

"I'm glad that your shoulder wasn't too much of a problem," Grannie smiled, "but if it ever does I'll come and kiss it better! But one thing still puzzles me. Our affair was in April, so you had more than three months before the Allied breakout, and I'm surprised that you didn't manage to trace Marie-Claire and Albert. Why were you unable to find them?"

Herr Heldorff looked at her for a few moments, then said, "Do you remember that after the shooting, and when I was playing possum, you phoned your family doctor and arranged to bring young Albert and his mother to his clinic? I can even still remember his name – M. Jeanfils – and I am sure that if we had made enquiries there we could easily have found where they had been hidden. But there was my promise to you, and anyway I didn't see that it would give us Germans any advantage to trace them. So although we had to go through the motions of a search, I did my best to keep it well away from the clinic."

It was Albert who found his voice first, "I've often wondered about this, Willi, but just concluded that we must have been lucky. But it wasn't luck at all, just another thing we have to thank you for."

"Yes," he said, "I could do that for you and your mother, but as for you, Hélène and your soldier friend – your husband-to-be – I could do nothing by way of taking the heat off the pair of you. The search, you see, was carried out by troops from an infantry division, helped by the Milice. I can tell you that there was a monumental row when you were not traced. Tell me, how did you manage to get away?"

And that story lasted for much of the rest of the evening, which proved to be the calm before the storm.

We had hoped that the daily papers would be more sympathetic to Grannie, but we were appalled when we read them. Every one of them, with the exception of the *Daily Telegraph* had gone bingo on patriotism. While they stopped short of calling Herr Heldorff a Nazi, and Grannie a French bitch, they went as close as they dared. Even the *Daily Telegraph*, which did provide a little more weight to her case, gave her, at best, a "Not Proven" verdict.

All the stories went on at length about the stupidity of trying to establish either innocence or guilt when all the evidence came from suspect records and the unreliable memories of old people. Not a single paper had a kind word to say to Grannie for bringing the case into the open. In particular they made much of the fact that the case had been ended prematurely, before Herr Heldorff had been cross-examined. It was all very distressing to her, as it had turned out to be a Pyrrhic victory. Certainly she would get all her costs back, and would not have to pay any damages, but overnight she had become notorious.

It was an obvious decision that she could not go back to Henley where she would have no protection from the media. She was very happy to agree that the best place for her was at Mélitour, and the sooner the better. This wasn't altogether easy as the media pack were still camped outside the hotel.

However, the staff were used to situations like this. We had to wait until that night when, under the cover of darkness, the four of us and Willi Heldorff were smuggled out through a staff entrance and into an anonymous van.

It was upsetting for all of us to have to make our departure in this way as if we were wanted criminals, but at least there were no unpleasant incidents. Not too many hours later we were safely back home, and Willi was back in his apartment in Berlin with a warm invitation to come and see us in Mélitour.

It had been a very unsatisfactory end to the affair. Life went on, and the media attention quickly died away. Grannie became old news. Back in the secure shelter of what had once been her home she found peace again.

Anyway, we soon had more important things to think about as my first child, an eight-pound son, was born on 15th May, almost a honeymoon baby. The Christening was a very grand affair in the estate chapel. The choice of names was easy, Jean Albert Andrew de Mélitour; Jean for my dear husband, Jean Pierre, and also for my father, John; Albert and Andrew for his two grandfathers.

The arrival of my son was the best possible therapy for all of us, and particularly for Grannie who was delighted to find herself a nursemaid at Mélitour again, more than sixty years after the first time.

Chapter Twenty-Two

It was a beautiful afternoon, early in July, when to my dismay the affair came alive again.

Pierre and I had played a few holes of golf late in the morning, followed by lunch in the clubhouse, but I had to hurry home to breast-feed my beloved young son. I had gone out to the terrace to sit beside Grannie while I did so. It was beautifully peaceful out there. When he had finished and I had buttoned up my dress, I handed him over to her as she liked to make him give his final "burp". She must have decided this was a good time for reminiscences. She turned to me saying, "Yvette, my dear, I am a lucky old woman. My adult life really started right here on that day in 1938 when I came to be interviewed by my dear Marie-Claire for the post of nursemaid to Albert, her baby son. I remember thinking how grand it was to be interviewed by a Comtesse. Now that baby is your father-in-law. There have been some funny twists in our family history, and I still wonder sometimes whether it was wise of me to confront Lord Hempson with the truth. It caused all of you a great deal of worry and effort. We struggled so hard to achieve the opportunity to prove his guilt in open court. In the end that opportunity was lost. We failed to convince the world that he was a traitor responsible for so much misery and so many deaths. But at least I did manage to embarrass the bastard"

She paused and smiled at me, "Funny, I can never speak

of him without swearing, and I never swear about anything or anybody else!

"Yvette, I am rambling on with regretful memories and my intentions were different. What I really wanted to say was that I have decided to lay these matters to rest. They are over and done with and I am so very content to be here with you and your family. As you get older, Yvette, you may find that the years tend to telescope. You are my grand-daughter, I know, but I have come to think of you as my child, and Pierre as my son-in-law. This in some way brings me closer to you both and to our little Jean." She rocked him gently as he by now was fast asleep, "He is so like that year-old baby whom I came to look after in 1938. At my age, love is the only important thing. The reality of time doesn't seem to concern me"

She went over then and settled young Jean in his pram, carefully adjusting the hood to keep him out of direct sunlight. When she came back to sit beside me I put my arm round her shoulders and we sat together for quite a while in perfect amity.

Our peace was disturbed by the sound of a car coming up to the front door. I wondered who it could be, and a few minutes later our major-domo came out to tell me that an Englishman, Captain Hector Shaw, wished to see either me or Pierre. I couldn't think who it could be, and as Pierre was going through estate accounts with Albert I excused myself from Grannie and went to see him. He was a tall young chap and he introduced himself in perfect French saying firstly that he wanted to apologise for the intrusion, but also that he wanted to give some information which he believed was of importance to us.

Hearing his voice, suddenly the penny dropped, "Damn it, you are one of the thugs who kidnapped us. I'll bet the other chap in the car is smaller than you and doesn't speak French!"

"Guilty exactly as charged," he smiled. "However, I do suggest you hear what we have to say. It is too absurd for us to have invented it. I hope, when you hear the tale, you will be able to forgive me and my friend Lieutenant David Sloan. Certainly, we owe you a huge apology. Leaving aside the issues of guilt and forgiveness, we believe our account contains matters that you and your family should know about."

At first I felt like telling him to leave, after all I had just heard from Grannie that she wanted to have nothing more to do with the affair. These two had played a dirty part in it. I was still thinking how to reply when I heard Pierre's footsteps behind me. I reckoned that I'd better involve him, so I said, "I wonder, darling, if you remember our Captain Shaw from the spring last year?"

Pierre looked blank, so I gave him a small hint, "You may remember that he speaks excellent French but his colleague only speaks English."

That was enough to make the penny drop for him too. Pierre's curiosity overcame my reservations so we were soon being introduced to David Sloan, the other man. We also decided that there was no point in keeping the meeting to ourselves and we got Albert to join us before we took the two of them out to the terrace to meet Grannie.

So, in just a few minutes, there we were, sitting on the terrace on comfortable chairs. To anybody watching it would look as though it was just a pleasant social occasion. But Grannie was not pleased, and she said to Shaw, "As I understand it, you two abducted these two young people last spring. I fail to see why we bother to let you talk to us. We should be telephoning the Gendarmerie to have you arrested!"

"You are probably right, Mrs. Dallachy; but I can tell you

that the abduction was instigated by a gentleman whom I think you have met. Certainly your grand-daughter has."

"And who was that?"

But I could guess the answer for her. This was immediately confirmed when he said, "Why Mr. James Butler of the Ministry of Defence. I suppose that I should now say, Sir James Butler, as he got the KBE in the last Honours list."

Suddenly Grannie was on his side as she said, "That smug little so-and-so! I never trusted him. Tell us more"

"Thank you, Mrs. Dallachy, I think you will find it interesting. To begin with let me say that both David and I find it very embarrassing because we did, indeed, kidnap these two young people. But we were tricked into it; I'll explain how it all came about. We are both members of a rather special SAS unit, and back in March of last year we had both returned to England after three months in Norway. We were part of a NATO group which had been gaining experience in the skills of working and surviving in Arctic conditions. We then got two weeks leave and were back in our base at the beginning of April. We were preparing to fly off with an all-British group to Australia to cooperate with the Australian army in an exercise in the Antarctic. We were to spend almost a year in a camp not all that far from the South Pole. I say all this just to paint in the background.

"Anyway, on the first Tuesday in April of last year, only a few days before we were due to go off, we were called into the CO's office in the late afternoon. He told us that we had to go at once to the Ministry of Defence and report there to a Mr. James Butler regarding a small operation which we were to be involved in. Our CO was as puzzled as we were; all he knew was that it was very urgent. David and I got to the Ministry shortly before seven o'clock that evening where we met this

Mr. Butler. He was obviously a very senior civil servant, who…"

But I couldn't help breaking in there, "All of us know this smooth civil servant. When I met him first it was earlier in the day on that same Tuesday in April of last year. I went there that morning and he gave me lunch. I wanted to get some information from him that I believed should have been in the MOD archives. Apart from that nice lunch I got nothing from him except a brush-ff"

"I already knew that," he smiled, "you see, your name was mentioned to us! Anyway the now Sir James began by reminding us that he knew we had both signed the Official Secrets Act, and that everything we would hear was Top Secret as it involved sensitive matters of Anglo-French relations." He paused there, and then said, "I can tell you that we should have smelt a rat right there, as he must have known that our unit was used in the field of so-called Special Operations. To remind us of our security clearances was an insult.

"He went on to explain that as a legacy of the war there were still some nasty secrets about. This was particularly true of France, where Britain was deeply involved in covert operations. There was always a danger when one of these rose to the surface that it could cause painful embarrassment. If any finger could be pointed at Britain, the evidence of dirty-tricks would be eagerly seized on by the many Anglophobes in France to whom La Perfide Albion is a fact of life. He also explained that the Germans were well aware of this latent distrust of the British by the French, and that they made good use of it during the war. Frequently they would allow the French Resistance to 'find' items of misinformation designed to throw doubt on the sincerity of British assistance. At the time these could usually be disproved and the damaged trust repaired. But today, if any were to be uncovered, they would be treated as Gospel Truth by many.

"I can tell you," he went on, "that he was very persuasive, and although more than a year has passed I can still remember his exact words…

"'Captain Shaw and Lieutenant Sloan, you two have a chance to do your country a considerable service. Unfortunately, some perfectly innocent people may be about to open a Pandora's Box of horrors in the Department of Yonne, deep in the heart of France.'

"I needn't," he said, "report all that he said, but we learned about the Mélitour escape line, about Marie-Claire, Comtesse de Mélitour who ran it, and about the young Hélène Duclos her number two."

He stopped there again, and turned to Grannie, "Let me say, Mrs. Dallachy that it is a privilege to meet you, and I hope that you will be kind enough to tell me some of your wartime adventures one day. I may say that the success of your late husband, Brigadier Dallachy, in stealing the V1 secrets is a legend in the SAS."

I could see that Grannie quite liked the flattery, and I had the uncharitable thought that the Captain had rehearsed this part of his speech before he came. However he was going on with Butler's explanation of the penetration of the escape line, about the many deaths, the torture of Marie-Claire by Major Kretzer, and how Major Dallachy had killed him.

Captain Shaw continued, "Both Lieutenant Sloan and I listened to this account with great interest. Peacetime soldiers spend their time rehearsing for war. I suspect Butler was baiting the hook, knowing how the promise of some real action would appeal. I can't remember exactly what he said, but it went something like this. 'You two gentlemen may think that all this is ancient history and of no significance now, but you would be wrong. After the war there were some unpleasant rumours regarding the penetration of this escape line. As a result we British undertook a carefully investigation. We found, as we had suspected all along, that it had been betrayed by a Frenchman. The surprise was that the young man responsible was son of one of General de Gaulle's closest associates. What followed was one of those grubby deals which our Secret Service sometimes gets up to. I may say that the lad denied everything but the evidence we had against him was overwhelming. There is no point in mincing words; our people blackmailed both the father and the son. It was our silence in exchange for their information and influence on French foreign policy.'

"We were fascinated by this story and had no idea that Butler was fabricating the whole thing. He went on to tell us more fanciful lies, saying, 'You can appreciate the reaction of the French if any of this became known. Frankly, I think the whole blackmail operation was incredibly stupid. Be that as it may, the business has become my responsibility and it appears as though it may rise up and hit us in the face. I say this because in just the last few days we have learned that the same Major Kretzer had a ploy of his own. Put yourself in his shoes. He had all the information he needed to destroy the escape line. The Frenchman who had betrayed the line was no longer of any use; to employ a current expression, he has passed his sell-by date. Kretzer's plan was devised to extract one last service from the Frenchman in the Nazi cause. He had plenty of evidence that would establish the Frenchman's identity and prove his guilt. Apparently he assembled this evidence and buried it so that it would appear as though a member of the escape line had done so in a last desperate act to pass the information onto his colleagues before meeting his own death. I suppose that Kretzer intended to leak the existence of the plant at some appropriate moment. Certainly it was a bomb that he could, at any time, choose explode which would throw dissent amongst the French and fire the tensions between them and the British. The irony is that Major Kretzer was killed before he could do anything and his bomb still lies where he buried it.'"

Captain Shaw broke off there, and said to Grannie, "Butler was very convincing, and went on about the possibility of quite innocent people finding plants such as this one. He then switched to talk about you people here. Considering your family's involvement with the escape line, and the tragic consequence which you suffered when the line was smashed, he said that it was not unreasonable for the de Mélitour family to have something of an obsession about the affair. He said that you, Mrs. Dallachy, your late husband, and your grand-daughter were equally obsessed.

"It was quite a tale he spun, and then he went on to say, 'Unfortunately we now know that some information has come to light which, we fear, could lead them to this old German plant. This danger was shown by an enquiry we received last week from Brigadier Dallachy, and subsequently a visit here today by Miss Yvette Dallachy. Both were seeking information from the records we have about the escape line. In fact, we didn't have that much so there was little to tell. However she told us that she had good reason to visit the de Mélitour family, and that she was leaving for France the next day to stay at the Chateau where she hoped that new information would be uncovered about the escape line.'"

Captain Shaw stopped yet again, "I can tell you that Butler spoke very sincerely. In retrospect, we can appreciate how clever his fabrication was. You will see that he stuck to the truth whenever it could be checked. On this framework he draped his tissue of lies.   .

"I am about to reach the purpose of Butler's deception. Let me continue with Butlers words as best as I can remember them. 'You can see what a difficult position we are in. We dare not tell the truth to the de Mélitour family, who would never forgive us for hiding the identity of the traitor who caused them so much distress. The trouble is that the evidence which we found back in 1945 is irrefutable. If we were to tell them I could not blame them if they exposed the guilt of that young Frenchman. He now is, I can tell you, a very senior politician, and even now has to cooperate with us so long as we still have this hold over him. The scandal would be horrendous and our Secret Service would be vilified throughout the world. I shudder to think how our relationship with France would suffer.

"'Now, if Miss Dallachy is to be believed, either she or the de Mélitour family may soon discover instructions which will lead them to the place where Kretzer planted the damning evidence against our young Frenchman. I am afraid that we do not know in what form they were hidden It could be reports, photographs or documents; we don't know. Neither do we know if Kretzer packed them with sufficient care for them to have survived for sixty years. Whatever the case, we simply can't take the risk that Miss Dallachy will explode Kretzer's bomb. The ensuing devastation would go far beyond Kretzer's wildest dreams. In a nutshell, Gentlemen, your mission is to prevent that from happening.'

"So there we were," Captain Shaw went on, "he had brainwashed us into believing that the four of you here were a threat to British National security. He went on to suggest how we might thwart you. He suggested that we should keep the

Chateau under surveillance and to follow Yvette Dallachy wherever she went. Then, whenever we suspected that she, and whoever was with her, had found something, we were to stage a mock abduction for ransom, take the information from them and, after a day or so, allow our captives to escape. The whole exercise had to look authentic and the loss of the information had to appear incidental.

"He then went on with a bit of flattery. 'Now, gentlemen, you are both experienced SAS officers. I won't insult you by suggesting how you should do this. I have arranged that Station-R will let you have anything you may ask for.'"

Captain Shaw stopped there, and smiled at us, "You'll remember from the 007 films that James Bond gets things from 'Q'. Well, the tools of our trade are supplied from Station-R. But don't tell anybody. It's supposed to be a secret!

"Butler was now ready to bring the meeting to a close. 'For your own safety I must tell you that secrecy is all-important. If you are caught we shall deny all knowledge of your actions. Now, obviously, you will need money, and you mustn't use credit cards, so here is ten thousand francs which should be ample to cover your expenses. As I have just said, we shall always deny knowing you, so we can't ask you to return any surplus funds. Please just treat them as a bonus.'

"He handed over a bulky envelope, shook hand with us, and wished us luck. And that was that; except for one thing. As David and I were walking downstairs it suddenly occurred to us that in all his instructions he never said what we were to do with the German package once it was in our possession. So, back up we went, and when we got to his door we just knocked and went in. To our surprise there were two men with him, one of whom we recognized as Lord Hempson and the other as Michael Marshall our Secretary of State for Defence.

"As we stammered our apologies the two turned their backs on us. Butler, clearly annoyed, said, 'What do you want? Our business is concluded!' I explained the question to him, and the reply was, 'Surely I made myself abundantly clear. Destroy it! Now please leave'

"So that was it, neither of them said a word, and we were on our way again. However on our way to Station-R we did wonder a bit. Several things were not right. Firstly there was Butler's insulting warning about secrecy. Secondly there was matter of the ten thousand francs. His offer to 'just keep the change' came across as a bribe and another insult. Lastly, there was that tense little drama when we returned uninvited. We couldn't make sense of it. But, damn it, he was in a position of power and we decided everything must be A-OK. It certainly became clear at Station-R that the instructions must have come from high places as our every request was provided immediately with no questions asked. The main things were:

A British car to get us into France

British civilian passports and driving licences, not in our names.

Civilian French passports and driving licences.

Nerve gas and some syringes of dope.

Two authentic handguns without bullets

"Yes," he smiled, "I'm afraid that the guns were empty; we couldn't risk hurting you!"

"The rest of it," he went on, "I am sure that you can guess. We got to France next morning, hired a motor bike and the Mercedes, and then drove to Tonnere where we made enquires about a secluded house to rent, and we found that chalet which was ideal. That was on Wednesday, and we began our surveillance of the chateau late that day. You, Mme. De

Mélitour didn't arrive until the following afternoon, and I can tell you that we weren't too pleased to see that XK8 Jag in case you out-ran our Merc! On Friday afternoon we were watching you when you went to that graveyard. We figured that this was the moment we were waiting for."

Captain Shaw had the good grace to look sheepish. "Well, let's just skip over the next part. After we let you escape on the Saturday evening, we returned to quickly clean up the chalet; drove north as fast as possible; turned in the Merc and the bike; collected our own car; and we were back in Britain early on the Sunday morning."

He stopped there, I'm quite sure just to tease us, and Grannie, impatient as always, burst out with, "But what about the film? Did you keep the original one?"

"That's interesting," he smiled, "so you found out that the one we left you with was a replacement. I confess we were surprised and disappointed to find that the Kretzer plant was just a film capsule. We hoped that we would be able to satisfy our curiosity immediately by reading documents and looking through old photographs. However, we did find something else besides the film. When we looked inside the mustard pot, there was in addition as small piece of paper and on it was a scribbled note."

"A note!" exclaimed Grannie, "What did it say!"

He smiled and handed her a small crumpled piece of paper, obviously torn off something. I couldn't resist jumping up so that I could read it over her shoulder. It was written in pencil and read (translated into English):

Dear friends, Hélène, Alicia, and Michelle, I am so glad that you have found this film. It was taken this morning in Troyes. It will prove that M Brume betrayed the escape line. Use it to expose the

318   Shadow of Treachery

bastard. I daren't tell you the truth now in case you
are taken. Marie-Claire

"This is so poignant," Grannie said, "it is as if she were
reaching out her hand to me from the grave. But can you tell
us about the film itself?"

"Let me satisfy your impatience, Mrs Dallachy. Yes, we
did keep it. We could easily have concocted some charade
whereby our two 'captives' could witness its accidental destruction. Then it occurred to us that we could have our cake
and eat it too. All we needed to do was to convince you two
that the film had been exposed to satisfy Mr Butler's require-
ment. We realised that the film was actually a blessing in disguise. Had the evidence been in document form we really
would have had to destroy it.

"We decided to keep the film, not only out of curiosity,
but because we didn't trust Butler. Certainly, the little note
convinced us that it contained the information he had described. But we were wary and frankly a bit paranoid. Civil
Servants have been known to regard members of the military
as being 'expendable'. The film was to be our piece of insurance.

"As I said, we got back to England early on the Sunday
morning. We immediately phoned Butler on the number he
had given us and he instructed us to meet him at his home.
That was another surprise but we duly followed his directions.
On our arrival we were shown into his study. Butler was his
usual effusively pleasant self so it was several minutes before
we were invited to make our report. He was full of congratulations, praise and flattery. He was particularly pleased with our
handling of the film. 'That was masterly piece of deception.
Now there is nobody who knows, or will ever know, what exactly Kretzer had intended reveal.'

"As we left, we wondered about his choice of words. They suggested that he would have been less than pleased if somebody – namely the two of us – did know about Kretzer's intentions.

"From Butler's home we went immediately back to our base. There we asked our unit photographic officer to develop the old film for us. It was on the morning of the day we were due to fly to Australia that we got the prints back. Here they are, Mrs. Dallachy, the pictures from that old film that your friend Marie-Claire buried all those years ago."

The photographs were in a little folder like the ones used for holiday snaps. She opened the folder, and I saw her face change from expectation to bitter disappointment as she looked at the photographs it contained. "Look, Albert," she said, "and you two, Yvette and Pierre. Look what they are like. Thank God Marie-Claire never saw this mess!"

Dreadful was the only word for it! The long internment in the graveyard had damaged the film and the pictures were grainy, faded and covered with blotches. It was just possible to see that they were of a group of people in a street, and one seemed to be of a newspaper, but it was quite impossible to see any detail, or who the people were. We were all silent, until Grannie said, "Well, that's it! All that trouble for a set of useless old pictures."

But I was then surprised to see a light come back to her eyes. "Tell me," she said, turning to the soldiers, "Why then are two gentlemen here? Has something else turned up to bring you so far?"

"Before I go into all that," said Captain Shaw, "let me tell you that we too were disappointed when we saw these prints. We had no time to do anything about it as we were to fly off later that day. That was in April of last year, and we got back to Britain only three weeks ago. At that time our priorities were only to get back to our families again, so we didn't immediately bother to do anything more about the affair in France. It was while we were away that you, Mrs. Dallachy, made your accusations against Lord Hempson. The libel court case was in March of this year, so the whole affair was over and done with by the time we got back. We'd probably never have heard about it but for a happy accident, and that part of the story belongs to David."

"It was an unlikely accident," Lieutenant Sloan began, "and all due to the fact that my mother is an old-fashioned Scottish housewife who lines all the drawers in the house with used newspapers. I went home on leave after getting back from Australia, and when I was putting some of my things away in a drawer I happened to see a headline dealing with Lord Hempson's case and the name de Mélitour caught my eye. Fortunately my mother had used the pages from this same issue in my room, so I pieced them together and it was immediately clear to me that Butler had taken the two of us for a whopping ride.

"When Hector and I met up after our leave he saw immediately, as I had done, that the story which we had been told turned the truth on its head. Butler's tale of a renegade French youth was nonsense. The real culprit was a British officer – now the venerated Lord Hempson. Our exercise in France was not to protect British National security, but to cover-up the fact that the great man was actually a traitor. We supposed that our mission had been instigated by his son, now the Secretary of State for Defence, and his Civil Service aide Mr. Butler, whose pay-off had been his recent KBE. The problem was, of course, that we are both serving officers and as such we have a duty to do what our masters tell us to do. But here, we thought, the circumstances were unusual, so we spoke to my father"

For a few moments there was a silence while we wondered just who that could be, but then David went on, "My father is Sir Edward Sloan who, until he retired last year, was a High Court Judge. His is advice to us was that, at this stage, we should pursue the case on our own. He warned us to be very careful not to let anybody know what we were up to. He didn't think that Butler would be inclined to take any action against us. Although Butler probably realised that we would get to hear of the liable case eventually, he would probably reasoned that, without any evidence, there was little damage we could do. Besides which our mission was 'deniable', and we both knew the meaning of 'deniable missions'. In the first place my father suggested that we should see if the photographs could be digitally improved. Hector mentioned Station-R, and while they could not do the job themselves, we have a friend there who knows the way into many secret government establishments. I can tell you that we live in a wonderful age of technological miracles, just think about the marvellous photographs which come back from space craft, and the military satellites which can take pictures of a newspaper from a hundred miles away, all thanks to computer enhancement. So our friend could arrange for the old film be processed at the government facility which specialises in image recovery and enhancement. I hate to think how many hundred pounds the job cost. Certainly it took them quite a time to do the work – but here is the result."

He opened his briefcase and produced a set of glossy prints, each about half the size of a tabloid newspaper sheet, and handed them to Grannie. I was still looking over her shoulder and I could see that they were of crystal clarity, not a speck of grain or a blotch to be seen. She gave a sudden squeal of excitement, and exclaimed, "I know that street; it is a small one on the west side of Troyes. And look, there is Major Kretzer and there is the young Henry Marshall bedside him."

The photographs had been shot in numbered sequence and they showed a group of Frenchmen, with their hands and their feet tied, hobbling out of a building. In the later ones they were being loaded into a truck under German guns. In the foreground young Marshall seemed to be enjoying the spectacle with Kretzer and, towards the end, even had a friendly arm round his shoulders. The sequence was broken by one picture of the front page of the *Figaro* showing the date – April 19th 1944.

"That's the clincher!" said Grannie happily, "and I must thank you two very sincerely for doing all this work and for coming to see us. Your detective work has certainly put the last nails in Lord Hempson's coffin."

She then turned to Pierre and me, saying, "As for my grand-daughter and her husband, I am sure that they forgave you a long time ago for abducting them. Maybe you don't know that it accelerated their romance in a quite remarkable fashion!"

And then she turned to Albert, "I think this is a case for first things first, so how about some of your de Mélitour Chablis so that we can drink a toast to Hempson and his perdition!"

So after all that we were a very friendly group, but it wasn't long before the sun went in and a little breeze got up and Albert led us back to the house. I saw Albert look at me with a question in his eyes, and I gave him a tiny nod which was enough for him to say to the soldiers, "We really are most grateful to you both and I hope you will do us the honour of being our guests tonight. I am sure you have stories to tell, and you mentioned that you would like to hear some tales from my dear Hélène. I can tell you that they are incredible."

It was in fact a very pleasant evening, and after dinner when we were sitting with our coffees and cognacs, Grannie did what she always did and turned on the BBC News at Ten. We were not particularly interested, but that soon changed as the lead item was about the death of Lord Hempson. He had been playing golf in the morning, but had suddenly died of a heart attack.

It was very odd. Surely we should have been pleased that our arch enemy was dead, but no, we weren't! Grannie in particular had been looking forward to disgracing him in the full glare of publicity, but to bring forward the evidence now would be to insult the dead. For her that was quite impossible. So we were all a quiet group as we went to our beds rather earlier than might have been expected.

It was after breakfast next morning when Captain Shaw asked if he could have a word with us. We all sat down with the two soldiers side by side. That this was significant was immediately obvious when he started by saying, "Last night when we went upstairs David and I had a long talk, and while we cannot go after the dead, what about the living? That creep Butler made monkeys out of David and me. In all this he must have been acting for, and aided and abetted by, none other than Her Majesty's Secretary of State for Defence. It was a disgraceful abuse of power, and I'm damned if they should get away with it. I can tell you that we have an idea how to go about it…"

But before he could go on, Grannie broke in, "No, Captain Shaw, I do not want any more worries, there have been too many ups and downs in this affair already. Now that

Hempson is dead, and I cannot humiliate him, I really don't care about his son or that crooked civil servant."

She paused for a moment, and this gave Albert, who had taken hardly any part in the discussion the previous evening, a chance to break in, "Hélène, I can very well see why you say that, but just pause and think for a little while. As for me I don't at all like the idea of those two fat cats getting away with it. We know they manipulated these two soldiers here to hide the treachery of a senior politician. I think it is only fair to at least hear what Captain Shaw has to say."

Pierre looked at me and shrugged his shoulders as if to say, "Whatever now?" For myself, part of me agreed with Grannie, the other bit was curious, and that bit won, so I said, "I agree Albert, let's listen." It was then Grannie's turn to shrug her shoulders in resignation.

Captain Shaw began by saying, "It was you, M. le Comte, who said the right thing when you called them fat cats, that is what they are and if we do nothing they will get fatter still. First of all Michael Marshall is still a plain 'Mister', and unless he gets a title of his own that's how he will remain. Although his father is now dead, he had only a Life Peerage. I'm sure, though, that his prospects are rosy and he is probably the most likely candidate to be the next leader of his party. The age fifty is quite young to be where he is and he has glittering future before him. The chances are good that he will one day become Prime Minister.

"Also there is Sir James Butler, and his progress up the ladder had been uninterrupted since the early '60's when, as a young trainee, he was in the Ministry of Defence when old Hempson was the Minister. I reckon he was involved in some way even back then."

"He surely was!" I broke in, and explained about the

highly sanitised records regarding the escape line after the originals had mysteriously been recorded as lost.

"That's good," he smiled, "more grist to the mill."

Then he turned to Grannie, "I can certainly see, Mrs. Dallachy, why you want no more publicity. The media have treated you very badly, and you must be sick and tired of it all. But how would you like it if we were to arrange, very quietly and with no fuss, for Michael Marshall to resign his Cabinet appointment and to see the Chiltern Hundreds, saying that he wished to give up public life. As for Sir James he would also resign on a much reduced pension. Neither of them would ever take up any of those lucrative Directorships, so beloved by elderly statesmen and civil servants."

He stopped there and looked at Grannie, "So, tell me, Mrs. Dallachy, do I carry on and explain?"

Chapter Twenty-Three

It was after breakfast next morning that we sat down for our conference, and Grannie began by saying "I'm sure you will think me an old fool to have doubts at this eleventh hour, but I am beginning to wonder if we should be doing this. We were, I think, almost reconciled to the end of the affair, yet here we are again on the merry-go-round. What good will it do? The old bastard Hempson is dead, so why bother?"

I could almost agree with her, but to my surprise it was Pierre who spoke, "Hélène, please don't lose heart now when we are almost at the end. Just remember my grandmother, your old friend Marie-Claire who, in the final act of her real life, buried the evidence of Hempson's treachery, the evidence which we had all given up any hope of finding. For me, and I think for the rest of us, the affair doesn't end with his death. Surely we can't let his son and Sir James get away with it? They abused their powers in the Defence Ministry in an endeavour to hide the truth. For Sir James I'm sure that his wrongdoing goes back to the 1960's when Hempson was the Defence Minister. Now we are in a position to do something about that." He paused before going on, "Come on Grannie, you old fraud, you do agree with me, don't you?"

But she wasn't convinced and said to the two soldiers, "Well, I'll listen, but there is no hurry to make up our minds. We would have to wait a decent interval – at least a month after Hempson's funeral. We owe him at least that much."

Captain Shaw smiled at her, "You are a hard nut to crack, Mrs. Dallachy, but our scheme is really very simple. You see, all we suggest is that you write a short letter to Michael Marshall enclosing one of photographs, and instruct him to come with Butler to meet you and your family at a time and place to be arranged. You will say that unless they come to the meeting you will publish the photographs, showing Hempson's guilt. At the meeting, which I am sure they will have to agree to attend, you will insist that they both resign their positions, and perhaps also agree to a reduction in their pensions. I can't see that they will dare to refuse as the scandal would be enormous if you were to go public. I've even drafted a letter for you to send, but I suggest that we have it checked over by your lawyer, and maybe Sloan's father could give his opinion as well."

There was a few moments' silence and then Grannie said, "Well let's see your letter." And this is what he handed over:

Chateau de Mélitour
Department de Yonne
France
23rd August

The Rt. Hon. Michael Marshall
Ministry of Defence
London

Dear Mr. Marshall
    The enclosed photograph, one of a set of ten, will explain why I now write to you.
    These photographs recently came into my possession. It was my intention to arrange for them to be published as final proof of your father's treachery and of the truth of my accusations. But now with his death, there is possibly no reason why I should do so.

I say "possibly" because, although my family and I have good reason to believe that both you and Sir James Butler have quite improperly sought to hide the truth, we can perhaps reach an understanding, and so avoid publicity.

I shall be staying at <give your address in London and mention times and dates> and shall be accompanied by Comte Albert de Mélitour, his son Jean Pierre de Mélitour, and his wife Yvette who is also my granddaughter. I suggest that it will be to the advantage of both of you to come to see us at <state date and time>. I trust that you will make the necessary arrangements with Sir James. I look forward to receiving a reply from you to confirm you attendance not later than <state date>.

You will understand that in the event of our having this meeting, our decision as to whether or not to publish will depend on its outcome. I must also emphasise that if we do not have your confirmation I shall take it that you do not wish to see us. We shall then take such steps as we think necessary to publish the facts.

Yours faithfully,
Hélène Dallachy

Captain Shaw sat back in his chair with a rather satisfied smile, and Albert, Pierre and I congratulated him on such an easy solution to our problem. But then I noticed that Grannie was silent and she suddenly shook her head decisively. "Look, I can see that you are keen to go ahead with this, but I'm afraid that I am not. I said earlier that I want to wait for at least a month, and after that time I'm sure that you will agree that it must then be my decision and mine alone whether or not to proceed. I am now so happy and contented living here in Mélitour that I just don't want to be disturbed. That old bastard Hempson is dead and I don't want anything to break my peaceful idyll. Maybe I'll change my mind sometime, but certainly not now."

And that was that, none of us felt we should argue the matter and the two soldiers left with a promise to respect Grannie's feelings and to keep confidence about the matter, and to remain silent. I could see that they were very disappointed, but I was sure that we could trust them.

Things rested like that for about six weeks. It may have done so for much longer but one morning Grannie received an astonishing letter. I was with her when she opened it and I saw her frown, but then she laughed and said, "There is no escape from this damn affair, just read this letter!"

Highbury House
Chelsea
London SW3
4th October

Dear Mrs Dallachy,

In the time since my father died I have had the opportunity to go through some of his confidential papers. To my surprise I have discovered that your accusation of his treachery during the Second World War were, unfortunately, all too true.

I hope therefore you will agree to meet me. I am coming to Paris next week and I wonder if I might come down to Mélitour on Saturday 11th October, in the early afternoon, say at two-thirty.

I believe a lot can be explained and dealt with at that meeting. I do hope that you agree to see me, and I look forward to your reply.
Yours sincerely,
Michael Marshall

I looked up after I had read it and she was still smiling, so

I said, "It's incredible, isn't it? It's a nice letter too; will you agree to see him?"

And she did. So on that Saturday afternoon we were all gathered in the drawing room after lunch, and I for one was curious to see what this hated man, Michael Marshall, would be like. In the event he turned out to be charming. He said to Grannie, "For me it all began last year in April when my father asked to see me urgently in my office at the Ministry of Defence. He told me about a problem which had arisen regarding an old piece of German information, long hidden in France, which could be very embarrassing to Britain if it were to be found..."

But Grannie interrupted him saying, "Don't waste our time telling us about that. It may surprise you when I tell you that the two SAS officers you employed were recently here in Mélitour, so we know all about it!"

"Well, well," he smiled, "that simplifies my job today. My father arrived in my office together with Mr Butler. I can tell you that Butler was very convincing. I remonstrated about the need to bring in the army people. I thought that a direct appeal to you, Mrs. Dallachy, your husband and Count de Mélitour would be the better approach. As I saw it you would be unlikely to do something that would result in a massive scandal and would be content to see the traitorous Frenchman removed from his high office and our Secret Service severely censured for their stupidity. But Butler and my father were adamant, so eventually I gave them my agreement. What a fool I was! Eleven months later you sent out those letters and my father raised his case against you. It didn't look like you had a leg to stand on but I was forced to look at Butler's story from a different point of view. At the trial the evidence of your German witness, despite what the papers may have said at the time, devastated my father's case. My father was indeed ill but its severity was conveniently exaggerated to allow him to gracefully withdraw before his case collapsed publically. Frankly I was afraid, but like a foolish coward, I again did nothing. But now that my father has died, everything has changed. Lawyers have been sorting out his affairs but the task of going through his papers, some of which are highly confidential, I elected to undertake myself. There I discovered things which horrified me. One of them was a copy of an original MOD document. All the pages bear the Ministry's official catalogue stamp indicating that they formed part of our wartime archive. It dealt with my father's time in France during 1944 and I have brought a second copy with me.

He then turned to Grannie and passed her a clip with several sheets of paper. They were photocopies of somewhat grubby typewritten originals. The typewriter was old and its ribbon needed to be replaced, so the words were difficult to read. After just a quick glance, she turned to me saying, "Read it to us, Yvette, your eyes are better than mine, and at least English is your first tongue."

As I skimmed over the contents I realised that most of it had initially been written in French and then translated rather badly into English. But it was legible and I read it to them, and what I give here is just a summary. It began, after the war, with a note to the effect that the statements of several French Resistance members had been taken by a Captain Anderson, acting on behalf of the Historical Section of the Special Operations Executive. It was headed:

Troyes, 17th August 1946.
Statements from M. Jacques Denis and Others

It was quite a lengthy document mostly containing tran-

scripts of statements taken from a number of members of the
French resistance. The majority was irrelevant to us but one of
the statements gave an account of M. Brume. It said that initially a man with the code name of M. Ombre had been the
British liaison officer in the area around Troyes. He was gen-
erally liked and trusted. Then in late March 1944 he was unex-
pectedly replaced by another with the code name M. Brume.
At a time when the burdens and dangers were increasing this
was a most unwelcome change. On the night of the 14th of
April a sabotage party supposedly led by M. Brume was surprised by a German patrol while laying explosives on a railway
bridge. It was a disaster and all the members of the party were
killed.

The report went on to say that there was some suspicion
regarding M. Brume. His body was not returned by the Germans along with those of the sabotage party. Rumours started
to circulate that he had not been with the party at all. Also
several people claimed that they had seen him in the town a
few days later. This was the day when six people were arrested.
One person claimed that M. Brume was smartly dressed and
in the company of Major Kretzer.

There was a small item in another report from a woman
member of the Resistance who was working for the Germans
as a clerk in their transport section. She saw a requisition order
signed by Lieutenant Heldorff, dated 20th April, for an ambulance to take a patient to a hospital in Cologne. She noticed
this because usually Major Kretzer would have signed such an
order. This was particularly true because the patient was a
British officer whose name was given as Lieutenant Henry
Marshall. Normally she would have passed this information
onto her contact but he had disappeared and indeed she never
saw him again.

Further notes had been added on 31st August 1946 by an Investigating Officer of Special Operations Executive. The typewriting was easier to read but it didn't add anything new. Mainly the officer was complaining that there were several matters in the statements from the members of the French Resistance which warranted closer investigation but he was constrained by time limits and lack of resources. He drew particular attention to the apparently treacherous behaviour of the British operative, codenamed Brume. He linked this to the special ambulance that had taken Lieutenant Henry Marshall to Cologne and pointed out that such treatment was normally reserved for senior German officer. Why was he not treated "rough" as were almost all Allied officers captured at this time in France? The Germans never gave them the protection of the Geneva Convention covering Prisoners of War. Anyway he concluded that M. Brume was Lieutenant Marshall and that he had been "turned". He finished on a note frustration with the SOE policy of never keeping written records that would reveal the identity of codenamed operative.

When I stopped reading Marshall said, "As you see, that report was written in 1946, but by then it must already have been a case of 'live and let live'. The war was over, and few people were interested in turning over stones to see what was under them, so it would seem that no further questions were asked. The report along with thousands and thousands of other documents was consigned to the archives.

"There it should have remained. But, come 1964, the young Butler must have stumbled upon the report and recognised the name of his Minister. What I do know is that from then on my father kept complete records, showing dates and amounts, of payment he made to Butler. These accounts were also among my father's confidential papers. I also know that

Butler removed the original document from the archive. The archive index card referencing the document has been marked 'missing and presumed to have been destroyed in error' then signed and dated by James Butler. On it was also a cross reference to another document that purports to be a replacement prepared by Butler in 1968. That document is very short and the subject matter is completely different. I am sure that Butler would have shown it you to fob you off.

I might add that Butler's rapid rise through the ranks must have been assisted by my father. He always treated Butler with great respect. I should have thought this odd, for despite his outwardly suave appearance and convincing talk, I wasn't really that impressed with his abilities as a civil servant. Yet again, I didn't think to question this.

He paused there and said to Grannie, "I am sure Mrs. Dallachy that you feel that I must be a very wicked man. A mere apology from me would be an insult. I fully intend to resign my appointment as Defence Minister. I have been guilty of stupidity, cowardice and misuse of power. However, I stop well short of calling myself a villain. It has been Sir James who was the nasty piece of works in all of this. Shall I tell you how I suggest we bring him to justice?"

I wondered what he would say if he knew Grannie had changed her mind about going on, but I was glad when she said, "I can tell you, Mr. Marshall, that until meeting you this afternoon I had decided to do nothing further. I am very pleased with my quiet life here. I confess that I did lump you together with Butler but your father's treachery was the target of my anger. He committed treason and I wanted him exposed. Now that he is dead – well it's over. The rest of my family have been very understanding. But they would think badly of me if we didn't listen to what you propose. So please go ahead and say what you want to do."

Marshall started, "I would like you, Mrs. Dallachy, to write a letter asking me to meet you with Sir James. In the letter you should state that you have evidence as to our wrongdoing. I will give you these sheets which you can produce at the meeting. When you do, I will express shock and say that I have no option but to resign from my position at once. I hope that he'll feel so alarmed at being found out that he too may agree to resign"

Suddenly Grannie was her old vengeful self again as she beamed at him, "Your plan is good. Indeed, we devised something similar ourselves some weeks ago but decided to put it on ice. You see, we were given some new evidence – actually very old evidence – which totally damns your father." She turned to me, "Yvette go and get our draft letter and the photographs. It is time to let Mr. Marshall see what we have."

I am afraid that Mr. Marshall was horrified by the pictures. After all Hempson was his father and, while the papers he had brought with him established his father's guilt, these pictures brought home the harsh reality of his treachery.

After a while Grannie told him about the two SAS soldiers, how they had taken the old film, and had it cleaned up and printed. Soon we were involved with Mr. Marshall in a friendly discussion. We decided to proceed by doing just what we might have done earlier, although Marshall was now going to be a collaborator and not an enemy. Mr. Marshall confirmed that he would arrange for Sir James to meet us, without in any way revealing the hand he intended to play Just for good measure we promised to have the two soldiers on call at the meeting to provide another shock for him.

It was such a friendly discussion that Grannie surprised us by saying, "Mr. Marshall, I can see that you are not to blame at all in this affair, so I suggest that there is no reason whatsoever for you to resign."

He shook his head rather sadly, "I'm afraid there is. I have to admit what I did, and my actions were quite out of order for a Minister of the Crown. Maybe someday I'll get another invitation to serve, but for now I have to go."

But Grannie was quite serious and tried to get him to stay for dinner and even stay the night. However he laughed and said, "I'd love to, but as you can guess I have business in Paris and right now my "minders" will be wondering where on earth I am. You see, in my position I am a target for terrorists so I should never wander about on my own. I just told them this morning that despite the rules I wanted to do a little shopping, and went off despite their disapproval. Now I'd better get off at once and return this hired car to Hertz."

So that was it! We arranged that we would send him the letter immediately and suggested a date a fortnight later for the meeting. Albert said that he would set up the venue once more in Grosvenor House. There was a round of handshakes as he left. I saw that Grannie couldn't resist temptation. She gave him a conspirator's wink as well.

Chapter Twenty-Four

So now six weeks later we were back in our suite in Grosvenor house, late on an October afternoon. We had driven up from Mélitour in the luxury of Albert's new Rolls. But I soon began to worry, as I was concerned lest Grannie might be having second thoughts.

I lay in bed that night wide awake, beside my slumbering Pierre. I remembered that it had been just the same before the day of the libel case, and now I could see in my mind our trying to get Butler to admit to his guilt and to retire quietly. But what if he didn't? However eventually the problem began to blur in my mind, and I did get to sleep. By morning I had sufficient sense to keep my reservations to myself, as it was bad enough to see Grannie worrying without my making things worse. Then I had a brain-wave and despite her protests I got a taxi and took her to Harrods, where I was glad to see her worries seemed to vanish. There is nothing like shopping to take female minds off more serious matters, and it was the best possible therapy both for her and for me. We got back to the hotel in time for lunch, maybe a little tired, but festooned with green plastic bags…and happy!

We were joined for lunch by our two soldiers. We had seen them for a little conference about a week ago, and they now were Hector and David and good friends. That also was a good arrangement as Grannie could shed half a century of her years when she was with congenial young people. On this occasion they had interesting news to tell her. They were due to leave the army by mid September at the end of their Short Service Commissions, and they had plans to open an adventure training school. When she heard that it was to be near Gairloch I saw her eyes light up like a young girl's. She told them of her times gone by in that part of the world. To Grannie it was still an enchanted spot where she had spent her honeymoon, and also the early times in her marriage when Granddad got leave. Not only that, it was also where my father had been born.

She was so much recovered after the brief talk with them that she even agreed to go off for a short nap before we met Marshall and Butler at 4 o'clock. Come the time we were all ready for them. The dining-room had again been turned into a conference suite, just as we had done back in March. Only Grannie and Albert were there with me as we sat at the big table, and I felt as if I were a soldier about to go "over the top."

Pierre had gone down to the foyer to meet Michael Marshall and Sir James, and bring them up to our apartment. In an adjoining room were the two soldiers and John Carson. We had installed a sophisticated CCTV system, so that everything in the conference room could be recorded both in picture and sound. Similar cameras had been concealed in a small bedroom which we were keeping in reserve.

A few minutes before they were due I got a quick call from Pierre to say that they had arrived. After a minute or two he came in with both of them, Michael Marshall looking suave and elegant in a grey suit and the distinguished Sir James in black pin-stripe trousers and jacket, every inch a civil service mandarin. I could see that Grannie was slumped in her chair with her hands trembling, and I was suddenly angry and impatient for Sir James to receive his comeuppance.

There was a moment of embarrassed silence, and then Sir James came forward and bowed to Grannie, saying, "Mrs. Dallachy, it is both a privilege and a pleasure to meet you again. Let me say how sorry I was to hear of the death of your husband – he was a great man."

Then he turned to me, "And you, Yvette, how nice to see you, and my congratulations on your marriage." He stopped there and smiled at me, "I do hope that you will forgive me for not addressing you more formally as Mme. de Mélitour."

Well, if Grannie had lost her voice, I certainly had not. "Sir James – and you will see that do I have the courtesy to address you formally – it gives me no pleasure whatsoever to meet you again, or indeed Mr. Marshall, so please let there be no pretence of friendship where none exists!"

That was just the tonic which Grannie needed, and she sat up straight, saying, "Well, gentlemen, my grand-daughter has spoken for all of us. Sir James you have already met M. Pierre de Mélitour, and at the head of the table is M. Albert le Comte de Mélitour, son of the late Comtesse Marie-Claire de Mélitour with whom I had the privilege to work during my years in the resistance."

I had been watching them as Grannie spoke, and Marshall showed all his politician's skill as he sat down and smiled at her, as we had arranged, saying, "Mrs. Dallachy, let me say that I can well appreciate your feelings, and those of your family. That photograph you sent to me was a great shock, as my father was always a hero to me, and when you first made your accusations he just laughed them off. Then, even after the sudden end of the libel action, because of his illness he still denied everything, saying, 'I couldn't stand any more of the damn case, the trouble is that after all these years it is impossible to prove innocence. The whole thing was a travesty, a reversal of British justice.' Well, I cannot say that I didn't have some doubts, but he was an old man and I took the easy way out and went along with what he said, and so I may say did most of his friends. But now things have changed, and I can see that he lived a lie for all those years, and I can see all too clearly why you hated him. The truth has taken a very long time to come out, and I presume that you wish to discuss this with us. I am curious, where did this photograph come from?"

"That," Grannie smiled, "is an interesting story. In fact there are nine more such photographs. We got them because of the stupidity of Sir James here!"

That was the last thing he expected to hear, and he spluttered, "What do you mean by that?"

"Just be patient, Sir James. First I must tell you that we know all about your ill conceived operation with the two SAS soldiers, which you arranged just after my grand-daughter been to see you. She had spoken then about possibly finding some information about the de Mélitour escape line, and Mr. Marshall here, and probably also Lord Hempson, must have taken fright. You then ordered Captain Shaw and Lieutenant Sloan to go to France and try to track Yvette's movements, and steal or destroy anything she found. I can tell you that those two SAS officers are in an adjoining room with our solicitor. Your scheme might well have worked except, as I said before, for your stupidity."

There was a moment of dead silence, and I could almost see the cogs whizzing round in his head, as he wondered what would come next. "You see, Sir James," she went on, "your first mistake was when the two soldiers came to your office, and you made a point of emphasising the fact that they had signed the necessary forms in connection with the Official Secrets Act. It was an insult to remind SAS officers of this. They might have excused you but then you gave them ten thousand francs to finance the operation. You told them that they needn't bother to return any un-spent francs. That was just like telling a waiter to keep the change."

As Grannie talked I could see Marshall shaking his head as if to say "What a fool", but she was going on, "So, although they went on with the operation it was with reservations, and when they found that the buried package was an old tin containing a film capsule, they kept the original film, and showed the two young people here, Pierre and Yvette, another film being exposed and made useless. They did in fact have the original film developed, but they were about to go off on an exercise, and they didn't get the pictures until the very day that they flew off to Australia. It was only after they got back to this country a year later – about two months ago – that they could do anything about it."

She paused there, and Marshall broke in as we had arranged, "Fancy that film surviving so well after being buried for more than fifty years."

"But I'm afraid it didn't," Grannie said, "Look, here are the photographs that came out."

And she handed them the folder with the original useless pictures, and I could see that Sir James was examining them closely, and seemed to be enjoying doing so. "These photographs are unintelligible," he smiled, "Are we to understand that the photograph you sent was of some kind of imaginary enactment intended to deceive?"

Grannie grinned right back at him, saying, "These old useless pictures would have been the end of it had Captain Shaw and Lieutenant Sloan not been suspicious after their treatment by you, Sir James. Being in the SAS they knew who to approach to have the film treated and computer enhanced. It is an interesting thought that if they hadn't had their suspicions aroused they would probable just have discarded the old film as useless. Here are the other nine photographs courtesy of modern technology. They are the final and conclusive proof that Lord Hempson was a traitor."

Grannie paused there, then handed the batch of photographs to them. While Marshall just glanced at them quickly I could see that Sir James couldn't hide his astonishment. He was about to break in but she refused to give way, and went on, "So the guilt of Lord Hempson is now established beyond any possible doubt, but now he is dead. I am prepared to do nothing further, subject however to assurances that neither of you continues to benefit from his patronage. The steps which you have to take in order to meet our requirements, which are both simple and non-negotiable, are as follows." She sat back in her chair and numbered the items off on her fingers:

"Firstly you, Mr. Marshall, will announce that following the death of your father you wish to retire from public life. You will resign your Ministerial appointment, and apply for the Chiltern Hundreds. You may retain the pension due to an ex-Member of Parliament, but the excess due to you as Minister of the Crown must be transferred to the Earl Haig Poppy Fund, a charity dear to the heart of my late husband. The arrangements for this need not be made public, but we shall require proof.

"Secondly you, Sir James, will issue a statement saying how much you regret the retirement of Mr. Marshall, and that you feel it is an appropriate time for you too to go. As regards your pension, one half of it must be transferred to the Poppy Fund, under the same arrangements as Mr. Marshall.

"Thirdly, all these arrangements must be completed and

confirmed by each of you within the next week.

"Fourthly, neither of you must make any complaint or approach to the army authorities regarding the actions of Captain Shaw and Lieutenant Sloan, who in any case are due to retire from their Short Service Commissions in the middle of next month

"These four things," she went on, "are the sum total of our requirements. They are so simple that we see no necessity for them to be written down, but unless both of you adhere to them to them in every detail, we shall go public about the whole affair, starting with Lord Hempson's treachery and ending with your botched attempts to stop us finding the truth."

I saw that Marshall was now pretending to be deep in thought, but Sir James managed to smile at Grannie before saying, "Mrs. Dallachy, your story is fascinating, but whatever Lord Hempson and Mr. Marshall have done, I must now make it quite clear to you that I am not guilty of any wrongdoing. However, I request your permission to apologise to the two soldiers. It just shows that a civilian like me should never be put in the position of giving orders to the military.

"In April of last year I received the call from Brigadier Dallachy, followed by your grand-daughter's visit. When I got out those old papers for her I was reminded that Lord Hempson had been my Minister at that time. I was stupid enough to phone him. I was astonished by what happened next. I found myself being ordered by my Minister, Mr. Marshall here, to set up the operation with the soldiers. He explained the necessity for it by telling me a tale about a renegade Frenchman, and about his entrapment by our Secret Service. Unfortunately I fell for it, and you know what happened thereafter."

He stopped there for a moment to clear his throat, "I can

tell you that I was unhappy about things, and some time afterwards, off my own bat, I got some research done through
the German army records department. You have seen what I
found, the papers which seemed to completely exonerate the
young Lord Hempson of any involvement in treachery. Not
only that, but he was a hero, and in hospital when the tragedy
happened. Anyway, as you know, I believed the papers and
gave evidence on his behalf at the libel trial."

He stopped and smiled round to us, saying. "You will see
that my only guilt has been that of believing my friends rather
than questioning them too closely. I have done nothing im-
proper, so with your permission, Mrs. Dallachy, I shall withdraw now and leave you to have a private discussion with Mr.
Marshall."

It might have been quite convincing, but then Marshall
slapped the table saying, "James, I must congratulate you. I'll
bet these nice people here are wondering if your story might
indeed be true. Both you and I know, of course, that it is all a
tissue of clever lies.

"Listen carefully, James, I must warn you now that I know
a great deal more about your duplicity that you might imagine.
For example, I know that up until 1964 the MOD had records
on file which show that the British officer code named Brume
was a traitor. Furthermore, I know that these records clearly
point to the fact that Brume and my father were one and the
same person. Do you want me to go on, James? Do you want
me to explain how these incriminating documents were stolen
from the archives and replaced by innocuous one? You know,
don't you James, the vile purpose of that theft…the blackmail
of my poor father!"

It was now the turn of Sir James to bang the table furi-
ously, "Michael, you are talking nonsense! As I have already

said I have been guilty only of taking instructions both from you and your father without asking too many questions. That is all! If, as you say, the original records in the Ministry archives had been stolen then it's obvious that your father must have done it to destroy the evidence against him. Damn it, he was the Minister! He could do whatever he wanted! It was he who instructed me, the junior clerk, what to put in the replacement document once I had reported the absence of the originals. I suppose I did wonder at the time why the Minister would concern himself with such a trivial matter. But now we know, don't we Michael, that it was to cover up his treachery. Anyway, as I said earlier, my conscience is clear and I have no guilty secrets. As to your suggestion that your father was being blackmailed…well that's just absurd. So I'll leave the rest of you to your further discussions."

But Marshall shook his head, "You are a fool, James, so for God's sake shut up! You must be blind if you don't realise that your whole rickety fabrication of lies has come tumbling down. I can tell you that for the last few days I have been agonising as to what I should do this afternoon. Before you spoke I was inclined to accept Mrs Dallachy's conditions even though they are far too generous to you!"

Sir James reared up in anger, "Michael, what the hell do you mean, I admit nothing except being stupid enough to believe your lies and those of your father. Certainly I am not guilty of any wrongdoing apart from that."

"All right," said Marshall, "we'll do it the hard way. I did warn you, but your stubbornness convinces me that it is now time for me to lay all my cards on the table. You see, James, underneath all your suave cunning there lies no great intelligence. You are unable to comprehend that, under the same set of circumstances, other people may act differently to the way you would choose. You would not have appreciated what a meticulous man my father was. I am sure that you believed without question that he would not keep anything which would indicate that he was a traitor. But he did – indeed, he kept a great deal! He kept records of the whole affair and left them where he knew I would find them after his death. My father may have been a coward and a traitor, but he was compelled by the torment of guilt to at least preserve the truth about himself and in the end pass it onto his son. Yes, James, it was a very financially rewarding day when you were given the tedious job of sorting through the old archives covering the French resistance in 1944. Eventually, you came to read one such paper dealing with events in the Department of Yonne in April 1944. May I remind you what it looks like? I brought a copy along with me today."

He stopped and fished a paper from his breast pocket, "There, would you like me to read it out aloud?"

But Sir James, whose colour had changed to an alarmingly vivid red and whose eyes flickered around like a trapped rabbit, interrupted, "Where the hell did you get that...there were no other..."

And he stopped there as if realising that he was digging his grave even deeper. Then he seemed to recover himself, and turned again to Marshall, "Before you go on, Michael, it is essential that we have a brief private chat. I wouldn't like you to make a fool of yourself, and it won't take long to explain something to you, so let's go into a side room if that can be arranged."

For a moment Marshall was puzzled but then said, "James, surely there is nothing more we have to say to each other , but come on, let's get it over with."

Pierre showed them into the small bedroom which we had

prepared and I pushed a switch which I had beside me. The TV set in our conference room began to show the two of them. Their voices were crystal clear. It was Sir James who began, "Look, Michael, there is no point whatsoever for the two of us to fall out, what has been done can't be undone. We can't deny your father's guilt, but we must limit whatever damage we can. The most important thing is for you to destroy the copy of that old MOD paper you have in your hand. Do that and we will have nothing more to worry about, will we? We cannot deny that we have been foolish, but the excuse for both of us is that we acted as we did because we believed what your father told us. Don't be an idiot; if we stick together we are fireproof!"

"Rubbish, James, you are wasting your time and mine. How can you expect me to do a deal with you? You have not been listening. It is not just that one piece of paper. I know everything about you and have my father's records as evidence of your villainy. You are a blood-sucking leech who has been preying on my father for forty years. I've been waiting for this moment ever since I discovered the details of his blackmail payments. You're finished, James. I'm off to join the others."

But then we heard Sir James say, very quietly, "Just wait a minute, Michael, you would be very unwise to do that!"

"Unwise! What the hell do you mean?"

"Well, I did hope that it wouldn't come to this, but unless you listen and do as I tell you, there will be most unpleasant consequence – for you."

Marshall sounded very quiet and composed as he said, "Don't try to frighten me, there are no skeletons in my cupboard, so what the devil are you trying to hatch up now?"

"What I have found out, my dear Michael, is that you have a cheek with all this 'holier than thou' nonsense. You are not above a bit of villainy yourself, are you? But don't worry as I'll keep quiet if you are sensible now."

I think that the four of us were struck dumb with astonishment, and it was Grannie who first found her voice, "I'd never have imagined it, and I was quite coming round to liking Marshall. Darn it, they are a pair, aren't they?"

Listening to her I missed a bit of what was said next door, but I picked up the conversation with Marshall saying, "...only suppose you have taken leave of your senses, what mischief are you up to now?"

"Me up to some mischief? Certainly not! But for you it is quite different!"

Sir James paused for a moment, as if to tease Marshall, then went on, "But talking of telling the truth, I sincerely hope that I shall not be required to do so, as that would ruin your career. Remember that about a fortnight ago you made a very powerful speech in the House in which you opposed an Opposition motion to restrict the involvement of non-EC companies in North Sea projects?"

"James," Marshall broke in, "you must for heaven's sake stop all this nonsense. You well know I have held this view for ages. It is totally irrelevant."

"You are a bloody good actor," said Sir James, "and you know damn well what I am talking about. You see, I was in your office quite early one morning just the other day. There was a letter on your desk which I found very interesting. Anyway, I managed to get a number of photocopies done, and the original one was back on your desk before you came in. Here is one of these copies just to refresh your memory."

We were all riveted, but were then surprised to hear Marshall give a great shout of laughter and say, "James you have missed your vocation, you should have been the court jester!

Come on, we must share this joke with our friends next door!"

We then heard some indistinct noises before Marshall came back into the room, holding a letter in his hand, with Sir James following behind, no longer flushed, but chalk white.

"Have you both come to some conclusion?" Grannie said politely.

"I don't know about that," Marshall said, "but certainly I have come to this one, and that is that James is even more of a fool than I had thought. You see, I made a speech in the House recently about North Sea oil, in support of non-EC firms being allowed to continue with their work there in the field of development and production. May I show you this remarkable letter, one with which Sir James thinks he can blackmail me into sealing my lips. It is in fact from the Managing Director of one of the major oil companies in Brazil, and probably about number three in the world. As you will see from his letter, he is a very good friend of mine."

He then passed the letter to Grannie, saying, "You and the others may find it interesting reading!" I was sitting next to her, and she showed the letter to me as she read it. The letterhead was certainly very imposing but letter itself was an informal hand-written one:

Óleo Internacional de Brazil

Dear Michael,

Very many thanks for your help; it was kind of you to take the trouble to do this great favour. It will resolve what could have been a major problem. I have today arranged for an immediate transfer into you current account of £60,000 which will clear my indebtedness.

Maria and I are looking forward very much to your visit next spring (autumn to us!), and we'll be there to meet you when you land in Rio.

```
Remember - Minha casa é tua casa,
With my best wishes,
José
```

Grannie looked puzzled as she passed the letter on to Albert, and there was, shall I say, a thoughtful pause as we digested its contents, which seemed absolutely damning. However Marshall looked round at our serious faces and laughed again. "I can see that you are all taken in just like James here, and what a pity that is for him. You see, my old friend José is, as I said, the MD of this major international oil company, but although they are a huge concern, the oils they deal with are all edible ones – olives, sunflower, rape seed, and a dozen more varieties. I can tell you that they are about number three in the world for margarine. So you can see that they have not even a jot of interest in the North Sea. But you may be wondering what that sixty-thousand pounds is for. Well, he and I share an interest in vintage cars, and he is at present rebuilding an 8-litre 1930 Bentley. Unfortunately, however, there were major problems with the engine of his car which had been inexpertly modified over the years. I noticed that an engine in good condition was being sold at auction some weeks ago, and by arrangement with José I bought it for him. You may question why on earth I paid so much for an old car engine, but let me tell you that his car will be worth over half a million pounds when it is complete."

He paused for a moment, and then went on "Hard luck, James, but it wasn't even a good try!"

Butler looked puzzled, "I'm sorry Michael but I don't know what you are talking about!"

Marshall frowned, and then said to him, "Surely you aren't going to deny our conversation just now?"

"No, of course I am not. But where did an oil company

come into it? And what's all this nonsense about a letter?"

I could feel almost sorry for Butler when Pierre went over and rewound some of the tape we had of their meeting, and turned on the TV set which displayed the two of them in the bedroom, with Sir James saying, "…you made a very powerful speech in the House in which you opposed an Opposition motion to restrict the involvement of non-EC countries in North Sea oil projects…"

"Turn it off, Pierre," Grannie said, "I reckon that's enough."

And she turned to Sir James, "The time has passed for any more talk, but I must advise you that I now feel that we were too generous with the terms which we offered to you previously. Everything stands except the question of your pension, and you must now retain only a third of it and pass the rest to the Poppy Fund."

He began to splutter but she would have none of it, "I told you that we do not wish to hear anything more from you, so now I'll ask our lawyer, John Carson, to take you into another room and arrange with you the details of the transfer of your pension moneys. But the draft of your retirement announcement will have to wait a little while as we want a further talk with Mr. Marshall."

But before he could go Marshall broke in, "Mrs. Dallachy, there is something else which you should know before you stipulate the term which James has to meet. Once you have heard what I have to say I think you will agree that they still far too generous. I'll be brief."

I glanced at Sir James, and saw him sitting slumped down in his chair. Obviously all the fight had gone out of him. Marshall also looked at him, and there was no sign of pity as he started, "One of the many papers which I found in my father's files was a complete account of the blackmail money given to this villain since 1964. You all know this, but what I didn't tell you was the magnitude of those payments."

He stopped there held up some papers for Sir James, "It's all here. If you think it is wrong then just let us see your records. I'm sure you must have had many happy times looking at them!"

He then passed copies over to Grannie, "Mrs. Dallachy, these will show you the colossal hold that Sir James had over my father. Since 1964 he collected over three hundred thousand pounds in blackmail money. Another of my failures was never to wonder how a civil servant could live in such a beautiful Georgian manor house in Surrey with grounds extending to some ten acres. I suggest that a nice round sum of half a million pounds, allowing for interest received, should also be transferred by him to the Poppy Fund. If that leaves him a little short I reckon he'll be able to sell his house for at least a million. That will enable him to buy a much smaller house, more in keeping with his position as a retired civil servant."

He stopped there and surprised me by putting his hand on Sir James' shoulder, and saying, "I'm sorry, James, that things have come to this. Accept the terms which she has outlined plus this extra payment and you can resign still with your title and with the respect of your friends and colleagues. As for me I am most grateful to them for giving me the option, one which I gladly accept."

I wondered what his reaction would be, but he was a broken man and just gave a quick nod, before he went off with John Carson.

Grannie said to Marshall. "This has made my day, and all this talking has made me thirsty, so I think we could all do with a glass of wine."

We talked trivialities for a while, and it was after the first bottle of Chablis was finished when she said, "Now, Mr. Marshall, we are all very indebted to you for coming here today, and having done so in such a friendly way. It is now clear who the villain in the piece was. You know, I have hated your father for most of my adult life but these recent dramas with their twists and turns have somehow cleansed my heart. Extraordinarily, I find that I can no longer bear him any ill will. I imagine the dreadful pressures that Kretzer must have inflicted on him. He must have been tortured for the remainder of his life by the shame of his surrender and capitulation. Cowardice and vanity are weaknesses but few of us are tested as he was.

"But as for you, Mr. Marshall," and again she put her hand onto his, "we have no quarrel whatsoever with you, as we can see how you were deceived. But we have to arrange Butler's resignation, so how do we do that without mentioning your father, or you?"

"That's easy," he smiled, "as that problem doesn't exist. You see we must now tell the truth about my father, and because of that I have no alternative but to resign my Ministerial appointment. It would be generous if you could see your way to allow me to retain my Parliamentary seat. There will in any case be an election in the spring of next year, and my constituents can then decide if they still want me as their member."

He paused there, and put his hand on Grannie's, "I think that's almost the end, but we still have to tie up Butler, and that will be quite easy, as it isn't unusual for a top civil servant to resign at the same time as his Minister. And it's easier in his case as he is not far off retirement age. So let's see your lawyer and we'll get busy with my press release and his."

Chapter Twenty-Five

Pierre and I decided to let Grannie and Albert continue without us. We went through to the adjoining room where the two soldiers, Hector and David, had been patiently waiting and eager to learn from us what had happened. As we were leaving, John Carson returned with Butler and went to join the others around the little conference table to bring matters to a conclusion. The press statement he drew up for Michael Marshall was rather cleverly done and I have shown it in Appendix 2. The one for Sir James Butler was not arrived at so amicably but he had to accept what had been written for him, and it is given in Appendix 3. When it was finished we all assembled again and watched in silence as Sir James stood up and walked slowly out of the room. If ever I saw a beaten man, it was he, and I couldn't help having a thrill of delight as he went off.

A second bottle of Chablis seemed to be in order and Pierre went round filling up the glasses while Grannie and Marshall put their signatures to their joint document. Then, rather shyly, they both stood up and shook hands. She said to him, "Look Michael – I'm darned if I am going to call you Mr. Marshall after all this – you said that it was essential that we are all seen to be good friends, so are you by any chance free to have dinner with us here in the hotel this evening? I'll bet that there will be some sharp eyes that will see us and wonder."

He smiled at her, "Hélène, I'm going to steal some words from you and say that I am darned if I am going to call you Mrs Dallachy after all this. I can tell you now that I came this afternoon in trepidation. I knew that my father's treachery could no longer be hidden, and I was determined bring about Sir James' downfall. I am well please with the outcome and I look forward to a new beginning with the dirt washed from my own hands. So…SO!…I shall be delighted to accept your most kind invitation. I don't think I told you that I arranged for my wife to bury herself in a little country hotel tonight, as I feared she could be besieged by pressmen. But now that danger is over. If I may use your phone, I would like to give her a call to tell her that all is well and let her know that I will be joining her later."

While he was away, Grannie went over to Hector and David and linked arms with both of them. She grinned, and said, "Boys, I have always had a soft spot for a soldier. Would the two of you care to escort an old lady to dinner? By the sounds of things we may be getting to know one another quite well."

Michael returned looking more relaxed, "My wife is greatly relieved and sends her congratulation and good wishes. May I return briefly to business? I suggest that, as regards our statements, we arrange to release them at perhaps noon tomorrow. That will enable me to attend to the matter of my resignation with the Prime Minister in the morning. Also, if you wish, it will allow you to make your escape to France before the balloon goes up. There is bound to be some speculation in the media. If there is seen to be friendship between you and me that should kill much of the sensational comment."

When we entered the dining room Grannie was still arm in arm with Hector and David. The three of them were putting on a good show and Grannie beamed at all and sundry. Meanwhile Albert had taken the precaution of mentioning to the Head Waiter that we were entertaining Mr. Marshall and we were seated with much fuss and attention. Not one person in the room could have failed to notice us and I knew that news of our dinner party would filter back quickly to the press.

We discovered over dinner that Pierre and Albert had expressed an interest in Hector and David's proposed Adventure Complex which had now gained sufficient stature to warrant the use of capital letters. An involvement in the Adventure Complex had in fact been discussed with the soldiers in the morning while Grannie and I were out shopping. I suspected that what had given Pierre the idea of going in with them was the thought that maybe our young son, Jean, could learn his fishing skills on the same waters as his grandfather back in August 1956. Certainly when Albert and Pierre told us what they were thinking about they got very enthusiastic kisses from Grannie – and from me too!

It was a most enjoyable dinner, and it didn't come as a great surprise when Grannie asked Mr. Marshall – or rather Michael we were calling him now – to come with his wife and stay with us at Mélitour. He thanked her but he also was a wise guest who knew that he shouldn't linger too long. We were back in our apartment not long after ten o'clock. The two soldiers came back with us so that we could talk some more about the project. With limited resources their initial ideas had been rather modest. Now, with Albert's financial backing and business acumen they could aim at the top end of the market and incorporate first rate fishing tuition into the Adventure School. Before the evening was out we were considering the possibility of a small luxury hotel, and making plans to acquire enough ground right away in anticipation of the scheme going ahead. Nothing concrete could happen until after Hector and David were demobbed and it was agreed that they would come down to Mélitour as soon as they were free when the real work could start.

It was just when we getting into bed that Pierre said to me very seriously. "Look, darling, why don't we get another three hundred acres so that we can build a golf course up there sometime?"

"That, Pierre," I replied equally seriously, "is an excellent idea. You see with this motherhood you have forced on me I doubt if I'll ever get back up to scratch again. But, as owners of the course, we'll be able to pick our own handicaps!"

In the morning we made an early start. I suppose that John Carson arranged for the press releases to go out at noon as we had planned. However by then we were already in France, and home in time for a late lunch. We were very lucky in our timing as on that same morning the Special Branch back in London had a spectacular success against a gang of bank robbers who made their get-away in a super-charged Jaguar which contrived to out-run the pursuing police cars, but was then tracked by helicopters. It all ended more than fifty miles away in a shoot-out in which two innocent civilians, two police, and three of the four robbers were injured, the fourth being killed. One lucky passer-by had managed to get a video of the affair, which no doubt made him quite rich, and all the gory pictures kept down the space which could be given to our affair.

Certainly we had one or two visits at Mélitour from the British press, but they went off very smoothly. In the reports there were even a few kind mentions of Grannie and how right she had been to libel Lord Hempson. Most of them said that Michael Marshall's retirement was a sad loss to both the government and to the country, and expressed the hope that he would soon be reappointed to some high office of state. One thing that we were all pleased about was that Butler's retirement hardly got mentioned – after all, he was just a civil servant.

Inevitably the French papers also picked up the story. There were some snide remarks about how a man who had caused the death, and sometimes a painful death, of many brave Frenchmen and Frenchwomen had gone on to become a top politician in Britain. We then had an influx of reporters from Paris. Grannie was magnificent when she told them that there were always two sides to matters like this. She reminded them that it was a British soldier, her late husband Brigadier Andrew Dallachy, who had exacted some revenge by killing the Germans involved.

So, once again we all settled down to a quiet life in Mélitour, and I was glad to see how much happier Grannie now was, with the affair behind her. She was also very pleased that good relations were re-established between her and Michelle and Alicia. She even arranged for them to come down for a few days, and I was touched to see how much they enjoyed seeing the Château again after so many years.

Also I could cheer her up even more just a month after that, when I told her that I had missed two periods and was pregnant again.

In late September of the following year, I reckoned that I was a very clever girl when I produced an eight pound baby daughter which meant once again the Château Mélitour could have a Marie-Claire in the house.

Appendix One

Gairloch
Henley-in-Arden
West Midlands
5th February

Dr. Peter Liddle
The Second World War Experience Centre
5 Feast Street
Hornsforth
Leeds
West Yorkshire
LS18 4TJ

Dear Dr. Liddle,

I refer to our recent correspondence and you will see hereunder the story of how, in April 1944, I was involved in trying to get performance figures for the V1 flying bombs. It is rather an unlikely story, but it really did happen.

It begins when I was on leave staying with my grandparents in Gairloch, after spending nearly three years in France. Much of my work there had been with the SOE and involved the setting up maquis groups. Anyway one morning I was surprised to be collected by a helicopter and then flown down to Farnborough by a Mosquito from Lossiemouth, without being given any information for all the haste.

I can still remember the flight, it sounds like

nothing now, but less than an hour and a half after
taking off we were landing at RAF Farnborough. I was
taken to an office building where a Flight Lieutenant
was waiting on the steps, who at once rushed me along
a long corridor and into an office which had been set
up for a conference.

There were a thee men waiting for me including
Wing Commander Jack Thompson, my boss in the SOE, who
gave me a smile of welcome and a wiggle of his
fingers to show me that the affair was none of his
doing. The other two were civilians. The first was
rather scruffy, but the other was very much a civil
servant mandarin, in an immaculate dark suit, and
highly polished shoes. I may say that I was suddenly
embarrassed as I remembered that in my hurry this
morning to get myself dressed in uniform I'd had no
time to polish my brass buttons or indeed clean my
shoes.

It was the mandarin who seemed to be in charge,
and to begin with it was just like a social occasion.
Coffee and biscuits appeared, and he even managed to
make a polite enquiry about the prevailing weather in
the Scottish Highlands. He introduced himself as
Harold Beamish of the Ministry of Home Security, and
the other civilian as James Pettie from GCHQ. This
rather puzzled me as I while I knew about that outfit
being involved with code breaking, I would have
expected that the Army or the Air Force to be in
charge of things - whatever they were. He then
puzzled me further by saying that we would have to
wait for the Chairman of the meeting.

He filled in some time by telling me about what he
called the V-type Weapons, about how their existence
had been suspected some eighteen months ago, but had
remained undiscovered until a clever WAAF officer had
spotted what looked like a flying bomb - now called a
V1 - in a photo-reconnaissance picture of Peenemunde,

a huge research and development complex on the shores of the Baltic. He also talked about the raid by some six hundred bombers last autumn, one of the most difficult - and expensive - raids undertaken by the RAF.

"It was very costly," he went on, "we lost forty bombers, but it must be considered a success. But for that raid the V1 attacks would probably already have started and God alone knows what would have happened."

Just as he said that the missing Chairman arrived, and limped in to take his place at the head of the table. He nodded to the others, but it was to me that he spoke, "Good morning, Major Dallachy, I gather that you have been dragged away from some very well-earned leave. Well, I'm sorry about that, however, desperate situations require desperate measures. But let me introduce myself, I am Duncan Sandys, and early last year Mr. Churchill asked me to take charge of our arrangements to deal with what was then a quite unknown threat by new and deadly weapons. I believe that you have been told something about the V1, and there is also what we have called the V2 which is a rocket-powered bomb, but it is the V1s which worry us more. Already we know quite a lot about them but critically we lack vital information regarding their performance. For example, we do not know their flight speed."

He stopped there, and I suddenly realised who he was - Mr. Churchill's son-in-law - but I was so puzzled about the whole affair that I broke in to say, "Mr. Sandys, forgive me, my mission would seem to be important, but I've been told nothing about it, don't you think that it is time to tell me just what I am supposed to do?"

Such plain speaking horrified Mr. Beamish, the posh civil servant, and he said, "Major Dallachy, do

please give Mr. Sandys the courtesy of listening to
his explanation, you will be told all about your
mission in due course."

But Mr. Sandys laughed, "Major, it is I who should
apologise; you see I am getting corrupted by spending
so much of my time now in Whitehall. I am glad that
Mr. Churchill hasn't heard me this morning, as he is
all for writing things on just one side of a sheet of
paper. So you want to hear to hear about your
mission, well it really is very simple. You have to
arrive tomorrow afternoon at one of the V1 launch
sites in northern France. We call these ski-sites.
You must arrange things so that you arrive in a
German staff car with a German soldier as the driver.
You must then spend the rest of that day and the
following day finding out all that we want to know
about the V1. That night you fly back here and
report. That's all - any questions?"

It was all so absurd that the only response I
could think of was to continue on the same lines, so
I said, "That sounds quite simple, Mr. Sandys,
perhaps you would be kind enough to arrange a car to
take me to Croydon so that I can catch the Imperial
Airways afternoon flight to Paris."

I saw the posh civil servant rear up at my
audacity in matching fun with fun, but Mr. Sandys was
more human. "Touché, Major, I deserved that, as
things are far too serious for jokes. No, you won't
be lucky enough to be flying to France by Imperial
Airways, and neither will it be in the luxury of a
Hannibal or Heracles. You will, of course, be in a
Lysander, and I'd better stop fooling around and
explain why you are such a very special candidate for
this enterprise.

"Mr Beamish will have told you about Peenemunde.
For the past many months we have tried our damnedest
to get an agent into the complex. We have failed and

several brave men have lost their lives in the
enterprise. We have also tried to lure, and in some
cases to blackmail, both German soldiers and
civilians, but here again we completely failed. That
is until just a month ago. We then had only one agent
left, and not a very promising one at that. He is an
elderly Polish exile and six months ago he was
infiltrated into Germany and has since managed to set
himself up running a little tobacconist shop in
Griefswald, a little town about fifteen miles from
Peenemunde.

"The break came when a German soldier came into
the shop and, to his horror, the Pole recognised him.
The German, however, simply completed his purchase
and left. Our man heaved a sigh of relief, believing
that he had not been recognised in turn. But he was
wrong. The German was waiting for him outside when he
closed up that evening. Naturally he was paralysed
with fear believing that the game was up. Again he
was wrong. Before he could do anything, the German
had embraced him and announced that he was still his
friend.

"The link between them was that the soldier had a
Polish grandmother whom he had visited several times
before the war, and our man was then a near
neighbour. It soon emerged that the soldier was
disaffected as he had been with the army which had
invaded Poland in 1939 and he soon found that all his
Polish relatives had been massacred. At the time he
had the good sense to keep quiet, but now he was
willing and eager to help. He had been wounded in
Russia, which left him lame, and now, as a non-
combatant, his job at Peenemunde was that of an army
driver. The miraculous bit of good luck for us is
that he sometimes takes scientific officers of the
German army to visit the V1 weapon sites. As soon as
we found that out we did two things, the first was to

parachute another agent into the area, who
fortunately got in safely and was able to contact the
Pole, and to speak to him and the German soldier. He
brought with him a new small radio set, and the plan
which they discussed was to try to intercept the car
on such a visit and then substitute a British officer
for the German one. The other thing we did was to set
up a special team at GCHQ to listen day and night for
any message from the Pole or our agent, and Mr.
Petrie here is the head of that team. Tell the Major
about it."

Up till then Petrie had hardly spoken, but now he
almost fizzed with enthusiasm. "Major, you can't
understand how exciting it is when you have waited
for hours, days, weeks, or even months for a message
to come through, then at last, through the crackle of
atmospherics you can make out the regular dots and
dashes of a Morse message. That message, the first
since our team was set up twenty-seven days ago, came
in at 3 a.m. this morning. It was, of course,
originally transmitted in coded form and written in
Polish, but here is a translation of it."

He handed me a single flimsy sheet of paper which
I spread out and read. Certainly I knew that it had
to be important, but I couldn't have guessed just how
important that sheet of paper was going to be. It
changed my life and, believe it or not, I still have
it. Remember that such messages have no punctuation
marks, and there is no distinction between upper and
lower case. Here is what was written:

JOHANN BRANDT LEAVES TODAY WITH SCIEN-
TIFIC OFFICER MAJOR ABERHART BORMANN FOR
VISIT TO SKI SITES CALAIS TO CAP GRIS NEZ
HE WILL BE IN ESSEN TONIGHT AND WILL AP-
PROACH ARDRES AND ROAD TO GUINES 1600
HOURS TOMORROW WILL FAKE BREAKDOWN 3KM
NORTH ARDRES AT WAYSIDE SHRINE BORMANN

185 CM RED HAIR RAISED IN ALSACE AND
SPEAKS WITH REGIONAL ACCENT.

"You can see now, Major, why we had to get you. A
large team scanned army records throughout the
remainder of the night. Like magic, your name
appeared. You were brought up in Alsace and so speak
German with the correct regional accent. You have
studied physics at university and should at least not
be a complete babe-in-the-woods when it comes to
missile science. The best bit of all is that you
would seem to be a dead ringer for the German officer
– about the same height and with red hair. I can tell
you that you are our only chance, so although it is a
lot to ask, and is a very risky business, will you
please try?"

What could I say but "yes" and surprisingly the
operation did work, and work like a charm, right up
to the very end when disaster came.

With my agreement things then went quickly but I
confess to wondering, even if I did get to the ski
site, how on earth I could successfully pretend to be
a German officer, an expert on flying bombs, when I
knew damn all about them. However, having been up in
the stratosphere, I was now passed down to much more
down-to-earth people, and probably more intelligent
ones at that.

Only Petrie of GCHQ and my Wing Commander came
with me as I went from groups of experts to further
groups of experts. A genuine German officer taught me
the basics of how I should behave, and also the
current German army slang, then a scientist from RAE
taught me what little they knew about flying bombs
and tried to anticipate the sort of questions I might
be asked. After that another German tried to teach me
the ABC of the hierarchy of the Nazi party, in case I
got involved in a conversation and had to make a

comment.

Probably the most useful lesson came from an elderly professor of mathematics who said to me, "An old philosopher of the eighteenth century - maybe Descartes - said that nobody could properly ask a question unless they already knew the answer. Well, maybe that does seem nonsense, but use the idea. So, if you are asked a question, and have no idea how to answer it, just say something like, 'That's interesting, but before I answer, tell me your opinion, I should like to hear it,' and nine times out of ten they will hazard something and you can agree with them! I can tell you that I have been doing that with my indecently bright students for the last forty years!"

On the question of details, I learned that an SOE group in the Pas de Calais area had already been alerted to stop everything they were engaged on, so that they could meet my Lysander in the early hours of the coming night, and act as my back-up. I was to take a special small radio set which was locked onto just one frequency on which there would be a permanent listening watch. I had to give it to the party who met me, so that on my return trip I could use it to send back any brief performance figures for the bombs just in case anything happened to me on my return journey by Lysander.

At last it was time to go, and I was greeted at the airfield by my pilot, Flight Lieutenant John Hawthorne. "Hello, Major, I gather that for the next couple of days I am going to be your personal pilot. Don't worry, I have never yet lost a fare-paying passenger."

To begin with everything went like magic. I landed in France at about two a.m. in a field about thirty miles back from the coast, and was met by an army SOE Captain, a tough Scot - "No names here, call me

Jock." - and four of his French team. We spent the
night at a farm just north of St. Omer and next
afternoon we drove in an ancient Citroen van, the
five of them dressed in somewhat rough clothes. I was
dressed in the casual clothes of a French student -
this I can explain later. As instructed in the
message, we went up the little road from Ardres and
stopped just beyond the shrine. It still seemed too
much to hope for that the German car would come, but
just on cue it did. Almost on the tick of four
o'clock I looked down the road and saw a Mercedes
staff car - an open tourer - drive up and stop quite
near us by the shrine.

The Captain and his men then leapt out from behind
our van, and in just a few minutes it was all over,
with the officer stripped of his uniform and put into
the back of the van, and with me dressed very smartly
as a German officer. Fortunately the clothes fitted
me very well.

There was quite a lot to do, and when Major
Bormann saw me in his uniform there was dismay on his
face. I said to him, "You can see what we are going
to do, I am taking your place, and I need certain
information. If you tell me the truth, then I should
be able to get away with the deception, but if you
lie then I will be caught. As for you, if I succeed
then your life will be spared, but if I get caught -
well, you think about that"

Certainly he didn't look like a German superman,
in fact more like a frightened back-room boy, and I
felt we'd have no trouble. I began with a question to
which we already knew the answer, just as a check:

"Where were you going?"

"To the control centre of ski sites Calais to Cap-
Gris-Nez."

"What were you going to do?"

"Visit the sites and help them with any problems."

"Have you been here before?"

"No."

"Have you others to contact?"

"Er, Yes"

His voice faded away, and Jock raised his gun and cocked the trigger with a loud click, "Answer now – or else."

The German's shoulders drooped, as if to admit defeat, "Yes, yes, I have to go to Calais tomorrow evening to give my report, and to have dinner with General Hartz. He is at the HQ and is responsible for overseeing the construction of all the ski sites in the area."

We had a few other questions, but his answer had defined exactly how I could get away. If I were still lucky enough to be undiscovered by the next night I could leave with what I hoped was now my trusty driver – ostensibly going to Calais for dinner – but really to make my rendezvous with Jock and his men at the same airfield where I had landed.

While all this was going on, one of the Frenchmen, a printer by trade with calligraphy as his hobby, was working to replace the photograph in the German's papers with mine. That was easy, but the hard bit was to fake the stamps which overlapped it, and although his facilities were basic, the result looked good enough to pass a cursory examination, surely all that would happen when I arrived in an official car with a real German driver.

While he was finishing his work, Jock and I talked with the young driver, Johann Brandt, who wanted further reassurance as to our plans for him. He was delighted to be told that he would be flown to England with me and would be enrolled as a valued member of an SOE team. I also had got a promise from the people at Farnborough, and could tell him that he would be very welcome to settle anywhere he wanted in

Britain after the war was over.

With everything we could do now done, all was haste. Jock and his team with the German officer went off in the van, leaving Johann and me in the Mercedes on that quiet by-road surrounded by peaceful French countryside - or so it looked. But I confess that I felt very lonely sitting there in my German uniform. Johann was keen to get off at once so that I could look at the papers in the officer's brief case. My first discovery was a real gem, a twenty page booklet of the kind one gets with a new car but this was a User's Manual for a V1. I also found that I had to complete a report covering my visits to each site with the questions ranging from my opinion of the site commander to the state of readiness of his unit.

Fortunately he also had with him a copy of the reports made by another officer who had visited the sites three weeks previously, and it gave me an idea of what to expect from the various commanding officers. At the time it seemed a ridiculous idea that I could fool a whole bunch of Germans into thinking that I was an expert on the V1s.

Surprisingly, I had very few problems. When I reported to the local headquarters I was assigned a middle-aged corporal whose job it was to direct my driver to each of the sites which were camouflaged and difficult to find. There were a large number and I had little time to hang about and engage in idle chat which could have proved dangerous.

I was sorry to see that the group of launch teams all seemed to be well advanced as regards their training, and were raring to go. The target date for operational readiness was early June, and it looked all too likely that it would be met. I shuddered to think that thousands of these ingenious horrors would soon be flying off to southern England.

I spent the night back at the local HQ. By the

nature of my position as an inspector, I was
something of a threat to the others in the mess, and
could sense their relief when I excused myself and
took of early to my room. By late in my second
afternoon there I had amassed a huge quantity of data
including the vital performance figures:
     Speed: 625-655 kilometres per hour.
     Cruising Altitude: From 600 to 900 meters.
     Operational Range: 250 kilometres.
     So there I was with my job done with never a
breath of suspicion. All I had to do was to wait for
an hour or so, during which I could occupy myself by
pretending to write up my reports, and then get
myself ready to go off, ostensibly to meet the German
General and have dinner with him in Calais.
     But I had relaxed too soon, as the local
Commanding officer sought me out in the mess where I
was ensconced with an impressive spread of papers
around me. "I must apologise for disturbing you," he
said, "but one of the senior engineers from
Organisation Todt has just arrived to see me, and
will spend the night here. I understand that he is
doing a tour of the French sites, just to assure
himself that all is well regarding the constructional
work. Anyway I am sure that he will want to meet
you." It didn't sound dangerous, but I wondered
whether by any chance he had met Major Bormann,
perhaps on some other visit?
     In the event, however, he had not, and shortly he
came and introduced himself to me, suggesting that I
join him in a beer. He turned out be a pleasant
enough fellow which struck me as odd given the
monstrous reports about Organisation Todt which
claimed that it employed over a million slave labours
from occupied Europe in the construction of the Nazi
war machine. Anyway, in the course of our
conversation he mentioned that this was his first

trip to this area, and went on, "I can tell you that
my predecessor told me that we had done
extraordinarily well by way of camouflaging the
sites, in fact making some of them quite difficult to
find and he was able to save me some time by giving
me a list of them, complete with their map
references." ·

That certainly woke me up because on my own tour
of inspection I was given no such list and had
depended on the directions of my assigned corporal. I
had tried to memorise the route we had taken but
without reliable success. Trying to keep my voice
neutral, I said, "I'm sure you will find that very
useful, as I too have had a few problems. Do you by
any chance have a spare copy of the list, just in
case I come back again?" I held my breath in hope,
then, "Yes, it happens that I do have a spare carbon
copy I can let you have." It was as easy that, and to
get that list of all the ski sites complete with
their map references was a treasure beyond anything I
had expected. It was an enormous bonus. Of course,
when the Germans discovered that they had been duped,
I knew that my friendly engineer would divulge,
either voluntarily or under interrogation, what had
happened. I had the heart to feel sorry for him
knowing that at the very least his career would be
ruined. The Germans would now have to waste
considerable effort in relocating each one of these
ski sites, and during that time the RAF would have
the opportunity to do considerable damage.

So I was very pleased with myself as Johann and I
drove out of the camp that evening, and headed for
the road to Calais. But as soon as we were well out
of sight of the camp we turned off up a side road,
and made tracks for our rendezvous with Jock at the
same field south of St. Omer where I had landed. In
one respect we were lucky, as it was a wretched

night, with torrential rain and a driving wind, so
there were few people on the roads to see us. Jock
and his team were ready, and I got a warm welcome
from him as he gave me a bear hug, saying, "It's a
bloody miracle, I didn't give much for your chances.
Did you get what you were looking for?"

When I nodded, he went on, "Right, I'll tell you
one thing, you and I are going to meet up when all
this nonsense is over, and we'll have a night on the
town, one which we'll long remember," and we shook
hands on the deal.

The Mercedes was whisked off to be hidden in a
nearby barn, and Johann and I were also taken there
so that we could get out of our German uniforms, and
into civilian clothes. Mine were to fit my emergency
plan if things went wrong, and I was casually dressed
and carrying papers which showed me as a student in
the third year of my studies at the University of
Reims. I had selected this identity just in case
there was a problem with the Lysander return flight,
and my choice of Reims was because I had many friends
in the maquis there. If the worse came to the worst,
they could put me in touch with the escape lines.

Another part of the back-up plan was that I could
use the radio to send back the key V1 figures before
getting into the Lysander – just in case of accidents
– but, sadly this was not possible. Jock was very
embarrassed about it, saying, "There has been a
stupid accident, I contacted your base late this
afternoon to confirm the flight, and the radio was OK
then, so tonight's pick up is on and it is arranged
for ten-thirty in this field. Unfortunately, however,
one of my team dropped the radio set as we loaded the
van to come here, and it is absolutely buggered.
Anyway, thank God the message about the flight
tonight did get through, so no harm is done."

We had more than two hours to wait, two long hours

which I spent worrying. I had left the mess a little
after 7 o'clock, so by now surely I had been reported
missing and the alarm bells would be ringing. A large
scale search must be getting under way, and I worried
that they would they find me before the Lysander
came, if indeed it came at all in these terrible
conditions. But Jock was optimistic, "Of course he
will come, old John Hawthorne is the best Lysander
pilot they have. We'll get the lights ready just
before he is due. Don't worry, he'll be here."

And indeed he was, as at about half past ten we
heard the sound of an aircraft engine and Jock lit
our lights. It was very dark and I peered up through
the rain trying to see the plane. Then, suddenly,
Jock grabbed my arm, "There he is! But hold on, he's
off line, there are trees there. Climb you bugger,
CLIMB!"

But he didn't climb fast enough, although he
nearly - oh so nearly - manage to clear the trees. He
struck the top of one, and in just a moment the plane
crashed into the ground, and became a ball of fire,
cartwheeling towards us. It did stop eventually, but
there was no hope for the pilot.

I confess I didn't know what the hell to do, but
Jock was a good officer, and he took only a moment to
issue his orders. His four Frenchmen had bicycles and
were told to scatter, get home if they could, but
otherwise to lie up somewhere for the night. Then he
turned to Johann and to me, "We'll need to get the
hell away from here, and risk using the van."

It was a hair-raising trip as he drove like a
madman - mostly without lights - on narrow side
roads, and by not long after eleven we were an
incredible thirty miles away, south of Bethune. He
knew a farmer there who took us in and gave us
glasses of rough Calvados to drink while his wife
supplied us with bowls of rich soup; people like that

old farmer and his wife were among the unsung heroes
and heroines of the war. They risked their lives - or
worse - to help people like me.

Jock and Johann departed the next morning. I
learned later that they were lucky enough to get off
scot-free and both of them reached Britain a few
months later when the Allies came. As for me the
farmer took me to Arras in a truck with some young
lambs which he was taking to market. From there I
took a chance and bought a ticket for Reims, and
caught a mid-morning train. My only disguise was that
the farmer lent me a beret to hide that damn red hair
of mine. Anyway, I got there safely and was able to
contact one of my old friends in town who made some
very quick arrangements, and I was taken in another
truck to Epernay, right in the middle of the
Champagne district, where I spent a very convivial
night in one of the immense cellars, one of the
ancient Roman chalk pits below the city, surrounded
by what looked like millions of bottles. By very
early next morning I was off again in a wine
merchant's car for Troyes, where I was put in touch
with the escape line there, and introduced to yet
another truck driver who was taking a load of wine
down to Chaource on the afternoon of 19th April 1944.

I mention the date because this turned out to a
rather special day for me. It was then that I met a
member of the French team who specialised in getting
Allied personnel out of France and into Portugal. My
good luck was that she was a beautiful young woman
and with her assistance we did get to Portugal before
flying to England, but not before I had the good
sense to marry her, and we are still married now
nearly sixty years later.

Yours sincerely,
Andrew Dallachy

Appendix 2

This is a Joint Statement by Mrs. Hélène Dallachy
(née Duclos), widow of the late Brigadier Andrew
Dallachy DSO, and the Rt. Hon. Michael Marshall, Her
Majesty's Secretary of State for Defence.

By Mrs. Hélène Dallachy:
   In November of last year I issued a letter with a
wide circulation in which I accused the late Lord
Hempson of treachery during the Second World War. It
stated that he had betrayed a French Resistance group
to the Germans.
   My accusation was based on a single event when my
husband and I, along with two Frenchmen, broke into a
German HQ in an endeavour to rescue Marie-Claire,
Comtesse de Mélitour, the leader of our French
Resistance group, and her young seven-year-old son.
We did save their lives but not before they had been
tortured. She received permanent brain damage and,
until her death last year, had no quality of life
whatsoever. Also injured was her young son, Albert,
now the Comte de Mélitour.
   During the rescue we killed most of the Germans
present including Major Kretzer the officer who was
responsible for the torture. Also present was an
unknown young man in civilian clothes who, despite
wounds to his shoulder, managed to make his escape.

My husband and I did nothing about this matter for
nearly sixty years. However, in the spring of last
year we saw a photograph of Lord Hempson as a young
man taken in 1944. We both recognised him as the
unknown civilian whom we had seen in the torture
room.

It is a matter of record that, after I sent out my
letters, Lord Hempson raised an action for libel
against me. The case was nearing its end when he
suffered a heart attack and decided to abandon the
case. Although evidence was then piling up against
him we regretfully decided that further action would
not be appropriate.

Recently Lord Hempson's son, Michael Marshall,
contacted me. He informed me that, after his father's
death, he had found documents which showed that my
accusation had been correct. Mr. Marshall has agreed
to publically state that his father betrayed his
country during the War and was guilty of concealing
the truth in the years thereafter. This is sufficient
for me, and I now consider that I have repaid my
obligations to Marie-Claire and to those compatriots
of mine in the French Resistance.

I greatly regret that Lord Hempson's son, Michael
Marshall, feels compelled to relinquish his
Ministerial appointment. He is, in my view,
completely free of any wrongdoing. I wish him well
and hope that he may someday serve his country again
as a Minister of the Crown.

By the Rt. Hon. Michael Marshall:
I have little to add to the above statement by
Mrs. Dallachy except to say that after the court case
last year I did have some concerns, but my father was
ill and to my regret, I did nothing.

However after my father's death I found certain
papers of his which made it quite clear that Mrs.

Dallachy's accusations were completely correct. The
record now must state that he was a traitor who
cooperated with the Germans and was responsible for
the death of many members of the French Resistance.
The discovery of my father's treachery was very
traumatic for me personally. Not only did my father
deceive me. He led me to compromise my actions in
order to help him conceal the truth of Mrs.
Dallachy's accusations.

As I saw it, I had an obligation to contact Mrs.
Dallachy and inform her of what I had discovered. We
had two meetings, one in France a few weeks ago and
another in London which took place yesterday.

I had grave concerns regarding Mrs. Dallachy's
possible reactions to the information I gave her. I
knew that she had lived through many horrors which
arose from my father's treachery. In the event our
meeting was completely friendly. She took some time
to explain the dreadful pressures that would have
been applied to him. As for me she understood that my
misdeeds originated from my desire to help my father
and that I had been only guilty of believing what my
father had told me.

However, under the circumstances, I am unable stay
on as Defence Minister. I have already seen the Prime
Minister and he has done me the courtesy of accepting
my resignation. Copies of the relevant letters will
be made available in due course.

As to my Parliamentary Seat, the Prime Minister
has persuaded me to remain a Member for the present.
There will have to be a general election next year,
and my constituents can then make their own
decisions.

Appendix Three

30th. October

By Sir James Butler:
  I have today learned with great regret of the
decision by Mr. Michael Marshall to resign his
appointment as Her Majesty's Secretary for Defence.
He is a brilliant man and it has been both a
privilege and a pleasure to work with him, and I may
say also with his father, Lord Hempson.
  As for me I have been thinking for some time of
taking early retirement so that I can spend more time
with my family, and this would seem to be a most
appropriate time for me to go.
  I shall of course stay at my post until my
successor is established in the position, but this
should not take long and I would hope to leave no
later than the end of November.
  I shall go with some regrets, but I shall take
with me a great many happy memories of the colleagues
and of the Ministers with whom I have been fortunate
enough to serve.

About the Author

Gray Laidlaw was born in 1918 and has spent most of his life in west Scotland. He now lives in Erskine Home beside the river Clyde where, in very comfortable surroundings, he was able to complete this novel.

He attended St Andrews University and received a first class honours degree in physics. By then the Second World War was underway so, immediately after graduating, he joined the RAF and worked primarily in the development of early radar. Towards the end of the war, Squadron Leader Laidlaw was posted to HQ RAF Fighter Command in charge of radar on all night fighters. It was there, in 1943, that he met his wife Margaret who was a WRAF Section Officer. They were married later that year and subsequently had two children.

After the war, Gray enjoyed a successful business career in Glasgow, only taking up writing at the suggestion of his wife after he retired from the glass trade. "I've been very lucky to have had wonderful years at St Andrews University and in the RAF, and a long and happy marriage to my dear wife," says Gray. *Shadow of Treachery*, like his first novel, *Past but Very Present*, is dedicated to his wife who died in 1998.